# MIDNIGHT IN VIENNA

## JANE THYNNE

QUERCUS

First published in Great Britain in 2024 by

**QUERCUS**

Quercus Editions Ltd
Carmelite House
50 Victoria Embankment
London EC4Y 0DZ

An Hachette UK company

A CIP catalogue record for this book is available
from the British Library

HB ISBN 978 1 5294 3 066 0
TPB ISBN 978 1 52943 067 7
EB ISBN 978 1 52943 069 1

1

Typeset by CC Book Production

Printed and bound in Great Britain by Clays Ltd, Elcograf S.p.A

Papers used by Quercus are from well-managed forests and other responsible sources.

*For Jane Wood*

*All men make mistakes, but a good man yields when he knows his course is wrong and repairs the evil.*

Sophocles

*And the Lord said unto Cain, where is thy brother?*

King James Bible

# PROLOGUE

Someone had crashed their car into the Admiralty Arch – the folly of trying to manoeuvre a large Austin 7 through such a narrow space alongside a bicycle. Voices were raised indignantly, a man was shouting, a woman was weeping and traffic was backing up. The hot evening air smelled of petrol fumes.

Not far away from this commotion, Hubert Newman made his way erratically along Pall Mall. Momentarily he stumbled and was forced to stop, reaching out a hand to the wall to steady himself. At first glance he might have been just another middle-aged gentleman returning from his club, having consumed enough alcohol to dull the drumbeat of war sounding through the city. And he was, indeed, returning from his club – the Athenaeum – where he had spent the afternoon in the comforting embrace of a cracked leather chair, fenced in by furniture as old as Trafalgar, attending to letters and matters of business.

He was in his mid-forties, with a portly frame rounded by good living, and pale, anxious eyes behind heavy spectacles. He wore an ill-fitting tweed jacket, suggesting an academic profession, a don perhaps, or a writer of some kind – an impression cemented by the clashing purple tie, chosen with no regard to fashion.

Continuing southwards, he turned right past Carlton House Terrace and descended the difficult steps into the Mall.

He blinked again. This wasn't fatigue – his vision had been blurred all afternoon. At first, he had attributed his condition to an event he had attended the previous evening, organized to welcome German refugees. The dinner consisted of sausages, presumably to make the newcomers feel at home, potato salad – ditto – and quantities of home-made elderflower wine. The wine was deceptively sweet, like some of the hostesses there: apparently syrupy but with a hidden strength.

Yet this was no hangover. He was sure of that now. He had the answer, if he could only summon it.

Titles pattered though his head. *The Mystery of the Missing Message.* One of his earliest. But that wasn't it. *The Horror at Henderson Grange,* perhaps? *A Dozen Layers of Dark?*

Crossing the Mall, he staggered in halting fashion towards a plane tree, in whose shade he clutched his chest. His body was torpid, yet his heart was racing – a tachycardiac pulse, well over a hundred beats a minute, signalling the muscles of the failing organ needed more oxygen.

That much he understood. He had studied the symptoms

of a heart attack for *Death in the Drawing Room*. But was this it? Or a stroke maybe?

As he passed a newspaper stand, his eyes scanned the headlines. The British locomotive Mallard had set a record for steam engines of 126 miles per hour. Thirty million gas masks were ready to be issued to the entire civilian population. The evacuation of children from London in case of war had been approved by government committee. Hitler's sabre-rattling speech at the Nuremberg Rally (printed in full in the inside pages) demanded self-determination in the Sudetenland and an end to slavery for Sudeten Germans.

Yet at the same time, he saw none of them.

Newman was acutely aware of his unsteady gait. Lurching onwards, he wondered if anyone might stop to help, before reminding himself that this was England, where personal privacy was an inviolable law, and people would as soon strip naked as accost a total stranger in the street. Polite avoidance was as English as the hiss of the gas street lamps, the perpetual rain or the native mixture of human warmth and freezing snobbery.

He gulped at the air. In direct contrast to his physical state, his mind was fizzing, ideas firing and colliding in fruitless, panicked combinations through his brain.

A pretty brunette passed on a bicycle, her scarf decorated with cherries trailing in the breeze, and a Jack Russell perched imperiously in the wicker basket. The girl didn't give him a glance, but the terrier's eyes followed his progress with beady curiosity.

Overcome by nausea, Newman sagged onto a bench and tried to slow his heartbeat. His breath was now coming in gasps, both from the exertion of the walk and from the increasing constriction in his chest that felt like a lead weight pressing down on him. He massaged his brow with fingers stained by a lifetime of tobacco and lit a cigarette.

After a single drag he flung it away. Each inflation of his lungs was a physical exertion, yet his brain was spinning like a slot machine, a whirring mess of questions, attempting to match symptoms to outcomes and facts to suppositions.

*The Secret of the Soda Siphon.* Could that be the one? Or perhaps *Appointment in Paris?*

He staggered on. He could no longer feel the weather on his skin.

Above him, in Great George Street, windows glowed against the dusk. Yet it was getting harder to see them, and not only because of the fading light. The oppressive air felt heavy, like a physical weight, though it was not the air dragging the skin of his face downwards or making his eyelids droop.

A group of young men emerged from a pub in a miasma of hops and chatter. He caught snatches of conversation:

'*The idea that Britain could ever hold the balance of power in Europe is entirely outdated.*'

'*Did you hear that fool Wolfson's gone off to drive ambulances in Spain?*'

His tongue was thick in his mouth. He wanted to address them, to call out, but his throat was choked, and the words could not crawl through the furrows of his brain. His heart began to skip its rhythm, fluttering weakly like a bird in a cage.

He stumbled. His feet were turning to living lead.

He had ten minutes to live. Nine, maybe.

The scenery began to recede, and in his addled mind other streets arose — the cobbled lanes of his birthplace, through which he had toddled in his hard little boots, holding the rough hand of Martha, his nurse, to shop for cheese and ham at the market.

These floating vistas confused his failing sense of direction, and he headed leftwards, into Storey's Gate.

Nausea, dysphasia, creeping paralysis. These signs told him that he had very little time. He had written so much about death, yet he had never properly considered how it would feel to die. Now his end was near, and like all men, even atheists, he felt an atavistic urge towards the sacred.

Faltering his way to the entrance of Westminster Abbey he lurched through the massive oak doorway, hammered with iron rivets a thousand years old, and laboured across the nave. His legs barely obeyed him.

He was, in every sense, petrified.

Above him stained glass windows scattered sapphires and rubies over the choir stalls. It might be the wrong religion, but it would have to do. The chords of practising choristers arose, stopping and starting again, angelic in their pursuit of perfection, and, in that moment, Newman sensed himself becoming transfigured into everything around him, life seeping out of him, even as comprehension filtered in.

*Midnight in Vienna.* That was the one.

Staggering through the cloisters, cool and dark, laced with shadows of folded stone, he managed only a few steps before his legs gave way. The ground crashed towards him and the ferric tang of blood filled his nostrils. He thought himself back to his club; the must-scented library, cigars burning in the tallow light, the dining room serving shoe-leather beef drowned in gravy. It seemed like a version of heaven to him.

For one last time the face of his mother came into his mind, before his heart, besieged by chaotic electric activity, gave a frenzied squeeze and stuttered to a halt.

# CHAPTER 1

*September 12th, 1938*

London, in that long, sultry summer, smelled of melted tarmac and dust.

Just after five o'clock Stella Fry got off the tram and walked along Embankment. A train clattered past across the tracks from Victoria, and across the Thames the twin chimneys of Battersea Power Station sent clouds of smoke into a sky that hung pale and heavy as a blanket over the parched city. Horse chestnut leaves cast fretted shadows on the pavement and a snatch of mock orange blossom wafted from the shrubs poking through the railings. A cat sat on a wall, too saturated with sun even to flick its tail at her. It was holiday weather, yet the heat and the distant shouts of children in the park filled Stella with gloom.

More than half of September lay ahead and it would be about as exciting as a burst balloon.

She was torturing herself with memories of other, better summers; the one she had spent in the cool of the hills above Florence, taking the winding road up to Fiesole, with the scent of wild thyme and the high creak of the crickets. The South of France summer at Mougins, looking down towards the coast, linen blowing on the line and lavender fields shimmering in the heat. The fountains and manicured lawns of the Schönbrunn Palace in Vienna. The crystal-clear water of the lakes in the Grunewald around Berlin. September was her birthday month and she had always associated that season with excitement, adventure and travel. Her restlessness was so acute it was almost physical.

*Wanderlust*, the Germans called it.

Almost at once Stella chided herself for such mutinous feelings. No one was going on holiday to Italy and France now, let alone Spain, deep in civil war. Conflict with Germany was either coming or it wasn't, according to which newspaper you read, but the whole of Europe seemed to be holding its breath in anticipation. A trip abroad was out of the question. Best reconcile herself to the offer of a week's visit to her brother's country house in Cornwall, where disappointment would sting like the gnats around the campfire in the drizzle. Because it would almost certainly rain. How had George II described the English summer? Two sunny days and a thunderstorm.

No one passing Stella Fry on the pavement that day would discern this mood. Containment came as second nature to her. Her face in repose was appealingly regular, but when she smiled her entire demeanour became animated and then people described her as beautiful. She had typical English features: a fair complexion, watchful brown eyes, a slender nose and a way of tilting her chin in an unconscious gesture of defiance that had followed her through life. The intelligence and vivid emotions that lay beneath that sober appearance were only apparent to those prepared to look.

Close observers, however, might note that there was something French about the cut of her powder-blue jersey jacket and that her svelte summer skirt was not the kind that could be found in *Vogue*'s British sewing patterns. Her time abroad had instilled in her a love of Continental fashion that she indulged whenever she could afford it. She wore a tiny hat, embroidered with beads, and her legs were clad in stockings, though she had stowed the equally obligatory gloves in a capacious Liberty's leather handbag, along with keys, a powder compact, lipstick and a library copy of *Rebecca*.

Plunging her hand in her pocket she found a scrap of card and brought it out. It was an old, clipped train ticket to a village on the shores of the Starnberger See. Immediately she heard the voice of a tall blond man, looking down into her eyes.

'*What does it matter, what I believe? It doesn't change who we are.*'

'*I think it matters, what you believe.*'

At the memory, she clenched the ticket into a ball, as if she could make it disappear entirely.

Her thoughts were interrupted by the mournful tinkle of an ice cream van, like an elegy for the summer she would not be having. The van, with a jaunty green and white slogan along its side advertising 'Ice Cream for Everyone. Fresh Daily!' drew up beside her, trailing fumes, and its proprietor leaned out. He had the striped shirt of a gondolier, a twirly moustache and an Italian accent that was fooling nobody.

'Fresh ice cream, lady?'

Stella smiled but shook her head. The atmosphere seemed too sombre for ordinary summer enjoyments. Politics tinged the air like petrol. Britain was running out of time to answer Herr Hitler's demands. Events on the Continent cast a gloom that no amount of ice cream could dispel.

She turned right into Oakley Street, came to a red-brick mansion block, walked up three flights and pushed open the door to Flat 7. Navigating an ironing board in the hall, she entered a high-ceilinged room, whose best feature was the flood of light coming from the long window, filtered through the canopy of the plane tree outside. A fraying sofa was parked along one wall, and most of the surfaces were covered with an artfully arranged clutter of peacock feathers, seaside souvenirs, china dogs and shells that gave the shabby flat a chic and eclectic air. A needlepoint Bible verse hung on the wall and a gramophone was positioned on an old leather trunk, with a stack of records beside it. An abandoned cup of tea had been dumped on a side table, alongside a battered paperback.

A woman in a slinky emerald evening dress and three strands of pearls was standing in front of a mirror. A tangle of curls framed her face, and her mouth was a perfect, lip-sticked bow.

'Is that dress for a part?' asked Stella.

Evelyn Lamont tugged her décolletage to reveal more plump cleavage and posed, hands on hips. The clinging silk caressed every curve as she glanced over her shoulder.

'It's for a man. How do I look?'

'Glamorous. A little tarty.'

Evelyn buried her face for a second in the perfumed cave of her armpit.

'Good. That's exactly what I was aiming for.'

She moved over to the mirror and began shaping her eyebrows in a high, Marlene Dietrich arch that emphasized the moony roundness of her face. Although she wasn't exactly beautiful, she devoted considerable time to grooming and cultivated the demeanour of Sorel Bliss in Noël Coward's *Hay Fever*.

'Roger's taking me to the Ritz bar after the show.'

'You'll certainly stand out there.'

Stella went into the tiny kitchenette, lit the gas ring and put on the kettle. The badly cut loaf, scattering of toast crumbs and a lidless jar of jam suggested Evelyn had already eaten.

'That's the idea,' Evelyn called. 'And it's no more than he deserves. I'm fed up with skulking around in dingy hotels.'

Roger was the latest in a line of married men who bobbed like bad apples through Evelyn's romantic life.

'I told him, if he's going to take me out, I see no reason why I should hide. That's his problem.'

'What is it he does, exactly?' said Stella, coming back into the room with a hunk of bread and margarine.

'He's a playwright.'

'A playwright? Really?'

'Not the Shakespeare kind. More of a producer actually. They're doing his *Wanted for Murder* at the Lyceum and he thinks I have a lot to offer.'

'Doesn't mean you have to offer it.'

'Don't be a prude.' Evelyn shot her a glance. 'Though if we get on, well, you know . . . he might come back.'

Stella thought of Roger's predecessor, who had come crashing into the flat in the small hours with a volley of curses, and then into the adjoining bedroom with the kind of laughs and stage whispers that made her yearn to rap on the wall. After he had left, her door had creaked open as Evelyn crept in for a drunken post-mortem, based around the theme that she'd had enough of married men and their excuses.

Evelyn was an actress. Although actual fame eluded her, she had met Edith Evans and Margaret Lockwood and could imitate both with perfect mimicry. She had taught herself to hold a cigarette like Bette Davis and she studied *Vogue* like the Bible. All through school, as Stella recalled, Evelyn had lost no opportunity to act, in lessons and out, and when she left, she landed a place at RADA. Yet although she looked a lot like Celia Johnson, her big break remained out of reach.

'When you do meet Roger, please be nice to him. He doesn't like intellectual women.'

'What should I talk to him about?'

'As little as possible.'

Stella picked up her paperback and flopped down on the sagging purple divan. Privately, she chided herself for scorning Evelyn's romantic life. Perhaps, with an aching heart and no lover of her own, she was jealous. Maybe her friend's busy social life only reminded her of her own solitude. Anyway, Evelyn was easy company. The flat was homely, and perfectly situated. It may have several damp stains on the ceiling, and cracked plaster, but the Ascot provided enough hot water for two unless, as was usually the case, Evelyn required a long soak before she left for the theatre in the evening.

And yet – Stella felt restless in this strange state of limbo, amid unfamiliar faces in a city she only half remembered. She had hoped that her life was about to start again – that she was standing on the brink of a new beginning, even though she had no idea what that beginning might be. But increasingly, she sensed that was wrong. In her worst fears she suspected that there would be no new start, and she would instead be engulfed in a life of routine tedium until she had forgotten ever feeling excited or alive.

It was six months since she had returned from Europe and taken refuge in Evelyn's small spare room. She had spent the past five years as a private tutor, before the Austrian family she worked for and whose children she loved, had decided to leave Vienna and seek safety in New York. She thought of Herr Gatz, with his delicate moustache and punctilious courtesy, spreading his hands apologetically, as though he were a mâitre d' with no vacancies rather than a Jewish businessman with no nationality.

'*You are family to us, liebe Stella, and always will be, but these unfortunate circumstances impel us to leave.*'

Those were not the only farewells. Another, more painful, separation had already taken place, though amid a nation in turmoil, Stella's own emotional upheaval barely figured. The fact remained, after she had waved the Gatzes goodbye, she had returned to England, with three languages, no job and a broken heart.

By the time she had arrived at Victoria station, laden with her Royal typewriter and a huge carpet bag, she was practically broke. The only people she could have asked for money were her brother Alan, whose bank account was controlled entirely by his wife, and her widowed mother, who had decamped from their Victorian terrace in Chiswick and moved to the south coast, where she existed on a diet of gin and bridge. Luckily, Stella still had Evelyn's number.

Stella and Evelyn had known each other since they were thirteen. In contrast to the buttoned-up Frys, the Lamonts were wealthy, flamboyant and extravagant. Philip and Sidonie Lamont were renowned for their entertaining and left-leaning sentiments. Sidonie, who was White Russian in origin, thought of herself as an artist and regularly invited actors, writers and painters to their opulent Chelsea home. Evelyn was their only daughter, and from the moment the two girls met, the Lamonts had taken Stella to their bosom, including her in endless trips, family dinners and outings. Together, Stella and Evelyn had spent hours analysing their futures, wondering if and who they would marry.

When Stella called Evelyn from a telephone box at Victoria station, her friend reacted as if she had gone no further than the corner shop.

*Come and stay! It will be a party, at least until this war arrives!*

Within the hour, Stella had been installed in the cupboard of a spare bedroom, next to a bathroom containing a constantly dripping tap. Evelyn's disarray was in extreme contrast to Stella's own love of order, which had dogged her since her teenage years. Nonetheless, she had no hesitation in moving in, and straight into the tumult of Evelyn's life.

Evelyn turned from the mirror and frowned.

'The fact is, I didn't say, but my show has just closed.'

'Oh, I'm sorry!'

'I'm not. Once the accountants decided, there was no point in prolonging it, apparently. It was throwing good money after bad.'

Stella could see why. A lacklustre musical at the Hippodrome was no diversion when the cinema newsreels were filled with an alarming montage of troops filing across Europe and angry, slogan-chanting crowds.

'It's all the fault of Czechoslovakia. I don't see why it should matter so much.'

Evelyn raked crimson-tipped fingers through her hair. 'Anyhow. We're holding a wake tomorrow evening. You will come, won't you?'

'I won't know anyone.'

'All the better. You'll meet new people.'

'I don't have anything to wear.'

'Wear that apricot silk blouse. The French one. It makes you look mysterious and Continental.'

Stella smiled at her.

'You'll be fine, you know that.'

'I know.' Evelyn sprawled on the chair and flipped her legs over the arm. 'But that's why I'm so keen to get on with Roger. Especially since my father says war can't be avoided and we'll all have to join the ATS and become car mechanics or something dreadful.'

The note of despondency that had crept into her friend's habitual optimism was swiftly smothered.

'But Roger knows everyone. If anyone can find me work, it'll be him.'

'I'm sure he will.'

'Let's hope. And listen, it will be fun, and we need to have fun while we can. There are movie people going to the wake. A charming man called Emeric Pressburger. He's a Hungarian refugee. You'd like him. And there are rumours that Alexander Korda might even be there. He owns London Films! An entire movie company at Denham Studios. He's sure to be talent-spotting.'

She reached out and took a gulp from a bottle of cheap

Rioja that had been standing open since the previous evening.

'Anyway,' she went on, 'I have an audition tomorrow morning.'

'There you are, then.'

'I suppose. But you didn't say. Where've *you* been today?'

'I was interviewed for a job.'

'You dark horse! More teaching?'

'Typing, actually. It's a stopgap. I'm transcribing a manuscript for an author. I used to do a little of that, when I had that job in publishing. He placed an advertisement in *The Times* and it caught my eye. Author seeks typist.'

'So . . . what's he called?'

'Hubert Newman.'

'*The* Hubert Newman!' Evelyn sat up. 'Stella, he's famous!' Evelyn had never associated Stella with celebrity; she looked at her friend with fresh interest. 'He writes detective stories. Murder at the vicarage kind of thing. Everyone reads them. I've just finished one. My mother knows him. He's been to one of her soirées. What on earth did you make of him?'

# CHAPTER 2

What had Stella made of him?

The interview was at the Athenaeum in Pall Mall. Stella had never set foot in a gentleman's club and she had walked the gloomy grandeur of Pall Mall a couple of times to prepare herself, glancing through the windows, taking in the pediments, the iron lanterns and the soot-pocked columns. The Royal Automobile Club, the Travellers, the Reform – the splendour of their facades marred by untidy piles of sandbags freshly stacked against their walls. The long windows, where soft yellow light shafted through the heavy drapes, looked like portals to another, more stately age. Eventually she steeled herself to climb the washed stone steps of the Athenaeum, where the door opened before she could push it, as if by magic.

She informed a man in purple livery that a Miss Stella Fry was here to see Hubert Newman. While she waited, she gazed around at the pillared recesses, the vista of chequered tiles, gleaming woodwork and cracked burgundy leather chairs as though they formed a door into another universe. Nothing that was happening in the streets outside – not the newsboys shouting, or the teams of workers piling sandbags against the facades, or the distant sound of anti-aircraft construction – seemed to penetrate this world of polish and moneyed hush.

After a few minutes, Newman came hurrying across the lobby. Perhaps because of the thickness of his jacket or the September humidity, he looked uncomfortably hot. His brow was beaded with sweat. He was pallid, portly and probably fifty, dressed exactly how she imagined a detective novelist might dress, in a tweed suit, with the glint of a fob watch chain across his rotund middle. He had sad, soft eyes and a drooping bulldog face. But either from nerves or indigestion, Stella detected a tetchiness beneath the punctilious courtesy.

'Miss Fry. Apologies for the wait.'

He forged a path through the dining room, nodding to friends and acquaintances, and clasping a couple of them by the hand. '*Morning, Rex.*' '*How are you, Henry?*' '*Hello, old chap. It's been too long.*' Stella followed him to a table in the far corner of the room that was designated the Ladies' Area. Regardless of the warm weather outside, a fire roared in the grate. Almost every other table was occupied by middle-aged and elderly men in dark suits, their low chatter mingling with the clink of heavy silver cutlery and the glug of expensive claret.

After fussing over the lunch order – lamb chops, carrots, peas and potatoes – and selecting a bottle of wine, Newman leaned back and dabbed at the narrow line of perspiration on his upper lip.

'I'm not sure if you're familiar with my work.'

She had made a precautionary trip to Hatchards in Piccadilly that morning, where the assistant guided her to a section heaving with vivid novels decorated with daggers, corpses and beautiful women dripping blood. Charles Latimer's *A Bloody Shovel*. Dorothy L. Sayers's *Gaudy Night*. There was a decent stack of Newman's most recent work, *A Shot Across the Bows*, a murder mystery set on a transatlantic cruise liner, but his pile was dwarfed by a display of the latest Agatha Christie, *Appointment with Death*. Stella wondered if novelists, like other professionals, felt jealousy towards their artistic rivals. She guessed it was possible.

She had done her best to flick through a selection of Newman's other titles. They were not the kind of novels to grace any academic shelves, even if the plots were satisfyingly twisty. His murders tended to be committed in manor houses and vicarages, the libraries of rectories and stately homes. A few, however, took place in more exotic locations: Paris, the French Riviera, and one in the Munich opera house. Most of the murders were solved by Peverell Drake, an aristocratic art dealer with a lot of time on his hands, whose motto, wearisomely repeated, ran, 'I look for answers where nobody thought there were questions.' Sometimes Drake was assisted by a sidekick, a former police detective in the habit of making comments of astonishing stupidity.

Her eye was caught by a novel called *Midnight in Vienna*, and instinctively she picked it up. Unbidden, a series of images flashed before her eyes. Six months ago, in March. A crowd massing around a loudspeaker in the square, and the voice that emanated, harsh and shrill, like a pneumatic drill on the ears. Herr Gatz turning to her saying, '*I think it may be time to leave the party.*'

This one, she had bought.

Yet as hard as she had tried to focus on Newman's book, nothing stuck. The words had floated past her eyes and it had been impossible to take anything in. She hoped he wasn't going to quiz her.

'I know you write detective fiction.'

'*Detective.*' Newman winced. 'Yes. That's the term some readers use.'

Plainly he thought it inappropriate. Stella hadn't managed to visit several different countries without grasping that words had many more meanings than their official ones.

'Nobody can choose their readers, unfortunately, though don't think I don't appreciate them. I make a point of replying to every letter I receive. I'm my own worst enemy. But it means a lot to them.'

He removed his tortoiseshell glasses and prodded them with fingernails that were bitten to the quick.

'Forgive me. This is my spare pair. They're not a good fit.'

He extracted a handkerchief and began to polish the lenses.

'Despite what the . . . critics . . . may say about my work, Miss Fry, I have always considered my novels more than mere stories of crime. More than the *Death on the Nile* type of business. "Murderers walk among us", kind of thing. I like to flatter myself they are exercises in philosophy. We English don't like the inexplicable, you see. People need a world where the loose ends are tied up and justice is done. And that is what I have tried to give them.'

He paused to examine the spectacles minutely, as though searching for invisible particles.

'An intellectual exercise is not enough, of course. Sometimes a detective is motivated purely by gut instinct – something doesn't feel right and he, or even she, is compelled to investigate. He feels a stir in the blood and a certainty that something is awry. Never trust anyone who places the intellectual above the emotional.'

He was gazing across the room, as if he was talking to himself.

'The fact remains we English crave a universe of order and morality, in which reason and stability are restored. Chaos followed by order. I see that as my mission. To give comfort at difficult times. My novels tell you that the world makes sense.'

'And does it?' she asked. 'Make sense, I mean?'

He looked up at her sharply, as if his mind was miles away.

'That's my hope. Though I am worried . . .'

'Worried about the chance of war?'

'Hmm. Yes, that. Of course.' His gaze strayed back across the room, searching the tables, as though he had lost his train of thought, before returning to her.

'So, what was your last commission, Miss Fry?'

'Actually, I've just come back from Austria.'

At this remark he halted, his fork halfway to his mouth, loaded with a roast potato.

'Austria?'

'Vienna, in fact.'

'Vienna?' he repeated.

'It's a beautiful city.'

'Yes, yes, and you were there as what? A companion?'

'I was a tutor to a family with three children. But earlier this year they were obliged to relocate. They managed to get passage to America.'

Newman nodded, understanding the implication. Which was that Stella's employers had been Jewish and that nowhere in Continental Europe was likely to be safe for them.

'That must have been difficult . . . for you and them.'

'It was. I've found that most people here have no idea what it's like out there. In Germany and Austria. The aggression and persecution.'

He frowned gravely.

'Indeed. We're at a dangerous moment. Great sacrifices will be required of all of us. It behoves us all to pin our colours to the mast.'

'Do you think that war's coming? Or do you believe the Prime Minister might manage to avoid it?'

She waited for Newman to elaborate, but instead he only gave another uneasy glance around the room and cleared his throat.

'Perhaps we should focus on this commission. I wouldn't want to mislead you. The fact is, this particular book is not a detective novel at all. It's a literary investigation. It's called *Masquerade*. I decided to apply my skills as a sleuth to investigate all the alternative candidates for the "real" Shakespeare. It's a bit of a specialist's subject – the "authorship question" – but I hope that everyone will be interested in my attempts to find the truth.'

Stella nodded. As far as she could see, nothing just then was less important than finding the real Shakespeare, assuming he was even lost in the first place. And yet, in the anxious atmosphere that prevailed, an academic exercise like this might prove restful. Soothing even.

'Is there any real doubt? About who Shakespeare was?'

For the first time in their encounter, Newman's eyes lit up with enthusiasm.

'I should say! There's no shortage of suggestions. If there is such a thing as turning in one's grave, I would think Shakespeare gets a lot of exercise.'

'I thought he was the son of a glove merchant from Stratford-on-Avon.'

'My dear, I agree with you wholeheartedly. I'm a Stratfordian. But there are plenty of others who would like to think otherwise. People who are desperate to advance their own pretenders to the throne. The authorship question is a perennial one. I tend to think it resurfaces in times of trouble. In other words, that uncertainty over our greatest playwright becomes a metaphor for more general uncertainties.'

'I see,' she said hesitantly, as he warmed to his theme.

'Bacon has always been the strongest contender, though each imposter has their own following. Marlowe, Oxford, Neville – some even believe Shakespeare may have been a woman.'

At this absurdity he grimaced and scooped up the last peas from his plate.

'Some critics cannot bear the idea that the greatest author of English literature was not an aristocrat, but a man of relatively humble origins. They refuse to believe that a man educated at a provincial grammar school could possibly know foreign languages or be acquainted with different countries or understand Platonic philosophy.'

'And you think you've proved that he did?'

'Maybe. But the thrust of my work is to cast a spotlight on the disreputable doubters. It enrages me that pretenders should be tolerated merely on the basis of their social status and aristocratic standing.'

He beamed.

'You could say my book is a detective story in itself, only the weapon is a pen, the crime is snobbery and the motive is elitism.'

The beam widened. This string of metaphors clearly pleased him.

'But . . . if you like the work, does it matter, in the end, what you believe about the author?'

'Some say it doesn't. After all, Shakespeare himself said, "the play's the thing". But I happen to think it *does* matter what you believe. The truth of a person. Authors, as much as anyone. Don't you?'

For a moment, the question seemed to hover in the air between them. Once again, Stella heard herself on the shores of the Starnberger See. '*I think it matters, what you believe.*' But before she could reply, a man entered the room, spied Newman and glided soundlessly on the thick carpet towards them.

'I say, Newman, I do hope I'm not disturbing anything.'

It seemed to Stella that he hoped he was. He was tall, with an easy grace, and fair hair that fell forward into his face.

Newman made a fussy dab of his mouth with the napkin.

'Just a little business discussion.'

The interloper smiled and she caught the glint of a gold tooth. Keeping his eyes on Stella, he slid a spectacle case onto the tablecloth.

'It's lucky I caught you. You left these at the event last night.'

He bent down, bringing a waft of lime cologne and cigars. 'Who's your lovely companion, may I ask?'

'This lady may be helping me with a little editorial work,' Newman murmured.

Stella waited for him to introduce her properly, but instead her host paused awkwardly and stared down at the wine, fumbling for his glass. His fingers, with their bitten nails and amber stain of nicotine, trembled slightly. After an awkward pause, the tall man straightened up and said, 'The alchemy of authorship! It wouldn't do to interrupt that.'

At this point another diner approached and clapped a hand on Newman's shoulder.

'Congratulations from my lady wife, Hubert! She's just read your last and is impatient for the next. Can I let her know when to expect it?'

'Soon, Edward, soon.'

Once the two men had departed, Newman took a gulp of wine before refocusing on Stella.

'I'm sorry. Where were we?'

'Discussing the candidates for the real Shakespeare.'

'Of course.'

Yet his enthusiasm for the subject seemed to have evaporated. Distractedly, he took off the spare pair of spectacles and replaced them with his usual ones.

'Normally, my manuscripts are typed by my secretary, Mrs Harris. But she's getting on a bit and her eyes are no longer up to it. What's more, she's convinced that Herr Hitler plans to drop bombs on us all, so she's gone to keep chickens on her brother's farm in Scotland. I'm therefore left in the lurch. Do you think you can manage it? The typing? I'll need it done quickly. In a fortnight, if you can.'

'I'm sure I can. I've typed manuscripts before.'

'I'll have it sent to your address then, if you would.'

He produced a small leather notebook and proffered a pen with which Stella carefully inscribed the address in Oakley Street.

'I hope you can navigate my handwriting. Mrs Harris calls it 'esoteric'. My grammar is just occasionally off-piste, and my spelling can—'

Stella leaned forward, smiling.

'Please don't worry. I did a little proofreading and copy-editing for a small publishing company after university. I'm suited to it, actually. I like order. My mother always said it was an obsession. Needing everything in its place and liking to do things in a particular way.' She tucked a stray lock of hair behind her ear and continued. 'I don't know about that, but it does mean I have a good eye. I'm good at spotting mistakes.'

At this, to her great surprise, across the starched table-cloth, Newman took one of her hands in his own, damp palm. He was regarding her intently above the round, tortoiseshell lenses, and for the first time in their meeting, she sensed that she had his full attention.

'Spotting mistakes. Yes. *That*, Miss Fry, is *exactly* what I need.'

'So, did you get the job?'

Evelyn had snatched up her perfume and was waving the bottle around her, spritzing the air with a floral miasma.

'I did, actually.'

'Hubert Newman! Fancy that. All those bodies in libraries

and chocolate-box English villages. So, what's the new one called?'

'*Masquerade.*'

'And you'll be the first to read it! Just wait till I tell my mother. She'll be so jealous! She'll die!'

# CHAPTER 3

Sitting at a window table in Lyons' Corner House on the edge of Trafalgar Square, Harry Fox reflected that he knew George Orwell as well as some women knew their husbands. Better even. What woman, no matter how besotted, would know how long their man took to devour a sandwich – five bites – or in how many gulps he downed a cup of tea. Ten. Or in precisely what order he would read the *Manchester Guardian*. Sport first, then news, then obituaries, to check who was dead, before a sniff at the crossword. Despite the fact that Harry's entire livelihood relied on spotting patterns, just occasionally he ached for Orwell to surprise him.

From his adjoining table, Harry could observe every lineament of the gaunt, tubercular frame. He could have traced the monkish cast of the author's pale face in his sleep. It was part of his training to commit physical details to memory, so he knew the scar where a year ago the man had been wounded in the throat by a Spanish sniper's bullet.

He could recite the details from his passport application by heart: 'Height 6ft 2ins, eyes blue, hair brown, tattoo marks on the backs of both hands.' He could identify the man's knife-thin outline in the dark. He had even picked up some of his opinions. Orwell had especially firm views about tea – he had heard him expound them to the waitress. A china teapot was best, with strong Indian tea made with properly boiling water. The tea should always go first into the cup, then milk, and it should be taken without sugar – why spoil tea by sweetening it? And if any was left, cold tea was a good fertilizer for geraniums.

Harry knew what trousers Orwell wore and where he got his shirts. His file, under the name of Eric Blair, included the comment 'He dresses in a bohemian fashion both in his office and his leisure hours.' *Bohemian* was Special Branch code for wearing the same shabby sports jacket on every occasion. Harry was familiar with the wheeze from Orwell's damaged lungs just before he folded up the paper and returned it to the pocket of his mac, and the quick look around he always took before he rose and exited the café into the rain-edged air.

As expected, Orwell headed like a homing bird up the Strand. Leaving a beat, Harry followed. He frowned momentarily when Orwell stopped to talk to the man selling the *Evening Standard*. Why would he talk to a news vendor when he had only just finished the *Guardian*? Had some item of breaking news electrified him? It seemed unlikely. The headline on the wired newsstand said, 'Ashes Hope for England'.

But then he was off again, head down and moving surprisingly fast for a man whose lungs, according to his medical records, had the texture of old dishcloths.

Harry ploughed on as commuters swirled around him. There were advantages to tailing someone at rush hour. Sheer numbers made a shadow harder to detect. The trick to shadowing lay in allowing all the rest of the world – the commuters' hurry, the weather – to fade, so that one's entire attention was condensed into a single point. To let all possible distractions slip away.

Recently, however, for Harry, distractions were becoming harder to ignore.

It was beginning to drizzle and people were putting up umbrellas. Momentarily, the forest of black blocked his view. For a second he thought he had lost his mark. He quickened his step.

His guess was that Orwell was heading towards the home of his brother-in-law in Greenwich. Or perhaps to the Hampstead flat of Richard Rees, for whose literary magazine, the *Adelphi*, he occasionally wrote.

Harry thought back to some of the other details in the file . . . '*this man has advanced Communist views, and several of his Indian friends say that they have often seen him at Communist meetings.*' So far, there was scant evidence of Orwell attending any meetings at all. He hadn't even set foot in the Communist Party headquarters in King Street, which was comprehensively bugged and wired by MI5. The most eccentric thing he did was to frequent a bookshop called Booklovers' Corner in Hampstead, where Harry avidly followed him because his cover involved browsing in the stacks.

Harry Fox loved to read, yet he had a deep envy of those who read easily. To him, it had always been a struggle. Words and sentences seemed a jumbled mess of shapes and lines, a code which needed to be decrypted, rather than a scene in which to plunge. Through patience and persistence, he had taught his brain to seek patterns amid the sliding shapes of the letters, and to order the fonts which slipped and drifted before his eyes. Perhaps that was where he got this particular skill, the one he used for his day job: hunting for anomalies, pinning them down and decoding them.

Or perhaps he was just flattering himself.

He hadn't tried Orwell's stuff, mainly because detective fiction was his great love. '*Mindless thrillers*' was how his last date had described them, a haughty girl called Violet who fancied herself as an intellectual on the basis of working in a French restaurant. '*Trashy. Full of clichés and cheap emotions.*' She was probably right but Harry didn't care. One of his other surveillance subjects, Cecil Day Lewis, had produced a number of detective novels under the pen name Nicholas Blake, and Harry had just passed the latest, *Thou Shell of Death*, to his nephew Jack, who even at the age of ten was an avid reader.

The thought of Jack took him instantly to the previous evening and his sister Joan's tense white face when he dropped in at the house in Hammersmith. The house was a mean little two-up two-down in a terraced street off the Fulham Palace Road. Shutting the front door made the window-panes rattle. The front room was full of the hot smell of ironing, and a stack of linen was visible on the board. Joan was in the kitchen, cutting a loaf of bread with her back to him, but she had turned sharply when she heard the door, and the knife, coupled with the faint tracks of tears on her cheek, caused him to start in alarm.

'Don't fret. I'm not going to off myself, if that's what you thought. Making sandwiches for the boy's lunch.'

Harry went over to fill the kettle and put it on the hob. He assumed the false jollity that always came upon him when confronted with his sister.

'Had me worried there.'

His attempt at levity fell flat, as he guessed it would.

'Whoever told you you could save the world, Harry?'

He struck a match and lit the gas.

'I do my best.'

'Well, you'll have to try harder, the way things are going.'

She was pale as a sheet. Whereas Harry had inherited his father's darkly handsome swarthiness, Joan had mouse-coloured hair and a milksop complexion. It wasn't fair, with her being the girl, but then looks weren't everything, as Harry's last date, Violet, had kindly advised him.

At that moment, his nephew Jack came clattering down the stairs and Harry's heart lifted. Jack was short for his age, skinny and as pallid as his mother, with bony knees beneath his grey flannel shorts, jug ears and a clever face. He was rubbing his glasses on an ink-stained school tie but his eyes lit up when he saw Harry.

'How are you, Jack. Busy with prep?'

The boy grinned.

'Only maths. It's fine. Easy.'

His nephew was a whizz at maths, whereas Harry's mathematical skills had extended only as far as lying about his age so that he could join up for the war at seventeen. He still remembered the face of the maths master, Mr Grimwood, florid with rage. *Show your working, Fox! How else will you solve anything?*

'Good lad.'

He ruffled Jack's hair, close cropped and soft under his hand. Something about the cleft at the nape of the boy's neck induced a surge of protective feeling. Jack was wise for his years, with a quiet, watchful intelligence, and he tended to hang back from schoolboy interactions, unlike his uncle at the same age, who could always be found at the centre of a scrap.

Harry picked up a model aircraft, meticulously painted in green camouflage markings with a silver underside.

'Spitfire, is it?'

'Yes. If there's a war, they're going to beat the Messerschmitts hands down, if we make enough of them. I have a Wellington and a Hurricane too. Is there going to be a war, Uncle Harry?'

'We'll have to see.'

'Mum says not, but the man on the wireless said it was a

crisis, and he wouldn't've said that if it wasn't serious, would he? I shouldn't want a war, but I'd like to see a Jerry dive bomber.'

Harry was mystified where the boy's intelligence had come from – certainly not the kid's brute of a father, about whom the less said the better. He supposed Joan did have some brains before they were beaten out of her.

'And look at this, Uncle Harry.'

Jack withdrew an envelope from his pocket.

'It's a Penny Black. I'm about to put it in my album. Want to look?'

Of course he did.

Lingering now beside a lamp post, these thoughts evoked a twist of nausea and Harry clenched his hands in his pockets, focusing once more again on Orwell who was progressing, as expected, along Great Russell Street.

If you had to be a shadow, writers were the best kind of subject. They behaved, Harry had found, with extreme predictability. Another of his jobs was tailing a poet, once active in the brothels of Weimar Berlin but now established in Hampstead, in blissful matrimony. Harry had researched everything about him: his handwriting, his lovers, his choice of gin, the fact that some of his post was redirected to a cottage in Kent. And because he prided himself on his attention to detail, he had even read some of the man's stuff in a journal called *New Writing*, dedicated to social-realist literature. Apparently, reality was to be found in the life of the working class, and anyone who wanted to engage with it should go to the slums and grapple with genuine members of the proletariat. From what Harry knew, this particular writer had indeed grappled intimately with members of the proletariat, occasionally on his watch. But that was not his concern. Another of Harry's subjects, a journalist called Claud Cockburn, who had travelled with Graham Greene to the Rhineland and had an MI5 file the size of the *Encyclopaedia Britannica*, even knew he was being followed. Despite his distracted air and weak eyesight, he was adept at spotting shadows and would often make cheerful gestures to whichever operative had been assigned to him.

That didn't matter. What mattered was, writers always did what you expected.

At that moment George Orwell paused in front of an architectural heritage store featuring shabti figures, presumably looted from the Valley of the Kings, and a jumble of strange funerary objects from a previous civilization. Might he be checking the window for shadows? Harry hung back just in case, but almost immediately Orwell straightened up and turned left towards Tavistock Square.

He never did this. It was quite outside his normal pattern. The whole point of Orwell was that he never sprang surprises. Paddington station, Lyons' Corner House, Bloomsbury, bookshop, home. Clockwork. In all matters, from roll-ups to writing, Orwell valued routine.

Harry commenced a rapid, head-down stride as the crowd of commuters coursed around him. His view was momentarily blocked by a woman in the kind of waterproof hat worn on a deep-sea trawler, but when he looked up again, he saw that all was well. Orwell was merely posting a letter.

He sighed with relief. Thus far, God willing, he had never lost one.

# CHAPTER 4

*September 13th*

The following morning Stella came into the sitting room to find Evelyn sitting in an armchair, her head tilted back and last night's make-up in smudged rings around her eyes. She was still wearing her evening dress and had plainly not been to bed.

'What's the matter?'

'Oh, there you are, Stel.' She looked up. 'I'm afraid something rather awful's happened. You'll never guess.'

'Roger's decided not to leave his wife.'

'No. Well, yes. But that's not it.'

Once again, a terrible vision came to Stella in which the pair of them were still living and bickering together as old ladies. She flinched and shrugged it away.

'It's this,' Evelyn went on.

She turned the newspaper lying folded on her lap. Stella

read the headline: 'Chamberlain to Visit . . .' Alongside it, the Prime Minister loomed in a starched wing collar and striped trousers wearing his familiar grimace of beaky anxiety. He was about to board a twin-engine Lockheed 14 at Heston aerodrome.

'Where's he visiting? Is it something about war?'

Everything was about war, or at least the prospect of it. Since Hitler had marched into Austria that March, it was all anyone talked about.

'No, it's not war.' Evelyn pointed below the fold. 'It's him. That author you were talking about yesterday. The one who's given you work.'

'Mr Newman? What about him?'

'He's dead.'

Stella felt the breath catch in her mouth.

'He can't be!'

'He is. Found collapsed in Westminster Abbey. Yesterday evening. And to think you'd just seen him.'

Stella snatched the newspaper from Evelyn's hands:

'Thriller Writer Discovered Dead in Westminster Abbey. Fans Mourn Veteran Novelist. Agatha Christie Pays Tribute.'

It was accompanied by a photograph of Newman, evidently taken some years ago, wearing a smart suit with the flourish of a pocket handkerchief and a more abundant wave of hair slicked over his scalp.

The article said he had been found at six o'clock, just three hours after she had seen him.

'Apparently it was a heart attack,' said Evelyn. 'Or a stroke.'

The article continued on page seventeen under 'Home News', behind the sports pages. Once past the fact of the death, it dwelt at some length on the fact that Newman's most recent novel had been dramatized on the wireless, with a cast featuring the well-known actor Tommy Lazard, who had since relocated to Hollywood. A few paragraphs followed about Lazard, whose performance in the programme had been acclaimed. Eventually, the journalist returned to the subject of Newman himself. He was 'the most English of writers'. Critics had called his novels 'the quintessence of Englishness'. The country rectories and stately homes which so often formed his settings 'epitomized everything we Britons hold dear about our green and pleasant land.' Others speculated that 'the kind of comfortable mysteries which Newman wrote may feel out of place in our chilly and dangerous world. Yet it is for that very reason that he is cherished throughout the nation.'

Evelyn hauled herself up, draped a dressing gown over her dress and drifted across to the kitchen.

'I'm frightfully sorry. But you didn't actually know him, did you? I mean, not properly. Not like a friend or anything.'

'No. I only met him the once.'

'So it's a terrible shock, but . . .' Already, Evelyn was distracted.

'Darling, I'm whacked. I need to go to bed. I didn't get

in till six. Three of those cocktails at the Ritz and you feel like a bomb's gone off in your head.'

Stella barely heard her. Her head was ringing with a sense – one that had often come to her before – of foreboding. It was like the electric air before a storm, or the feeling of trepidation when knocking on a strange door.

'I don't suppose you bought Nescafé?' said Evelyn.

Automatically Stella nodded and Evelyn lifted a vague hand.

'Something came for you. It must have been the early post. I found it on the table in the hall when I came in.'

It was a heavy package. Inside an outer wrapping of brown paper was a large envelope, sealed with masking tape. The torn edges of the tape suggested that the sender had ripped it with their teeth, either in a fit of impatience or because they couldn't find scissors. Inside the envelope was a thick ream of paper which Stella withdrew carefully, in case the unbound pages spilled out onto the floor. As she looked more closely, her hands began to shake. The first page bore a single word in spidery black ink.

Masquerade.

She sank down onto a chair and tried to look at the page calmly and objectively, as she would have done just a day earlier. Yet the mass of paper resting on her lap felt like a living thing. As though Hubert Newman himself had assumed another form and risen up to find her. He must have parcelled it up and sent it immediately after their lunch.

Attached to the title page was an envelope inscribed

'Payment in advance', inside which was a cheque for five guineas from Coutts Bank, made out to her.

Tentatively, she flipped the title page and set it to one side by her feet. The remainder of the manuscript was composed in the same crabbed black hand, as though written by a scribe in the Dark Ages with a quill pen. The paper was fine quality, but the dense rows of tiny, forward-sloping sentences made her eyes glaze over. She knew it would be a devil to read. There were repeated crossings out and arrows pointing to additions in the margins. She frowned and turned back to the beginning.

The second page contained just a single line which she scanned at first swiftly, then again slowly, forcing herself to focus and refocus.

'To Stella, spotter of mistakes.'

She read it out loud, hearing Newman's voice clearly in her head.

'It's dedicated to me!'

Evelyn lifted an eyebrow.

'Touching.'

'I can't believe it. I barely knew him.'

'Well, you obviously made an impression.'

For a second, the air around Stella seemed to condense and she was acutely aware of Evelyn's half-smoked cigarette smouldering in an ashtray, the faint cry of children playing outside intercut with the hoot of a tug on the river. She felt a piercing sorrow that this manuscript on her lap represented Hubert Newman's last enterprise, the final statement of his existence. It was almost as though she held his life in her hands.

Immediately, she shook herself. That was shock talking. The responsible thing would be to track down Newman's publisher and hand the manuscript over. But first, perhaps, she owed it to him to complete her commission of typing and copy-editing.

As she squinted at the line on the page, Newman's waxy face swam once more before her.

'To Stella, spotter of mistakes.'

Somehow, it felt more like a demand than a dedication.

# CHAPTER 5

The basement of the Café de Paris was host to a cocktail of actors, journalists, writers and socialites who could be relied on to attend any party for any play, even a musical that had closed after only a few months at the Hippodrome. Perhaps it really was the machinations of politicians in faraway countries, rather than the show itself, that caused *Big Business* to falter. But whatever the cause, if attendances had been disappointing, the wake had drawn a capacity crowd.

Stella was milling around the fringes of the party, wondering when she could slip away.

She came to a halt at the foot of the twin staircases where a basement dance floor edged by gilt legged chairs was circled by guests smoking, laughing and embracing each other. To the backdrop of a band crooning 'Pennies from Heaven', the latest West End bankruptcy was discussed. Now that the curtain had fallen, no one was mincing their words.

'The reviews were an absolute horror story. Wretched press. All of them competing to outdo the others.'

'Careful what you say. That's the *Daily Express* over there.'

'What does it matter? That man has more blood on his hands than Herod. He likes nothing better than murdering plays.'

It did matter, though, Stella knew. Beneath the glitter and champagne, the theatrical life was savage, and a run cut short was enough to sabotage careers. Now, over that perennial fear, another one lay – that not only careers but lives might be cut short by another war.

Beside her, a group of journalists clustered, distinguishable by the notebooks in their top pockets and their air of vague discontent. One lifted his nose, as if sniffing for gossip.

'Is anyone here? I was assured Larry was coming.'

'No such luck.'

'Larry would attend the opening of an envelope.'

'He would, but this is a closing. Larry doesn't want to be seen around failure.'

'I've heard of first-night parties, but it's come to something when we're having parties for flops.'

'Not their fault, poor darlings.' It was a woman with a hard fringe and eyes etched in kohl. Stella vaguely remembered seeing her face above a byline in the *Daily Mail*.

'The mood's wrong. It's all politics now. That's all anyone's talking about.'

Disconsolately, the journalists surveyed the room.

'Look at them all. It might as well be a cocktail party for Winston. They're all his supporters.'

'Winston's the real leader of the opposition,' said the *Mail* woman.

'The country hasn't been so divided since the civil war. It's all Roundheads and Cavaliers, and the Cavaliers are so much more fun.'

Stella's attention was caught by a man standing on his own in the corner. Despite an outwardly languid demeanour, he was regarding the room with the kind of coiled attention of a big cat at the zoo. He was in his forties, probably, and strikingly handsome, with a hefty build and the kind of face that needed two shaves a day but only got one. Unlike the other male guests, his dark hair did not gleam with brilliantine. His tie was loosely knotted and the top button of his shirt was undone. The good looks were spoiled by a scar that ran from the corner of his left eye, tugging it slightly downwards before ending the other side of the cheekbone. He had a faint corrugation of lines on his forehead and a crinkle of smile lines fanning out at the sides of his eyes. What with the scar, and the stubble, he looked like what her mother would describe as 'a rough sort'. An actor, no doubt.

He was glancing covertly at a woman whom Stella assumed to be an actress, judging by the circle of admirers around her who were rocking with laughter at something she had just said. He was not the only person watching her.

Everyone was. She wore a clinging dress of indigo silk and her lips were boldly outlined in scarlet. Her peroxide hair and pearls glowed like neon in the murky basement light.

A booming voice to Stella's left made her jump and she turned to see a man in a dinner jacket lurching towards her.

'Stella Fry! Flatmate of the divine Evelyn.' He stuck out a hand. 'Roger Anson. I've heard a lot about you.'

'I've heard a little about you, too.'

'All bad, I hope.'

He gave a pantomime wink and tipped a dose of Scotch down his throat. He had a bristly ginger moustache and matching gingery strands extending across a gleaming scalp. Everything about him, from the raddled charm to the flabby figure and whisky breath, fulfilled Stella's expectations.

'Fancy coming on to a club after this?'

'Well, I'm not sure that—'

'It's on me, darling. It's my party.'

'I'm a bit tired.'

'Surely a little pleasure can't hurt. You look like you could do with some fun.'

Roger's eyes roved up and down, taking in her violet Jaeger dress – a favourite – and the single strand of pearls. She had secured her bobbed, shoulder-length brown hair with a rhinestone clip.

'Evelyn tells me you were working for the writer chap. The one who died.'

'Yes. I met him only yesterday. I can hardly believe it.'

'What a way to go. In the cloisters of Westminster Abbey!'

She paused a moment, then musingly uttered the thought that had been going through her mind.

'It's odd. He didn't look like a man about to die.'

'D'you think he might have planned it? Suicide? These writer chaps can get depressed. The Black Dog and so on.'

'Oh, I couldn't possibly say. As I said, I only met him once.'

Around them, ears were pricking up at the mention of Hubert Newman. Faces turned in their direction and Stella was riven by a fresh jolt of sympathy for the dead man, so swiftly reduced to an item of cocktail party gossip. She deployed a reliable exit strategy.

'Isn't that Ivor Novello over there? I hear he's in the new *Henry V* at Drury Lane.'

At the sniff of celebrity, Roger's eyes swivelled instantly away.

'I think you're right. Excuse me, would you? I must have a word. And remember, darling, the invitation stands!'

Looking around for Evelyn, she heard her friend's high laugh and caught sight of her following Roger's progress across the room. She felt a pang of tenderness. He was not remotely worthy of her, but Evelyn knew what she wanted, and if Roger Anson was what it took to achieve it, she would have to take him.

She went over and murmured in her friend's ear.

'I'm leaving.'

'You can't! We've only just begun. Roger's taking some of us on to the Astor Club.'

'Sorry.'

'We're having Chinese food.'

'I'm exhausted. I'll be fast asleep when you get back.'

It had rained during the party. A warm mist of drops still flickered across the neon facades of Piccadilly Circus and the wet pavement gleamed with strip-lit advertisements. Random words in red, yellow and green throbbed in the darkness. 'Craven "A" for Your Throat's Sake'. 'Esso'. 'Schweppes Ginger Ale'. 'Wrigley's Chewing Gum'.

She wanted to walk. Despite what she had told Evelyn, she was anything but exhausted. In the last twenty-four hours, the shock of Newman's death, and the surprise of the manuscript dedicated to her, had reverberated through her entire body, making her jittery and unsettled. A walk would calm her down, or at least tire her enough to sleep. She would head down Haymarket, then across to Northumberland Avenue and carry on southwards in the direction of the river.

She couldn't say how she first noticed that she was being followed. The pavements at this hour were quiet, the streets shadowy and the light of the street lamps interspersed with pools of darkness. Buses heaved their way up towards Regent Street and taxis passed, switching off their lights as the drivers headed to their homes south of the Thames. Other traffic was infrequent and the few pedestrians hurried, intent on getting home.

The footsteps behind her were not heavy or threatening, but merely regular, in a precise echo and distance from her own. A metronome, marking out her own restless tread. She gripped her clutch bag tighter under her arm and quickened her step.

Passing Suffolk Place, a quiet terrace of stucco and cream pillars, she diverted suddenly, but the footsteps followed and, before she had gone ten yards, a man drew level and she nearly jumped out of her skin.

'You're pretty elusive, Miss Fry.'

She turned to find a tall figure, whose hat cast a slanting shadow over his face.

'I took my eyes off you for one second to find another of those gin cocktails, and when I looked again, you'd vanished.'

She snatched a breath to quell her quickening heartbeat.

'I'm sorry. Do I know you?'

'My name's Harry Fox.'

It was the man she had noticed at the party. Beneath the hat he had a broad face and a wide, expressive mouth that reminded her, irrelevantly, of a Holbein painting. One of the Ambassadors in the National Gallery, powerful and composed, though somewhat less well dressed.

'Forgive me. Are you a friend of Evelyn's?'

'Not exactly.'

'Well, you'll have to excuse me, Mr Fox, but it's late.'

'I didn't mean to startle you. I wanted a word. If you're not in a hurry.'

She clutched her bag more tightly to her chest.

'I *am* in a hurry.'

Why would she not be? It was drizzling and nearly eleven o'clock.

'And can I ask how you know my name?'

'Chap with a voice like a foghorn was talking to you.'

'What were we talking about?'

'Hubert Newman.'

Instantly, a horrible thought struck her.

'Are you . . . a journalist?'

He seemed affronted.

'Do I look like a journalist?'

'I wouldn't know. I don't know any journalists.' She huddled further into her jacket. 'As I said, I need to be getting home, so I should say goodnight.'

She began to walk on, but immediately the man fell into step beside her, his pace exactly in sync.

'I'm approaching you in a private capacity.'

'Well, I'm sorry to disappoint you, but if you actually overheard our conversation, you'd have heard that I didn't really know Mr Newman.'

'I did.'

She looked up at him sharply.

'Oh. I'm sorry. Were you friends?'

'Yes. That is, we met recently. We corresponded.'

He shot a look at the sky, where a mist of rain was thickening.

'Perhaps we could find somewhere more comfortable to talk?'

'At this time of night?'

'I know a place that's still open. It's not far.'

She hesitated awkwardly, just for a few seconds, then agreed.

She would wonder, in retrospect, whether that had been the moment. The instant at which she might have refused and hurried home, perhaps even spending precious shillings on a taxi, before turning peacefully into her bed. After a night of good sleep, she would wake refreshed and ready to look for a full-time job – maybe another teaching position like the one she had applied for in a girls' school on the south coast. She would work hard, make new friends, and in the evenings she might show them her photographs of Vienna and Paris and Rome with a nostalgic smile. She would join a tennis club. Learn bridge. Her career would travel a path of quiet predictability and she would have been spared all the extraordinary events that subsequently engulfed her life.

The café was an Italian place with a jar of plastic geraniums in the window and a steamed-up glass door. Harry held it open, then followed her through. His confident tread, and the fact that he did not so much as glance around him, told her this was not his first visit.

He chose a table at the back with a sauce bottle and a sugar jar. As they sat down, a plump man in a stained apron hurried over and clasped his hand as though being reunited with a long-lost brother.

'Mr Fox! Is late! What can I do for you? You want food?'

'Just coffee please, Luigi.' Harry nodded at Stella. 'And for my friend.'

Still beaming, the man disappeared behind the counter and began to set out the cups. Stella looked around. The light was dim and the only other customer was an elderly chain-smoker studying the racing form who barely glanced up. How odd they must have appeared – the woman in the party dress and her companion in his shabby mac.

Harry slid a packet of Senior Service onto the table, offered her one which she declined, then lit one for himself. He rested one arm on the back of the chair and took a drag. Close up she caught his scent, a melange of undiluted masculinity made up of tobacco, alcohol and sweat.

Two cups were deposited in front of them on the scratched deal tabletop. The coffee was rich and aromatic and could not be less like the watery substance to be found in most London restaurants and tea shops. Instantly she was reminded of the Caffè Gille in Florence, whose stately mahogany fittings and high ceilings were in dramatic contrast to the tiny, exquisite cups of coffee they served. And of a handsome Austrian with a strong nose and ice-blue eyes sitting across from her, laughing. Reaching across to move the hair out of her eyes, then taking her hand in his. But she pushed the memory away. Now was no time for brooding, and besides, the man opposite her now was a complete stranger who was watching her every move, and acting as though they were already connected in a way she knew nothing about.

'Are you a regular here, Mr Fox?'

'I've helped Luigi in the past.'

'Helped him with what?'

His hand made a little horizontal gesture.

'This and that.'

'You said you knew Hubert Newman. I'm sorry for your loss. His death must have been a shock.'

'It was.' He rubbed the edge of his coffee cup, as though pondering a philosophical problem. 'When did you last see him?'

'Actually, we only met once. Yesterday. At the Athenaeum.'

He nodded and pushed the sugar towards her. He had large hands, with a curl of hair on the knuckles. The fingers were long and slender – piano player's hands, as such fingers were always described – though Harry Fox did not look like he spent much time with Beethoven.

'And why did you meet?'

She didn't have to explain to him, but she was here now, drinking delicious Italian coffee, and although Harry Fox looked a little rough, he didn't seem likely to attack her.

'I answered an advertisement in *The Times* to do some typing for him. I'm not a typist,' she added, surprised that she cared what he might think. 'I'm a tutor. I've lived abroad for the past five years.'

'Long time.'

'I suppose.'

He tilted his head and let out a jet of cigarette smoke.

'It must have taken some vim. For a young woman to

set out for the Continent on her own. I assume it was on your own?'

'It was.' And it had.

'D'you miss it? Abroad? Wish you were still there?'

'No point right now.'

Whether it was the warmth of the café, or the friendliness of Luigi, or the searching way that Harry Fox looked at her, Stella found her reserve melting. Something about him made her want to talk.

'How was it you came to be there?'

'The professor who taught me German at university was approached by a family in Vienna who were looking for someone to tutor their children. He remembered me, so he got in contact and I took the job.'

'How did that work out?'

'Beautifully. They were a wonderful family, the Gatzes. Herr Gatz had a shoe business, with a factory and a couple of shops. There were three clever children, two boys and a girl. We did everything together, played tennis and swam, travelled all round Europe. They treated me like one of the family. But in spring they had to leave in a hurry. They were Jewish, you see.'

He nodded solemnly.

'So I had to come back home too. And I needed work, which was why I replied to Mr Newman's advertisement.'

'To type his new novel.'

'Not a novel, actually. It was a work of non-fiction. About the Shakespeare authorship question.'

'The what?'

'The idea that Shakespeare didn't write his own plays. That someone else did, under a pen name.'

Harry Fox looked mystified, then shook his head.

'You mentioned – I couldn't help hearing – that Mr Newman didn't seem like a man about to die. What did you mean by that?'

'Nothing really. It was just a casual remark. I'm not a doctor. I wouldn't know how a man about to die might look.'

'So why did you say it?'

'It was . . .'

'It was a hunch?'

'I suppose.'

'You should always trust hunches. How did he seem? When you saw him?'

'He seemed . . .' Stella thought back to the pallid, frightened face with its sheen of sweat and the badly bitten nails. 'He said he was worried.'

'Did he say what he was worried about?'

She tried to recall the moment. Newman's lamb chop congealing in its gravy as he looked around distractedly.

'His exact words were "*I am worried*." I assume he meant because of the prospect of war and so on.'

'Why did you assume that?'

'It's pretty obvious, isn't it?'

The door banged open, bringing in a waft of night air, and Harry looked up sharply, not at the new customer, but at his reflection in the window. It was a cabbie, in a flat cap and neckerchief, who explained to the waitress that he had left his taxi around the corner and popped in for a cuppa as he was 'parched'. Having bought tea and a bun, he parked them on the adjacent table and settled down, unfolding a copy of *The Times* in front of him. As Stella finished her coffee, Harry said abruptly, 'Shall we go?'

He nodded goodnight to Luigi, left sixpence on the counter and walked ahead of her out of the café. Stella was obliged to follow, if only to thank him for the coffee and say a definitive farewell, but he kept walking, hands thrust in pockets, until he diverted down a narrow alley scattered with scraps of rubbish. Up ahead a chef in his whites was smoking at the back entrance of a restaurant, a plume of smoke catching in the wedge of light emanating from the kitchen door.

There he wheeled round to face her, leaning against a wall, his face in shadow.

'Did you notice anything unusual about that chap?'

'He said he was a cabbie but he was reading *The Times*?'

'Precisely. Perhaps he's not a cabbie and he was interested in our conversation.'

'Perhaps he's interested in current affairs. Or maybe someone left the paper in the back of his cab.'

Stella was no longer nervous of Harry Fox, although he was clearly eccentric.

'I'm afraid you're going to have to explain what this is about because, as I said, I'm in a hurry.'

Yet she wasn't really. She was wide awake and the caffeine was already buzzing through her veins. Her curiosity was piqued. 'If you're not from the newspapers, why are you asking all these questions?'

'Because my guess is that Hubert Newman did not die a natural death.'

Instinctively, she took a step back.

'What are you suggesting?'

'A number of things,' he said. 'I'll need to explain. But not here. I'd prefer you came to my office tomorrow.'

'Why not explain here?'

'Because it's wet and I have a hole in my shoe.'

He thrust a scrap of paper at her. It looked as though it had been torn from a notebook.

'The address is on there.'

'I'm not sure I'm free. I haven't said I'll come—'

'It's the top bell.'

Stella turned, and as she went, she sensed his eyes on her, appraising every inch of her as she walked swiftly down the street.

# CHAPTER 6

After she had left, Harry Fox hurried through the rain to Newman's home. The mansion flats in Paddington were tall, red-brick Edwardian affairs, with the names of the individual blocks inscribed in gold leaf behind glass above each door. The net-curtained facade was faded but eminently respectable, like its mostly elderly inhabitants. Its solidity suggested that if Herr Hitler did let loose bombs on London, as people were predicting, they would barely trouble the foundations.

At this time of night, the hall was plunged in darkness and it was a matter of moments to let himself in. He had made sure to keep an old set of skeleton keys from his time at Scotland Yard, which he had joined right after the war. While it would have gratified him to gain entry without them, the urgency of the situation, coupled with his personal interest, meant he couldn't afford to wait. Not that it would have bothered him to encounter resistance. Fox's First Law of Physics said that force equalled strength plus intelligence. Nobody, however, appeared out of the gloom, and the lock yielded softly to his key.

Once inside, with the door firmly closed, he pocketed his torch, switched on the light and the flat sprang into view. It was exactly as he'd imagined. Newman had lived there for several decades, though he kept a cottage in Shipton-under-Wychwood for weekends. Harry stood for a moment, as the sense impressions queued up to meet him. He smelled vacancy, as though the place itself could tell that it was now redundant. The air was filled with books and paper, and particles of furniture polish mingled with traces of sandalwood cologne. Yet when Harry sniffed for any trace of boot leather and damp mackintosh – the signature perfume of his erstwhile colleagues – he detected nothing.

It was a pleasure for him to exercise his skills; the idiosyncratic toolset that he had honed and developed over the years. Generally, the job of watching involved only elementary footwork, so given the opportunity, it was satisfying to interpret a swirl of information, test hypotheses and reach a conclusion.

He waited, allowing the same process as always to run through his mind. He was imagining himself looking at the scene through the eyes of Newman himself. What did he see? What did the room tell him about Newman's state of mind?

There was no sign that the author had known he was leaving it for the last time. In the small kitchen, a Royal

Doulton teacup sat in the sink and the larder contained a standard-issue bachelor kit of Prince's corned beef, tea, powdered milk and sugar that was strikingly similar to Harry's own. This he registered with a pang, recognizing also the half-used loaf of bread, draped with a tea towel on the counter, the scrap of butter in waxed paper, the Cooper's marmalade and remains of a boiled egg. He checked the insides of the saucepans and delved into the china cabinet, lifting up each of the cups.

Across the corridor, the bed clothes on the narrow divan were awry, but the disarray did not look romantic, mingled as it was with a tie and a couple of spare socks. Inside the wardrobe several pairs of hand-made Church's shoes, as polished as conkers, were lined up; he checked them, from habit, for signs of hollowed-out heels. The tiny bathroom cabinet contained a bottle of Sanatogen nerve tonic, a packet of Rennie's indigestion tablets and a pot of Brylcreem.

Somewhere above him a door slammed. He froze for a moment in his inventory-taking, listening acutely, before continuing his prowl to the drawing room.

It was dominated by stolid mahogany furniture and a chintz armchair under a brass reader's lamp with an oblong green shade. Harry observed it all carefully. Furniture spoke, if you were prepared to listen to it. On a recent job, posing as an employee of Wilson's Ltd, Painters and Decorators, he had noticed that every painting and drawing in the subject's home featured scenes of the British coastline. Exactly the kind that might come in useful to a foreign power contemplating invasion.

Newman's own paintings, however, were interesting in a different way. Far from the genteel watercolour tableaux that a well-to-do Englishman of advancing years might collect, the artwork on the walls resembled, at least to Harry, a lunatic mind laid bare. Slashed lines and harsh, jagged blocks of colour. Some were discernibly portraits of women, if not the kind of women Harry ever came across, with projectile breasts and aggressive, sprawling legs. Others were no more than jumbles and scrawls. Modernist, he got that, but all the same . . . odd. Anomalies bothered him. Inconsistencies, contradictions, unexpected quirks. He stood for a moment, taking them in, before turning away to continue the search.

Unlike the paintings, Newman's photographs held no such surprises. A glass-fronted cabinet was crowded with pictures: Newman receiving a prize, plumped up in evening dress. Newman outside his Oxfordshire home, clutching a white cat. The house, with hollyhocks and roses climbing over the door, recalled exactly the chocolate-box cottages that appeared in so many of his novels. Someone whom Harry took to be Newman's mother, a hard-faced harridan in a black felt hat. A college photograph featuring a set of youths, including the young novelist, lounging self-consciously in blazers and straw boaters, and another, trussed up in costume, performing some play in a quad. Harry tilted this towards him quizzically. He could clearly see the older Newman in his younger self. Poised, self-possessed, tight-lipped.

Another picture, from the same era, featured a group of men in somebody's flat, turning towards the camera. Newman was in wide trousers and braces, standing behind them with one hand resting on a chair. And then a further trio: a slightly more mature Newman in a polka dot bow tie, sandwiched between an older man and a dark-haired woman. This one he slipped out of its frame and tucked it in his jacket pocket for later.

The bookshelves ran across two walls, floor to ceiling. Harry upended a couple of volumes and probed them for cavities or folded scraps of paper, then ran a gloved finger enviously along the spines. The complete works of Shakespeare; a selection of rare volumes – Newman was clearly a fastidious collector; and above them a sentry line of every novel he had written, from *Traitor's Gate* onwards. On top was a shelf of poetry.

Poetry reminded Harry of the bad times, after his dismissal from the Yard, when a woman he'd cared about had left him, and every day felt like November. Gloom had hung over him like a low fog and he'd tried a bit of poetry for medicinal reasons but it hadn't worked. Since then, having tailed a few poets, he was astonished that anyone might consider them any guide to life.

He glanced at the foreigners – Baudelaire, Rimbaud, Rilke, Goethe – and then the home team: Wordsworth, Coleridge, Tennyson, Auden, Spender. The last name gave

Harry a start. Stephen Spender had been one of his marks for a time, and tailing the energetic poet had been a full-time job. He recalled the report of his predecessor, who had been obliged to attend an event at Hornsey town hall at which Mr Spender was speaking on the future of world socialism. Not most people's idea of an evening out, but the place had been packed and the policeman was obliged to conceal himself in the gents to avoid notice. Harry smirked at the memory of his report. 'I was unable to hear the majority of the proceedings owing to my obscure position in the lavatory and to the fact that a boy was standing in the cloakroom door the whole time. I heard someone say that the best thing would be for world socialism to triumph but I cannot vouch whether Spender himself confirmed this view.'

He drifted over to the roll-top desk, rifled through the pigeonholes and found an address book of soft brown leather with gilt edges which he flicked through, then slipped into his jacket pocket. He would comb through it later, not only for names, but for those names which might be something else altogether: codes or dates or places. He enjoyed this amateur cryptography. He was astonished how often intelligent men would resort to the enigmatic marks and mirror writing of a teenage girl's diary.

The surface of the desk was arranged with spinsterish tidiness: stamps, envelopes, ink and pens all in their allotted place. This order, however, was disturbed by a letter, ripped from its envelope and lying askew on the blotting pad.

He picked it up. The envelope was postmarked two days earlier. Newman must have read it the same day that he died.

The letterhead said: 'Professor Frederick Lindemann, Christ Church College, Oxford', and the note was at once brief and enigmatic.

*Dear Newman,*
*I find your allegations both grotesque and completely incredible.*
*Furthermore, your remarks reflect badly on you as a gentleman.*
*I would be grateful if you would refrain from contacting me again.*
*Yours sincerely,*
*F.A. Lindemann*

Harry frowned, and read it again, his heart gathering pace. Then he replaced the letter in its envelope and stashed it in his pocket. This seemed very far from fan mail. It confirmed his suspicion that something had been troubling Hubert Newman. Something that may have led to his death.

The letter also proved that the police had not bothered to visit, as otherwise they'd have taken it. They had quickly lost interest in Hubert Newman's sudden demise. The man was dead and buried, as far as officialdom was concerned.

Harry didn't know whether to be pleased or angry.

All the same, he could see this letter would be hard to follow up. Even with his forged Special Branch card, even with a search warrant he could write himself, the thought of fetching up at Christ Church College to quiz a bad-tempered professor about an unknown allegation was some way beyond his talents.

Then the face of Stella Fry, with her intelligent gaze and defiant tilt of the chin, came to his mind. The straight brows and the way she shrugged her slim shoulders at him as she stood her ground. Early thirties, five foot five, brown eyes, brunette hair secured with a clip at the side, slender build, regular features, good teeth, attractive. Single, or no visible wedding ring. No distinguishing marks. He had filed away her details as though she was a subject, for God's sake. It was a bad habit of his.

Beyond her physical attributes, though, she was a mystery.

The friend, Evelyn, was easier to assess. She looked like a piece of work. Sweet to look at but hard enough to break a tooth on. He'd met plenty of Evelyn's type over the years and courted them too, with some success.

Stella Fry, though, seemed different. Not softer, necessarily, but tough. Those brown eyes were unreadable, which was a quality he admired, and she seemed like someone who watched people herself. Observed and evaluated them.

She was resourceful too. She must be. It would have required a certain amount of pluck to go off to the Continent for five years on her own, but when he had probed, she wasn't giving anything away.

'*I haven't said I'll come.*'

He hoped to hell she did, because he didn't have any other ideas.

# CHAPTER 7

*September 14th*

'Thought you might need this.'

Evelyn appeared through the bedroom door around seven the following morning and placed a glass of water and an aspirin on Stella's bedside table. Not precisely on the table, but atop the stacked manuscript of Hubert Newman's *Masquerade*, onto which some water slopped, dampening the title page.

As soon as Stella had returned the previous night, she had rifled through the manuscript, hoping against hope that some clue to Newman's death might lie within. It was four hundred and thirty-four pages long, and such a doorstop that it hurt to hold for too long and she needed to wedge herself in bed with the manuscript against her knees, looking through a section at a time. It was divided into two parts. The first chapter was entitled 'The Child' and proceeded in the kind of pedestrian tone that made one wish the child had been strangled at birth. '*The genius we call William Shakespeare was born in Stratford-upon-Avon on April 23rd, 1564 . . .*'

Other chapters followed in similar vein. 'The Schoolboy', 'The Actor', 'The Manager', 'The Courtier', 'The Husband', 'The Pretenders', 'The Stratford Man'. Neither Shakespeare's sense of drama or Newman's apparent skill as a detective writer had been allowed to intrude on the narrative. What had he been thinking? Had he been cowed by the sanctity of his subject? It was like reading the telephone directory in the handwriting of a medieval monk.

Did he actually want anyone to read this book?

The two parts of the manuscript were different lengths. Part two was much shorter, only two chapters long. The first chapter, entitled 'The Pretenders', was a long discussion on the Shakespeare authorship question.

*Many have questioned the identity of the mind behind the greatest works in the English language. They have suggested that the name Shakespeare may be a pseudonym for a genius who preferred to remain anonymous. It has seemed incredible to scholars over the centuries that the humble son of a country glove maker could possibly possess the erudition or experience required to write these masterpieces.*

The chapter went into detail on the biographies of individuals including Sir Francis Bacon, and the Earl of Oxford who had at various times been suggested as the playwright himself.

Stella yawned. Simply deciphering the tiny, crabbed hieroglyphics was a migraine in the making. She wondered if Hubert Newman's secretary had really left because of impending war, or failing eyesight, or whether she just couldn't take any more. Eventually, her eyelids drooping, she had abandoned the attempt, surrendering to a sleep that was fractured by visions of the Gatz children playing in the cloisters of Westminster Abbey and discovering the body of Hubert Newman in the shadows. And of Harry Fox looming up out of the Piccadilly evening, telling her to trust her hunches.

'Thought you might have a bit of a head,' said Evelyn, indicating the aspirin.

'That's kind of you. How did yesterday's audition go?'

'The director said I'd be out of my depth. He's got a nerve. He gave the part to Daisy Delves and she'd be out of her depth in a bird bath. She must be pushing forty.'

'Where are you off to, then?'

Evelyn was fully dressed. Max Factor Scarlet Whisper lipstick. Hair newly curled off her face. Jaunty little hat with a velvet band. Jacket with a row of Perspex buttons. And Stella's own French silk blouse, she noted.

'As it happens, another audition's come up. It's a late stand-in for Michael MacOwan's *Troilus and Cressida* at the

Westminster Theatre. I'd be playing Cassandra and under-studying Diana Sowerby as Helen of Troy.'

'Who?'

'You must know her. Blonde. Brassy. Britain's answer to Jean Harlow. She's everywhere.'

'I've been abroad, remember.'

'Anyway,' Evelyn paused with one hand on the doorknob. 'If you don't have anything to do, Stella, would you mind awfully doing a little cleaning and tidying? I have someone coming back later. An awfully nice chap who paints murals. You don't have anything to do, do you?'

Stella didn't. And that, she told herself, was the only reason she was planning to visit the enigmatic Harry Fox.

The queue for gas masks outside Chelsea Town Hall stretched past the number 22 bus stop all the way to the fire station. Fathers and mothers, each with children attached, infants in prams and pushchairs, larger ones hanging off their mothers' hands, schoolboys fizzing with excitement, school-girls casting wide-eyed glances around them. Watching the little groups, Stella was reminded of the card game everyone had played when she was a child – Happy Families. To win, you needed to collect four of a kind. Mr Baker, Mrs Baker, Miss Baker, Master Baker. She had played it, too, with the Gatz children in Austria where it was called *Quartett*. That was what families were meant to be – everyone understood that. A father, mother, son and daughter. That was the win-ning hand in life.

But it was a long way from her own experience. Her Irish father had died when she was nine; killed by a freak lightning strike as he crossed Clapham Common in a rainstorm. After that, their mother had sold the house and taken Alan and Stella to live in a squashed little terrace in Chiswick with a damp basement, next door to a pub.

From the other side of the town hall, people were emerging with gas masks in cardboard boxes. A couple of boys were wearing theirs larkily, like some monstrous fancy dress, and the sight made her shiver. It couldn't really be possible, could it, that they might soon be dodging invisible poison gas? That the familiar facades of Chelsea might be smashed like children's bricks by dive bombers, and the birdsong drowned by the crump of shells?

The newspapers seemed certain of it. Every headline was a variation on 'Hitler Speaks Tomorrow', or 'Hitler's Speech'. The Prime Minister had taken an aeroplane from Croydon airport all the way to Bavaria in the hope of averting conflict. On an early autumn morning in Chelsea, war seemed utterly impossible, yet in the past few years Stella had already seen what was possible, not only for the Gatz family, but for thousands of others, and she was still trying to forget it.

As she stepped off the kerb she almost collided with a cyclist. He had come from nowhere, and she had only the chance to register the blur of a face beneath a cloth cap and a skitter of tyres before he wove around her and continued up the road without a backward glance.

How could she not have seen him? Almost certainly, she

realized, she had been too deep in thought. Perhaps it was a symptom of the times. The pace of international events had left them all jittery and unsettled. Everyone was distracted by the meetings of statesmen, the massing of distant armies and the uncertain future that awaited them.

She shook her head and looked again at the scrap of paper Harry Fox had given her.

Goodwin's Court was a tiny cobbled passageway six feet wide, with bay shopfronts, doors with Georgian fanlights and heavy iron lanterns. A passer-by might plausibly imagine that they had stepped off St Martin's Lane and straight into the eighteenth century. Tall, sooty buildings on each side shut out the light, and generations of pigeons had left their legacy on the brickwork. A pungent smell of beer emanated from the Seven Bells pub, and Stella could easily imagine figures from a Hogarth etching tumbling out of the door at last orders.

A scuffed sign beside the top bell of number 6 said Simpson Private Investigations and International Inquiries. A man was coming out so Stella slipped inside without buzzing, mounted the bare wooden stairs, and thrust open the glass door slightly too hard so that the pane rattled in the frame.

The office smelled of carbon paper and typewriter ink. Harry Fox was sitting behind the desk reading a magazine. An early five o'clock shadow dusted his jaw and his dark hair suggested no recent acquaintance with a brush. She doubted he had even been to bed.

He jumped up when she entered, and closed the magazine quickly, only giving her time to see a half-clothed woman on the cover and the title *Naturist*.

He turned it face down and said, 'Analysing this for signs of invisible ink.'

'Right.'

'Thank you for coming, Miss Fry. Would you like a cup of tea?'

He gestured towards a narrow, partitioned space containing a stove with a gas ring and a kettle, a packet of Tetley teabags and a cup containing sugar cubes.

'Yes, please. Thanks.'

As they waited for the kettle to boil, she stood awkwardly, arms folded, as though for a job interview, and looked around the cheap furniture and crowded shelves. The place was not exactly homely, but nor was it like any office she had ever seen. The paint on the wall was patchy and the leather chesterfield was sprouting horsehair from its cracks. A stained chaise longue on the far side of the room looked as though it might have done duty as a bed. The bookshelf was piled with magazines such as *Left Review* and *International Literature* and *New Writing*. On the mantelpiece, a half-obscured framed certificate said 'Officer of the Year'. A similar notice, with a crest and motto, was propped incongruously above a line of telephone directories. Next to this was a tarnished silver photograph frame displaying a sweet-faced boy in school uniform, with jug ears and a broad grin – Fox's son, presumably. In a Chinese plant pot on the mantelpiece, a spider plant was fighting for life and next to it a desk calendar, fluttering in a draught, displayed yesterday's date – September 13th. Splayed on the top of the desk, spine cracked, was a novel called *An Oxford Tragedy* by a J.C. Masterman.

Stella perched on the cracked chesterfield and crossed her legs.

'So, why's your business called Simpson Investigations? Who's Simpson?'

'It's a long story.'

He brought the teapot over, together with a pair of cups blotched with tea stains, and five digestive biscuits, fanned out on a plate in a stab at gentility. He nodded at the Masterman paperback.

'Are you keen on detective fiction?'

'It's not my favourite,' she said carefully.

She was about to say she preferred big European works – Tolstoy, Flaubert, Balzac, Thomas Mann – to cosy detective novels, but it sounded pretentious and besides, this was not a literary encounter. She was here because Harry Fox had made alarming suggestions about Hubert Newman's death.

'Don't know what you're missing,' said Harry, dropping three sugar cubes in his tea. 'I like a good mystery. A murder. That one there's by an Oxford don. Clever chap. What makes one person want to kill another?'

'I can't imagine.'

'Hubert Newman was the master, though. Superb. I've read them all. His best are locked-room thrillers.'

'What are they?'

'Where the crime takes place in a sealed environment. Like murder in a remote castle. Seemingly impossible.'

He blew on his tea, and Stella imagined her mother shuddering. Despite her reduced circumstances, or perhaps because of them, Nancy Fry clung to what she did possess, which was a comprehensive knowledge of correct behaviour. Her mother was a scholar of domestic etiquette, skilled in the proper use of fish knives and notepaper, and the correct distinctions between 'looking glass' and 'mirror'.

'And Newman's detective,' Harry went on, 'Peverell Drake. That man's a creation of genius. "I look for answers where nobody thought there were questions." That's his motto.'

'It's certainly catchy.'

'Not that Hubert Newman was my responsibility. I read him for pleasure. You wouldn't think they'd be my kind of thing, detective stories. Murders. Busman's holiday.'

'Oh! So, you're a policeman?'

He sniffed, and she guessed that getting any kind of information would be difficult. She suspected that Harry Fox was his own locked room.

He lit a Senior Service, waved the pack encouragingly in her direction and she took one.

'What did you mean when you said Hubert Newman was not your responsibility? What exactly is your responsibility?'

This question provoked a surprising response. Harry got up restlessly, walked to the end of the office and stared out of the window, hands in his pockets. He paused for so long, she began to wonder if something was wrong. If he was, actually, a little mad. Then he returned, sat down and leaned towards her.

'I'm only telling you this, Miss Fry, because you're in it now. You have a right to know. It affects you.'

He puffed his cheeks and blew on his tea again, leaving another meaningful pause, before saying, 'I'm a shadow. I follow people. Writers, mostly.'

'You follow *writers*?'

'Someone has to.'

'Which ones?'

'Not sure you'd know any of them.'

He reached for a file on his desk and fetched out a picture of a young man with a slick of oiled hair flopping over his brow, a bow tie and elephantine ears.

'This one for example.'

'Isn't that . . . W.H. Auden?'

Harry paused, as though disappointed.

'You know him?'

'Everyone does. He's a poet.'

Harry returned the photograph to the file. 'Not the easiest person to shadow, I can tell you. The man has the longest stride of anyone I've ever known.'

Stella looked around the shabby office. Through the sash windows, the first customers could be seen entering the pub opposite. This place was about as far from a police station as she could imagine. And Harry Fox's story seemed frankly incredible.

'Are you saying the police tell you to shadow these people?'

'I'm not in the police.'

'I thought you were.'

'I was suspended,' he clarified tersely.

Immediately, Stella longed to know why he was suspended, but something in his eye told her not to ask. Not then, at any rate.

'I'm an investigator now.'

'Then why are you—?'

'They still give me work because I'm good at it.'

'Who else do you shadow?'

'I can't give you names. I shouldn't have mentioned Auden. But it's any writer or artist thought to pose a threat of Soviet infiltration. Anyone who supports Communist activity on the British cultural scene. Agents, fellow travellers, sympathizers. Spies.'

She drank some tea to hide her astonishment.

'Is that why you were at the party?'

The reason for Harry's presence at the Café de Paris had been a little more prosaic.

He took on other work. God knows, he needed to. Marriage – or more specifically, infidelity – was his bread and butter. Adultery never went out of fashion, along with covetousness, envy, wrath, murder and all the other deadly sins that paid so many people's wages. He had been at the Café de Paris on the tail of an actress, Diana Sowerby, whose husband believed she was having an affair. Harry very much hoped she was. Not for the money, or the swift resolution of the case, but because the husband so richly deserved it. Sir Walter Heap was an immensely wealthy man – an executive on one of Britain's most popular newspapers – and he came possessed of every bad attribute Harry could think of: cruelty, abusiveness, brutishness and ignorance. The bad fairies must have had a ball at his christening.

'Are you saying there were Communists at the Café de Paris?'

Harry shrugged. 'Confidential, I'm afraid.'

'Well, even if there were, I refuse to believe Hubert Newman was one of them.'

'He wasn't.'

'So why—?'

'There are different reasons for my interest. As I said, we had an acquaintance.'

Stella Fry didn't need to know how brief that acquaintance was.

The impulse to contact Newman had arisen quite unexpectedly, but once there, it was impossible to ignore. Harry had read all of Hubert Newman's novels, several times, and it was after finishing the most recent, *A Shot Across the Bows*, that he had taken up his pen and crafted a fan letter. A number of false starts were screwed up and balled into the wastepaper bin and, frankly, he was amazed that he'd finished the letter, but he was thrilled to receive Newman's response, with the suggestion that perhaps Mr Fox would care to attend a forthcoming event at the Authors' Club. Harry had arrived promptly, and sat with rapt attention through his favourite author's talk, though he had to admit that Newman had a downbeat air, and tackled the audience questions with a marked lack of enthusiasm. At the signing table, Harry had introduced himself and Newman had asked what he did. As he scrawled his signature, the writer had said, *'Maybe you can offer me some assistance, Mr Fox? Become my official advisor on police procedure? Explain to me how police go about tackling their more delicate cases?'* He had seemed on the brink of saying more, but instead had closed the book, adding, *'Why don't we meet in the bar here next Wednesday? Unless events intervene.'*

Harry had immediately acquiesced but already Newman was squinting up at the next customer, a frump in a salmon twinset, who had pushed forward in the signing queue. Harry didn't care. The prospect of a personal meeting with Hubert Newman – of a genuine professional relationship – was an unlooked-for joy. He was to become a literary advisor, an expert amanuensis in the arts of detecting and surveilling.

*Unless events intervene.*

At the time, he had assumed Newman meant war, or bad weather, but now he wondered if death was the event that Newman feared.

'I admired his mind – he would have made a great detective.'

Stella frowned.

'But that's irrelevant now, isn't it? He had a heart attack. It said so in the newspaper. He was overweight, probably not in the best of health. Surely the police will—'

'The police will do the basics. They'll take witness statements and question his doctor about whether he was suffering chest pains. A terrible loss and gone too soon. Then they'll close the book. They probably have already. That's where I come in. As Peverell Drake said, a private investigator looks for answers where nobody even thought there were questions.'

'And have you actually found questions?'

'I reckon there's more to Newman's death, and I think you do too. You have natural intuition. I can tell.'

She frowned sceptically.

'When I was following you last night, you were aware of me, though most women would have been oblivious. But you didn't want me to know that you knew. You carried on just the same.'

'How could you tell?'

How did one describe the slight tension in the shoulders that changed the timbre of the footsteps? Harry didn't have the words for that kind of thing.

'Technical expertise. Tricks of the trade. You learn things in this game. You get inklings.'

'Is that another technical term?'

Her eyes were dancing. He could not tell if she was taking him entirely seriously.

'There are rules in detection. Ways of going about things. And one of them is to listen to your instincts.'

'The fact is, Mr Fox . . . whatever your *inklings*, why on earth would anyone want to kill Hubert Newman?'

He was rolling a halfpenny under his thumb, staring out of the window as he spoke.

'I don't know. But if I'm correct, then the questions we need to ask are, who would have motivation? What would their motivation be? And how was it carried out? If you ask me, I suspect it was nothing to do with his day job. I'd guess it was some other part of his life. And that's the part that interests me. Newman knew something, or someone, and it ended up killing him.'

'I still don't—'

He cut her off.

'You said you met him at the Athenaeum. Did you eat the same meal?'

'Exactly the same. Lamb chops, carrots, peas and roast potatoes. He had the suet pudding. I didn't.'

'Did you have anything to drink?'

'A bottle of wine. He had most of it.'

'And what kind of people were there?'

'I don't know. As far as I know, the club is popular with politicians, civil servants, government people. And writers, obviously. I'd never been to a Pall Mall club in my life till then.'

'Did you encounter anyone?'

'He said hello to a couple of people.'

'Any idea who?'

'One man called Rex, another called Henry. And somebody whose wife had read his novel. He didn't introduce me.'

She paused.

'There was another person — probably not a writer — who mentioned an event the evening before.'

'How do you know this chap was not a writer?'

'He said something about not wanting to interrupt the *alchemy of authorship*. I can't imagine actual writers talk like that.'

'And did Newman give you the job?'

'Yes.' She hesitated, and Harry waited attentively, like a doctor who knows that patients keep the most important facts for last.

'I suppose it doesn't hurt to tell you. As I said, he'd just finished a new manuscript. It's called *Masquerade*.'

'The Shakespeare thing?'

She nodded. 'He wanted it typed up. His usual secretary Mrs Harris is getting on a bit and her eyes are going, so he needed a typist. The manuscript arrived at my flat yesterday morning. He must have sent it straight after he saw me. And that's not the only surprising thing . . .'

'Yes?'

'He dedicated it to me, actually. He wrote "To Stella, spotter of mistakes".'

'Why do you think he wrote that?'

'It's just something trivial I'd said. It sounds boastful now, but it simply slipped out. I'd told him I was a good copy-editor.'

'Pretty brief acquaintance to merit a dedication.'

'I thought so too, but then I suppose he'd written so many books, perhaps he ran out of people to dedicate them to.'

'Where's the manuscript now?'

'On my bedside table. It's four hundred-odd pages long so it's going to take a while even to read it, but I thought I might get in touch with his publishers and offer to type it up anyhow. He did pay me in advance.'

'He paid in advance? Why?'

'It must be procedure. Only I haven't cashed the cheque. It seemed . . . improper. In the circumstances.'

Harry went over to the plant pot on the mantel, lifted it and extracted an envelope.

'When I visited Newman's flat earlier, I found this.'

He proffered the letter, which she unfolded and read.

'Who is this Lindemann?'

'Professor Lindemann. He's a physics chap. Head of the Clarendon Laboratory at Oxford.'

He sat down at the desk, opened a notebook and proceeded to recite.

'Born Baden-Baden in Germany, April 5th 1886. German father, American mother, schooled in Scotland and the University of Berlin. Physics research at the Sorbonne, fellow of the Royal Society, director of the Clarendon Laboratory at Oxford University where he works on nuclear energy, whatever that is. Keen tennis player. Unmarried.'

'Physics? What would Hubert Newman have to do with physics?'

'That's a sensible question.'

'Perhaps it was some kind of research. Maybe he was considering setting a novel in the world of science.'

'Again, entirely reasonable.'

'What does he mean by "grotesque allegations"?'

'Wish I knew.'

'Perhaps somebody should look into it.'

'Sure. I'll refer it to one of my assistants, shall I?'

She frowned at him a moment and then said, 'You can't possibly be asking *me* to look into it?'

'Perhaps you can get to see him. See if he'll bend to your charms.'

Already, she was shaking her head.

'That's completely impossible. I can't approach a total stranger out of the blue, and not just a stranger but a very important man. I'm sorry.'

'We need to go through everything – his publishers, his family if he had one, his friends.'

'Sorry . . . what do you mean "we"?'

'The fact is, if I'm going to find out anything, I'll need your help, Miss Fry.'

A pulse of excitement went through Stella. A thrilling lightning flash earthing the dull autumn that only three days earlier had stretched before her. It was as though she and this man, whom she had met just hours ago, were united by an invisible skein of events. Something entirely unexpected had brought them together and bound them in the moment.

Immediately, she doused the excitement. She began to

rebutton her jacket, as if physically repressing the impulse, and summoned a cool tone.

'I'm sorry, Mr Fox, but I can't help. I'm not cut out to be a shadow.'

'I disagree. I think you'd make a fine one.'

'The thing is, I need to find a job.'

'This is a job. I can't pay you much but I'd pay you.'

She hesitated. She had not cashed Hubert Newman's cheque, and was under the vague impression that bank accounts were closed or frozen once a person died. If so, she had no income, certainly not in the near future, which meant that the need for a job was now pressing. Already, she was fretting about how to find work. Charming though Evelyn could be – and rich though her family was – like all the upper classes she was gimlet-eyed when it came to the rent.

Harry Fox stretched his arms behind his head and leaned back in his chair for a moment, as though contemplating the nicotine-stained ceiling.

'I think we'd make a good team. Fox and Fry.'

'What on earth do you mean?'

'Your class and my know-how. In fact, the Security Service often pairs operatives like us together. An older man, and a classy young woman.'

Stella didn't know where to begin answering that, so she stood, picked up her bag and said, 'As I say, it's not the line of work I'm used to. And I absolutely don't see how any of this involves me.'

Her reply emerged a little stiffly, but it didn't seem to faze him. He was doodling circles on his notepad. He looked at her pleasantly, almost mildly, and said, 'You may not see it, Miss Fry, but I'm afraid you *are* involved, whether you like it or not. Hubert Newman dedicated his final work to you, hours before he died. If that death was not a natural one, and you saw something significant, there's every possibility you are under threat too.'

# CHAPTER 8

Two hours later, Harry walked past Lambeth Bridge and approached the looming Portland stone block with the enthusiasm of a man nearing the gates of hell. Thames House was the home of the domestic Security Service and its aesthetic, if it could be said to possess such a thing, was part prison, part cathedral. Either way, distinctly penal. All the fancy appurtenances, from the heavy, neoclassical lamp posts, to the giant brass doors and elaborately carved imperial arch gave the building a stately air in inverse proportion to its occupants. The staff of Thames House struck a balance somewhere between the eccentric and the humdrum. They were markedly different from their counterparts in the Secret Intelligence Service who dealt with foreign espionage and had recently relocated to a stately home called Bletchley Park. In the matter of intelligence, the British class system was at its most pure. SIS agents were drawn from the ranks of the top public schools and gentlemen's clubs – White's,

Boodles and the Reform – and they looked down with effortless superiority on the former policemen, shadows and mackintosh-wearers who dwelt in Thames House. Yet it had not taken long for Harry to realize that MI5's operatives were cut from a hardier cloth than their SIS equivalents – more Woolworths, less Savile Row.

'Mr Fox?'

The receptionist was a brunette who had once allowed him to buy her a gin and French, but now regarded him like a wasp at a picnic.

'I'm here to see Mr Flint.'

She picked up the telephone, murmured something, then passed him the receiver as if with cotton gloves.

The voice on the phone could have iced a Scotch.

'Hell are you doing here?'

'Good morning to you too, Mr Flint.'

'Christ, Harry. You might have let me know. I could have arranged something. You'll have to wait.'

Harry retreated to a green leather bench across the chequered tiled lobby, placed his trilby on the seat and assumed the posture of an oriental sage. If anyone glanced at him, he ignored it. He'd been a bartender in the course of duty, as well as a window cleaner and a hotel concierge, so he had no problem blanking inquisitive stares.

Yet despite his ability to project serenity, he was not experiencing complete relaxation.

He had no faith that Flint would know anything about

Hubert Newman's death, and even if he did, that he would reveal it. What was in it for Flint? Already, Harry sensed he had been wrong to come, and from across the hall he could feel the receptionist's gaze on him, radiating disdain.

He shifted a little. The whole point of his job was to look ordinary – it was important to dress unmemorably if you didn't want to be remembered, and to avoid any fancy after-shave, too. But his usual sartorial insouciance had possibly gone too far. The lining had come away from the inside of his jacket. There was a hole in his shoe, requiring the insertion of a small piece of card to keep out the damp. He noticed a threadbare patch in his trouser leg, the size of a shilling, and covered it with his hand. Since the last woman in his life had departed, and he didn't blame her, his personal grooming had taken a dive.

Fingering the knot in his tie, he wondered again how it had come to this.

There had been a time – a mere three years ago – when he was riding high. He was a force to be reckoned with. A rising star. Within Scotland Yard's Special Branch he was known as a master of the fine arts of covert entry, bug planting and photographing documents. He slipped into locked buildings like a shadow. In the matter of surveillance, he was as observant as an owl, and when breaking into houses, as furtive as his namesake fox. Thus, he was a natural choice when, in 1935, Superintendent Albert Canning, head of Special Branch, at the request of the Prime Minister, Stanley Baldwin, initiated a very delicate operation.

It was the King's idea. George V's main passions were shooting and stamp collecting, but the hobbies of his son, the Prince of Wales, were far more exotic; to wit: sex, gambling, drinking, drug taking and louche parties at his Windsor hideaway, Fort Belvedere. Fearing blackmail or worse arising from his son's entertainments, the old King had called in Special Branch and a unit of surveillance operatives was formed, called, informally, the Watchers.

Everything the Watchers did was highly sensitive. The Prince's personal bodyguard, Sir David Storrier, supplied confidential information on Edward's movements, conversations and what passed for his political views. Others bugged and shadowed him at home and abroad. Harry's role had been to keep track of the movements of the Prince's paramour, the rangy Wallis Simpson. Wallis herself was paranoid and convinced she was being tailed, though ironically, she suspected her pursuers were being paid either by her then husband, Ernest Simpson, or by the Prince himself. Harry had set up shop opposite the door of her Bryanston Court apartment and waited there like a cat at the hole of a particularly nervy mouse.

For months he followed her with dedication. To restaurants, to cocktail parties, to an antique shop in Kensington, whose owner was helpful on how Mrs Simpson had the Prince 'totally under her thumb'. But most regularly he tailed her to the Bruton Street flat of a married Ford car salesman called Guy Trundle, a man with a wide-boy suit and a smile as sharp as a knife in the back.

Soon enough, Mrs Simpson took to meeting Trundle at the salon of her dressmaker, Elsa Schiaparelli, in Upper Grosvenor Street – the one place where the infatuated prince would not accompany her – and Harry took up residence in the doorway opposite.

If only he could have stayed there.

But the job of watching Wallis involved other duties and it was in the course of them that Harry's downfall came. Someone made a mistake. It was more than a mistake, really; it was manslaughter. A man ended up dead and it was Harry who took the blame.

He had been lucky to escape a stretch behind bars. For a few months Harry inhabited a murky exile, constantly awaiting arrest. The job was lost, along with his reputation. Yet the arrest never happened. Instead, Flint came to his rescue. Former Detective Sergeant Flint to give him his full title, Prince of Policing, Earl of Undercover Infiltration, Duke of Dirty Tricks. At the Yard he had been Harry's boss but now he was Flint of MI5 B division. Five foot five of pinstriped flannel with rat-grey hair and a mind like a calculating machine.

Flint had come to him with a charm offensive, though as ever with Flint it was less charm and more offensive.

'No one wants to give you the time of day, Fox. You're the lowest of the low.'

'Thanks very much.'

'But I'm your fairy godfather. I have just the thing. You like reading, don't you?'

Cautiously, Harry issued a grunt.

'This is connected to reading. But it's strictly off the books.'

'What exactly is it?'

'It's about writers.'

That was how it started. The head of the Security Service, Sir Vernon Kell, had formed a joint MI5/Special Branch unit to monitor Communist and left-wing sympathies among the cultural elite. The names of the targets were noted down on the Red List, which was a detailed collection of subversives whose activities were to be followed at all times. Henceforth a large swathe of writers, actors and artists would have their every move logged, card-indexed and preserved in the filing cabinets of Thames House.

For this task they needed shadows, and who better than the Watchers? Harry would be one of those who did the shadowing. It was not a *job* in any way that the word might imply. His name would never appear on any payroll. Requiring limited violence, except when strictly necessary. Harry would be assigned subjects on a need-to-know basis. He was not to set foot in Thames House. He would take his instructions from Flint and report back to him alone.

Harry leaped at the work, yet there were times, increasingly often, when he wondered whether this kind of hanging around after people was entirely British. When had watching people and keeping notes of their daily lives become a full-time occupation? Tracking intellectuals and poets, their habits, their likes, their loves, even the books they read – didn't it smack of the same kind of Communist behaviour that they were supposed to be detecting?

These qualms, however, he ignored, because it paid the rent on his basement flat in Battersea and Harry was flattered, despite himself, that the men at counter-espionage needed to solicit his help. It was recognition of what they both knew – that he was a master in his field. It wasn't the spying he found interesting – there was only so much following you could do, and tailing usually turned up the same secrets and deceptions, the lies told to wives and employers, the petty betrayals for petty cash. Ultimately, what interested him was what it revealed about society. What you betrayed, where you pledged your loyalty.

Most of the people Harry tailed were the backbone of English society – the elite, the top drawer, the natural masters of every corridor they strode. Men who commanded the best table in restaurants and accepted the fawning of the lower orders as their due. Who attended the same schools, wore the same ties and played the same games. Hunting, shooting, Lord's cricket ground. The kind of people who went to church and addressed God like an old acquaintance. So why did they pledge allegiance to a different land? It was easy enough to see why he, Harry Fox, with a worn suit and a hole in his shoe, should feel like an outsider. But what made these people think themselves outsiders, when they should so effortlessly belong?

★

Flint's office overlooked the Thames. Through the window, Harry could see the vast, mud-coloured river flowing sluggishly by. Inside, the air tasted flat, as if it had been breathed too many times. On the sill a line of pigeons sat in a row, like parishioners waiting for communion. Opposite, in front of the balustrade of Millbank, a man in a shabby mackintosh, tartan scarf and dark glasses was selling matches. He was blind apparently, but it was clear to Harry from the way he darted furtive glances at the people going in and out of the doorway, that his vision was unaffected.

He turned to Flint. 'You realize that man's watching you?'

Flint strode across the room in frustration, took a look, then moved away with a grunt.

'He's blind, Fox, if you hadn't noticed. He's been there for months. Anyhow. What's this about? This had better be good.'

'It's about Hubert Newman.'

Behind the horn-rims, Flint's tiny eyes widened.

'What on earth? That's nothing to do with us. It was a natural death. A nation mourns.'

'It might not be that simple.'

'What are you getting at?'

'Just pulling together a few threads. I wondered if you could help. I'd like to know if there's anything behind it.'

'A forty-five-year-old portly gentleman of impeccable character suffers a heart attack? What the hell's got into you, Harry? It's not exactly "hold the front page".'

Flint was right. Harry had been to the Athenaeum an hour

ago, where a chap dressed as the Jack of Spades in a purple waistcoat and striped tie had confirmed that yes, he was the porter and that no, Mr Newman had not complained of feeling unwell during or after his lunch. Nor had he eaten anything out of the ordinary. For a further consideration, the porter also furnished the information that lunch had consisted of lamb chops, roast potatoes, steamed suet pudding and a bottle of Château Lafite Rothschild '33, drunk almost entirely by Newman himself.

'It's complicated.'

'No, it isn't. And even if it was, it would no longer be of any relevance to you. You're good, Harry, but even you aren't capable of tailing a dead man.'

Flint began tending to his noxious pipe. After a series of encouraging puffs, it smouldered back to life and he regarded Harry through curling wreaths of smoke.

'I know you, Harry. You're never satisfied. I'm telling you, you need to step away from this one. Focus on Auden and Isherwood. Those types are up to their ears in it. Commie lovers, apart from everything else. Pacifists. Cranks. Dissidence, disloyalty, *Oxbridge*.' At this word, Flint's tone shifted from distaste to contempt. 'That's the type we're dealing with.'

Behind Flint's head, Harry saw rows of publications. The *Daily Worker*, *Tribune*, the *Manchester Guardian*, the *Morning Star*, the *Times Literary Supplement*. It amused him to think of Flint grappling with them behind closed doors. Taking them out at home in Surbiton and asking Mrs Flint to turn down the Light Programme while he puzzled over articles entitled 'Is Art Propaganda?' or made his way joylessly through Title of the Month from the Left Book Club. What passed through Flint's mind when he read Auden's poetry? Did anything stir in his small, desiccated soul?

A flicker of sympathy crossed Flint's features. He was regarding Harry with what might have passed for pity, if he had been capable of that emotion.

'You're impetuous,' he said.

'Is that what they call it now?'

'I was being polite.'

'I'm just following a hunch, Mr Flint. I'm an investigator. It's in the job description.'

'Well, let me describe this job in a way you can understand. You can't afford to push the boundaries. Not any more. I don't care what you get up to in the rest of your time. You have to make a living. I understand that. But I don't want you freelancing in this neck of the woods.'

Through Harry's mind rang the words of Lindemann's letter. 'I find your allegations both grotesque and completely incredible.' Allegations. What grotesque allegations might Newman have levelled, and at whom? It seemed unlikely that they concerned the higher realms of theoretical physics or a dispute about the nature of atoms. He wondered whether to share his quandary with Flint, but a sixth sense advised him against it.

Flint was standing, hands thrust in his pockets, squinting down at the match seller.

'Fact is, I'm not sure there's much future in this, anyhow. Tailing the Commies. According to our overlords the Soviets are our best buddies now.'

'Oh yes?'

'That's the idea. Makes no sense to me.'

He sniffed, bitterly. Flint hated Communists in all their incarnations. 'Fellow travellers', 'comrades', 'progressives'. None of these soubriquets summed up how fiercely he felt.

'One moment the Russians are the end of civilization, the next moment we're all supposed to hold hands and fight the Nazis. If you ask me, they've got it wrong. It's the Red Menace we need to worry about. The Nazis are no real threat. They may be a problem on the Continent, but that's unlikely to affect us. The French have the Maginot Line. And I have every faith in Mr Chamberlain to keep us out of this show.'

From the corner of his eye, Harry noticed a copy of Walter Heap's newspaper on the far side of the desk with a headline reading 'Magistrate Condemns German Jews Pouring into the Country'. He thought again of the refugees he regularly encountered in Luigi's coffee shop in Soho, clustered together with hunched shoulders and nervy, haunted eyes, chain smoking and conversing in their native languages, always with a cup of bitter black coffee on the go.

He spread his hands.

'I don't know anything about politics, Mr Flint. Nazis, Bolsheviks – it's all the same to me. You decide who the bad guys are this week and I follow them.'

Flint frowned sceptically.

'Only, I just know there's something odd about Newman's death. I wouldn't have come if I didn't believe that. I wondered if you knew anything. I want to look into it.'

'Who's paying you for this?'

'No one.'

'You mean it's a hobby? I've never known you do something without getting paid.'

Flint's assessment was brutal but accurate. Harry had never done anything like this before. But how could he explain the churning disappointment and disquiet that was fuelling his quest? He couldn't even explain it to himself.

'It's personal.'

'Well, whatever it is, I know nothing about this man and I can't help you. You're getting distracted, Harry. You drink too much. Step away from this one. There's plenty of trouble in the world without you going looking for more. I have no idea why you're even interested. Keep tabs on that Orwell chap. What news on him?'

'He's meeting John Strachey tonight at the Shanghai Club in Soho.'

'Then tail him. There's more to him than meets the eye. I'll be wanting a report by the end of the week. And don't, for God's sake, come here again.'

'*There's plenty of trouble in the world without you going looking for more.*' As the door closed all too swiftly on him, Harry could not help but ponder his urge to probe Newman's death. That was what Stella Fry had questioned, and she had every reason to.

People dropped dead every day. It was hardly a surprise that Newman, a man for whom belts were made for loosening, should expire suddenly. His last meal had involved an entire bottle of red wine and enough suet pudding to fell a horse. He had merely suffered Death by Lunch.

Was Harry's unease merely because he felt cheated out of a further meeting with the man, and a chance to discuss in person the policing details of *Midnight in Vienna*? The offer of a new career as literary consultant. '*Become my official advisor on police procedure. Unless events intervene.*'

Or was it because he had a hunch? Harry had faith in a hunch. It wasn't scientific, but then nor was science a lot of the time. To him, intuition was a kind of invisible force, as powerful as the particles that held atoms together, and no less important because it couldn't be seen or defined.

He had a hunch now, and as he trudged down the corridor, something about Flint's reaction bothered him.

'*Step away from this one.*'

How quickly Flint had closed him down. He might just as easily have smiled and acknowledged that Harry was not on the staff of either Special Branch or MI5 and was thus entirely free to embark on whichever wild goose chase took his fancy. Instead, he put a lid on it.

Might it be that someone wanted Hubert Newman's death to be unexplored?

Whoever it was, Harry was sent to defy them.

# CHAPTER 9

Stella and Evelyn were hurrying along the street to Cheyne Walk, the home of Evelyn's parents, Philip and Sidonie Lamont. The news that Stella had met Hubert Newman, however briefly, just hours before his tragic death, had prompted Sidonie to issue an immediate invitation. Stella was well aware that Sidonie, who had danced for Stravinsky in her youth and considered herself more of a cultural force than a socialite, was also a declared fan of detective fiction. A number of famous writers – Agatha Christie, Dorothy L. Sayers and Ngaio Marsh – had attended her soirées. Stella's brief acquaintance with Hubert Newman had merited an immediate invitation to tonight's party in support of European refugees. No actual refugees would be there, but those who spoke in their favour would be toasting them with fine champagne.

Despite the mildness of the night, Stella could not shake off the chill of Harry Fox's words.

'*There's every possibility you are under threat too.*'

The thought of it prompted her to glance behind her, as if she were at that very moment being followed. Her senses sharpened, taking in the flutter of music and voices from wireless sets behind long curtains, and the soft lapping of the river beyond the Embankment.

She shook herself. Nobody was following her. Harry Fox was obviously a fantasist. She had never encountered anybody like him. His manner was extraordinarily cocksure. As to his professional situation, she scarcely knew what to make of it, except that the award certificates on the bookcase seemed genuine. He might be a fantasist, but he was a fantasist with commendations. And the little boy in the photograph looked sweet. Nonetheless, there was no chance she would take him up on his offer.

All the same, everything felt surreal. Three days ago, she had been a children's tutor with no job and now, it seemed, she was a children's tutor with no job and a death threat. All because she had gone for an interview.

Beside her, Evelyn was deep in her own existential crisis.

'Don't know how much longer I'm going to be able to act.'

'I don't see why not. You're never unemployed. You'll go on forever.'

'It's not that. It's events. My mother thinks I'll have to abandon the stage. She says war is coming and all the theatres will go dark. I should be thinking of being a nurse or a VAD but frankly I couldn't possibly. Have you seen the uniform?'

'Thought you liked dressing up.'

'In a grey blouse and apron? With a bedpan in one hand? No thanks. And it's not like I know how to do anything else. I'm not brainy like you.'

'There are plenty of—'

'Anyhow,' Evelyn interrupted, clearly uninterested in the alternatives, 'I'm having some new studio portraits done. I'm going to look irresistible.'

'You already do,' said Stella, surveying Evelyn's dark flannel trousers, tight cotton blouse and tie, which, combined with her glossy tumble of curls, lent her a boyish sexiness. Stella, who was wearing her sole smart evening dress, black with a flared skirt, felt drably conventional beside her.

'You're bound to get the *Troilus and Cressida*. Even if you don't, there'll be other plays.'

'You're right. Why should the theatres go dark? There'll always be a need for entertainment, won't there? And who says there will even be a war? You must know. You listen to the wireless. You listen to politicians. What do they say?'

'They all say different things. That's the point of politics.'

Outside Evelyn's family home a man in dark livery with silver buttons was buffing a gleaming Rolls-Royce so efficiently that they could glimpse themselves in its polished flanks as they passed. Evelyn trotted up the steps to the porch.

'Roger thinks *you* should take up acting. He said, "Why doesn't Stella go on the stage herself? She has the looks for it." I said there's a difference between being nice-looking and being a classically trained actress and he said, "If you say so." Charming.'

Evelyn paused to ring the bell, and the maid opened the door to a blast of warm air and laughter.

'What will you do, Stel? Do you have any ideas for jobs?'

'Not yet. But I'm sure something will come up.'

On the threshold of the room, Stella watched Evelyn brace herself with inherent theatricality. She always entered a party as though it was the stage at Drury Lane. Mentally, Stella braced herself too, preparing to penetrate the wall of conversation and condescension.

She had known this house for half her life. It was a handsome Victorian edifice whose capacious first-floor drawing room provided a regular forum for actors, writers, artists and assorted London intelligentsia. The long windows gave a panoramic view of the Thames, its water turning iridescent beneath the Embankment lamps and flowing under the graceful span of the Albert Bridge. Rex Whistler had contributed a fresco to one panelled wall and the others were hung with ancestral oils, a John Singer Sergeant of Sidonie in her younger days, swathed in ivory silk, and a study of her head in charcoal by Henri Matisse. Side tables gleamed with glass and silver and the Steinway grand was clustered with photographs. There were flowers everywhere, and even the candlelight felt expensive as it fell on the press of brightly dressed women in satin gowns and pearls and men in dinner jackets.

No matter how long she had known the Lamonts, Stella

would never truly get used to their affluence, their Bohemian insouciance, their sense that somehow, for people like themselves, everything would always turn out all right. Even a war, probably. They were as politically connected as they were culturally on the pulse. They could not be further from the narrow world in which she had grown up: the pebbledash semi in Chiswick, the shouts and thuds from the pub next door at closing time.

Yet again the feeling rose to the surface, the feeling she hated, that she would never belong. She would never know the ease or social confidence possessed by these people. She wondered if it was something deep within that thwarted all her attempts to feel comfortable. She had belonged once – for a while. After school she had got a scholarship to Oxford to study French and German at Somerville. She had worn a long scholar's gown and befriended men in baggy trousers and downed little glasses of sherry in wood-panelled rooms. She had drunk cocoa and blown smoke rings and recited medieval French poetry and Shelley and Baudelaire. But three years later the need to earn her living had cut her off from all those friends and forced her out into the world. She had dropped out of those gilded circles as fast as she'd joined them.

'My parents are just back from the Riviera,' said Evelyn. 'They say it's getting a bit gloomy out there.'

The Lamonts lived for exotic travel. In the South of France, they generally stayed at the Hotel du Cap, and there was a photograph of them on the piano to prove it, set against a background of umbrella pines and a sparkling sea. By contrast, Stella's mother, Nancy, had barely set foot on foreign soil, other than a single trip to France when Stella was ten. She remembered Nancy coming back with a pair of gloves, wrapped in tissue like priceless treasure. '*Lovely kid, they are, Stella.*' To buy gloves in a Parisian boutique was, for Stella's mother, the apogee of sophistication. As she thought of it, it occurred to Stella that perhaps Hubert Newman had felt the same. His aristocrats, the stuffy lords and ladies of his mysteries, seemed somehow to be painted with an outsider's eye. Yet that couldn't be true because Newman himself was the heart of the establishment. He dined in gentlemen's clubs, after all.

'Stella!' Sidonie appeared in a gust of Mitsouko. She was an imperious presence, who appeared taller than she was because her training as a ballerina had taught her to stand abnormally straight in a way which felt perversely judgemental. Her hair was immaculate, raven black and centre parted with Continental precision, and her eyes were a penetrating, gentian blue. Her cut-glass accent was sharpened with an icy, White Russian edge.

'We're so happy to have you back. And many sympathies on the loss of dear Hubert. Such a wonderful man. We're all absolutely distraught. We knew him, you know.'

'Evelyn told me.'

'*The Chocolate Cream Poisoner*, that was my favourite. I always suspected that he may have modelled one of his characters on me. The ballerina, you remember? In *Curtain Call*?

He would never have let on, of course. I've always loved
detective novels, though other people do seem to be catching
up with me now. They say they're an absolute craze.'

'Isn't it something about people wanting to forget the
war?' A woman in twinset and pearls had inserted herself
into the conversation. 'Taking refuge in mysteries? Seeking
comfort? It's all the fashion.'

'Oh, I've never been one to follow fashions,' said Sidonie,
who preferred to believe that she set them. 'All I know is,
I've loved Hubert Newman since his very first story.'

'*Traitor's Gate!*' chimed the guest.

'I only met him once,' repeated Stella. But Sidonie seemed
not to hear.

'Hubert was such a supporter of our efforts to help the
refugees. We liaise with the centre in Bloomsbury. Poor
souls. They're terrified that if the Germans invade, they'll
be sent off to camps, just like the family they left behind.
It must be so hard. Tom has just been at a conference about
the refugees – to get some kind of international consensus.
You remember Tom, don't you?'

As if Stella could forget.

Evelyn's older brother Tom was everything Evelyn was
not: clean cut, serious, highly intelligent. Stolid looking,
rather than handsome. In him the family's high brow, dark
hair and grey eyes came together to express a sense of matu-
rity. Sidonie must know that in the past, when Stella had
visited the family at their Berkshire house, Tom Lamont
had nursed a passion for her.

The Lamonts' country house was a place of glory – a mansion of sober stone with a long drive flanked by elms, a rose garden and lawns running down to a stream. Stella had spent a brief, sunlit month there after university, which was when she came to know Tom properly. He was ten years older than her. Following the war, he had won a scholarship to study natural sciences at Cambridge and gained a fencing blue. But instead of becoming a scientist, he had taken exams both for the civil service and the Foreign Office, coming top in both. He chose the Foreign Office, where he was said to excel.

Did Sidonie know what had passed between the two of them? Almost certainly. She had a nose as sharp as any detective. Yet also, Stella knew, she had far grander ambitions for her only son.

'How is Tom?'

'Oh, he's at the Foreign Office, working for our dear friend Aubrey North. Aubrey's *very* close to Churchill, and he says it's getting rather desperate. The whole of Europe's on the edge of a precipice. You know Hitler's threatening to annexe the Sudetenland; he says it is in all reality part of Germany because of the size of the ethnic German population. Well, Tom is convinced he won't stop there. The Czechs are next in his sights. And now the Prime Minister is meeting Hitler at the Berghof. Churchill's telling everyone not to be taken in, and his friend Lindemann agrees.'

Stella gripped her wine glass more tightly.

'Frederick Lindemann?'

'Yes. Do you know him?'

'No. I mean . . . I've heard of him. What's he like?'

'The Prof? Pick your adjective, my dear. Prickly, eccentric, sarcastic, opinionated, arrogant. Puts a lot of backs up. The only person who really loves him is his valet. They say no man's a hero to his valet but this one's the exception. The Prof rescued the poor man from life as a fairground boxer and Lindemann treats him like a son. And, of course, he's frightfully close to Churchill, even if they're chalk and cheese. They stay up till three in the morning, talking, after everyone else has gone to bed. Why do you ask?'

Stella faltered. It was impossible to say any more, let alone that she had seen a cryptic private letter that this professor had sent to Hubert Newman.

'He just sounds so interesting. His work on physics and so on.'

'Oh, he is. That's the most fascinating side of him. It's developments in physics that will decide our future now, Lindemann says. He's full of the most astonishing ideas that I wouldn't pretend to understand. He says Hitler is squandering his nation's scientists. That's why he's so involved with the refugee crisis. It's why he came tonight.'

The breath caught in Stella's throat.

'Are you saying Professor Lindemann's here?'

'Not here, darling.' Sidonie smiled. 'But out on the terrace, I think.'

A few minutes later, Stella detached herself and ventured outside. After the heat of the drawing room, the air was chill and smelled of damp grass. Her bare arms goose-pimpled. The distant hum of traffic was scarcely enough to trouble the tranquillity of the evening. The lawn was separated from the flagstone terrace by a balustrade, and the light spilling from the long windows framed the outline of a man, leaning silently against it, gazing into the darkness beyond. He was rigidly still, as though he was straining to hear the calls of some distant night bird, and although he must have heard Stella, he neither turned nor showed any sign of registering her approach. Instinctively, she dropped the cigarette she was holding and stubbed it under her shoe.

Her stomach clenched as she summoned the nerve to address him.

'Professor Lindemann?'

The man turned on a heel, and the light from the windows illuminated a commanding figure with ramrod posture, cropped silver hair and a salt-and-pepper moustache.

'Mrs Lamont said you would be here. I wonder, would it be possible to have a word?'

Lindemann's face registered the polite distaste typical of men of stature when accosted by strangers, particularly female ones.

'Of course, Miss . . .'

'Fry. Stella Fry.'

Churchill's closest confidant dug his hands into his pockets and inclined his head in a little bow.

'How can I help?'

'It's about Hubert Newman.'

An imperious frown.

'I'm sorry. Who?'

'The novelist. The one who just died.'

This did elicit a response. The ramrod figure braced, and the grey eyes widened.

'Forgive me, Miss Fry, are you telling me—?'

'I thought you might have heard. It was in the newspapers.'

'I don't have time for newspapers. When was this? How did he die?'

'From a heart attack, apparently. Two days ago. I saw him just a couple of hours before it happened.'

The shock that had flickered across Lindemann's face disappeared just as quickly, and a mask of indifference came down.

'Who are you? Are you some kind of relative?'

'No.'

'Not, heaven help us, a member of the police force?'

'I was his employee.'

'I see. Well, I'm sorry for your loss, but I'm afraid it's no concern of mine.'

'I think it might be. You see, sir, he had received a letter. Shortly before he died, and I was hoping you might—'

'A letter. What letter?'

'A letter from you.'

'And how would you know about any letter?'

'He left it open on his desk.'

'Where is this letter now?'

'I don't know. But in it you referred to Mr Newman making allegations. And I wanted to know . . . It could be significant, you see. What allegations did he make?'

'I can't possibly tell you that. Nor should you expect me to. It's a private matter.'

'Can I ask who he was referring to?'

Lindemann's complexion was purpling to a degree out of all proportion to her questioning.

'I'm too busy for this nonsense, madam. I have more important things to do than discuss the wild imaginings of some detective writer. Please don't trouble me further.'

Marching past her, he strode back through the French windows and was lost in the throng.

Stella stood frozen on the flagstone patio, chiding herself for the disastrous conversation. She had been too abrupt, too forward. She had broached the question in entirely the wrong way. And in doing so, she had lost the chance of eliciting any information whatsoever. The chill of the evening crept into her blood and she shivered.

A crunch of footsteps startled her and she turned to see a man with the battered face of a boxer approaching awkwardly. It was the chauffeur who had been polishing the Rolls-Royce in the street outside.

'I'm Harvey, miss, the Prof's valet.' He was twisting his cap in his hands in agonized apology. 'Don't be upset, miss, if the Prof was direct, like. He means nothing by it. The

Prof can seem ungentlemanly, but I assure you he's a man of the highest quality.'

'It's fine. We were talking about Hubert Newman.'

'I heard, miss. And believe me, I was that sorry when I saw the gentleman had died. I've read all his books. Do you mind me asking, was he a friend of yours?'

'I knew him professionally.' She hesitated. 'We were just . . . discussing his recent visit to Professor Lindemann.'

'That's right. Mr Newman came the other week. To the Prof's rooms at the Clarendon Laboratory. He seemed upset, but whatever poor Mr Newman had to say, the Prof was pretty much incensed by it. He was cursing for hours, calling him a cheap thriller writer and all kinds of names.'

'He didn't seem to know that Mr Newman had died.'

'I'm afraid, miss, he was so worked up, I hadn't presumed to mention it as yet. Hence you got both barrels just now. It must have been a shock for the Prof.'

'That explains it.'

'I wonder, did you . . . did you hear what happened to Mr Newman? Any idea what carried him off?'

'A heart attack, they think.'

'Well, my sympathies to you, miss.'

He cast a hasty glance back to the drawing room.

'I'd best be off. The Prof will be itching to leave.'

Stella felt the last chance of getting any answers retreating rapidly.

'Before you go, I wonder, do you have any idea what Mr Newman wanted with the Professor?'

Harvey shook his head.

'I'm not one for listening at doors, miss. More than my job's worth.'

'Of course. I wasn't suggesting—'

'But since you did know the gentleman, professionally, I will tell you a queer thing.'

She waited.

'After he'd left – Mr Newman – the Prof asked me to find one of his scientists and bring him straight round. I had to go and see the fellow, not just call up on the telephone. Actually see him and deliver the message personally that the Prof wanted him. I had to go straight to his house in St John Street, and tell Mr Grunfeld in person.'

'Mr Grunfeld?'

'The scientist. Dr Ernst Grunfeld, to be correct.'

'So, did you go?'

'That's the odd thing. When I got to his lodgings, the landlady, Mrs Forsyth, said Mr Grunfeld had left. Suddenly, out of the blue and not a word of explanation. Packed up and left a little extra on the dresser to cover the rent until the end of the month. Mrs Forsyth said she expected no more of foreigners, though Mr Grunfeld had seemed a decent type, and it just proved that you could never tell what went through their minds. I was about to leave when this lady's daughter came out of the parlour and said that a few days before he went, Mr Grunfeld had had a visitor. She'd bumped right into him in the hall and thought she heard his name – Robert or Roger or Roland Finch, she thought, but names are so difficult aren't they? Easy to confuse. But she remembered him because he was such a handsome chap, the kind of fellow who wore a suit well, she said. Spitting image of Clark Gable. This is only a young lady, you understand. Very free with her remarks. She had asked Mr Grunfeld if his friend was coming back, but Mr Grunfeld said not, because the chap lived in Vienna.'

'Vienna?'

'That's right. It's all I know, I'm afraid, miss. Now I'd better get going because the Prof is spending the weekend at Blenheim and it doesn't do to be late for Mr Churchill.'

# CHAPTER 10

*September 15th*

Nobody could have been more attentive to the marital problems of the rich and powerful than the *Daily Mail*, but when it came to his own issues, Sir Walter Heap preferred a confidential approach. Thus, when Harry arrived at the ornate brick behemoth at the far end of Fleet Street, past a waiting fleet of lorries carrying gigantic rolls of paper, he was ushered with speed through halls of fancy marble and gilded lamps up in a mirrored lift to the sixth floor.

The room was dominated by a walnut table the size of a tank, and probably twice the price, Harry thought, as he pictured the newspaper's executives gathered around it, debating how to steer the future of Europe. On the walls, other executives, gone to the Fleet Street in the sky, were memorialized in oils. The far wall was reserved for a medieval Madonna, one of the early kind with a pallid, incurious face and an elderly Christ child perched stiffly on her lap.

Heap had telephoned to express his dissatisfaction with the paucity of evidence against his wife. When Harry entered, he did not rise, but remained, legs splayed, a cigar wedged between fat fingers, dropping ash on the Turkish carpet.

'What's the news, eh, Fox?'

'Early days, Sir Walter. I have some leads, but—'

'Don't mess me around, fellow. You need to step it up. I want results for my money.'

'I understand that but—'

'Now listen. This is why I've asked you here. I've a dinner at White's tonight. She knows I'm out, and if I'm not wrong, she'll take the chance to visit him. Whoever he is.'

Harry fixed on Heap's unappealing face, blotched with an angry map of broken capillaries. It was an insult against God that anyone, let alone a beautiful woman, should be shackled to this brute. Back when he had any damns left to give, Harry might have offered up this opinion, and others, for free. But commercial considerations constrained him, so he contented himself with nodding sagely and drinking as much of the man's whisky as he could gulp.

'She needs my permission to go out. She knows that. But she doesn't care. I want you to watch her like a hawk. It's what I'm paying you for.'

Harry nodded. 'Sure.'

The truth was, watching this woman was no hardship. Platinum hair, deep-blue eyes, figure modelled on the Venus de Milo. A laugh that tinkled like ice in a cocktail shaker. He could watch her for hours on end. It helped that beautiful women were used to being watched. They spent their lives being looked at. Everything in the history of culture, every painting or statue, taught them to think about their image. How a woman appeared was essential to her success in life.

'I'm certainly paying you enough,' Heap added. 'Your time is expensive.'

Not as expensive as his own time, clamped to his wrist in Rolex form, but it was true, Harry had made sure to put in plenty of overtime on this job, including the evening at the Café de Paris where he had encountered Stella Fry. Given Heap's stinginess he was hoping to put plenty more on the meter before he delivered the photographs that would seal a society divorce.

'Any photos yet?'

'Nothing incriminating,' he murmured.

The pictures were essential – adultery being the only grounds on which a man could sue for divorce – and they needed to be compromising.

He fixed his gaze on the ornate fireplace, ripped from a Renaissance church. It was writhing with naked putti, as though even the fittings in this place could scarcely contain their lustful impulses. He dug his hands deeper into his pockets.

'You mentioned Lady Heap has a role in a new production?'

'*Troilus and Cressida* at the Westminster Theatre,' Heap

grunted. 'She'll be at the theatre most days in rehearsal until then. Or so she assures me. It's a Trojan War thing.'

From far beneath, the distant thrum and rumble of the presses could be heard, producing the first editions that would bring news of far more modern conflicts.

'Which part is Lady Heap playing?'

'Helen of Troy.'

What else? From what Harry could recall from long-ago lessons at Hammersmith Boys, Helen was the world's most beautiful woman, who was kidnapped from her husband by another man and carried away against her will. Or perhaps she went willingly, he wasn't sure. Either way, none of it seemed ideal to mention.

'It opens at the end of this month. That's if Herr Hitler has not grown tired of our empty warmongering by then and decided to invade us.'

Harry glanced around. His eyes were drawn to a sheaf of that morning's papers displayed on a side table. The *News Chronicle*, *Daily Graphic*, *Daily Herald* and the *Morning Post*. And Heap's own paper, carrying that day's sensational news. 'Prime Minister Arrives at the Summer Retreat of Herr Hitler at Berchtesgaden'. The splash was accompanied by a photograph of Chamberlain, flanked by Hitler and von Ribbentrop, trudging up the steps to the Führer's home against the backdrop of Bavarian Alps. The Nazis were in uniform. Chamberlain wore a wing collar and had a tightly furled umbrella hanging from his left arm. He looked hopelessly impotent against the might of the thugs ranged against him.

Heap followed his gaze.

'Whatever happens, war's good for newspapers. Even rumours of war. Rocket fuel for advertising revenue.'

Yet again Harry wondered at Heap's total lack of humanity, or even manners. He was living proof of what money couldn't buy.

'You think Chamberlain will succeed?'

'I very much hope so. I'm a modern man, Fox. Unsentimental. I detest this Winston hysteria. I don't get carried away by these feminine squalls of emotion. Nor does Herr Hitler. Serious times call for serious men.'

A rudimentary search on Heap had revealed that his recent travels included a visit to last year's Nuremberg rally as a special guest of the deputy führer, and regular outings to Fort Belvedere, the country home of the former King and Wallis Simpson, where he had partied with the Clivedon set, a group of grandees around Nancy Astor who advocated appeasing Hitler.

'I can't say much for the man, but what I would say is, remember that Chamberlain is an angler. That gives him patience. Determination. He's used to standing up to his waist in cold water coaxing a trout. He's playing these negotiations like a salmon fisher.'

'Right. About the play . . .'

'My wife says she's in full-time rehearsal. She dismissed the chauffeur because she likes to walk. More likely she's meeting her fancy man. Probably an actor.'

Heap gave a thin smile. He was as economical with his smile as he was with his cash.

'I want you to catch her red-handed. Trap her like a rabbit. It shouldn't be too hard.'

He was stroking the bulge of button-back upholstery with a thumb, as though caressing a woman's backside.

'You know what women are like. You just need to get inside their little heads.'

Could that be true? And if so, how did you do it? Despite his romantic successes, Harry Fox still found women, like books, difficult to read. They seemed straight enough on the surface, but as often as not when you reached deeper, all logic seemed to fall into jumbled chaos, like the last lines of an optician's chart.

'You get the evidence; I get the divorce. Clear off!'

This last was directed not to Harry but an underling who had stuck his head around the door and withdrew it hastily at Heap's curdled roar.

At this cue, Harry got to his feet. It was unpleasant even to be in the same room as Walter Heap. Aggression simmered constantly beneath the surface of his Savile Row suit. Suddenly, everything about this job was offensive to Harry and he felt ashamed to play any part in it. But work was work, and although the rent on his office was cheap, he could hardly pay it with thin air.

Sure enough, Heap's intuition was correct. One hour later, as he arrived at Belgrave Square, Harry was in time to observe Lady Heap, Diana Sowerby, slip out of the glossy black door and head at a swift clip towards Kensington. She was dressed in enough expensive fashion to buy a Spitfire. A tight crepe skirt reached to the middle of her slender calves. Her high-heeled shoes were, to his untrained eye, probably French or Italian. A stole made from silver fox looked as though it was actually enjoying clinging to her perfumed neck. Her platinum locks were freshly styled.

Whatever occasion she was heading for, it wasn't Bible class.

# CHAPTER 11

*September 16th*

'I can't cook. I never said I could. Except for mashed potato. There's not much here but corned beef, Carnation milk and pickled onions, and there's nothing you can make out of that, is there? Or *is* there? Maybe some kind of milky stew? Oh, I wish we could just go to the Ivy. Or L'Étoile. Or even the Blue Cockatoo. And what if war comes? I hate the idea of coupons and points and rationing.'

Evelyn was sitting at the table in the flat, her full lower lip thrust in a pout. Her hair was half in pipe-cleaner curlers and half in tangled disarray. She was wearing a kimono wrap. Beside her, a box of Charbonnel et Walker chocolates donated by Roger was down to its last violet cream. A quite different suitor – a Czech photographer called Lazlo – had invited himself to dinner, unaware of what awaited him.

'Should I give him my signature dish?'

She was referring to sardines mashed up with vinegar and curry powder then spread on toast.

'Not if you want to see him again,' said Stella.

'You're right. I'm going to have to persuade him to take me out. Or perhaps we could go back to his. It's so awful to think that everything normal might end.'

Normal, for Evelyn, was parties at the Ritz bar, drinks at the Café Royal and long evenings in Chelsea flats with artists and actors and poets.

'Just be grateful you're not living in Germany. They believe women's role is *Kinder, Küche, Kirche*. Children, kitchen and church. They don't like women smoking either. Or drinking.'

'I'd rather die.' Twirling the curlers in her hair, Evelyn said, 'Do you think you might ever have to cook for a man?'

'Maybe,' said Stella, absently. She was on the sofa, with her knees up and a copy of *Time and Tide* magazine propped in front of her glazed eyes.

'God help me if I do. But then, I don't expect I'll ever get married. I'm not a natural housekeeper.'

Stella cast a glance at the clutter of clothes, books, ornaments, old newspapers and used cups around them. Ancient shells collected on distant beaches. Theatre programmes, perfume bottles, an old wine bottle holding a spray of dried flowers. Tidiness was anathema to Evelyn – she said it was unartistic – whereas Stella was, by nature, exceptionally neat. Evelyn mocked her for it, but Stella's books were shelved, her clothes hung up and her two spare pairs of shoes always neatly ranged beneath them. Secretly, she hated herself for this neatness. She suspected it was indeed, as Evelyn said, a psychological condition. But it had been that way since the age of nine, when her father died. From that moment, when her own young life had spun out of control, she had tried instead to control her surroundings.

'D'you know, I used to long for you to marry Tom so we could call ourselves family.'

'I doubt your mother felt the same way.'

'Oh, she loves you, Stel. She thinks you're clever. But you're right. I can't really imagine you marrying Tom. Evenings with him would be frightfully dull. Translating Homer or listening to Bach or reading Proust in the original. Do you know, he recently translated *Winnie-the-Pooh* into Greek for a bet?'

'Did he win it?'

'Naturally. And he says things like, "Poetry is essential because how else can the dead talk to us?"'

'I remember.'

'It's probably just as well you don't marry him. Our mother wants Tom to be ambassador to Moscow, and if he was, you'd always be horribly cold.'

Evelyn glanced down at the script she was supposed to be learning, where she had underscored her lines in red crayon.

'Why are all the best parts written for men? I have hardly any lines. I was saying to Victor . . .' Victor was Evelyn's agent, who was entirely responsible for failing to progress her career, '. . . I said there are simply no plays where women get the most lines. Why do women have to skulk around in the shadows being secondary? Why can't we be the heroines?'

Stella tried harder to tune out Evelyn's voice. Her eyes were fixed on the article in front of her which was headlined, 'It May Never Happen but You've Got to Be Prepared'. It was a piece about how to turn a dining room into a gas-proof refuge. She had read the same paragraph several times now, but her mind was miles away.

'Our director, Mr MacOwan, says "Imagine every little bit of your dialogue as a code. Take the text seriously . . ."' Evelyn reached for the final violet cream. 'But as I have hardly any words, I can't see that it applies to me.'

Her voice was a fuzz of white noise, like wireless static.

'We open on the thirtieth and I'm never going to be ready. That's only a fortnight away.'

'Just as well you have hardly any lines, then.'

'That's true. But I have to *inhabit* the character.' She pulled a cartoonish grimace. 'That's what the director says. He says you need to find your inner motivation and project it. It's Stanislavski. Method acting. Psychological realism. But how am I supposed to do that with Cassandra? Pretend I'm a clairvoyant on the brink of war?'

'You like doing the tarot.'

'It's not the same.'

'You're a great actress. You'll find your motivation. How does Celia Johnson manage?'

'Mr MacOwan keeps talking about how in Shakespeare

each word means far more than it says. How you need to decipher him. But to be honest, I find the whole thing hard enough to read to begin with. Sometimes, I haven't the faintest idea what the dialogue even means.'

On the dining table before her, a small pool of red wine, spilled the previous evening, had etched a map of Ireland onto the tablecloth. The stain made Stella think of Hubert Newman's death, in the cloisters of Westminster Abbey. Had his skull cracked as he fell? Had his blood mottled the ancient flags? Had he lain on his back, lifeless, staring at the high roof, mouth agape, or was he face down on the cold stone, limbs crumpled askew as his life ebbed away? Was he killed by a blood clot that had formed silently over hours, or days, before making its deadly way through the deep tributaries to his heart? Or had someone else had a hand in his death?

'Have you worked it out yet?'

Stella jerked to attention.

'Worked out what?'

'What you'll do. About a job. I saw you had a letter.'

Stella glanced down at the floor, where a single sheet of paper protruded from its envelope:

'Regarding your application for the position of junior mistress in the instruction of French and German, the Lady Theresa School for Young Ladies would like to offer . . .'

'Oh. That.'

It was difficult to think clearly about the future. It was hard to think of anything at all, save the conversation with Professor Lindemann, and underlying that, the outlandish suggestion that her own life was at risk. For the past three days, Stella's entire body had hummed with unease. Could it be true, as Harry Fox had said, that she was in danger because of something she had inadvertently seen? It sounded fantastical, but Professor Lindemann's furious response when she had asked about his letter seemed odd. Hubert Newman's worried face came back to her. Was he scared of something more than approaching war?

In the light of all these questions, there was no chance of attending to anything else, let alone the prospect of a row of inattentive schoolgirls reciting German verbs, or detailing in halting French what they had done at the weekend. '*Très bien, Mademoiselle Fry. Je suis allée au cinema à Littlehampton.*'

Yet if she didn't take the teaching job, she would have to find another one. She was down to her last three pounds, and Evelyn was complaining about finances and not being able to afford anything without Stella's thirty shillings a week.

She tuned back into Evelyn's frequency.

'. . . he's frightfully sophisticated. And he's a major photographer who's offered to do my studio portrait for nothing, so I simply can't give him cheese on toast. I suppose the thing is . . . What I'm saying, darling, is, I don't want to be a bore, but could you possibly advance me the rent?'

That decided it.

# CHAPTER 12

A large part of Harry Fox's job involved hanging around, but mortuaries were his least favourite place to loiter. He had encountered more than enough corpses two decades ago in the trenches. After all those men staring empty-eyed at the sky, torn limbs akimbo, it seemed incredible that it might happen again. Did nobody remember? If so, he would love some of that amnesia. Remembering was his problem, and the only forgetting available to him came over the bar, in a glass of something rough.

Sometimes, though, a trip to the underworld could not be avoided.

The Westminster Public Mortuary in Horseferry Road was a gloomy edifice, housing a central, refrigerated hall and a series of other rooms including a private space for viewing. Alongside this space was a gallery with a draped window at which the bereaved would stand, before, at a signal, the curtain opened to reveal their beloved on a trolley. Harry had seen this ceremony more times than he liked, but that morning he short-circuited the performance by taking the back route and trotting briskly up the stairs to find Abel Edwards, the mortician, in his tiny room, walled in by files and drinking a cup of mahogany tea. He was a small, whiskery man, like a creature in its burrow, and he sprang up nervously at Harry's approach.

'Mr Fox. Long time no see.'

'Just a quick visit, Abel. It's about that writer, Hubert Newman.'

It was a guess, but as Newman had died just a few hundred yards away from here, this was the logical place for his body to end up.

'He was in, Mr Fox, but he's left already,' said Abel, with the apologetic air of a club receptionist noting the absence of a member.

'Already?'

'You've just missed him, actually.'

'Was there a post-mortem?'

This was the point at which Abel Edwards should have requested another look at Harry's credentials, or at the very least enquired as to his interest in the deceased's case, but the fact was, Harry had been extremely helpful on a past occasion when Abel was accused of being drunk in charge of a corpse. The fumes of formaldehyde, Harry assured the angry widow, caused symptoms similar to the ingestion of an entire bottle of whisky. It was an outrage to suggest that Mr Edwards was intoxicated on duty when he was, in fact, putting his own health at risk in the interests of the dead. Afterwards, Harry and Abel Edwards had celebrated privately in this very back room over a glass of Glenmorangie.

'No PM. It was an open and shut case. I saw he was in the papers, Mr Newman. He was quite a writer, apparently. Rest in peace. There's no issue, is there, Mr Fox? Nothing suspicious?'

Harry ignored this question.

'In what way was it open and shut?'

'Heart attack. Nothing untoward.'

'A heart attack is untoward.'

'Not round here, Mr Fox. I've seen plenty of gentlemen like him who enjoyed the good life, so to speak. We do have the Houses of Parliament on the doorstep.'

'So what did the investigating officer do?'

'Just examined him before he was took away.'

'How exactly did they examine him?'

'Very respectfully, sir. Respectfully and briefly.'

'Did they ask you questions?'

'They never do now. Not like you used to, Mr Fox.'

He paused and considered. Beneath the bushy eyebrows, the beady eyes narrowed. Abel Edwards, Harry knew, had seen death in all its incarnations.

'If you're asking me, though, Mr Fox, there is one thing I noticed. The deceased was still in *rigor mortis*, but he looked very calm, if that's any consolation to his loved ones. Sometimes they come here and you feel sorry for them, even though they've passed. You see a lot of pain and fear. But this gentleman had not a frown on his face. It was unnatural, almost. As though he was frozen.'

'Frozen?'

'Not with cold. More like he had turned to stone. It's hard to describe what I saw, Mr Fox, but it was like he had become his own statue.'

Heading back to his office, Harry was so absorbed in the implications of Abel Edward's remarks that he noticed nothing of his surroundings until he passed a bookshop and saw a selection of Hubert Newman's novels in the window. *Midnight in Vienna*, *Appointment in Paris*, *Traitor's Gate*, *A Shot Across the Bows*. He stopped in his tracks. He could recite those titles in his sleep. He'd read a lot of detective novels. Terrible ones, exciting ones, bestsellers. Those that were mysteriously praised to the skies, despite their leaden flaws, and those he unearthed dead and yellowed, on the shelves of a second-hand bookshop, which sprang instantly to life when he read them. He had grown familiar with the grammar – the formula of clues, red herrings and diversions, and the great reveal. It occurred to him that detective fiction employed much the same techniques as counter-espionage – notably, deduction, intuition, examination, counteraction and control.

That was what he had been planning to explain to Hubert Newman.

The pain of being cheated of that conversation struck him once again. It would have been a new departure. A new sideline, after so many low blows. Instead, it had been snatched from him by forces unknown.

The sight of the novels brought to mind his own boy – or as good as – Jack. Jack might as well be his son because he loved him, and felt a visceral need to protect him. But if he wanted to spend more time with Jack, he needed to repair things with Joan, and his sister was tricky. Sometimes she wanted him there and other times she didn't, and there was no way of telling what kind of a day it was going to be.

He'd gone round the other night to drop off *A Dozen Layers of Dark* for Jack. Joan had just made a shepherd's pie and the three of them ate around the table like a normal family. The air was filled with the scent of tomatoes growing in the glass lean-to at the back of the house, and the tiny garden was crowded with late roses. Birdsong came in from the opened window. He recognized a robin's call. Jack talked ten to the dozen about school, and the fact that he had, at last, been selected for the second eleven.

'No books at the table,' Joan intervened, removing the novel deftly from Jack's side. 'Always has his nose in a book, this boy. He needs a more useful hobby.'

'Let the lad read. He has a brain. Reading's important if you're going to get on.'

'What, detective thrillers?'

The snobbery was not entirely justified. Joan herself was an avid consumer of romances, acquired every week from

Boots' lending library, and fat lot of good that had done her. But Harry wasn't about to mention that.

'Any kind of reading. It's important. Helps him focus. Develops the brain.'

Joan raised her eyebrows.

'He's got plenty of brains as it is without developing more.'

She cleared the plates away, tight-lipped, as Jack disappeared upstairs to finish his homework. Then she came to sit at the table again, lit one of his cigarettes and said, 'If I need advice, Harry, I'll ask for it.'

'C'mon, Joan. I was only trying to help. Young boys need an older man around. I saw it in the war.'

'Oh, not the trenches again. There's plenty of men who suffered out there and haven't gone out doing what you did.'

She dragged on the cigarette, sucking in her cheeks, and then, more congenially, said, 'D'you enjoy your job?'

Did he? Following people in whom he had no interest, who may or may not be a threat to his country's interests. Could a few pamphlets, or the odd poem, really pose any kind of danger? He had seen danger, after all, and felt its breath whistle past his head and explode in the earth behind him. He'd seen it maim young men and rip the skin off their faces.

Perhaps the job had more to do with his origins, and the feelings he had about their own father, growing up. Stanley Fox had never been around for Harry and Joan. He was a rootless, enigmatic figure who had left Harry with no idea of how a father should be. When friends asked where his father was, Harry would repeat his dad's own lame excuses. He had gone to Italy on business. He was in Ireland, buying a racehorse. He was prospecting for gold in Ontario. They never believed him. Stanley Fox was a hole in the air. A farrago of paper-thin excuses and unlikely stories. A lasting enigma that his son could never unravel. Maybe that also explained his own admiration for Hubert Newman, because Harry Fox had never been much good at creating a story, so he envied people who could.

On impulse, he turned back to the bookshop and went inside.

He had to cough a couple of times before the bookseller deigned to notice, and then he said, 'How can I help you, sir?' as though asking if Harry required the tradesman's entrance.

'It's about Hubert Newman.'

The man swept his arm towards a display, in the midst of which was a framed photograph of Newman, decorated with a black ribbon.

'A tragic loss. We've been swamped with requests. We can't keep up. We have more on order. Does sir have a title in mind or do you prefer a recommendation?'

'I've read them all.'

'Oh. I see.' He blinked. 'Then could I ask why—?'

'I thought you could tell me a bit about him.'

'Well, sadly I never had the pleasure of—'

'As a writer.'

'Ah! Sir asks a fascinating question. Can I ask what prompts your interest?'

He could ask, but Harry would certainly not be telling him. The circumstances around Newman's death contained anomalies – the letter from Frederick Lindemann, the curious dedication to Stella Fry and the mysterious state of the corpse – but they failed to add up to anything. Everything told Harry that a logical evaluation of clues and suspects should lead to a solution, yet he still had not the faintest idea if anyone had killed Hubert Newman, or why. He was open to any ideas – and just that moment it had occurred to him that Newman himself might be able to help.

'I'm interested in the way he constructed the novels and so on.'

The bookseller relaxed back against a shelf and assumed a professorial stance, pushing his pince-nez further up his nose. There were no other customers in the shop and he was loath to pass up a chance to display his expertise.

'Indeed. Well, the reviewers would have us believe that when it comes to Newman, plotting was his forte. And that is certainly true. His plots are dovetailed like Chippendale. They twist like a knife. One can explore in the most forensic detail the puzzles he lays out – the plot, the clues, the solution – and watch in admiration as he gathers the facts in an orderly and methodical manner. He handles the who, the how, and the why like a science equation. He has a complete respect for the analytical method. And yet . . .'

Here, the man paused and flexed his fingers. He was loving this. Harry supposed he rarely got the chance to say much more than 'Two and six, sir,' or 'Would Madame like it delivered?'

'If sir was asking me, I would have to say that the psyche of the murderer – the secrets of the heart – those were Newman's interests. The Orient, the Riviera, the ocean liner and so on may have been his settings, but his true location was the human mind.'

'The mind?'

'The psychology of the crime and of the criminal. In every novel, if one reads attentively, one sees that Newman is far less interested in the execution of the murder than in the motive. His work is full of long-buried motives leading to festering feuds. Hidden pasts that lead to a bloody conclusion many years later. His murders, as you will be aware, often appear entirely random. But Peverell Drake excavates the past like an archaeologist, tunnelling through layers of cover-up until he unearths the bare facts of the case. That is why Newman is the perfect exemplar of the Golden Age.'

'I'm sorry. The what?'

'It's the name that we in the trade give for this particular style of detective novel. Because, as far as these novels go, we are very much in a Golden Age.'

'You mean Mrs Sayers and Mrs Christie and the rest?'

'Precisely. And, I don't mind saying, so much more popular with our customers than the American noir.'

'Which is?'

'Hard-boiled thrillers. Gumshoes, crime rackets. Gritty urban settings with ill-bred, ill-dressed characters who are morally compromised.'

Here, the bookseller cast Harry a pointed look.

'Detectives from the noir genre tend to be tough and cynical, whereas Golden Age detectives are intelligent and refined. They are heroes one can truly admire. Lord Peter Wimsey, Inspector Alan Grant, Hercule Poirot and of course, above all, Peverell Drake. Drake is a creation of genius. He reached his apogee, in my personal opinion, in *A Shot Across the Bows*.'

The bookseller sighed.

'There are many queens of the Golden Age: Dorothy L. Sayers, Agatha Christie, Margery Allingham, Ngaio Marsh, not to mention Josephine Tey. But Hubert Newman was the king. I don't know what we'll do without him.'

The door clanged, and an elderly man in a velvet-collared coat entered fussily, producing in the bookseller a Pavlovian spurt of energy. The seminar was over.

Briskly, he said, 'Is there anything else?' No 'sir' this time.

Harry demurred, and left the shop.

None of that was much help, but as he walked towards Soho, he realized for the first time that he understood something. Not about Newman, but about himself. He too had always admired detectives like Lord Peter Wimsey, Peverell Drake and Hercule Poirot, but he, Harry, was not cut from that cloth. He had never set foot in a vicarage. He hung out in backstreet cafés and was acquainted with the scum of the earth. Also, he was a cynic. You had to be one in his line of work. Cynicism was part of the equipment. A tool of the trade, as much as false identities and skeleton keys. Real detectives didn't go around believing people and acting aristocratic towards them. They went around distrusting people, just like politicians went around kissing babies.

He was that kind. He would never be a hero. He was tarnished and afraid, and 'Doubt Thy Neighbour' would be one of his ten commandments long after he had forgotten the other nine.

In Wardour Street he dropped in at a theatrical costumier called Willy Clarkson's. The shop was popular with all the West End theatres, but it was also the first choice of the Security Service, who deployed its wares for any number of disguises. Wigs, moustaches and false beards were difficult to carry off – they tended to look bizarre under the artificial light of pubs and underground trains. But Harry liked to keep a stash of other accessories: pipes, hats and glasses, to hand.

'I'd like some spectacles, please Toby. Clear lenses.'

'Certainly, sir. In the case over there. Any of those take your fancy?'

He tried on some horn-rims, then a pair with heavy black plastic frames, before settling on an elegant rimless style.

'Lovely sir, very academic.'

He experimented with a couple of hats. Despite appearances to the contrary, Harry was interested in fashion. He often wished that he had chosen a career that lent itself to more than Aquascutum raincoats and nondescript fedoras by way of uniform. He knew he looked good in well-cut clothes. Occasionally he would walk down Jermyn Street or Savile Row or Burlington Arcade, dreaming of shooting his cuffs in bespoke suits of fine pinstriped wool like the employees of MI6, who had the class to dress eccentrically, with the occasional flash of red sock and their fathers' old sports jacket from Gieves & Hawkes. The Watchers of MI5, however, needed to blend in. They weren't called plain clothes for nothing. Nobody wanted Sir Anthony Eden following them down the street.

Besides, it wasn't as if he could afford it.

But as he tilted a soft grey trilby raffishly on his head and peered in the mirror, he had an unsettling shock. Across the street, from the cover of a shop porch, a seedy, balding man was peering straight at him.

Gino.

Gino Lombardi was a nondescript Italian with a large Adam's apple, a wandering eye and features so forgettable that they slipped away like water. Until the previous year, he had been working as a waiter at the Hotel de Paris in Bray, Berkshire. When his workplace was selected by lawyers for Mr Ernest Simpson as the location of a staged adultery to procure a divorce from his wife Wallis, Gino had been required to observe the couple in bed and take notes. Subsequently he was asked to repeat his evidence to a packed court, which he did to great effect. The hotel sacked him for his efforts, but Gino's observation skills and lurking anonymity had attracted the attention of the Security Service, with the result that he had found a new life in the shadows.

What the hell was Gino doing here? And more importantly, skulking just feet away, looking directly at him?

Harry paid hurriedly, but by the time he had left the shop, Gino had vanished. He looked up and down the street in frustration before abandoning any attempt to find him. Gino was good at disappearing, and if he didn't want to be found, he wouldn't be. The only person who might know why Gino was there was Malone, and Harry had not spoken to Malone in a long while. Perhaps it was time to give Malone a call.

Disquieted, he made his way to the office, and it was only when he glanced at himself in a shop window that he realized the new glasses made him the living double of Heinrich Himmler.

# CHAPTER 13

When Stella arrived at Goodwin's Court she ran up the stairs quickly, flushed and slightly out of breath. She found Harry Fox with his head down, scrawling in a notebook, a grey trilby and a pair of rimless glasses on the desk in front of him. She could not help noticing that his eyes lit up when he saw her.

'This is a surprise. Have you considered my offer?'

She took off her jacket and hung it on the back of the chair as though she already worked there. Then she sat down, planting her elbows on the table.

'I have. I've come to discuss terms.'

'You're going to take the job?'

'Actually, I've already started. I met Professor Lindemann. As you suggested.'

He stared at her, incredulously.

'How? When?'

'Last night. Quite by chance. At a party for refugees. Well, not for refugees themselves, but for people who help them.'

'And you actually talked to him?'

'Briefly. He was on his way to see Winston Churchill. They're close, apparently.'

'So, you told him about finding the letter? Did he explain Newman's accusations?'

'No. In fact he seemed terribly cross to be asked. Furious. He wouldn't tell me a thing.'

'Damn.'

'But as I was leaving, his valet came after me and apologized for the Prof being so gruff. It was just his manner, he said. And he told me about Newman coming up to Oxford and visiting Lindemann's rooms.'

'Did he say what they talked about?'

'The valet didn't hear. But he did say that the moment Newman had left, Lindemann asked him to go and find one of his colleagues. A scientist called Ernst Grunfeld. He had to go straight to his digs in St John Street. But when the valet went to his house, his landlady said there was no chance, because the man had packed up quite suddenly and vanished.'

'How do you mean, vanished?'

'Totally disappeared. And that's not all. The landlady's daughter said that a few days before he went, Mr Grunfeld had a visit from a man called Robert or Roger or Roland Finch. She wasn't sure of the name, but she remembered him because he looked the image of Clark Gable. Anyway, this man had returned to where he lived. Vienna.'

'Where you used to live.'

'Exactly.'

Harry leaned back in his seat and twiddled a match between his fingers. His eyes dwelt on her thoughtfully, then he leaned forward and shrugged.

'You'll have to go back there.'

She laughed.

'Oh, of course. Why didn't I think of that?'

'You know the place. And you speak the language, don't you? Austrian.'

'German. I also speak French, and a little Italian, if you'd like me to make a tour of the Continent at the same time.'

'No. Vienna's the place.'

She shook her head in astonishment.

'You can't really mean it, Mr Fox. Harry. It's one thing agreeing to work with you, but there is absolutely no chance of me travelling all the way to Vienna. Firstly, I can't afford it. Secondly, the whole Continent is on the brink of war and thirdly, fourthly and fifthly, I don't have a clue who this man Finch is or what he looks like.'

'Give me a couple of hours.'

At five o'clock Stella was sitting in her chair in the flat, sewing a missing button on a skirt and wondering what she might make for that evening's supper from a tin of beans, a loaf of bread and a lump of cheese, when she heard a shuffling sound. A buff envelope had been pushed under the door. She opened the door, but the stairwell was empty. Bending to retrieve the envelope she found inside a wad of foreign notes secured with a paperclip, a ticket and a cutting from a magazine called *New Writing* dated September 1937. The cutting consisted of a grainy photograph, bylined *Roland Finch*, and a column about a fire that had destroyed Vienna's Rotunda, which was the largest domed structure in the world. Accompanying the cutting was a folded page torn from a notebook on which was inscribed a brief message that was, she realized, Harry Fox's version of top-flight professional advice.

'*Be careful.*'

# CHAPTER 14

*September 17th*

As the train left London the next morning, Stella sat back in the carriage, eased off her stiff jacket and felt her old life slide away. In a small suitcase she had packed two blouses, including the silk one Evelyn had purloined, underwear, a spare skirt and Evelyn's turquoise evening dress, though in what possible circumstances she might wear it, she could not imagine. In her handbag lay her passport, a wallet containing tickets to Vienna – via Dover, Ostend, Brussels, Aachen, Cologne, Frankfurt and Nuremberg – a sheaf of Austrian schillings and an envelope containing the cutting with its small black and white image of Roland Finch, or whoever he may really be. She stared again at the squarish, handsome face, with its cleft chin and quizzical eyes.

She had absolutely no idea what she was doing here.

Outside, as the city gave way to countryside, the landscape

rolled by with increasing speed. A flock of rooks rose like cinders from the edge of a wood, then drifted down again through the warm air. Stiff ghosts of cow parsley stood along the parched hedgerows.

Inside the carriage, however, all was luxury and refinement. The decor was art deco, with graceful carved lamps affixed to the walls, inlaid silver figuring on the side panels and plush crimson velvet seating. Although she had brought a package of tinned salmon sandwiches in her bag, Stella discovered that her ticket entitled her to a seat in the wood-panelled dining car, where each table was covered with a starched-linen tablecloth and a sleek bronze lamp. The delicate fragrance from a vase of white freesias mingled with the smooth fumes of cigar smoke and the rich scent of a pot of coffee that was being carried towards her by a white-coated waiter on a silver tray. Amid the clink of heavy silver cutlery on china and the murmured chatter of her fellow travellers, she attempted to reconcile the undercurrent of excitement with her sheer astonishment at being here.

In truth, if it hadn't been Vienna, she would never have dared.

The previous evening, half an hour after she had received the envelope from Harry, she had gone straight out to see her brother Alan.

Alan was her only sibling, and had managed, through a good marriage, to leave the pinched circumstances of their childhood far behind. He and his formidable wife Vanessa lived in a Georgian town house in Pimlico given to them by her parents, Sir Archie and Lady Beaumont. It boasted an oak-panelled dining room and a hall hung with oil paintings of Vanessa's ancestors, illustrating the evolution of the distinguished Beaumont nose. If Alan spent any time contemplating his cramped origins in Chiswick, he gave no sign of it. He had Stella's brown eyes and regular features, but they were overlaid with a mildness that contrasted with the acerbic nature of his wife.

Alan and Vanessa were heading out for a bridge evening, and Vanessa was sitting at her chintz-swagged dressing table, removing her old make-up with cotton wool and cold cream, then reapplying fresh. She paused, snatching impatient puffs of her cigarette, as Stella explained her plans.

'You're going where?'

'Vienna.'

'You can't be serious. On your own?'

'With a girlfriend,' lied Stella smoothly.

'For what possible reason?'

'I thought it would be interesting to see the city again. The art and so on.'

'See the art! Have you lost your mind? They're digging trenches in Hyde Park! We collected our gas masks this morning. I've laid in material for blackout curtains. And you talk about going to Austria?'

Stella shrugged with a nonchalance she did not feel.

'Honestly, Stella, you must have read the papers.'

'Mr Chamberlain seems close to a peace deal.'

Vanessa dignified this with an arch of her perfect brows.

'I thought you were looking for a job?'

'I'm going to start as soon as I get back.'

Any deviation from expected behaviour irritated Vanessa. As she squinted into the mirror to apply her mascara, brow furrowed, Stella could not help but admire her sister-in-law's reflection. The clear skin, waved chestnut hair and startling violet eyes concealed a character of fearsome determination. Sometimes it was hard to believe that Hitler would ever have the temerity to ruin her bridge evenings.

'The fact is, we're about to take Henry down to Cornwall. They're saying that children may have to be evacuated if things get worse, so I thought we would get ahead. Alan's staying in town, but if you need a break, why don't you come down with me? We've plenty of room.'

They owned a damp rectory buried in a valley on the south coast of Cornwall. It was draughty in summer, freezing in winter and slept six, but to hear Vanessa talk about it, it might have been Versailles.

'Alan!'

Stella's brother entered, tapping ostentatiously on his watch face before catching sight of Stella and grinning broadly.

'Hello, Stel! What are you doing here?'

'Alan, do talk to your sister. She says she's going on holiday to Austria. I said that's madness. A terrible idea right now. It's probably illegal. I said why doesn't she come to

Cornwall? She could spend some time with Henry. Henry loves his auntie playing with him.'

That would be the sensible thing to do and, as far as Vanessa was concerned, Stella was the most sensible of girls.

Alan's face took on an evasive expression. A lifelong conformist and taker of the easy option, he had never had the nerve to cross his younger sister and he wasn't about to start now.

'I'm sure Stella's old enough to know what she wants.'

Vanessa picked up the mascara and returned to her transformation. In her smoke-roughened voice, Stella detected a hint of concern.

'Well, I think it's an awfully bad idea at a time like this. Who's to say there will even be a peace deal? The whole notion seems to me completely mad.'

The truth was, Stella agreed with every word.

How had she managed to get caught up in this extraordinary enterprise? To return to Europe, just as the political situation was getting critical and thousands of others were flooding out. That morning's newspapers had all carried reports of Chamberlain returning from his meeting with Hitler in the Führer's mountain home in Berchtesgaden. The *Daily Express* was emblazoned with a gigantic headline 'No More War!' Others were urging the Prime Minister to 'Stand by Czecho!' Either way, the whole Continent was on edge.

And yet, Stella could not help feeling that all the events

of the past week – meeting Hubert Newman, going to the wake at the Café de Paris, being pursued by Harry Fox, her encounter with Professor Lindemann – were more than a succession of random occurrences. It was as though they were joined together by some invisible propulsive energy, a chain whose links were real, if unseen.

It was like something that Hubert Newman himself might have written. She recalled a theory she had once heard about detective stories – that the key character was either the victim, the detective, the criminal or someone completely innocent who just happened to become involved. If this was like a novel, then the latter was her.

She had considered bringing the manuscript of *Masquerade*, but its weight and tedium deterred her, so she had separated out Part One, whose chapters she had managed to read – 'The Schoolboy', 'The Actor', 'The Manager', 'The Courtier', 'The Husband' – and left them in the flat, resting pale and heavy on the bedside table. Part Two was much smaller, just two chapters, and these she fitted back into the brown envelope they had arrived in, and bundled them in her old leather suitcase, intending to read them on the train. She had also grabbed her copy of *Midnight in Vienna*. It seemed appropriate, and she had opened it several times. The novel began with the disappearance of a boy from an address in Berggasse in Alsergrund, in Vienna's ninth district.

*On the corner of Berggasse, not far from the home of the eminent Dr Freud, is a bookshop, and it was from that spot that Markus Friedkin, thirteen years old, vanished one night, while everyone was looking the other way.*

It was unsettling to hear Newman's voice in her head, so soon after his death. If the whole point of fiction was to draw you close to the author, to step into his shoes, then what would that calculating mind have made of his own end? And if she was going to find an explanation for what had happened to him, what were the chances that it would be found in Vienna?

Fragrant steam wafted from the coffee in her cup. In the cold light of day, the impossibility of the task she had taken on was all too apparent, and Stella felt a fraud for even trying. The chances of tracking down an unknown man in a city of two million people, armed with only a photograph for identification, were slender, to say the least.

The train was hundreds of miles from Vienna. There was still a chance to slip back to normality, if that was what she wanted. But what was normality now?

Her suitcase, on the rack above, bore travel labels from Milan, Munich, Paris and all the other places she had visited with the Gatz family. The Gatzes were wealthy, and they had loved to travel. She remembered their last jaunt, when they had stayed in a little Left Bank hotel in Paris in the Place Saint-Germain-des-Prés, and she had slipped out at night to drink red wine in cafés in Montparnasse and listen to Maurice Chevalier and Charles Trenet. How she had sat awestruck in the red and gold glory of the Opéra and one evening had seen Josephine Baker on stage.

In those five years there had only been one boyfriend. Franz Lehner was a lawyer from a prosperous family in Vienna's first district. Tall, blond and broad shouldered, he possessed an aquiline profile and a cheerful straightforwardness which Stella liked to believe concealed a tender sensitivity. In the past few months she had tried so hard not to think of him, but now, before she could catch it, her mind ducked down the rabbit hole of her thoughts and into the joy and anguish of their time together.

The long-suppressed memories returned in a flood: dining at Sacher's, whose crimson salons and high mirrors seemed to reflect a last glimpse of Austria-Hungary. Sitting in the taverns of Grinzing drinking the new wine of the season which would be passed around in huge mugs as a band played folk songs and everyone joined in. Visiting the Belvedere and the Schönbrunn Palace, the opera house and the Prater's ferris wheel. Sunday afternoons when Franz drove his Opel convertible out of the city to explore the mountains. Physically, at least, she still craved Franz. Not a day passed when she did not yearn to feel his arms around her and rest her face against his strong neck.

Had she loved him? She believed so. Yet perhaps she had only admired his confidence, which was so attractive to someone always hedged around with doubts. Franz seemed sure that their relationship would end in marriage, and although Stella was by nature cautious, she was flattered by such blithe certainty. Until the last time – on a weekend trip to the Starnberger See, discussing where they might marry – when casually, almost as an afterthought, he said, 'Oh, and I've joined the Austrian National Socialists.'

'You don't mean it. You can't have.'

Stella could barely get the words out. She freed her hand from his and turned to face him.

'It's just a precaution. In Germany all lawyers must become members of the National Socialist Legal Professionals associ-ation if they want to practise. Who's to know what's going to happen here, but I've always thought Austria would be safer as part of the German Reich.'

She stared up at the fine, aristocratic features. How could she have got Franz so wrong? How was it possible to know someone so well, and yet not know them at all? For a person to seem one thing, and to be another entirely.

'You can't believe all that nonsense.'

Franz's handsome face had frowned in incomprehension.

'It's a detail, Stella. No more. Just bureaucracy.'

'If you believe that, I can't possibly marry you.'

'Darling. You're being absurd.'

'I'm completely serious.'

'What does it matter, what I believe? It doesn't change who we are.'

But it did. And it always would.

Now, scrutinizing herself in the train window, she

wondered if she had returned to Vienna, not to seek out one man, but another. To staunch the unbearable ache she had felt since the day she last saw him.

A guard arrived to check her papers. Outside, the afternoon light was fading over the Rhineland, turning the broad, lazy curve of the river silver and tinting the horizon with a melon-pink glow. The wide plains of the landscape were interspersed with dark outcrops of woods and the occasional village, whose pretty, gabled houses were unchanged since medieval times. The landscape of Germany tugged at her heart as the train raced on and her own face stared back at her in the dust-smudged window.

How different her life would have been if she had married Franz. Or Tom Lamont, with his serious grey eyes and his youthful crush. Or any of the boyfriends from her Oxford years. She felt them all around her, those other lives she might have lived. The man she might have lain beside each night, the children whose heads she might have kissed. The houses she might have inhabited and furnished and loved.

Then the train was swallowed in a tunnel, and she and all the other Stellas vanished back into the dark.

# CHAPTER 15

The train wheezed and sighed to a halt, and the noises of the Westbahnhof rose up around her in a cacophony of sound. Yet it was the local accent that transported Stella more efficiently than any locomotive to the Vienna she knew. The call of porters and the shouts of tradesmen, all expressed in the high-toned, harsh pitched accents of Wienerisch, caused her unused language muscles to flex with delight. Torn scraps of words floated through the air, a babel of Austrian, Hungarian, French and other tongues she didn't recognize.

'*Schnell, schnell!*' A couple trotted by, dragging a small boy disgruntled at being trussed up in a loden coat in late summer, past a newspaper vendor advertising his titles, '*Wiener Zietung! Reichspost, Weiner Journal!*' Together with a chestnut seller, whose trolley of candied nuts issued the sharp fragrance of burnt sugar, they produced a counterpoint as fine as any from the Vienna Boys' Choir.

Stella showed her papers at the entry barrier, entered a

street full of carts, buses and trams and was transported immediately to the city she loved. The Ring, with its baroque and self-important buildings, adorned with urns and caryatids and figurines whose chiselled faces stared down with stony hauteur. Fashionable Kärntnerstrasse, where fur-clad women trawled the boutiques and lofty cafés imbued with the city's famous *gemütlichkeit* – the cosy warmth essential for combatting the long winters that came across Eastern Europe and blew icy wind round every street corner. The clatter of horses' hooves as the Lipizzaners crossed from the Hofburg towards the Riding School.

Only now, six months later, everything was changed.

In the surroundings of the station, it was impossible to ignore the groups of Jews standing in small huddles with their luggage bidding tearful farewells. The men had pouchy shadows beneath their eyes and the mothers had deliberately bright smiles, as if to convince their children that somewhere, at the end of the train line, a kinder world existed. With a shiver of apprehension, Stella moved out into the street.

The familiar buildings were now festooned with swastika banners, the elegant facades wearing their brash decorations in frozen dignity. Towards the city centre, brown-clad storm troopers were stationed on each corner. Restaurants bulged with German officers, spilling out onto the pavement cafés. Several shopfronts were shuttered, with 'No Jews or Dogs' scrawled in black paint across them. Outside a doctor's surgery, a tin-plated sign read 'No Prescriptions for Jews'.

The faces of the Viennese around her were just as bland and self-satisfied as she remembered, yet their circumstances had changed beyond measure.

Stella and the Gatz family had left before the *Anschluss*, so it was in a cinema in London that she had witnessed the occupation. She had sat horrified watching events unfold on the Pathé newsreel. The massed crowds ten deep shouting '*Wir wollen unseren Führer!*' A field-grey tide of men and tanks and horse-drawn gun carriages rolling beneath a sky turned black by Luftwaffe bombers. Propaganda leaflets wheeling like giant snowflakes to the ground. The flanks of the horses steaming and the church bells ringing out. Nazi supporters spilling onto the streets, or driving around in lorries, their weapons barely concealed. The fleets of open-topped Mercedes-Benz 770s flanked by SS and storm troopers, their swirling exhaust fumes blackening the slush as they progressed to the Hofburg Palace. Then, as the motorcade neared the Heldenplatz – Heroes' Square – the hundreds of thousands of adoring citizens extending their right arms as Hitler ascended a balcony and surveyed the land of his birth. And other, more brutal celebrations. Jews were dragged out of their homes onto the streets, humiliated and forced to scrub the pavements.

Vienna now felt both familiar, and intensely alien.

She passed a bakery, and the sugar and butter smells assailed her with memories of her favourite Austrian treats: *Apfelstrudel, Sachertorte, Kaiserschmarrn* and *Kastanienreis*, which was a heap of puréed chestnuts soaked in liqueur and topped with a mound of whipped cream. That thought led on to an image of the Christmas display at Demel's, in which an entire manger scene was made of *Lebkuchen*, embroidered in coloured icing.

Yet this sweet nostalgia was intercut with sharp reality. The old familiar streets were now filled with troop carriers and armoured cars. Cartoon Jews with crooked noses were daubed on walls and shopfronts. As a tram sailed past with a new slogan on its side – 'Jewry Is Criminality' – a wave of nausea hit her. The signs had been there for years, so how had they not had more impact on her? The graffiti, the taunts, the children's bewildered faces. The jeers of the bullies. '*Jude! Jude!*'

'*Take no notice of them. They're ignorant.*'

How could she not have seen what was in front of her eyes?

Yet even the Gatzes themselves had not seen, until it was almost too late.

The larger hotels were thronged with German staff officers and orderlies, so she decided on a small *Gasthaus* near Stephansplatz, the city's central square. It looked cheap enough, and was the kind of place that in past times would have been busy with vacationers, come to see the Secession building, or the opera, or the art. Now, though, it was deserted. In the dimly lit lobby, no tourists busied themselves for outings. There were no visitors with tickets for the theatre. Only the owner, a languid man in a shabby suit, who was sitting behind a desk, picking his teeth. Despite the lack of custom, he seemed in no hurry to register her presence.

'Are you busy, *mein Herr*?'

'I can offer you a room, *Fräulein*.'

Heaving himself up and taking her luggage with a cursory grunt, he laboured up to a small room on the fourth floor whose window offered a narrow slice of view through the rooftops to the yellow and ochre chequerboard tiles of the cathedral. The mantelpiece bore a lone swastika pennant, stuck in a vase like a daffodil. A pair of sun-faded pamphlets splayed on the table advertised the delights of the opera and the Grinzing vineyards. A washstand offered a hard little sliver of soap. There was a pervasive smell of mothballs, overlaid with old cooking and the sour tang of sweat.

Once the owner had departed, Stella sat on the bed and recalled again the time, just six months earlier, when the Gatzes had left.

It had been a long, cold winter. The statues in their stone robes seemed to flinch at the freezing wind that rolled all the way across Europe from the Russian Steppes to the Alps. The wind circled the columns of the opera house and whipped the chiselled facades of the Belvedere Palace. It howled down the cobbled maze of the inner city. It rattled the imperial stables and made the horses kick at their stable doors. One morning, Herr Gatz had shivered in his astrakhan-collared overcoat and said, '*I think it may be time to leave the party.*'

Eventually, visas were secured. On the morning of their

departure, the two boys, Jacob and Daniel, had shaken her hand solemnly, before she gathered them into a hug. Ruth, the youngest, had cried and clung to her neck and showered her with kisses.

'*Come to New York, Stella! I don't want you to leave us.*'

Herr and Frau Gatz hid their own apprehension in affectionate concern for her. '*It will be wonderful to see your family again, Stella. They will be so happy to see you after all this time. But you won't forget us, will you? We will see you again.*'

She felt suddenly, irredeemably, alone. Apart from the slow trudge of the owner up and down the wooden stairs, the *Gasthaus* was silent. In all her time with the Gatzes, there had always been a background sound of children's voices, or piano playing or the soft murmur of the wireless. Being properly alone was a different, more unsettling experience.

She questioned again what had prompted this impulsive venture. How reckless she had been to return to a country in turmoil, and under Nazi rule. She was generally the most rational of people. Recklessness was not a trait that Franz would have recognized in her. She wondered where her former fiancé was that night, and if he was thinking of her.

Opening the tiny window, she leaned out. Looking over the patchwork of rooftops she remembered the happiness of her first arrival here, exploring the winding alleyways and quirky, crooked streets, admiring the baroque statues and golden domes.

Perhaps, being in Vienna was not only to do with Franz Lehner or Roland Finch but also with herself. She remembered something her revered German teacher at Oxford, Cecil Fairfax, had liked to say. That there were two kinds of people, those who made something of their life and those to whom life merely happened.

Was that what she had been trying to prove for the last five years? That she could make something of her life?

She turned, opened the suitcase and hung up the evening dress and her French blouse, then she settled down to read a few more chapters of *Midnight in Vienna*.

# CHAPTER 16

*September 18th*

For just a second the next morning, the sound of St Stephan's bells tricked her into imagining she was back in her life at Oxford, where the clocks of the colleges and chapels would chime the hour with a charming lack of synchronicity and she would stretch luxuriantly in her bed before cycling off to a lecture or a library. Then she looked around at the cheap wooden furniture, the tassel-fringed lamps and shabby chairs with their moth-eaten plush and faux-gilt legs and remembered. She was on an ill-judged and possibly dangerous mission, for reasons that Sigmund Freud might have a chance of fathoming, but she herself could not begin to understand.

She got up, washed at the basin, clipped on her stockings and dressed in the French blouse and a dark skirt. Then she dragged a brush through her hair and fastened it tightly off her face. As she looked at herself in the mean little mirror above the basin, she realized yet again what an asset was the tranquil demeanour that she had inherited from her Irish father. Nobody studying that face would have any clue of the turmoil of emotion behind it.

She walked along Dorotheergasse and found the Café Ludwig and drank a *mélange*, a shot of the Continental coffee, thick and potent, that she had missed so badly. Then she ordered a plate of *Buchteln*, little jam-filled sugared buns that the Café Ludwig made better than anywhere in the city. The warm air, filled with the aroma of hot, roasted beans and the fug of energetic conversations, was instantly evocative. It was consoling to be back in a place she knew so well, when everything else about the city had dramatically changed. She scanned a copy of the *Neue Freie Presse*, the newspaper that the Gatzes had always preferred. Its owners were Jewish and it had a strong liberal heritage – it had defended Dreyfuss back in the day – but the idea that it might contain a news article about a mysterious Roland Finch was too much to hope.

All the same, the combined effects of coffee and glucose provided the necessary jolt of optimism that her mission might – just might – succeed.

Dabbing a finger on the last traces of sugar and licking her lips, she formulated a plan. She would comb the city systematically, district by district, in her search. She had no idea if there were rules for this kind of thing, but even a bizarre hunt like this could be improved with a routine.

Routine, after all, was her speciality.

She began with the Ringstrasse, Vienna's central boule-vard that circled the inner city in a necklace of fine stucco palaces and neo-Baroque mansions.

As she walked, she was intensely watchful. She knew she was naturally observant, yet she was astounded at how little she had noticed in her previous life. This was vigilance of a different order. Every edifice seemed charged with meaning. Each face she passed was studied for significance and every street corner was a potential turning point at which she might encounter her target.

But nothing.

Once she had explored the first district, the Innere Stadt, Leopoldstadt was next on her list. Yet as soon as she entered the slum district, common sense began to dampen her hopes and her earlier optimism started to fade. Here on the other side of the Ring, away from the banks, the palaces, the theatre and the opera, was the centre of Jewish poverty, per-vaded by the smell of cooking fat. There were blocks with peeling plaster, smeared windows and broken doors, where families lived eight to a room without running water. Stella threaded along alleyways and peered into small bars with bare board floors and unwashed tablecloths. But nobody resembling Roland Finch could be seen.

Beneath bridges and arches, past iron-grilled houses smelling of coal dust, Vienna's medieval backstreets twisted apparently at random, up steps and down, the narrow walkways doubling back on themselves like a frustrating argument. After several hours, her feet were aching from the cobbles, and following her initial surge of adrenaline, she was beginning to feel the effects of her exhausting journey. Increasingly, she realized that she was on a fool's errand. How could she possibly find a man she had never met in a city of this size? How far did she propose to comb the streets? As far as the sixteenth district and the tenements of Ottakring? Or right out to the industrial district of Simmering?

As she left the Danube behind and progressed up Turkenstrasse, back towards the city centre, a sense of despondency enveloped her. Now that she was here, her journey seemed more impulsive than ever. She had acted without sober evaluation of the risks or the likelihood of success. She thought of Harry Fox, back in his ramshackle office in Soho. Why had *he* not come to Vienna, or at the very least volunteered to accompany her, if he was so keen to investigate Hubert Newman's death? *I think we would make a good team.* What on earth had he meant by that? They had nothing in common at all.

The fact was, she knew next to nothing about Harry Fox. She had no idea if he was married, or had family, or even the misdemeanour for which he had been suspended, and which he refused to discuss. She had no clue what motivated his desire to explore Hubert Newman's death. And yet, for reasons she could not explain, she was drawn to him. Harry Fox was unlike any man she had known. His face, though handsome, had a careworn quality, and his eyes contained a darkness that made her wonder what they had seen.

None of that changed the fact that she had come halfway across Europe at the behest of a complete stranger.

# CHAPTER 17

The sour-faced man with the full Viennese moustache, and an expression that could curdle a tray of Gerstner's cream cakes, shrugged insouciantly.

'English no more. Austrian now.'

The British Passport Office at 6 Metternichgasse, a stately slab of stucco in the leafy diplomatic district close to the Schloss Belvedere, had been sold. The place where, on a freezing winter day, the Gatzes had come seeking visas to leave Vienna now bore the flag of the *Nationalsozialistische Fliegerkorps*, the Nazi Flyers Corps.

Instead, the Passport Office had been downgraded to a legation and the business of issuing British passports and visas had squeezed into a narrow building in Wallnerstrasse in the Innere Stadt.

The idea of checking at the British legation had come to Stella as a sudden inspiration. If Roland Finch was British, there was every possibility that they might have some trace of him. If some central register of British subjects existed, this surely would be the place to find it.

At Wallnerstrasse she had to bypass a queue stretching out of the door and along the pavement, and through the narrow hall, bulging with people. The queue massed along the chequerboard tiled floor, and snaked up the stairway, everyone waving papers and carrying suitcases. Men with anxious faces, women trying to keep their children quiet, as if any spark of youthful vivacity might spoil their chances, elderly couples supporting each other. Amid the subdued frenzy, a low moan was issuing from a corner of the hall, where a very pregnant woman was sitting, legs akimbo, attended by her flustered husband.

'That poor woman,' murmured Stella to a smart *Hausfrau* in a headscarf beside her. 'She should be at home.'

'She's come deliberately,' said the woman acerbically. 'She's hoping she'll give birth on British territory and they won't be able to refuse her a passport.'

Stella followed directions to a cubbyhole of an office on the top floor where a card in a brass frame announced its occupant as 'Passport Officer Eric Wilson'. She knocked at the door.

'Come!'

Eric Wilson was a harried young man who looked as though he had not slept for a week. As Stella entered, he jumped up and frowned.

'My name is Stella Fry. I'm looking for someone. He's

in Vienna, but I haven't a clue where to find him and I wondered—'

Wilson flapped a hand impatiently.

'Have you seen what it's like out there, Miss Fry?'

'Yes, but I—'

'Then I don't need to explain. You've come at a terrible time. Half of Vienna is seeking an exit visa. We are quite simply overwhelmed. Captain Kendrick – our head of consulate – has been arrested and expelled. He was crossing the border with his wife when the Gestapo got him. They're alleging he was spying on German troops. The secretaries have been obliged to leave too. Our office manager is being detained at Gestapo HQ.'

He gestured at the pile of papers that threatened to topple over on the desk.

'I'm all that's left and I'm leaving any moment now. I'm emptying the drawers and dealing with documents.'

He glanced across at a bin, overflowing with a pile of paper that had already been shredded, and fished off his spectacles to clean them with his tie.

'Kendrick was trying to do as much as he could in the time we have left. We've been stamping temporary visas for weeks. But there are half a million non-Aryans in Vienna and we can't give visas to them all. Kendrick must have granted entry permits to Palestine to at least 10,000 Jews this summer. The local staff are so overwrought they keep bursting into tears. I confess I often feel the same.'

He shook his head, as if surprised at this departure from his normal, bureaucratic self.

'So the possibility of trying to track down a friend of yours who may or may not be in this city, is not, I'm afraid, at the top of my agenda.'

Stella hesitated for a moment, uncertain what next to do, and Wilson's demeanour softened.

'Who exactly is this person you're looking for?'

'His name's Roland Finch.'

Wilson shrugged.

'Can you describe him?'

'About five foot ten,' she guessed. It seemed trivial to suggest he looked like a film star. 'Dark hair, slightly wavy, brown eyes.'

'And he's disappeared, you say?'

'Completely.'

'I would imagine he's had the good sense to leave the country. Either that or he's been arrested. I don't want to alarm you, Miss Fry, but they have lists. A card index of every suspected anti-Nazi drawn up by the Gestapo. Bankers, politicians, artists. The arrests are constant. I'm sorry. What does your friend do?'

She had no real clue. But he had contributed a column to *New Writing* the previous year.

'He's a writer.'

'Well, the only thing I can advise is, if you're looking for a writer, you'll want to go to the Café Louvre, across from the central telegraph office. All the writers go there, or at

least they did before the *Anschluss*. It's a magnet for jour-
nalists. An intelligence-gathering hotspot. Eric Gedye, John
Gunther, William Shirer, all the foreign correspondents.
They swap news, get updates on the political situation.
Journalistically speaking, the Café Louvre's pretty much
the centre of Europe.'

He picked up his pen and returned to the pile of papers in
front of him; then, as she remained, frozen with indecision,
looked up again from behind his pince-nez.

'Miss Fry, if I can speak to you seriously. This is no place
to be either a Jew or a Communist, but it's also not the place
for a British woman to be asking vague questions about her
missing friends. You must leave as soon as you can. Do you
need help to arrange it?'

'I won't be here long. I'm only staying a day or two.'

He knitted his fingers together, leaned forward on the
desk, and contemplated her soberly.

'I have no idea what you're really doing here, Miss Fry,
and I suspect you're not going to tell me, but I repeat, it's
not safe to stay. I've already told you that the head of our
consulate has been arrested and accused of spying. Going
around talking about missing people is exactly the kind of
thing that attracts attention. The Nazis are on a hair trigger
here and the residents are all too eager to report anything
unusual to their new overlords. They'd accuse you of spying
as soon as look at you, and it would be the devil to have you
released. You must take great care with whom you speak

and where you go. Trust nobody, and for the love of God, please leave as soon as you can.'

Stella walked back from the British legation, sick with nerves. She had no idea where to go or how to proceed. Eric Wilson's warning had only added to the feeling – the one she had back in London – that eyes were tracking her. She told herself that was normal for Vienna – no one could move in this city for statues and figurines, and at every turn an angry Titan or a marble Atlas would be staring down. Architecturally at least, Vienna's citizens were under constant surveillance. Most likely, she was just exhausted by hyper vigilance.

Her feet led her on the familiar route to the apartment where she had lived for several years. The Gatz home was a handsome art nouveau building with an ornate balustrade, bulging with caryatids and acanthus leaves. The family had been long established in Vienna and looked askance on the tens of thousands of *Ostjuden* who had more recently poured into the city from the east – the kind of impoverished immigrants who settled in Leopoldstadt. The Gatzes valued their social standing. They had a library of books with marbled leaves, an enclosed courtyard made into a winter garden, and a grand piano which was beautifully played by their daughter, Ruth, in recitals for family and friends.

It had taken a great deal for Herr Gatz to leave such a place.

Standing across the road, she tried to imagine how it

must have felt for Herr Gatz to abandon his ancestral home with little money or security. Whereas she had a passport to peace and safety, Herr Gatz had launched his entire family into the unknown, throwing himself on the mercy of a cousin in New York with whom he hoped to go into business.

Perhaps his consultations with the celebrated Dr Freud had helped. Herr Gatz was an unlikely character to lie on a psychoanalyst's couch. He was a genial businessman with a jovial demeanour, but he had enjoyed discussing history and art with Stella, and he guessed she might be interested in Freud's ideas. The doctor had a theory of a 'double self', he told her, all to do with shadows, opposites and telepathy, and his consulting room was filled with precious antiquities. Tiny women with fat pot bellies. Monkey's paws, heads, cats, and a marble baboon that was Thoth, the ancient Egyptian god of the intellect.

At the thought of Freud, a line came to Stella from the first page of *Midnight in Vienna*.

*On the corner of Berggasse, not far from the home of the eminent Dr Freud, is a bookshop, and it was from that spot that Markus Friedkin, thirteen years old, vanished one night, while everyone was looking the other way.*

She decided to take a look.

★

Alsergrund, just north of the Innere Stadt, was a district of wide cobbled streets flanked by elegant nineteenth-century buildings that were popular with doctors, academics and artists. The blocks were massive and solemn, as if their very stone embodied the decades of sombre discourse and philosophical enquiry that had been debated within them. As she approached the neo-Gothic Votivkirche she tensed. Even the churches now required an armed guard. A pair of sentries in steel helmets, their hands clasped on the barrels of their rifles, stared ahead.

Berggasse 19, the home of Dr Freud, had a traditional wooden double door that led, in the Viennese custom, to a tiled corridor. Beyond was a courtyard and from the corridor, several doors led off. On the ground floor was a butcher's shop, and opposite, a flight of broad stone stairs, wrought with elaborate iron banisters, that led to the psychoanalyst's consulting room. Freud himself, she knew, had already left for England after the apartment was raided and his daughter, Anna, questioned by the Gestapo.

As she stood outside the building her attention was caught by a commotion. A knot of people was milling and a tangle of excitement hung in the air. A slogan, '*Ein Volk, Ein Reich, Ein Führer*', had been daubed in impatient black paint across the frontage of a shop.

Moving closer she saw that it was a bookshop, but nobody was selling books that day. Instead, the door gaped open and the interior was in the process of being ransacked. Brown-jacketed storm troopers were emerging, bearing stacks of volumes which they piled carelessly on the pavement. In the midst of these piles an officer sat on an upturned crate, opening each flyleaf, scrutinizing it, then stamping the front pages with a rubber swastika stamp.

A small man, whom she took to be the bookshop owner, was standing helplessly in shirtsleeves and braces to one side, wringing his bony hands.

Hanging back, Stella edged closer to an elderly man with a tattered overcoat and a fraying suitcase.

'What's happening?'

'They're saying it's a suspect place.'

'The bookshop?'

'*Ja.*'

He turned away. Nobody wanted to be seen talking. Gossip was one step from treason now, especially in the presence of so many soldiers, broiling with aggression. Conversation was too close to confrontation.

She remembered the slow creep of it. The coughing fit she had feigned the first time someone said '*Heil Hitler*'. The decision to no longer shop at the grocery store that offered 'Aryan eggs'. The shock at the opera when audience members offered a right-armed salute during the encore. People stopped greeting each other, for fear of compromising their neighbours, and they avoided each other on their daily walks.

And in that instant, she was also reminded of something else.

The flicker of fear on Hubert Newman's face when she

had sat across the table from him in the Athenaeum. Now she understood where she had seen that expression before. It had been written on the faces of Jews in Vienna, in cafés, or shops, or hurrying along the streets, because they knew danger – mortal danger – lay just around the corner.

It occurred to her that if the bookshop Hubert Newman wrote about was a real place, perhaps he had visited it once. Crossing the road to avoid the attention of the soldiers, Stella stood at a tram stop opposite and watched the Germans going systematically through the stacks of books, piling some to one side and tossing others on a jumbled heap. Several of the rejects, she noticed, had foreign titles.

Momentarily a tram blocked her view, lurching along the street with a screech of metal and a splinter of electric blue sparking from its wires. Then, as it passed, she caught a glimpse of a man emerging from the house next door to the shop. He had a dark brush of hair, a cleft chin and tight-set mouth. He wore a green loden coat and soft black hat.

It was like being struck by a ghost.

She knew that face. She had it in her pocket.

The man set off at a brisk pace and Stella followed, sticking to the opposite side of the street, trying to hang back sufficiently far so as not to attract attention, all the while keeping him in her sights. He had a fast, purposeful forward sloping stride, and he kept his hands deep in the pockets of his coat.

He turned left, skirting a small park and the front of the

ornate neo-Gothic Rathaus, and marched west along the Ring, passing the Café Landtmann, whose elegant metal chairs were warming in the sun. At the entrance to the university Stella lost him momentarily when he disappeared behind a knot of students, but his height meant the black fedora was soon visible again, several hundred yards away. She increased her pace so that she was almost trotting to keep up, but as she reached the crenellated, ivory portico of the Burgtheater she was caught up in a surge of theatregoers pouring out of a matinee, pushing past as they made their way to taxis and trams, and by the time she had threaded her way through, he had vanished.

She paused. Had he disappeared along one of the paths of the Volkspark, or was he heading for the grand parade ground of Heldenplatz? Maybe he had vanished into one of the massive apartment blocks that lined the Ring.

There was no sign of him. It was as though he had vanished into thin air.

She stopped in frustration, heart pounding. She looked both ways and chose left, back through the Innere Stadt, moving without conviction up through the streets.

It was not until a couple of minutes later that she caught sight of a shape ahead, turning a corner, and she accelerated.

He was about ten yards away with his back to her. When he turned the corner of Wipplingerstrasse she realized with some astonishment that Mr Wilson at the legation had been exactly right – he must be heading for the Café Louvre.

For a moment she lingered behind an advertising pillar,

pretending to read the flyers for Hermansky's department store and another for a parade at the Spanish Riding School. Yet again she checked her surroundings lest some other watcher might be observing her. It seemed extraordinary that she should have sighted Roland Finch by sheer coincidence as she was visiting Freud's house. What business could he have in that street? The doctor himself was long gone. Perhaps Finch had been planning to visit the bookshop before he noticed the unwelcome intruders.

Seconds pulsed through her like the throb of her veins. She forced herself to breathe deeply until her heartbeat gradually slowed. She scanned the scene, watching for anyone Finch might be meeting, or perhaps even another person following him. A policeman passed wearing the traditional Viennese belted, gold-buttoned greatcoat, but now with a swastika armband, and she intensified her scrutiny of the advertisements.

For a moment she wished she was an actor. Evelyn was always talking about how acting worked. You embodied the character you intended to present by studying their gait and their hand gestures and how they held their cigarette or their teacup. You had your props and your costume and your imagination, but ultimately acting was a form of psychological deception. What had Evelyn's director told her? *'You have to inhabit the character. Find your inner motivation and project it.'*

Inhabiting the character was the easy bit. Though her German was perfect, any native speaker could detect an accent, so it was no good pretending to be anything but British. Stella was a young Englishwoman living in Vienna, out for an afternoon stroll. The clothes she was wearing were entirely appropriate for the role because they had been bought on the Continent. Her neat green jacket was Austrian in style – it had been bought here a couple of years ago – and her dark skirt was nondescript. She was wearing her French silk blouse. Her hair was tidily brushed back from her brow, her lips were lightly painted. She had dabbed a little perfume behind her ears and on her wrists.

The inner motivation was harder. Because rather than projecting it, she was desperate to keep it concealed.

She waited a few minutes after he entered the café, then followed.

Inside was a dazzle of marble, mahogany and red velvet, the chandeliers and mirrors reflecting back to customers all the glimmering gilt-edged world of yesterday. Little golden putti peered from the cornices. Waiters in black aprons with trays held at shoulder height wove through customers reading newspapers on long wooden poles, or reclining in front of tiny round tables, puffing clouds of smoke. On a central stand, an array of glistening cakes, glazed with chocolate and oozing cream, flaky strudels and cloud-shaped choux pastries, stood like an offering to the gods, or rather to the cherubs and deities who peered down from the painted ceiling.

The least colourful part of the scene was the field-grey knot of German officers, who had annexed a large part of the café by commandeering a number of tables and pushing them together and were discoursing in loud Prussian accents.

Finch had taken a table in the corner.

He was sitting there absorbed, preoccupied by the pages of a newspaper that half obscured his face. His soft hat sat on the table beside him.

Bracing herself, she crossed the café and settled at the vacant table next to him. Almost immediately a waiter appeared with a napkin over his arm and she ordered *Kaffee mit Schlagobers*. She sensed Finch register her arrival and glance upwards, return to his coffee, then look at her again more fixedly. Yet she kept her eyes firmly down, taking off her jacket, fussing with the flap of her bag, calculating what she might say if they spoke. She chided herself for failing to work out a backstory. She ran through her character again. Was it plausible to say that she was an art student, studying the masterworks at the Kunsthistorisches Museum? Or should her cover be more broad-brush? She was a keen tourist, interested to see Europe while she still could? Each explanation seemed less convincing than the last. The best thing to say was that she was a tutor, teaching English in Vienna. That life was at least familiar to her.

Her coffee arrived but Finch remained absorbed in his newspaper. Occasionally he turned a page. Closer up she noted that the nose was slightly broken, and twin cliffs of cheekbones stood out sharply on the wide face. He seemed entirely relaxed, with the measured poise of a character in a Dutch interior for whom time is immaterial and the ceremony of coffee is one to revere. His jacket was patched with leather at the elbows, and the edges of one cuff were stained. His cup stood on the marble table in front of him, next to a glass of water, a sugar bowl and a packet of Balkan Sobranie cigarettes.

Her next move came without thinking. Spontaneously, she reached over to the sugar bowl and knocked the glass of water over, causing him to spring to his feet, brushing down his jacket and trousers.

'Oh, I'm so sorry. Please forgive me!'

It was an instant, foolish slip-up. She had used her native tongue. No resident of Vienna would speak English in the first instance to a stranger. The man's annoyed face composed itself into a smile and he replied, 'No. No matter. Don't concern yourself.'

He dabbed at the remaining water on his clothes, picked up the cigarette packet and turned towards her, graciously.

'Fortunately, my cigarettes have survived the flood. Do you have a light?'

'Of course.'

She fumbled in her bag for her lighter.

'Will you have one? They're Turkish, but the tobacco is grown on the edges of Albania. It's really something special.'

She took one, then he leaned over and steadied her hand as she held out the flame. Their eyes met briefly, before she quickly looked away.

'You're British?'

'Yes.'

'Gracious, what's a young British woman doing in Vienna now?'

Without thinking, she said, 'I've just come from the Kunsthistorisches Museum. I was looking at the art.'

'My favourite occupation too. Which is your favourite?'

'*The Conversion of Saint Paul* by Parmigianino. I like the look on his face as he sees the light.'

'Interesting.' He nodded and seemed to consider this. 'I prefer his *Self-Portrait in a Convex Mirror*. It's such a clever distortion. It makes you unsure what you're looking at. That painting was the rave of Renaissance Italy, apparently. The Pope was stupefied.'

His voice was deep and cultivated. He exhaled, and she caught the aroma of his cigarette, rich and acrid. As he blew the smoke away he said, 'And what do you do when you're not looking at art?'

'I'm a tutor. I teach English.'

'Is that so?'

His demeanour was intelligent, almost sceptical. The sensual lips turned upwards in the suggestion of a smile and his deep-set eyes seemed to focus on her alone, as though entirely devoid of peripheral vision.

'I'd have thought all the people who need to learn English are either leaving or have left.'

'It's true. Work's running a bit dry. That's why I'm wasting my time sipping coffee in the middle of the afternoon.'

'But surely you know by now, coffee's not a time-waster in Vienna. *Kaffeehaus* culture is a state of mind. A cult. A national religion. Where else would you find so many varieties? I counted them once, for an article. Thirty-eight, I made it. *Melange Mitte, Melange Dunkel, Melange Ganz Hell, mit Schlag, ohne Schlag, Schale nuss, Türkish natur, Gespritzer, Mokka, Kapuziner* – it's called that because it's the exact shade of a Capuchin monk's robe, did you know? – *Eiskaffee, Einspänner*, and so on. Compare that with a cup of Nescafé in London.'

He spoke with the droll delivery she recognized so well, bred on English public school playing fields and echoed down the corridors of Westminster and Whitehall.

Smiling cautiously, she said, 'Seeing as you asked me, I hope it wouldn't be too rude to ask in return . . . why are *you* here?'

He pivoted towards her and held out a hand.

'Forgive me. I should introduce myself. My name is Roland Finch. I'm a journalist.'

'Who do you work for?'

He laughed.

'Anyone who'll have me. I'm freelance, you see. Newspapers, magazines. The wireless too, sometimes.'

'And what do you write?'

'Whatever comes to mind. Reportage, even the odd book review.'

'And you're British, too. Do you miss home?'

He leaned back, cigarette lightly extended in one hand.

'Oh, I spend plenty of time there as it is. I'm just back, actually.'

Her skin prickled. So, it was true. He had been in England, which confirmed the idea that he was the same man who had visited Oxford. Yet how could she begin to ask what had taken him there, what had passed between himself and Ernst Grunfeld, or what he knew of Newman's '*grotesque allegations*'?

'Yet you live here? In Vienna.'

'But of course. To me, Vienna's the centre of the world. The meeting point of philosophy, art and psychology. The city of Freud, Wittgenstein, Mahler and Klimt. The crucible of sex and death. This city's so much darker than all those Mozart tunes and Strauss waltzes that bring the tourists clamouring. Which makes it all the sadder that current events will oblige me to move on pretty soon.'

He shot her a keen glance.

'I assume you're contemplating that too.'

'Oh, I'm not interested in any of that. Politics. War.'

'You may not be interested in war, but war is interested in you.'

'Is that a quote?'

'Leon Trotsky.'

Finch surveyed the café around them, taking in the knot of German officers who were seated at a central table, their conversation heedlessly loud and their long boots out-stretched, obliging the waiting staff to manoeuvre carefully around them.

'Have a look around. This is Germany now. The Austrians may have voted for this *Anschluss* but nobody can possibly doubt that Hitler's ambitions go further than dear little Austria. There's plenty more conflict to come. From what I hear, a reckoning may be just days away.'

'But Chamberlain's in Germany right now, isn't he, discussing a peaceful solution? He's talking to Hitler about an accommodation regarding the Czechs.'

'I'm sure he is. Chamberlain's a coward, he will appease the brutes. I can't bear to look at the man. We can't rely on Britain for courage. And I speak as one who has witnessed great courage.'

'Where was that?'

'Well, miss . . .'

'Fry. Stella Fry.'

He moved closer, as if even amid the hubbub of the café, his sentiments might get him arrested.

'I was in Spain for a while in '36. As a journalist. It was a foreshadowing of what was to come. It taught me a lot. Truthfully, it changed me.'

As he spoke, Stella was trying to make sense of him. Despite the seriousness of the subject matter, he talked with a kind of languid assurance, stirring sugar into his coffee.

'I've noticed, since then, that most people distract themselves with trivialities to keep the threat out of sight. They don't want to look it in the face. They don't want to acknowledge the thunder in the air. Perhaps they should have been at the *Reichsparteitag Grossdeutschland* – the rally at Nuremberg, to celebrate the *Anschluss*, earlier this month. They would have heard a thing or two about believing protestations of peace. Thirty thousand Germans cheering the Führer to the rafters. And the British government wants to handle him with kid gloves.'

There followed a moment when the encounter might have gone either way. The waitress appeared, with a questioning look, and Stella shook her head to stave off the interruption, but the thread of their conversation was lost. They were once again two strangers who had struck up a chance discussion while enjoying a passing cup of coffee in a foreign city. Finch picked up his newspaper again, as though to return to his article, and Stella resumed her coffee, keeping an eye on the Nazi officers across the room.

A moment later, he lowered his paper and said, 'Forgive me for talking politics. I should know better, in polite company. And impolite company even more.' He nodded over at the Germans. 'It's the height of discourtesy.'

'I suppose it's hard to avoid right now.'

He smiled. A smile so different from the saccharine Viennese smiles she saw all about her. A warm, reassuring beam that said England, and home.

'It's good that you were at the gallery. We should all see as much art as we can while there's still time. See that chap over there, getting drunk with the officers?'

He nodded towards a man in a grey suit, raising a glass to his uniformed companions.

'He's a member of the Reich Chamber of Culture. He's here to oversee every painting, play and book that the

Viennese produce. He decides what's degenerate and what people can and can't read.'

'That explains it. I saw a bookshop being ransacked.'

She was about to say, 'when I first saw you', but managed to stop herself.

'I assume they were looking for subversive texts,' she continued. 'They were going through all the books and putting them in different piles.'

'The Nazis won't find much to excite them. It's been years since the Viennese have had the taste for subversion.'

'Maybe they're just hiding it.'

Finch laughed.

'Good point. The psychologists tell us we all hide our subversive urges. We present our best faces to the world and conceal the other parts of ourselves. Dr Jung says the work of our life should be reconciling those parts that we allow the world to see and those that we hide.'

'Do you mind?'

He reached over for the half-smoked cigarette that she had abandoned in the ashtray.

'Oh. Not at all.'

He relit it, and put its crimson-lipsticked stub to his lips, like a kiss. The intimacy of the gesture prompted an unexpected shiver to travel down her body.

'So, Miss Fry, what do you hide?'

Where to start? The shabby house in Chiswick and a fatherless family unable to afford the clothes or food that others at school took for granted. The tub of margarine that replaced the greaseproof pat of butter. The sting of rejection. The void of heartache. Her suspicion that she had made no sense of her own life whatever.

'Oh, not much. Just the usual. Ladders in my stockings.'

He looked down at her legs, clad in Paris Sand, then all the way up her figure to her eyes again, in a way that contained no ambiguity.

'In that case, your cover is flawless.'

'Thank you.'

'No, thank *you*. It's a pleasure to have such an interesting and unlooked-for conversation. And in English, too. What a joy to converse in one's native tongue, with all its complexity and nuance. Ours is such a subtle language, with so many inherent contradictions, don't you find?'

'That's what I tell my pupils.'

'English is so good at hiding things. It might as well have been designed to baffle outsiders.'

'What do you mean?'

'Oh, you know. You can say somebody *is* a character, and that's not a good thing, or you can say someone *has* character, and that is undeniably a compliment. You can say Chamberlain has a slim chance of succeeding in thwarting another war, or he has a fat chance of succeeding. Or take "quite". Quite charming can mean a little charming, or very charming. I think, Miss Fry, that's what you are . . .'

'Charming?'

'*Quite* charming.'

'Well, that's nice.'

He laughed, rolled the stub in the ashtray to end it, and began to fold his newspaper into his briefcase.

'I'm sorry to say, I have an appointment now. But I wonder . . . I'm sure you're busy, but if not . . . I mean this is inappropriate, but we live in inappropriate times . . . I have business this evening, but I'll be free tomorrow. Would you do me the honour of having a drink with me at the Reiss Bar? Say eight o'clock?'

# CHAPTER 18

She had a whole day to contemplate the evening ahead, yet still she could not stop brooding on the past. She managed to prevent herself passing the building where Franz lived, or the offices of his legal firm, or the Burggarten, the flower-filled park in front of the Hofburg where they would take coffee on sunny lunchtimes beside the elegant Palmenhaus. But still she could not quell an urgent longing for the old Vienna – not only the food, the *Leberknödelsuppe* and the chocolate and cream desserts – but the places which had meant most to her. Inevitably, she found herself heading for Morzinplatz, on the edge of the Danube, and the grand, neoclassical Hotel Metropol.

The Metropol was the glory of late Habsburg Vienna and a destination for VIP travellers and celebrities alike. It boasted three hundred and sixty-five lavishly decorated rooms, one for each day of the year, a magnificent painted dining room and a great glass-covered central courtyard for fashionable partying. It was the place to be seen and also the place where, exactly twelve months earlier, Franz Lehner had taken her for a sumptuous dinner of oysters and roast turbot and asked her to be his wife.

Given what she had witnessed elsewhere in the city, Stella should have been prepared, yet still it was a shock to see the building's vast frontage transformed. Long scarlet swastika banners billowed between the ornate Corinthian pillars and sentries stood guard at the doors. Instead of well-dressed tourists, officers in German uniform were passing in and out of the porticoed entrance.

She made for a glove shop on the opposite side of the square, a narrow boutique with a musty smell, lined with glass cabinets, and she toyed with a particularly expensive pair, kid leather and fur-trimmed, turning her hands this way and that and glancing covertly through the window while the proprietor waited attentively, scenting a good sale.

'I haven't been back here for a while. What's going on with the Metropol?'

The glove seller was a small man with a drooping, handlebar moustache and a sardonic expression more appropriate for a cabaret performer than an upmarket shopkeeper. He shrugged.

'Let's just say, you wouldn't want to be a guest any more.'

'Oh, really?'

'You must have been away for some time, *Fräulein*. It's Gestapo headquarters now. Still plenty of people checking in, but the service is not so good. They say the better rooms are in the basement.'

'What do you mean?'

'If you're an ordinary fellow, you get a cell on the ground floor, but important guests are detained in the lower ground. They kept our old chancellor Kurt Schuschnigg there, and Louis Rothschild. Upstairs is all offices. Plenty of rooms, but then, the Gestapo, they do have plenty of files.'

She stared down at the counter in shock. So this was where Captain Kendrick, the head of the British legation, had been detained, along with his office manager. Not to mention the thousands of others who had been taken for processing before being sent away. With a shudder she peeled off the gloves as if they were contaminated.

'Sorry to disappoint you, *Fräulein*.' The shopkeeper filed away the gloves in their case with a sarcastic look. 'I hope you weren't planning to take tea there.'

'Thank you. No.'

She left the shop and moved quickly across the square. A man in a long raincoat and SS cap was leaving the Metropol and climbing into a waiting Mercedes. Through the doors she caught a glimpse of the lobby and a mass of uniforms. It seemed incredible to think that just a year ago this place had been synonymous with luxury and pleasure. A top choice for dances and film premieres and private parties. What did the sumptuous dining room look like now? The place where Franz had leaned across a starched linen tablecloth proffering a sapphire and diamond ring?

'*We are well suited, Stella, both in temperament and intellect. I think we will make a good match.*'

She remembered her flustered acceptance, which went against all her deeper instincts. She had always believed love would start with a juddering thrill at the touch of another's hand, or an unexpected moment of excitement that would change her entire life's path. Not a proposal that was more like a legal document than a romantic declaration. Yet Franz had always valued pragmatism over passion. She recalled again their final meeting at the Starnberger See, and the single moment when her life's path had indeed changed.

'*What does it matter, what I believe? It doesn't change who we are.*'

'*I think it matters, what you believe.*'

As she hesitated, lost in thought, a posse of four men emerged, two in field-grey uniforms and two others in business suits, carrying the same, ribbon-tied document folders that Franz had used for his briefs. With a start she realized that this pair must be lawyers engaged on Gestapo business, either overseeing arrests or interviews, or formulating fresh decrees against Jewish residents. Possibly they were colleagues of Franz. Maybe she had even met these men at a dinner dance of the Austrian Bar Association, where they would have greeted her, fleetingly, with a *gnädiges Fräulein* and a handkiss. As they approached, she scrutinized them closely, noting how they talked and smiled, glancing with deference at their German companions who were staring, grim-faced, straight ahead.

The men passed without registering her and Stella flinched. With sudden clarity she knew that if Franz ever came here now, it would not be as a guest or a would-be fiancé, but as a Nazi-accredited lawyer.

The thought turned in her heart like a key in a lock, and she realized she was free.

# CHAPTER 19

Every piece of clothing she had brought from London felt wrong — too fussy or dull or practical — but luckily she'd brought Evelyn's turquoise silk dress which made her feel more elegant and adventurous than she was. To complement it, she sprayed herself with the only perfume she possessed, Lanvin's Arpège, a fragrant cloud of roses, jasmine and lily of the valley, and fixed her hair up. Then she pulled on stockings, outlined her lips in scarlet, smoothed her face with Max Factor and dabbed on a little powder. Drawing her jacket around her, she surveyed her reflection in the mirror with satisfaction. She looked nothing like her normal self. But wasn't that the whole idea?

The sunset was lowering itself gently on the skeletal spires of St Stephan's and a moon, young and sharp, pierced the soft evening. Just off the Kärtnerstrasse, past the German travel agency in whose window an enormous portrait of Hitler loomed, was the Reiss Bar. With its long mahogany counter, leather chairs, shining glasses and chrome fittings, the Reiss did its best to offer the anxious citizens of Vienna a little escapist glamour. It was a place, it seemed to Stella, that reaffirmed the eternal verities of life. In the light of its red silk lamps young women looked younger, old men looked richer and everyone mellowed in a soft mist of schnapps.

The fact that she had had a day to think about this meeting made it even more nerve wracking than their first encounter. She had no idea if Roland Finch was what he said he was, nor had she yet worked out how she might raise the events of the past week. What possible relationship might exist between a journalist like Finch and an obscure German scientist? Or, indeed, the death of an English novelist in Westminster Abbey. Merely managing to track Finch down had already surpassed her wildest expectations. On the other hand, she was relieved to have brought an evening dress. Her story of living in Vienna would be far less credible if she had nothing suitable to wear.

Through the Reiss Bar's glass-panelled doors she found a low-ceilinged room, its walls crowded with elaborate mirrors interspersed with paintings of women in bustiers and stockings and gentlemen in top hats. The linen-covered tables were busy with groups of men conversing, and at the back was a doorway covered with a plush curtain, beyond which waiters were coming and going. She found Roland Finch sitting at a table against the far wall, surveying the clientele with a laconic air. A chilled bottle of Gumpoldskirchner, wearing a white napkin, was waiting.

'Most of the beer here is no better than coloured water, and I had no idea what you'd like so I made a choice, based entirely on my assumptions. Was I right?'

'Thank you.' He poured her a glass of the soft golden liquid and she took a sip. 'I love this wine. I've visited the village where they make it.'

'The Viennese like their wines sweet. Strange, isn't it, when their nature is so brutal?'

She raised her eyebrows.

'Oh, all that Strauss, I mean. *Die Fledermaus*, the waltzes, the chocolate cake at Sacher's. The gilded ballrooms and manicured gardens. It's a rotten kind of sweetness, don't you think? It's sugaring over the truth. The Viennese like to disguise the ugly face of fascism with a splendid stucco facade.'

'I'd say Vienna's far more than that.'

'Oh yes? What is it to you?'

How could she explain what she had realized that day, as she walked around the streets, thinking of Franz and why she had left him? Vienna was more than a place to her – it was a point on a moral compass. Not just for herself but for the Gatzes and so many others.

'It's a complicated city. It's a centre of art and philosophy and psychology. You said so yourself yesterday. You said Vienna's the centre of the world.'

'Did I? How dramatic of me. Well, that Vienna's as dead as the Habsburgs now.'

He glanced across the bar, where a group of four men,

already loosened by drink, were engaged in loud, competitive conversation.

'Those gentlemen over there – Jewish, I'd guess – must have been coming to this place for years. It makes them feel safe, but it's false security. All these people, they thought they would be here forever and now they find everything around them falling apart. The Nazis will take their homes and their businesses. There's an SS man called Adolf Eichmann who's just been put in charge of expelling Jews. He particularly likes arresting the middle classes – doctors and lawyers and the like – in public view. Simply to show that he can. He's also arrested a number of Austrian aristocrats and sent them to Dachau.'

'Remind me what that is?'

'They call it a concentration camp. A prison. But of course, if you've been living in Vienna, you'll have seen what's going on.'

'I have.'

She remembered a moment, a year ago, when a sackful of coloured paper had been emptied in the street, and the children had seized on the scraps, opening tiny bright strips imprinted with mottos: 'Hitler Will Bring Us Bread. Hitler Gives Us Hope'. And the first day that someone had chalked a swastika on the Gatzes' doorstep. '*We should be grateful,*' Herr Gatz had said, '*for this. At least in Austria, no Jew can be in doubt of what's coming. Berliners are more sophisticated. In Berlin, some Jews still feel safe. Prussians are different but these Austrians are bigots. Jew haters.*'

She forced herself to focus. Why had Finch said, '*If you've been living in Vienna*'? Was he testing the details of her story? Or was she being paranoid? More likely he was merely enjoying an unexpected evening with one of his compatriots and the particular camaraderie that such encounters bring. The intimacy of his manner did indeed put her at ease, when it was essential that she maintain her guard. She decided to change the subject. Fiddling with her drink, she said, 'You mentioned you were in Spain. I knew some fighters there too. Some of my contemporaries from Oxford went out to fight for the International Brigades. One of them died in Barcelona.'

'Then you'll understand. Fighting against Franco changed so many people. Whether they were there as journalists or fighters, they came back broken men who will never be whole again. The Japanese have a word – *kintsuji* – ever heard of it?'

She shook her head.

'It means, broken things that become more beautiful for being mended. I met Spanish fighters who had watched their cities shatter, and their houses and churches fall into ruins, and they said it didn't matter. Because one day, when they had triumphed, they would build a new city in their hearts.'

'That's a beautiful thought.'

'No, it's a foolish one. They won't triumph and there's plenty more breaking to come. Civilization itself is breaking up. Though I sometimes think maybe we should count ourselves lucky to live at a time of chaos.'

'Not many people would agree with that.'

'They will, when the new world has swept all this away. Everything you see here in Vienna — all these towers and spires — they're no more than a sarcophagus. They'll burn like the topless towers of Ilium. Ever read Gibbon's *Decline and Fall?*'

'Sorry, but no.'

'Gibbon says the Roman empire fell because it became decadent. That's the West now. The system is rotten. Nobody understands just how turbulent the future is. They have no idea what they're up against. For far too long, these people have flattered themselves that their world view is the only one that counts and their values are the only ones that can be described as civilized. Well, the chess pieces of the world are moving. The whole — entitlement — of these people is what dooms them.'

'Dooms them to what?'

He sipped his wine, considering the question.

'You mentioned the Kunsthistorisches Museum. Have you ever seen that tiny devil, caught in a cube of glass? It's seventeenth-century. A spirit driven out in an exorcism and captured *in vitro*.'

'Oh yes, I have!'

The Gatz children had always been fascinated by the curio and demanded to see it when she had taken them to visit the gallery. It was a tiny demon, vitrified in a glass prism and trapped for eternity, flailing its arms as if it might manage to escape. The label described it as 'a *spiritus familiaris* that was driven out of one possessed and banned to this glass'.

'It's so macabre,' she said. 'Apparently, the message of the piece is that we should keep our demons in close sight. But it gives me the shivers.'

'It must have been so much easier then, when they believed they could trap the devil in a glass. Now Europe has its own devil, there's no prism on earth big enough to contain him. Except one.'

'And what's that?'

'A technological prism maybe. Something invisible. That can control the world, and even more, can destroy it.'

'You mean . . . like a weapon?'

'Yes. It has to do with the most basic building blocks of life. Atoms.'

'A weapon made out of atoms?'

'It's secret knowledge, right now. But whoever owns this knowledge can change the world.'

'I've no clue what you're talking about, but you sound as if you're familiar with it,' she said lightly.

He laughed. 'Sadly, not at all. It's way beyond me. But new ideas matter and I'm interested in those who have them. One idea in particular. It may not be perfect, but the alternatives are worse.'

'Which idea would that be?'

He was tenser than before. Less jocular. He hesitated a moment, as though wondering whether to trust her, then with a shrug said, 'I'm talking about Communism.'

'Are you a Communist?'

'Since you ask, yes. You might think that a little contradictory. I'm a journalist, after all. Journalists pride themselves on asking questions, whereas Communists are interested in answers, not questions.'

Stella glanced around her. In London it was not unusual to talk about Communism. At Oxford, friends quite openly had declared themselves Reds. But here in Austria, and especially since its rule by Nazi Germany, such declarations were foolhardy if not downright dangerous.

'That's a perilous way to think in Vienna right now.'

'It is. They're arresting Communists constantly. It won't make a difference. We're everywhere, and that's why they'll never defeat us. The authorities may be paranoid about Communism, but paranoia weakens them. It stops them thinking straight. Besides, in Vienna Communists have some places of safety.'

'Safe houses?'

He laughed.

'Not exactly. Right now, the places of safety are under our feet. If you've finished your drink, why don't you come for a walk with me?'

The flat moonlight turned the city into a film set. The centre, which might normally have been full of people going home from restaurants, theatres or bars, was unnaturally silent. The streets were practically empty, winding off into small squares. The dark gathered deeply in the corners and striped the shuttered shopfronts. The glinting, irregular cobbles and the narrow lanes reminded Stella of an Expressionist film, all sharp angles and drunken perspectives.

Vienna was a city of shadows.

She was glad that they were walking side by side, so he could not see her face. Despite Finch's languid demeanour, it was impossible for her to relax. She had to stay entirely focused if she was to discover if this man had any part in Hubert Newman's death.

They had gone some way in silence before he stopped beside an iron advertising column and leaned against it, pulling out his cigarettes.

'You asked about safe spaces.' He tapped the pillar. 'Beneath here is a vast network of tunnels. In truth, it's the sewers, but Vienna's sewer system is like an entire city. It's a labyrinth – it goes miles out from the Florisdorf district. Plenty of people have been smuggled out that way.'

'That sounds horrible. And risky.'

'Not as risky as walking the streets. These are dangerous times for everyone. But personally I believe the greatest danger lies in failing to pick your side.'

'And you really think your side is better? Morally better?'

'I think you choose a side. Like chess. Black or white. And I have no doubt about the verdict of history. Anyway, Stella, enough of this.'

He lit the cigarette, then shook his wrist to douse the match and tossed it away.

'Did anyone ever tell you, you have gorgeous eyes?

They're gold-flecked and chestnut brown. They remind me of a tiger's eye.'

'The gem or the animal?'

'Oh, the animal, definitely. You're not cold and expensive. You strike me as fierce and alive.'

He reached towards her shoulder and at his touch she felt a quiver go through her. It felt like sexual attraction but it wasn't. It was harder and sharper than that, like a shaft of iron.

It was fear.

As she flinched, he withdrew his hand and said, 'I couldn't help noticing you're reading Hubert Newman. I saw the book in your bag.'

With a jolt of horror, she realized that she had been careless. She must have allowed the flap of her leather satchel to fall open. She had meant to conceal *Midnight in Vienna*, and instead she had left it in plain sight.

'Oh, yes. I love detective stories.'

'Do you?' His tone was light and level. 'I'd never have guessed. I'd have thought the greats were more your style. I would have said you were more of a Flaubert woman, or at the very least George Eliot.'

'Oh, Newman makes such complicated plots. So intriguing.'

'Really? Then I will have to defer to your judgement. Maybe he has some skills as a writer. Or *had*, because I saw he died the other day. There was a down-page paragraph in the *Wiener Zeitung*. How did he die, do you know?'

She was so close to him she could see a pulse throb at the side of his neck.

'Nobody's sure. They discovered him in the cloisters of Westminster Abbey.'

'How dramatic. What did the papers say about him?'

She tried to recall the obituary in *The Times*.

'They said he was the essence of Englishness.'

'And isn't that the funny thing?' Finch paused for a moment and picked a strand of tobacco from his lip before taking a deep drag on his cigarette.

'Because Hubert Newman wasn't English at all.'

In the beat of silence that followed, the words seemed to hang, vibrating, in the air between them. Then Finch took off again in the direction of Neuer Markt and she followed him.

'What do you mean, he wasn't English?'

'Everyone hailed him as the quintessential English gentleman, but he was as far from that as you can imagine. He was Jewish – an Austrian Jew. Once his family had moved to England, Newman became perfectly assimilated, if there is such a thing. As if you can ever take the blood out of a person and wash it clean. Which is of course the fervent wish of many people on this Continent.'

'That's impossible.'

'Seems so, doesn't it? And yet, he grew up very close to here. Hubert Newman. Or Neumann perhaps I should say.'

'Neumann?'

'His father was an academic at the University of Vienna.

He taught mathematics. Logic. Presumably it was logic which helped him see the writing on the wall. Persecution of the Jews is one of those age-old Viennese pastimes, like philosophy or ballroom dancing, and Herr Professor Neumann could see that his fellow citizens were not going to abandon anti-Semitism any more than they were going to give up Sachertorte. So when Hubert was thirteen, his father took his family off to London. They left Berggasse forever.'

The line came to her instantly.

*On the corner of Berggasse, not far from the home of the eminent Dr Freud, is a bookshop and it was from that spot that Markus Friedkin, thirteen years old, vanished, while everyone was looking the other way.*

Hubert Newman had been telling his own story. In a way that nobody could possibly guess.

'The father anglicized their name. Neumann became Newman. Changing a name can do so much. People rarely look below the surface.'

'I would never have imagined.'

'Perhaps not. And he wouldn't have wanted you to. Hubert learned another language, and that gave him the ability to remake himself. In a different language, you're always a different person. I suppose because you express yourself in a new way. Hubert Neumann had been passionate, enquiring and lively, but Hubert Newman the Englishman was precise and correct. You might even call him ponderous.'

'You sound as though you've met him.'

'I have. We met the same way all writers and journalists meet in England. At university. One of those interminable parties in a room overlooking a quad, full of self-aggrandizing undergraduates who think they're learning about philosophy when their chief education is in how to hold their drink. Endless evenings sitting on the cold steps of a college staircase arguing about history or politics or poetry. People who think they're going to change the world when they can barely change their own bed linen.'

'And you stayed friends?'

'Not really. We lost touch for a few years. After we both moved to London, we saw each other at the odd book launch, house party or cocktail party, those occasions full of dead-beat poets and blocked novelists. Literary society, it's called, though really, it's no more than a circle of hypocrites who read each other's poems and review each other's novels in their little magazines, then snipe about them behind their backs. It was sometime around then that I learned the truth about Hubert's background and it accounted for something I'd long sensed about him. He was never at home in England. Always terrified that he might be unmasked.'

'Unmasked?'

'As a foreigner. That someone might detect a faint edge to his accent, might catch a little piece of grit carried in the wind from *Mitteleuropa*. He was terrified that someone might rumble him for who he was. He wanted so badly to belong to all that gilded literary culture. Those writerly circles. To be accepted in Britain, his adopted home. Yet he always felt an outsider. Can you understand that?'

She could. She had felt that way for years. Even at Oxford, whose golden arches and gables had given structure to her life when she most needed it, she had never sensed that she belonged.

'When did you last see him?'

'Oh, a while ago. You know, it's one of history's ironies that Hubert's novels should sell so well here in Austria, the land of his birth. His countrymen can't get enough of them. But no doubt that will be over in time. The Nazis will dispense with them soon enough. Stack them on one of their bonfires.'

'That sounds a little dismissive.'

'Does it? Well, in this case, I'd say the Nazis have it right. I despise the kind of art that Hubert specialized in. Ersatz country houses, vicarages. Designed to comfort readers with a vision of Little England that was never real. That's not the kind of art that serves humanity.'

'It's asking rather a lot of detective novels that they should serve humanity.'

'Is it?' Finch's eyes gleamed with humour and she realized that he was enjoying this intellectual digression, as much as he must once have enjoyed the spats on the student staircase.

'I tend to think we don't ask enough of art. Aren't novels supposed to challenge the world? Hubert allowed himself to become a tool for the forces of conservatism. He refused to challenge society or to improve it. His novels aren't books, they're anaesthetics. They poison us with cliché.'

'I wasn't expecting an evening of literary criticism.'

'Then you shouldn't drink with a literary critic. It was consorting with the enemy, that nonsense Hubert wrote.'

'What do you mean, "consorting with the enemy"?'

Finch came to a halt in front of the ochre-brown Capuchin Church and leaned against the wall.

'You ask a lot of questions, Stella Fry. So now it's my turn. Why are you here?'

'I told you—'

'Yes. I remember, you're an English tutor with a passion for detective fiction.'

He reached out and his fingers traced the length of her arm. His hand curved down the thin silk of her dress, then reached up to cup her chin in his hand.

'I like you, Stella. I think if I knew you better, I'd like you even more.'

'Do you?'

'Yes. I recognize myself in you.'

She shivered in the chill night air and disciplined every fibre of her being to remain still under his penetrating gaze.

'That's a strange thing to say.'

'Is it?'

He drew closer, so that his face was only inches from hers.

'Maybe I say it because unfortunately, like me, you're not all you seem.'

He moved back again and inhaled on his Balkan Sobranie, his face silhouetted in the light from the nearby street lamp.

'You see, I knew as soon as we met that you were no simple Englishwoman biding her time before saying goodbye to Vienna. I knew you were searching for me.'

She remained intensely still, watched by her own silent shadow on the wall behind him.

'What a mad thing to say! It was a coincidence. I sat next to you in a café.'

'And why did you not look at me? You looked everywhere but at me, even though you were aware of me watching you. What woman reacts like that? At the very least she bats her eyelashes, lowers her gaze flirtatiously, or if she doesn't like the look of me then she gives me a stare and the cold shoulder. But you – not a glance. I knew there was something odd, but I couldn't tell what it was.'

'Your imagination is running away with you.'

'Is it? This evening that instinct has only grown stronger. If I had to guess, I'd say you were in Vienna specifically to find me.'

Before she could frame an answer, a pair of German officers in SS livery approached, their uniforms blacker than the night. Their heels clattered sharply on the cobbles and their cap insignia glinted in the moonlight. As they came nearer, they slowed and Stella sensed Finch stiffen, before, in a single fluid movement, he stepped towards her and drew her into his arms, pressing his soft mouth against hers.

For a second she felt his breath hot against her cheek, before, instinctively, she pushed him away. The officers paused, alert to the possibility of a romantic contretemps.

Still gripping her arm, Finch continued smiling, but his voice was a harsh whisper.

'I don't know who you are, but I think I have the measure of you. You may have tracked me down but there are others you'll never uncover. Fortunately, I leave in the morning.'

'Where are you going?'

'It doesn't matter.'

He threw the stub of his cigarette away.

'Somewhere nobody, not even clever Stella Fry, will find me.'

With that, he turned on his heel and walked rapidly away.

Her dream was terrible. She was with the Gatzes again and the Gestapo was coming. She was to be arrested and imprisoned, with no way to alert anyone. She needed to escape, but as the heavy linen sheets knotted around her, she dreamed she was being tied down, and any amount of restless twisting only made it worse.

The prison was in London, for some reason, and her heart was galloping.

A steel door opened and a man dressed in the black livery of the SS had entered her cell. He was holding out a note – the note that would condemn her – and when she looked, she saw that it bore Newman's spidery black-ink handwriting.

'To Stella, spotter of mistakes.'

The officer said, 'What is this mistake?'

'I don't know. I don't know. It's just an inscription. It means nothing.'

'You expect me to believe that?'

'But it's true.'

Her mind was in a maze, fighting in the darkness.

'Then you'll stay here until you tell me what it does mean.'

The officer turned on his heel. The steel door clanged behind him and she heard the key turn in the lock.

Then she was calling out for help, and what surprised her – if it was even possible to be surprised in dreams – was that the person she called for was Harry Fox.

# CHAPTER 20

*Cry, Trojans, cry! Practise your eyes with tears!*
*Troy must not be, nor goodly Ilion stand;*
*Our firebrand brother, Paris, burns us all.*

'Darling. No. Darling. Please. Just stop!'

Evelyn froze as the director, Michael MacOwan, stood up from his place in the stalls, wrenched off his glasses and placed his hands on his hips.

'Listen, darling. War is coming. Actual, dreadful, barbaric war. Hmm? Terrible disaster lies ahead. It will consume Troy and all your compatriots. You, Princess Cassandra, can see the future, but no one's listening. Is it too much to ask that one might convey a little of that? You've lost your entire future, darling, not your bus ticket.'

'Yes . . . I . . .'

He blew out his cheeks.

'Once more with passion, Evelyn. From "Tis our mad sister / I do know her voice".'

Evelyn squeezed her eyes to banish the tears and gave her shoulders a little, symbolic shake. This was quite different from her role in the chorus line at the Hippodrome, but even so, it was hardly out of her range. It wasn't as if she had never done Shakespeare before. She had Titania and Portia under her belt. When she had done *All's Well* in rep she'd had to share a dressing room with a live piglet, so nobody could say she hadn't grafted. But MacOwan was different. He was so demanding, constantly jumping up and down from his place in the stalls and bouncing on the balls of his feet. He was obsessed with the idea that Shakespeare should carry 'contemporary resonance'. The play must debunk the romantic and heroic view of war. With the result that all the cast was in modern dress and everyone had to navigate their way around a set dotted with field telephones and large-scale territorial maps and rolls of barbed wire.

He was also keen on psychoanalytic interpretations. 'We need to decrypt Shakespeare. He is writing, my dear, in code.'

That was as may be, but if so, Evelyn was no code breaker. It was all she could do to keep up with the words on the page. The production opened in less than a fortnight and it was frankly a miracle that she had managed to learn the part so fast. But it would be worth it. MacOwan's prestige promised a starry audience on the first night. J.B. Priestley was coming. Max Reinhardt, the famous Berlin theatre director, who had arrived in England after the *Anschluss*, was attending the dresser. There was talk of Alfred Hitchcock coming to talent-scout for his next production. Perhaps that was why the director was being such a terror, slicing the air with his hands, windmilling his arms at Hector, who was dressed in full Nazi uniform, with jackboots and an iron cross at his neck, stressfully demanding reruns, and, as now, vaulting onto the stage and gripping the sides of his skull, eyes wide, reciting her lines.

'"Cry, Trojans, cry! Practise your eyes with tears!" Do you see now, darling?'

Evelyn nodded dumbly. But MacOwan was just getting going.

'Whom do we trust in the fog of war? Shakespeare lived in a world of spies and plots, of danger from foreign parts and secret threats to the state. His actors inhabited a surveillance culture. His rulers commanded clandestine intelligence. Shakespeare was saying that people who live in a world of lies don't recognize the truth when they see it. Understand, darling?'

Evelyn didn't.

'Of course.'

'Good. Two more lights at the back, please, and raise the spotlight.'

Evelyn was just running her hands through her curtain of hair to make it look more ancient Greek and opening her mouth to begin the wretched lines again, when MacOwan wheeled round distractedly, 'Where the hell is Helen?'

This was the third time Diana Sowerby had been late for a call. In fact, her mind seemed to be elsewhere much of the time. Technically, this was good news for Evelyn, who was understudying her. Given Diana's erratic attendance, it was not too much of a fantasy to imagine that she might absent herself altogether and Evelyn would get to play the part. Then who knew what that might lead to? Perhaps a part in Hitchcock's next project – a spy film called *The Lady Vanishes* about a British agent with vital information for the Foreign Office.

'Not seen her this morning,' volunteered the stage manager, a weedy young man in a tank top.

Behind her, in the shadow of the wings, Evelyn could hear the assistant stage managers murmuring.

'Diana Sowerby's going round the bend, poor darling.'

'She's already gone round several bends.'

'Unstable?'

'Must be that husband of hers.'

'I heard he's friends with Hitler.'

'If Walter Heap's the person talking to Hitler, he's bound to invade.'

'Diana's wasted on him, poor love. Imagine sleeping with that man.'

'Who says that *is* the man she's sleeping with?'

The ASMs were always gossiping. Their chat was a distant buzz from the wings, distracting and irresistible in equal measure. They knew everything.

And it made sense that they would gossip about Diana Sowerby. She had the kind of looks that made people crash into lamp posts, even if she was the daughter of a public house owner in Herne Hill, who had danced half naked in the chorus line at the Windmill Theatre until she had her big break. Contrary to expectations, Evelyn was surprised to find that she liked her. Although Diana now lived in Belgrave Square, with hot and cold running servants, and spoke in a refined and dovelike coo, she had not lost the barmaid's ability to strike up casual friendships, and when they were assigned the same dressing room, the two women had instantly bonded.

MacOwan was fanning himself tetchily with the script.

'OK, let's break there. Evelyn, can you please go and discover when Miss Sowerby will deign to grace us with her presence?'

Evelyn was grateful for the distraction. Though it went against her nature, just occasionally it was a relief when the spotlight shifted onto someone else.

She threaded her way back to dressing room two, through the shadowy wings where technicians huddled playing cards on an upturned orange box. Priam was doing the crossword and other actors lounged, smoking and chatting. '*I was standing behind Noël Coward at the Eaton Place depot when he was issued with his gas mask today. He couldn't get the wretched thing on. It was too funny.*'

The dressing room was a jumble of clothes, empty bottles, tubes of foundation and opened jars of make-up. Diana was there, half dressed, applying a hurried stripe of lipstick to her Botticelli face. She smelled of gardenia perfume and there was a high flush on her cheeks. She had obviously just arrived.

'The director's waiting for you. You missed your call.'

'That man.' She turned her back. 'Can you do me up? I can hardly breathe in this dress.'

Her voice was as soft as candy floss.

Evelyn did her buttons up rapidly.

'The fact is, darling, I'll need to leave early too. Could you cover for me, do you think?'

'What should I say?'

'Say I'm off for an appointment. Tell him my husband and I are meeting with very senior politicians at Downing Street. Or say I've got the curse.'

It was strikingly obvious that Diana had not thought through her excuses. And her motivation, theatrical or otherwise, remained a mystery.

'Which one?'

She giggled. 'You choose. I don't mind what you say.'

She had a gurgling laugh, like champagne being tipped down a sink.

'Where are you actually going?'

'Can you keep a secret, darling?'

Evelyn nodded eagerly, but from the distant stage, along the stone recesses of the corridors, past the dressing rooms and through the door, came the muffled bellow of MacOwan, querying her absence.

'Damn that man.'

'He's just impatient. So, what's this secret?'

'It'll have to wait.'

Diana patted her hair with a hand that bore an enormous diamond cluster ring.

'But if you can keep it, I promise you can come and meet Vivien Leigh at Claridge's next week. Would you like to? She's fallen in love with Laurence Olivier and they can't keep their hands off each other.'

'Isn't Olivier—?'

'Married? Yes, of course, and so's she, but I suppose they think they might as well live while they can. Don't we all think that? My husband says Mr Hitler has far more aircraft than we do and he will be flying his bombers over London this time next week.'

'Next week?'

'Or soon, anyway. We might be going dark before we even open.'

'Do you really think Hitler will bomb London?'

'Didn't you see that film, *Things to Come*? Where the city is wiped out by an aerial bombing raid and it leads to world war? It was made by Alexander Korda and I'm telling you, that man's a genius. He knows far more than we do about what's going to happen.'

For one unsettling moment, Evelyn allowed herself to contemplate that the black clouds on the horizon might actually turn into a storm. Did Alexander Korda really know more than anyone else? Or Diana's husband? Sir Walter Heap knew important people, he met politicians all the time, and he presumably had some private insight. Really, Evelyn ought to ask Tom. Her brother detested Walter Heap, but then Tom hated anyone who didn't support Churchill, so he would be bound to offer some opposing view.

And yet . . . if it did come, if war arrived, as everyone seemed to think, would it really bring bombs and terror raids and attacks from the sky? Her artist friend, Peter, who painted murals, had shown her a terrifying picture by Picasso portraying a Spanish town called Guernica being devastated by Nazi bombers. It was horrifying to think that might happen to Chelsea too, but that was what the public information films told you every time you went to the cinema. And Chelsea was at particular risk, because even in a blackout, German aircraft would use the moonlit river to navigate their flight path, and if that happened then she would be needing an air raid shelter too. She could hardly bear the idea of it. It was one thing squashing up with actors in the theatre basement in a press of flirting and giggles, but what if an air raid happened when she was at home? Going to a smelly, public shelter in the middle of the night, full of dreary neighbours moaning in their damp coats, was quite another.

Her mother had said that in the event of war she would shut up the London house and move to the country. She had already hired a van to transport some of the artworks and the better pieces of furniture. Like everyone, Sidonie had received a letter asking if she would be willing to take in refugees and she had said she would explore the potential of some of the outbuildings in Berkshire.

Then, as she contemplated war, the focus of Evelyn's questions widened. What would happen to all the men she knew? All the nice ones would join up, or be conscripted, leaving only the halt and the lame. What, most importantly, would happen to Tom?

She calmed herself by recalling that morning's news bulletin, which had reported Mr Chamberlain's peace negotiations. Whatever Mr MacOwan said, the twentieth century was very far from Trojan times. Evelyn sent a prayer up that the Prime Minister would make Hitler see sense. It was boring how everyone was obsessed with the news, and war would only make that worse. It would be so inconvenient.

War would spoil everything.

For a moment, she felt a flicker of anxiety for Stella, off on a jaunt to God knows where. She had left a few days ago with only a brief explanation about wanting to see art in Vienna, or something, but Evelyn had been lying drowsily in bed only half awake, and besides, Stella always exuded confidence about foreign travel. She had a mind of her own and the truth was, Evelyn rather admired the intrepid way that she travelled, not with taxis and trunks and luxury hotels like her own parents, but fearlessly, with not much more than her tatty old valise. Yet even Evelyn could see that a holiday on the Continent right now was ill-advised.

She hoped that Stella was not in any trouble.

# CHAPTER 21

The office of Hubert Newman's publisher in Bedford Square was up several creaking flights of stairs, at the top of which Harry Fox held a minute's silence out of respect for his smoke-blackened lungs. Then he opened the door to find an effete young man in rolled shirtsleeves, a Fair Isle knitted vest and dapper bow tie, presiding over a tower of books and dog-eared manuscripts tied with pink ribbon. He had a soft, girlish face and a complexion shrapnelled with acne.

'Mr Fanshaw's on holiday. I'm his assistant. If it's about a manuscript, I'm afraid we're closed for submissions. As you can see, we're absolutely drowning in fiction here and I'm spending all my time writing regrets.'

He had a theatrical delivery, which suggested he saw his natural home as the stage rather than a cramped box room fenced in by books and papers.

Once Harry had identified himself, the young man dispensed with the niceties and leaned forward, eyes agleam.

'A detective! Why didn't you say? If you're investigating his death, you must be thinking it wasn't a heart attack, then? I mean, I know Hubert Newman didn't have much of a heart, but it said in the newspaper—'

'It's early days. Did he have family that you know of?'

'Only his mama. He was devoted to her, but she died quite recently.'

'Girlfriend?' suggested Harry, without hope.

'Not unless he was keeping her *very* quiet. The only ladies I ever saw Hubert with were his mother and his secretary.'

Harry brought out a magazine cutting from his pocket.

'Ever see him with this man? A Mr Roland Finch?'

The young man held the picture at arm's length and squinted at it.

'Ooh. Is he an actor?'

'No idea.'

'Well, he should be. With looks like that. Could have taken him for Clark Gable if you hadn't told me.' He pursed his lips. 'No? More's the pity.'

'How about this one?'

Harry proffered a photograph of an earnest man with hair swept back and wire-rimmed spectacles.

'Ernst Grunfeld. Scientist of some sort. Possibly a chemist. Born in Germany.'

'Sorry.' The young man performed an arch shrug. 'I don't know any chemists except Boots. But even if he was a friend of Mr Newman's, I'd be none the wiser because he wouldn't have confided in the likes of me. He kept himself to himself.

Some authors love to pop in for a gossip – anything to distract them from their desks – but that was not Mr Newman. He might have chatted to Mr Fanshaw, but he's just left for the Isle of Wight and he's not back for a fortnight.'

He sighed, and arranged his features into a philosophical cast.

'It's been a terrible business. The last novel, *A Shot Across the Bows*, was out last autumn and it was a bestseller. It's awful to think that there'll be no more Hubert Newmans. Everybody here's terribly affected. We've lost a brick in the cultural edifice, that's what Mr Fanshaw said. The press has been phenomenal. The *Daily Telegraph* called him "The Spirit of the Age". We were all frightfully pleased.'

A thought struck him. 'There *are* no more, are there? Have the police explored that? He didn't leave us another, by any chance? Something in the drawer?'

Instinctively, Harry shook his head.

'Shame. The readers won't know what to do with themselves, and it's no good saying "Go and try Ngaio Marsh." People know what they like and they like what they know. That's how publishing works. Readers want more of the same.'

'I was hoping to focus on Mr Newman's personal circumstances.'

The young man shuffled into a more confidential pose.

'But of *course*. Does this mean you're thinking of someone he knew? Maybe a friend or family member?'

Harry nodded at the display of titles ranged along a shelf

behind the young man, most of which featured the word 'murder' on their jackets in a variety of fonts and sizes.

'If you've read all those you'll be familiar with police procedure, so you'll know I couldn't share information like that.'

'Oh, yes. Sorry.' The young man mimed a zipping of his lips. 'Anyhow, I won't say a word.'

'Was Mr Newman worried about anything, do you think?'

'I don't know. I promise I'd tell you if I did. But I'm only the assistant and as I said, he kept himself to himself. Even if he did talk, Mr Newman was never going to gossip with the likes of me. If you did want to find out more, you might ask at the Detection Club.'

'What's that?'

'I shouldn't say.' He tossed his head like a show pony and flicked a strand of hair from his brow.

Harry waited.

'But you *are* the police, aren't you?'

He issued a grunt that might have signalled assent.

'It's secret. Invitation only. A club where they meet.'

'Who's they?'

'Detective writers. You can't apply. Only existing members can elect another. Apparently, there's a frightful initiation ceremony with a rope and a sword and a skull. Everything conducted by candlelight. Gives me the shivers.'

'And Hubert Newman was a member of this club?'

'Goodness, yes. Terribly proud of it. Even though he wasn't supposed to say.'

'Is there an address for this place?'

The young man made a little moue with his lips.

'I wouldn't know. As I said, it's deadly secret. It's like the Freemasons. If you tell anyone, they cut your tongue out and slit your throat.'

He drew a finger across his neck.

'So how would I go about . . .?'

'Well, I know Dorothy L. Sayers is in it.'

He was already burrowing in a drawer.

'I can give you her address if you like.'

Harry left the office and trudged through the red brick and pale stucco of the Bloomsbury streets. In Lincoln's Inn Fields, local council workers equipped with spades were hacking up the grass of the communal garden and digging trenches. Already, the iron railings around the edge of the square had been ripped up and removed, ready to be melted down into aeroplanes or guns or bullets. It was the same in Kensington Gardens and Hyde Park. In the space of a month, the entire city had been transformed. You could walk along a street that was perfectly normal, but then come upon a garden or a square that was completely unrecognizable: either stacked with sandbags, dug into trenches or fenced off with corrugated iron for an air raid shelter.

The landscape of London seemed to believe that war was coming, no matter what the politicians might say.

★

His mood palled. In normal times, the idea that he was about to call on a famous writer to investigate a secret literary society would have been an enormous thrill, but now, what was the point? Just like the gardens, his own life too had been ripped up and remodelled. He was forty now, and he felt barely recognizable as the young man who had come out of the war with military distinction, good looks and a bright future ahead of him. Forty years, and what did he have to show for it but a succession of broken relationships and a basement flat in Battersea with a fine view of a brick wall?

He thought of his father, with his tattered tapestry of stories: the villa he was buying in a place called Villefranche; the business cartel with whom he had purchased land for gold mining in Ontario, Canada; the car dealership in northern Germany. If Stanley Fox was that rich, why were they living in a semi-detached house in Hammersmith with no maid?

Despite all his fantasies, Stanley Fox had always retained the bright confidence of the chancer, whose imaginative life was rich and for whom success was always just around the corner. He was a great lover of the classics, and invoked their old watchwords – Nemesis, Hubris and Catharsis – at the most mundane of moments: a childish spat, a car breakdown, a missed train. He knew the Bible and Shakespeare backwards and would intone long passages in his deep baritone, especially when drunk.

Ah yes, that was what they had in common: the drink. And maybe, Harry thought, he was more like his father than he cared to believe. Wasn't this same enterprise, tracking down the killer of Hubert Newman, just as fantastical, born of the refusal to accept reality and a vanity that he might join a different, gilded literary world? Whereas the truth was, war was coming, Newman was dead and what did it matter how he died? As Flint had stated so brutally, Harry wasn't even getting paid for this. He was the only person in the world who cared, apart from Stella Fry, and God knows where she was now.

Stepping back from this inviting abyss of self-pity, he consulted again the address he had been given and came to a halt.

Number 24, Great James Street was a handsome brick building with a pillared portico and an elaborately decorated pediment featuring a rearing phoenix in immaculate white plaster. A stout, wholesome-looking woman in her forties, with a tanned complexion and hair in an immaculate bun, answered the door. She had a broad, mannish face, with apple cheeks, a short nose and intelligent, sceptical eyes. Her masculine looks were set off by long dangly amber earrings, and a chunky bead necklace complemented the enormous exotic jewelled ring on her hand.

Harry showed his specially adjusted Special Branch card which she scrutinized for several seconds through rimless spectacles before stepping aside to allow him in. He wondered what kind of detective writer she was if she couldn't spot the place where the date had been amended, but followed her up a flight of stairs and into a drawing room on the first floor.

If he had been expecting a decor replete with occult objects, ropes and skulls, he was disappointed. Instead of theatricality, it exuded extreme Englishness, from the watercolour landscapes of the Lake District and sketches of cathedral interiors, to the fringed chintz of the armchairs, single-bar electric fire and the pervasive, unmistakeable old lady smell of lavender polish and talcum powder. One wall was devoted to framed photographs of what appeared to be fellow writers, judging by their poses with pen and paper; beneath, on a simple oak desk, lay a clutter of paper and notebooks.

'You're lucky to catch me in. I don't use this flat often any more. Only when I'm up in London overnight. I would offer you tea, but I'm afraid I have no milk or lemon. How can I help you, Mr Fox?'

'I've come about Hubert Newman.'

'I see.'

Was it his imagination, or did a shade come down over those sceptical eyes? Instead of answering immediately, Sayers busied herself with gesturing at the sofa and moving a pile of knitting and a pair of reading glasses onto a side table before settling herself on a button-backed armchair.

'Poor Hubert. God rest his soul. That's why I'm here, as it happens. I've just come from his funeral. I'm catching the train home to Essex shortly.'

'He was buried today? Already?'

'His agent said that was what he would have wanted. It was in Oxfordshire. A churchyard close to his country home. It was a small, private ceremony. He had no family.'

'So who was there?'

'Just a few writing colleagues and fellow members of our club.'

'That would be the Detection Club.'

A brisk smile dimpled the apple cheeks.

'Are you sure you won't have something? A glass of water, perhaps? I have some Amontillado sherry if . . .' here she glanced at the clock, whose hands registered 11.30 a.m., 'if it's not too early for you?'

Harry forced himself to refuse a drink. Sucking down a tumbler of something this early was not going to improve his credibility with the author of *Catholic Tales and Christian Songs*, but when she extended a silver cigarette case, he took one gratefully.

'You mentioned the club.'

'I did.'

She settled herself further back in the chair, smoothing her tweed skirt fastidiously across her knees, as if to iron out any misinterpretations, and regarded him beadily.

'How long had Hubert Newman belonged?'

'Right from the start – 1930. He was one of our most loyal members. He rarely missed a meeting.'

'What happens in the Detection Club?'

'I like to say the first rule of the Detection Club is, we don't discuss the Detection Club.' She laughed, lightly. 'That does tend to be the way with secret societies, does it not? But then, you'd know all about secrecy, Mr Fox, in your line of work.'

'You could say secrecy is my specialism.'

'Yes. I'm not sure I understood your credentials, precisely. You work with Special Branch?'

'In the cultural department.'

'How fascinating.'

She waited for further enlightenment, and when it didn't come said, 'Normally, I wouldn't dream of discussing our activities outside of the club walls. But as you're a detective, it obviously behoves me to give you an outline. The Detection Club is the oldest society of crime writers in the world. Some have called us the aristocracy of detective writing.'

Despite himself, Harry winced. All aristocracies, self-elected or otherwise, were inherently obnoxious to him.

'You could see a photograph, if you'd like.'

She rose and fetched a large, silver-framed picture from the mantelpiece. It portrayed Newman, swamped in a scarlet cloak and flanked by a group of frumps, the myrmidons of the mystery world, done up in dark smocks and holding flickering black candles. On closer inspection he identified Agatha Christie, Baroness Orczy and, at the centre of the group, directly in front of Newman, Sayers herself, dressed in a fur coat and holding not a candle but a human skull, perched on a cushion.

'Looks like a great night out.' He handed the picture back.

'Certainly beats the Metropolitan Police social.'

'It was taken during an initiation ceremony at the Northumberland Avenue Hotel. The membership process is very strict. Our members are elected by secret ballot and we require that they go through the ceremony and swear an oath before they are admitted. All the costumes and accessories do make candidates a little apprehensive, and I suppose that's understandable, but in truth it's all perfectly pleasant. Which isn't to say we don't take our vows seriously.'

'Vows?'

'We operate by a strict code in our writing. All our members swear an initiation oath promising that their detectives . . .' here she adopted a tone of jokey formality, '. . . shall well and truly detect the crimes presented to them using those wits bestowed on them and not placing reliance on or making use of Divine Revelation, Feminine Intuition, Mumbo Jumbo, Jiggery-Pokery, Coincidence, or Act of God. No hitherto undiscovered poisons, secret passages or identical twins.'

'Who dreamed that up?'

'It was devised by our founder member, Ronald Knox. I'm sure you've heard of him. The guidelines are fairly well known. The criminal must be mentioned in the early part of the story. The solution must derive from the clues that the reader already possesses. No vital clue must be omitted.'

'How about hunches?'

'Hunches?' her smile lifted in a soft, sceptical curl.

'Do hunches count as a clue?'

'Hunches are not a clue in themselves. Indeed, we forbid the detective from following an unaccountable insight that later proves correct. But to my mind, hunches may suggest something of which the detective is not yet aware. A powerful, yet invisible force. Therefore, it's perfectly fair to include them in the narrative, so long as they are not the defining feature. The most important thing is to play by the rules.'

'Like cricket?'

'Precisely. In fact, Mr Fox, I think there's something in that. Conan Doyle was a first-class cricketer. And I've come to understand that rules are essential for civilization, as much as for detective fiction. We ignore them at our peril. It's my belief that observing certain rules leads to the mastery of many mysteries. Take, the medieval trivium subjects — grammar, logic and rhetoric . . .'

She had lost him here, but he managed a sage nod.

'The ancients regarded these as essential tools to master every other subject. I think it applies to writing, as to anything else.'

Observing his countenance, she stopped herself with a laugh.

'Oh dear. Forgive me. I'm making our club sound rather sombre, when in reality, it's anything but. It's not a science, it's an art, and while we take our art seriously, we are determined to enjoy ourselves in the process. We meet up at the Café Royal and talk shop. We also have premises at Gerrard Street and we regularly host lectures by those with relevant expertise: coroners, psychoanalysts, philosophers. We even like to pick the brains of policemen like you . . .' This last remark struck Harry with an almost physical pain, 'But most of all, Mr Fox, it's the social aspect that we treasure. We all enjoy getting together to discuss the process of writing. We critique each other's works. Writing can be a lonely business, stuck in a room for hours a day on your own, thinking about different kinds of violence.'

'Sounds a lot like my life.'

'Indeed. Please don't think that any of us regard detective fiction as a lifeless set of rules. There's no instruction manual for murder. In fact, quite the opposite. None of us wants to be constrained by our form. To me, our novels should always contain a human dilemma at their heart.'

'And Hubert Newman believed that, do you think?'

'Most certainly.'

Harry stubbed his cigarette out on a china ashtray painted with an image of Felixstowe docks, and stretched his legs.

'What I was wondering, Mrs Sayers . . .'

'Miss.'

'Miss Sayers . . . was whether Hubert Newman was experiencing any specific human dilemma in his own life before he died.'

'Ah!' A beam broke across her face. 'So now we come to the nub of it.'

She was far less surprised at the question than he had expected. Indeed, she seemed to relish the moment. He guessed that death was never just death to a detective writer.

Death was a device, a plot point, a mystery. Death was the central event.

She was leaning towards him, a glint ignited in the depths of her flat brown eyes.

'I did assume, from your visit, that it was not only the cardiologists who were interested in poor Hubert's passing. Even while we have been talking, I've been racking my memory for any hint of disquiet that he might have shown before he died, but I'm afraid I detected nothing. Nor was I aware of any change in his circumstances.'

'How long ago did you see him?'

'In July. At the club. We had a ceremony.'

'And how did he seem?'

'You mean, did he have foresight of impending death? Was he thinking of dispensing with himself, or did he worry that someone else desired his death?'

'Any of those.'

'Sorry, but no.'

'Perhaps he had encountered an aggressive reader. A stalker. I know people get upset with detective writers because they disagree with some detail of a plot, or think the wrong character did it.'

'On the contrary, most people seem to love us. They feel we lend an order to the chaos of life.'

Harry realized that was true. It was why people liked detective fiction. It was why he liked it. The books persuaded you that everything would be all right in the end, even if it wouldn't be all right. It never had been and wouldn't be now.

'Generally, we do give comfort. But with Hubert, I think it's the opposite. All those vicarages and libraries and home counties houses, they were killing fields. The college quads and luxurious hotels were never remotely safe. They were replete with menace and threat. For some reason I think Hubert was saying, perhaps even to himself, that there has never been any place you can really feel safe.'

Sayers had removed her rimless spectacles and was polishing them thoughtfully on a spotless lace handkerchief.

'The fact is, even though we had been acquaintances for years, I never felt that I *knew* Hubert Newman. Perhaps he was a difficult person to get close to. Some people are like that. Peel back the onion and you find only another layer beneath. He was a shy man. He did very few public readings. He always said he preferred to meet his readers on the page.'

'I met him at a public reading,' Harry couldn't help offering.

'Did you indeed?' Her expression warmed suddenly, as if she was lowering her defences. He had revealed himself as a fan. She had the measure of him now.

'I'm glad. If his death must be investigated, that it should be by someone familiar with his work. There's no better way of understanding a person than to read their novels. Everything you need to know about them is right there on the page. And something about Hubert's novels tell me that perhaps one should not be searching for murderous hatred as a motive. Maybe we should be looking for love.'

He could see the shrewd eyes calculating, and the brain behind them whirring through the possibilities.

'Do you ever think about love, Mr Fox?'

'Constantly.'

He had been in love more times than he cared to remember, and it always seemed to burn brightly, until the flame guttered and he awoke in the cold ashes of his dreams. Since Violet departed, the nearest he got to a romantic relationship was to investigate it and report the perpetrators.

'I always sensed that Hubert was a romantic. And love is more powerful than hate. Love makes us do crazy things, don't you agree?'

It had in her case, he knew. Dorothy Sayers had, despite her strict Christian observance and all her tracts on theology, given birth to an illegitimate child. He thought of the Prince of Wales, throwing away a kingdom for a woman who had already burned through two husbands. Of his sister Joan, and the brute she married. Of Walter Heap, and a love that had turned to hatred.

'Love is dangerous. It can turn bad. Love is sometimes a destroyer.'

'But Hubert Newman was a bachelor. Unless . . . you were aware of any . . . entanglements?'

'Entanglements?'

She gave a bright, delighted laugh, like a bird.

'Hubert was the last person on earth to be entangled. In all his dealings, he was a person of order and precision. I never met him with a woman. Or a man, for that matter. And yet . . .'

She paused, thoughtfully.

'There's a description of a woman in one of his novels, *Midnight in Vienna*, which I think could only have been written by a man who had once been in love.'

She glanced at her watch and rose abruptly.

'I'm so sorry, but I do need to hurry if I'm to make the 4.45. My husband, Mac, is not in good health and he does like his supper on time.'

'Of course.'

'If there's anything else, don't hesitate to call.'

As she was letting him out, she paused.

'And Mr Fox . . . please don't think the flaw in your credentials escaped me. My husband used to be a crime reporter for the *News of the World*, so I can tell a fake at ten paces.'

She closed the door and he stood for a while in the street, silently, tasting the air.

# CHAPTER 22

*September 23rd*

Stella reached Paris by six the next evening and caught the boat train at the Gare du Nord. From Dover, a breakfast of eggs, bacon and kippers was available in the Pullman carriage, but she could manage nothing more than toast. Throughout the long train ride from Austria, recriminations had rung in her ears. Why had she not pressed Roland Finch further on Newman's death? That, surely, was the whole point of her journey. Why, also, had she been so foolish as to tell him her name, even if he could not possibly have discovered where she lived? She knew the answer, and it was lack of courage. Put simply, she was scared. She might have found the man she was searching for, but in all other respects she had failed, utterly, and returned with more questions than answers.

She wondered yet again about Finch's comments.

'Something invisible. That can control the world, and even more, can destroy it. Whoever owns this knowledge can change the world'.

What was this knowledge? And who possessed it?

The moment she stepped off the train, still lugging her valise, she found a telephone box and called Harry Fox. He did not pick up. Undeterred she headed straight for his office, but the bell at number 6, Goodwin's Court rang without immediate answer. After a short while a sallow-faced boy emerged from one of the lower floors, scrutinized her for a moment wordlessly, then let her through the outside door, disappearing back into his own office. Stella climbed the stairs to Simpson Private Investigations and International Inquiries, but when she reached the top, she found it locked. She dumped her case on the floor and leaned her head against the door in tearful exhaustion.

*Where are you, Harry Fox?*

Fatigue and frustration warred within her. She had travelled all the way to Vienna and back at his suggestion, and now Harry was nowhere to be found. She had put herself at risk, when for all she knew Harry Fox was ensconced in one of his Soho watering holes. She realized, to her dismay, that although the two of them were bound in the most perplexing and secret of ventures, she had absolutely no idea where he lived.

In that instant, she was assailed by an uncomfortably familiar emotion and realized that she was thinking of her father, that beloved, charming, exuberant Irishman, who had deserted her at the age of nine. Maybe calling it desertion was unfair, though death was a kind of desertion, and those left behind feel the same sense of abandonment and loss.

After a few minutes she gathered herself and brushed the hair from her tired eyes. This was no time for maudlin reminiscence. She needed to work out how to communicate her news. And then decide what to do with it.

# CHAPTER 23

The garage, in a suburban road near Clapham Junction, just round the corner from Arding and Hobbs, was the place where used cars were kept for Watcher operations. It catered for everything from routine servicing to the equipment of specialist vehicles. A cracked sign read: 'K. Jessop Coachworks, Oil Changes and Service' and a rusting door led onto a rough space, its cement floor darkened with oil and littered with stray car parts, ramps, jacks and random pieces of scrap metal. A lank Alsatian, curled on a mat in the corner, raised its nose at Harry's arrival, then lowered it again to its paws.

Dodging the Riley Imp suspended above a repair pit, Harry approached a small cabin to one side, and cocked his head at the girl inside until she turned her wireless down.

'Mr Jessop in?'

She blinked incuriously.

'Dad?'

Jessop emerged from the back of the shop, wiping oily hands on a rag. He was a burly, beef-faced figure, who looked like he would be useful in a brawl, yet he spoke with the elaborate courtesy of a gentleman's butler. He turned to the girl and inclined his head.

'Thank you, Katy. I'll deal with this.'

Katy got up and left.

'Mr Fox. Pleasure to see you, sir. It's been a while. How are you keeping?'

Jessop was a resource. Meaning he maintained service cars and provided new ones. Humbers, Jaguars, sports cars. He spray-painted them in new colours and changed their plates every three months. Back in the day, Harry had used Jessop for all kinds of transport needs. He could secure everything, from bikes to buses. He could adjust, repair, adapt and retro-fit. On their last meeting Jessop had managed to insert a camera into the wing mirror of an Austin 10, and create a space on the indicator light casing large enough to contain a rolled-up note.

He had a crafty manner, as though the whole world was engaged in some under-the-counter enterprise, and short cuts were always available if you knew where to look.

'Good, thank you. And how are you doing, Kenny?'

'Can't complain, sir. What can I do for you?'

Harry had no idea if the news of his suspension had reached Jessop, but very little escaped the Irishman from his berth in the Falcon pub on nearby Clapham Junction. The beefy face registered little, but he absorbed everything.

Although he had made himself available to the Service for a number of years on motoring specialisms, Jessop's original trade was entirely different. For a long time, just after the war, he had worked in the Bertram Mills circus, with an act in which he hypnotized crocodiles and persuaded chimpanzees to drink tea. This expertise led him to source a number of exotic animals for Maxwell Knight, the head of B1F, who was a passionate keeper of unusual pets. Outside Knight's job as an agent runner, he had a penchant for rare creatures which he tended in the confines of his Dolphin Square apartment. Over a number of years, Jessop had supplied monkeys, mongooses, baboons, bushbabies and snakes. And, legend had it, a small bear.

Now, however, Jessop's creatures were purely mechanical.

'I remember you had a cab,' said Harry.

'My pride and joy. A 1936 Austin Low Loader. All fittings chrome plated. Want to take a look at her?'

He led the way to the back of the garage and flicked up a tarpaulin to reveal a shiny black London taxi.

'She's the genuine article. Good condition, with a few adjustments. Internal locks, for added privacy. Just press here,' he stabbed a meaty finger at the dashboard, 'and the doors won't open from the inside. Not much on the clock. Used one before?'

'Once or twice.'

'It's quite straightforward, sir. Don't switch on the light until you need or you'll attract the attention of every Tom, Dick and Harry. Why don't you let me buff her up a bit?'

Harry leaned against the wall as he went to work on the already gleaming bonnet.

'Still in the animal trade, Jessop?'

'No call for it, sir. Very few takers. A lot of folks are saying pets will be put to sleep by law if the Jerries invade. Hard to feed them, too. People are queuing up at the vets with their dogs and cats. Very sad. I can get you a parrot for a song, if you're interested.'

'I don't like anything that talks too much.'

'A parrot's only going to say what the owner says.'

'All the more reason. It's bad enough saying what I do, without hearing it repeated in polite company.'

'Fair enough.' Jessop finished the polishing, slipped the cloth over his shoulder and handed the keys to Harry.

'There's half a tank in there and she's a dream to drive. Very smooth.'

'I'll bring it back within a day. Thank you, Jessop.'

'Not at all sir. We do what we can.'

From the small glass-fronted cabin, Katy gave him an expressionless stare.

A few minutes later, Harry turned out of the drive in the taxi cab and switched off the yellow light.

He had used cabs before. A taxi was the perfect surveillance vehicle in London. They were so commonplace as to be almost invisible. He pulled into Belgrave Square, admiring the pretty wrought-iron railings and the glimpses of opulent interiors within. The little front gardens were full of obedient flowers and manicured topiary that got shaved, he guessed, more often than he did. The imposing stucco houses glistened like ocean liners and the black doors looked more bulletproof than any amount of air raid shelters. When Hitler's bombs came, nobody here was going to be stuck on a platform of the Northern Line with a blanket and a Thermos. War, as he recalled, was a great respecter of class.

He had supposed he might need to circulate a while, but by sheer chance as he cruised the square for the first time, Diana Sowerby was emerging from number 5 and trotting down the immaculate white steps. Suddenly, to his shock, she caught sight of him, and even though his light was off, stepped forward on the pavement with a hand in the air. Panicked, he considered ignoring her, but this was an opportunity, so he drew up and she opened the door.

She looked quickly around before she got in the back.

'Where to, miss?'

'Mayfair, please. Bond Street.'

'Certainly, miss. Shopping, is it?'

She said, 'Hmm.'

His eyes met hers in the mirror and she looked swiftly away.

Harry made a couple more attempts to engage her in conversation. He observed that the weather was lovely, but that rain threatened. Then again, they had nothing to complain about, did they, after the summer they'd had? To these insights, Diana Sowerby appeared oblivious, alternatively burrowing in her handbag and looking out of the window with quick, anxious glances, until he fell silent.

A bus sailed by. The advertisement on its side said the Alhambra was offering *Waltzes from Vienna* and Harry experienced once again a dyspeptic jolt. His initial bravado at persuading Stella Fry to take a train to Vienna had, over the past few days, resolved into a mass of guilt that sat indigestibly in the pit of his stomach. What could he have been thinking? Picturing her that first morning, coming up the stairs to his office with a flush on her cheeks and a girlish sprinkling of freckles on her face, every protective instinct rose up to choke him. No matter that she had lived in Austria before, and spoke the language, and was an adult, Harry had exposed her to quite unnecessary peril. He wondered where she was now, and hoped desperately that she was safe.

He tried to analyse how he felt about Stella Fry. It wasn't the usual thing he had for a woman. He'd loved all types of women. Forthright women, and those pushed to the sides of their own lives. Young women, and others who had found their looks in later life, when their cheekbones sharpened to reveal a beauty no one expected.

But Stella Fry was none of those. She was certainly pretty, with her dark, glossy hair, neat figure and beautiful eyes, yet she was adamantly not his type. Not his usual type, anyway. She was a woman with thoughts and ideas and a whole internal life of her own. He found himself wanting to talk to her more. Much more. He recalled what his last girlfriend, Violet, had once asked him. '*Don't you ever want anyone close? Someone you can talk to? Someone to confide in?*' At the time he had interpreted this remark as yet another veiled criticism and responded with a sardonic laugh, but now he began to see her point.

The other woman, the one who was his current job, was rapping on the glass divide.

'Miss?'

'I've changed my mind. I'd like to go a little further. Can you take me to Bermondsey?'

He almost said no.

'Bermondsey? You joking, miss?'

This remark was accompanied by what he hoped was a cockney grin.

She had been staring out of the window, and did not bother to break gaze.

'Just drive, please.'

Why? Why had she not said so to start with? Was she suspicious, as well she should be, that her husband was not the trusting kind? That her destination might have been overheard?

Grimly, he signalled a left turn and swung the cab south.

For Harry, every part of the metropolis throbbed and pulsed with its own particular energy, but this area had especially bad vibrations. Consciously, he avoided it. Not far away, the Thames widened and dragged past the Tower of London, its surface flecked with oil from the barges and houseboats. The green spaces were left behind, leaving the city a tableau of dirty brown and grey.

He drove on, a creep of menace running its fingertips across his skin. What was a woman like Diana Sowerby planning to do in a place like this?

He crossed Tower Bridge, and was driving down towards the Old Kent Road, through a dense network of narrow, Georgian streets, largely inhabited by dockers and those who worked on the river. This was the kind of district where youths lingered in alleyways, bulldogs clenched at their feet. Between the houses, washing lines were strung, and clothes hung like a line of white flags, as though signalling surrender to potential invaders.

He was turning into a dreary terrace, with a church on the corner, when she leaned forward and said, 'Just let me off here, will you?'

Damn. He had no choice. And it would be difficult to follow her without being seen.

'Want me to wait for you, miss?'

'No, thank you.'

'Might be hard to find another cab around here.'

'I'll manage.'

She fumbled in her purse for the fare, gave him a generous tip and slammed the door behind her.

A group of lads were kicking a football in the street. A couple of women in aprons, arms crossed, were engaged in conversation. Fox backed the cab round a corner, then as fast as he could, got out and sheltered in the church porch. Opposite was a poster appealing for air raid wardens: 'Protect Yourself and Your Neighbours: Volunteer for Training', over which someone had painted a swastika.

He had misjudged the woman. It wasn't the first time he had misjudged a woman, by any means, but Diane Sowerby quite perplexed him. Until a couple of days ago he thought he had the measure of her – sweet Miranda to her husband's Caliban – but now it appeared that Diana Sowerby had hidden depths.

At the heart of every skill Harry possessed was the ability to know routine and patterns and pick out the anomaly. The anomaly might be tiny, and well hidden, but it was everything – the flaw in the carpet, the fly in the ointment. Hubert Newman's modernist art had been an anomaly, as was the discovery of a letter from an intemperate professor on his blotter. Some anomalies were hard to spot, but this one was glaring.

Why should Diana Sowerby, Lady Heap, of number 5, Belgrave Square, find herself in this impoverished corner of south-east London, knocking at the door of a house she could probably buy for the price of her own fur stole?

Thirty minutes passed. A tortoiseshell cat came by and he bent to stroke it. Its body was as round as an owl and soft as a moth. Harry loved cats. He had not had one since childhood – a scratchy, thistledown creature of streaked silver and black, with smoky gold eyes and a ferocious mousing instinct, and he still missed it. Perhaps he would find a kitten for Jack. Get Jessop to source one, maybe. Whatever they said about people having their pets put to sleep, Joan had a soft heart and she would never be capable of that.

He fingered the camera in his pocket. It was a specially designed Leica with a false lens at the front and a real lens at the side, so that one could point it at a view and take the picture you wanted without anyone realizing.

But there was no point in taking a picture now.

When he looked up again, something crossed the edge of his eyeline, leaving the house. It was the back of a man in a fawn overcoat with heavily padded shoulders, a trilby pulled tightly down, and a rapid gait. Harry cursed softly and considered tailing him, but Diana Sowerby was still inside and she was the job.

It was another ten minutes before the door opened and she reappeared, wearing a headscarf over her bright blonde hair. She looked distractedly about her and glanced up and down the street. Harry drew back, fingering the miniature camera in his pocket. He had no idea how she was going to get home – taxis were hardly ten a penny around here – but he couldn't risk triggering her suspicions by reappearing. Eventually she set off briskly up the street and rounded the corner.

Once she had disappeared from sight, he went and rang the bell.

It sounded emptily. A couple of knocks got the same answer.

After a few minutes, the neighbouring door was opened by a squat, peroxided woman in a housecoat, with a piece of cloth wound turban style on her head. Harry introduced himself as Edward Stephens, a solicitor from Weatherby and Co. He had a card for this purpose, and a notepad with the name of his firm etched in gilt letters on the cover, which he now proceeded to extract.

She scrutinized the card for less than a second and folded her arms, expectantly.

Harry explained that he needed to make contact with the occupant of this house, because the address had been mentioned in the will of a distant relation. The occupant was out, evidently, but he and his firm were keen to track them down. If Mrs . . .

'Jones. Molly Jones.'

If Mrs Jones might be able to assist, it might help him and his firm to establish contact. He couldn't say anything, because he was professionally bound, but in confidence he was sure that Mrs Jones's neighbour would have good cause to thank her. He wondered, if it was not too much trouble, et cetera, whether she might possibly . . .

The first thing he detected was that Mrs Molly Jones was not the neighbourly type. Wasting no time on formalities, she leaned against the door jamb and began to unleash her observations.

Not much had escaped her. She was wasted as a housewife. Frankly, he should forward her details to Vernon Kell.

'I know her. Wouldn't call her a friend.'

He unpeeled a pack of Senior Service and offered her one.

'Her name is . . .?'

'Name's Vera. Foreign. No better than she should be, by the looks of her.'

'What kind of foreign?'

Mrs Jones shrugged and wrinkled her nose.

'Just foreign.'

'What makes you say that?'

'Funny accent. And clothes.'

'Married lady, is she?'

'Calls herself a widow, but there's no end of men friends.'

'What sort?'

'All sorts. Coming and going.'

'Does she have a job?'

'No idea. She's not the type you want to ask. Very la-di-da.'

Harry knew better than to interrupt. He was a Watcher by trade, yet all watchers were honorary members of the world of professional listeners, that cabal which included priests and publicans, whose skill lay in sifting conversations for the nugget of detail and panning for the golden glint of information. He contented himself with making stray jottings in the pad.

'Any lady visitors?'

'Not seen one. At least, not before her.'

She cast a long glance down the street, as if Diana Sowerby might reappear at any moment.

'She anything to do with this? The will?'

'I couldn't say, I'm afraid.'

'So what's coming to Vera, then?'

'Again, it's not for me to divulge, Mrs Jones, but I think it will come as quite a surprise.'

Despite her willingness to co-operate, there seemed little more of substance to add. Harry said goodbye and headed back to where he had parked the cab.

He was rounding the corner when it came. The dull glint of iron arced through the darkness, delivering a heavy, knuckle-dusting dose of déjà vu. An uppercut to the face, then a second, winding blow to the stomach.

Harry had, in his time, sampled an entire menu of street violence, both à la carte and specials, so he recognized this for what it was. It was fast, professional and designed to wound, not kill.

Still, it left him on his knees, fighting for breath like a drowning man. His heart flapped behind his ribs like a paper bag as his legs folded beneath him.

Then he began to lose consciousness and, as he went down, all he could think was that he was supposed to be meeting Malone.

# CHAPTER 24

Stella hurried down Whitehall, threading her way through a sea of cloth caps and bowler hats, and women in heels clipping their way to work. A group of young men passed, already in uniform. In the street outside the War Office a police car with a loudspeaker on its roof was cruising, telling everyone who had not already got a gas mask to equip themselves straight away. An advertisement for air raid warden volunteers loomed over a bus stop, next to a hoarding urging all eligible young men to join a Supplementary Reserve.

Here, amid the stolid, neoclassical heart of government, the atmosphere of prevailing crisis was tangible. A fleet of black cars swung into Downing Street, passing a small gaggle of protestors. There were two rival groups, one side holding banners saying 'Support Czechoslovakia!' And the other with hand-painted posters that said 'Stop the War'. It felt eminently plausible that the pendulum might swing either way.

Only that morning the wireless had reported that the Prime Minister was meeting Hitler for a second time, this time at Bad Godesberg, a small spa town near Bonn. The BBC said the conference would be held at the Hotel Dreesen, where Hitler had a suite with bulletproof windows, over-looking the Rhine. There were hopes that an agreement could be reached for a peaceful partition of Czechoslovakia, with a commission settling the mixed population and decreeing where the transfers of population would take place.

The idea had come to Stella out of the blue, though like most strokes of inspiration, it was only the inevitable rising to the surface. And the inevitable was that she would seek out Tom Lamont. Evelyn's brother was working at the Foreign Office – was that not what his mother had said? Perhaps he could make sense of what Roland Finch had told her.

Past the War Office she came to King Charles Street and the grand arched main entrance of the Foreign and Colonial Office. Over-riding her natural hesitation, she went inside.

The entrance led to a courtyard and then a hall filled with balustrades and a floor made of elaborate mosaics. It was more like a cathedral than a place of work. The walls were dressed in gilt-spotted wallpaper. Statues of ancient statesmen looked down on a vast, marble staircase, its steps covered in plush red carpet, and traversed by men in chalk striped suits and club ties making their way to other, equally gilded halls. Despite the smooth elegance of the personnel, there was a vibration in the air. The tectonic plates of politics were shifting, and even the genteel calm of the Foreign Office was affected.

She checked in with an official behind a desk at reception, inscribed herself awkwardly in the visiting book as 'personal acquaintance of Mr Lamont' eliciting from him an appraising smile, and followed directions to the top floor. At the far end of a corridor of glossy parquet she found an office in which a plump woman in pearls was frowning behind a typewriter. When she looked up enquiringly, Stella forestalled objections by announcing herself as 'a friend of Tom' and knocking at the inner door.

'Come!'

Tom Lamont was bent over a green leather-topped desk piled with papers, dispatches, telegrams and manila files. He looked up wearily, but when he saw her, the grey eyes widened and he sprang to his feet.

'Stella Fry! My God!'

He was exactly the same stolid old Tom, except for a faint tracery of lines around his eyes which made him seem older, and threads of grey in his brush of wavy hair. Already stocky, she could see at once the man he would be at fifty, or sixty even. He had the same manner of plunging his hands in his pockets, his brow furrowed and expression grave. The same aura of authority and competence that she remembered so well from the past, whether it was changing her bicycle tyre, or identifying songbirds, or walking round the National Gallery talking about Impressionists. Images she had forgotten for years rushed before her eyes.

She felt suddenly awkward at how much she herself must have changed. Perhaps she, too, looked tired and lined, fading like an old flame.

'What brings you here?'

She patted her hair automatically, as if she could smooth her internal disarray.

'I'm just back from a few days in Vienna.'

'Vienna! But I thought you'd returned to London. What on earth were you up to in Vienna?'

'I went for a holiday.'

Even as she said it, it sounded insane, but Tom must have been knee deep in insanity, because, seizing her by the sleeve, he shut the door behind her. The tapping of the typewriter from the outer office resumed. He continued in an urgent whisper.

'Thank God you're safe, then. I'm only just back in the country myself. I was at a conference in Évian-les-Bains. Representatives from thirty-two countries discussing what to do about the refugee problem.'

'Was it a success?'

'It was what we call in diplomatic circles an *uneven outcome*.' A terse laugh. 'In other words, a disaster.'

'But why?' she said, uselessly.

'Where can the refugees go? The United States is not fulfilling its immigration quota. Canada has said no, the

French say they're saturated, the rest say they would only be importing "racial problems".'

'What about Russia?'

'We can't look to Russia for help. Do you have any idea what it's like out there? Stalin's been responsible for a great famine. Millions have died in the Ukraine. His entire regime is built on lies. Show trials, gulags, history rewritten. The purges are terrifying. The newspapers print lists of the condemned – government officials, professionals, artists – then police squads called the Black Ravens come in the night and take them away. A quarter of the Union of Writers has been arrested.'

He was talking with the frantic speed of too little sleep and too much coffee.

'Even without Russia, surely other countries could get together and plan.'

'They've tried . . .'

Then he frowned and shook his head, as though her previous words had only just registered in his mind.

'A holiday? I'm sorry. What do you mean, you went on holiday?'

Although her explanation was ridiculous, Stella's actual motivation seemed suddenly equally absurd. How could she explain that she had been in pursuit of a man called Roland Finch who might possibly be connected with the death of an English crime writer? How futile it sounded, compared to the huge international crises in which Tom was engaged. And yet, that was why she was here.

'It's a complicated story. It wasn't exactly a holiday, to be honest. That's why I came. There's something important I need to discuss.'

Tom was glancing about, distractedly.

'Of course. But not here. Why don't we take a walk? I could do with a breath of fresh air. Afraid I can't be long.'

He led her through an ante room and called out 'Back in twenty minutes, Margery' to the secretary, who glanced up from her typewriter saying 'Certainly, Mr Lamont' and shot a suspicious glance at Stella. Then they walked out into St James's Park.

'Forgive me if I seem tense.'

Tom was moving swiftly, his brow knitted.

'The fact is, we're at a point of very great peril for the whole of Europe. A lot of us aren't sleeping. People are waking up at three in the morning worrying about the possibility of calamity. Yet a large part of the population – and indeed the government – would prefer to believe that it's all made up. They have no idea of what's coming.'

He inclined his head.

'Unlike you, Stella. You were living on the Continent for what, five years? I imagine you've seen a lot first hand.'

'I have.'

'You probably have a greater idea of what's coming than I do. I'd like to hear about it.'

They fell silent as a group of laughing schoolgirls passed by. The sight of them, armed with sketchbooks and pencils, heading to what must be an outdoor art lesson, shrieking with laughter at some irreverent joke, struck Stella with an almost physical pang. How long would these girls' life continue like this, routine and innocent, unbothered by the threat of bombs and raids?

'Are you optimistic, Tom? For Chamberlain's efforts?'

'It depends what outcome you think is a good one. Whether Chamberlain genuinely manages to stop Hitler in his tracks, which strikes me as entirely impossible, or if by giving him free rein to take the Sudetenland he merely gains a pause. But if he does, at what cost? Why on earth do we imagine that if we give Hitler what he wants he'll go back to his gardening? And the idea that Britain should be used to compel a small, democratic country to mutilate itself and dismember its own land is deeply wrong. Or so most of us believe. Churchill says we're choosing between war and shame, and if we choose shame, we'll get war soon enough too. Either way, we can expect an ever-increasing flood of refugees.'

'Your mother had a party for the refugees the other night.'

'Yes. I'm sorry I missed it. I'm working late most nights.'

'I met Professor Lindemann there.'

'The Prof!' He gave a terse laugh.

'Your mother said you knew him. What's he like?'

'Oh, he's a remarkable character.'

Just the thought of it seemed to soothe him.

'The Prof relaxes by studying prime numbers. He considers *The Times* crossword trivial and he doesn't smoke or drink. He eats only salad and egg whites. He's famously hard to get on with. They say when he walks in a room, the temperature falls ten degrees. The only two things he possesses are a piano and a world-class collection of enemies.'

'Do you see him much?'

'As it happens, I do. My boss works for Churchill directly, and the Prof is best friends with Churchill, so North encounters him frequently. Or as frequently as he can bear, because like most people, he and Lindemann do not get on. They go down to Chartwell – that's Churchill's country house – for their more private discussions. Sometimes, I accompany them.'

They came to a stop at a bench beside the lake. The beds were bright with Michaelmas daisies and the air was punctuated by the distant cries of children. The perfection of the day seemed chilled by the shadow of events far away. The thought that this might be the last season of freedom, before the world plunged back into war, made Stella shiver.

Tom removed his jacket and draped it over her shoulders, and the residual warmth of his body, along with the old familiar scent of him rose up around her.

'You're cold. Do you want to go back?'

'No.'

He regarded her solemnly, with the same, unsettling intensity that she remembered.

'You haven't explained why you're here. I don't suppose it's a social call.'

She caught the edge in his voice but couldn't tell if it was reproach, or regret.

'I came because I thought you might be able to help. The fact is, I was asking about Professor Lindemann because I need to see him.'

'Stella, my dear,' he frowned, baffled. 'I think he may be a little tied up right now. Besides which, he's never been very good with ladies.'

'Wait. Let me explain.'

Tom listened quietly while she related her first encounter with Hubert Newman, and the growing suspicion that his death was not a natural one. At one point he glanced around, as though somewhere in the shrubbery, or among the school-girls or the mothers pushing prams, eavesdroppers might be concealed, but he listened attentively and did not interrupt.

'Then a friend of mine, an . . . an ex-policeman . . . found a letter in Newman's apartment, from Professor Lindemann, dismissing what he called "grotesque allegations" that Newman had made. Only we don't know what those alle-gations might be, or why on earth Hubert Newman should have gone to see him. All we know is that a few days later, Newman was dead. And I discovered that one of the men who might be involved in those allegations had left for Vienna, so I went to see if I could track him down.'

Simply articulating the sequence of events made it sound even more extraordinary, if not absurd.

'You went all the way to Vienna for that?'

There was admiration as well as astonishment in Tom's voice and she realized, for the first time, how reckless she had been. What a wild card she must seem to his responsible, diplomatic eyes. Evelyn had been far more blasé about her journey, but then Evelyn was wrapped up in her own world of acting and romance and had no time for other people's adventures.

'Yes. And a little nostalgia too, I suppose.'

'Of course,' he said quickly, as if to forestall her. 'You must have friends there. Relationships.'

A tiny hiatus hovered, before she decided to ignore the last remark.

'Anyhow, I need to tell Professor Lindemann what I found.'

Tom must have longed to take charge at this point, and relieve her, a mere civilian, and a woman to boot, of the matters in which she was dabbling. Instead of which, with familiar decisiveness, he rose to his feet and plunged his hands in his pockets.

'As it happens, this could be your chance. Tomorrow morning I'm driving down to Chartwell. The Prof is a great friend of Clemmie, Churchill's wife, and he'll be there. They like to play tennis together.'

'You're going to play tennis?'

'Not me. I'm not staying. I just need to pick something up. It's a little errand for Lindemann, as it happens. He asked for me specially because, as I said, he doesn't get on with most people. Social encounters with Lindemann are never easy.'

'So, how does this affect me?'

'You could come along too, if you like.'

'To Chartwell?'

'Yes. If we thought of some reason why you would be with me.'

Impulsively, and before she had time to hate herself for it, she said, 'Let's tell them I'm your girlfriend.'

# CHAPTER 25

*September 24th*

It was perfect September weather. The road towards Kent rolled through fields deep with late-summer green. Above, the trees hung heavy with dusty leaves and on each side, hedgerows bulged with cow parsley and rose campion. In any other circumstances, it would have been a glorious day out. Day trippers on bicycles enjoying the last breath of holiday were out in force. Couples passed, with picnic baskets piled in the backs of their cars.

Tom and Stella might have been day trippers too, he in his tweed jacket and no tie, and Stella in a royal-blue cotton print skirt and matching jacket, decorated with small pink birds. But her mood was far from relaxed. In the passenger seat of Tom's dark-green Morgan, she tightened her headscarf and tried to suppress the churn of nerves. She had attempted, several more times, to contact

Harry Fox. But each time she telephoned his office, there was no answer.

What he would make of her visiting the home of Winston Churchill, she could only imagine.

'Are you sure this is OK? Won't Mr Churchill or the family want to know who I am?'

'I shouldn't imagine you'll meet too many people. They have rather a lot on their minds right now. But if there are any questions, let's stick to the story you suggested.'

Only minutely did his jaw tense, but she noticed it all the same.

'There are other concerns to focus on. A correspondent at the *News Chronicle* has come back from Prague with a secret document belonging to Konrad Heinlein, a Nazi official in Czechoslovakia, showing detailed plans for an invasion of the country. Chamberlain lands in Cologne today and the feeling is, he absolutely must challenge Hitler this time, rather than roll over and appease him. Churchill has warned there will be grave consequences if Czechoslovakia is partitioned.'

'You mean . . .?'

'Yes. War. Japan and Italy have said they'll stand by Germany. Russia is readying its fleet. But it's vital that we fight to prevent Germany dominating Europe. It's a struggle between the principle of law and the principle of violence.'

He shook his head.

'This whole enterprise is sickening. That the leader of the British government should be going cap in hand to a monstrous dictator. To allow himself to be duped. Churchill says it's the stupidest thing Chamberlain has ever done.'

'But if it means a chance of peace . . .'

His voice hardened.

'I'm amazed you can say that, Stella. You've just been in Vienna. You told me how it was. You've had the benefit of seeing the Nazis close up. You must know there's no chance of peace with a man like Hitler.'

She nodded.

'If he's appeased now, it will only embolden him. It would be a defeat without a war. Hitler wouldn't have drawn up invasion plans for Czechoslovakia if he didn't mean to follow through. Churchill wants the Prime Minister to issue an immediate ultimatum threatening war if he dares invade.'

He smiled, wryly.

'And, I probably don't need to say this, but if you do meet anyone today, don't for God's sake express any sympathy for Chamberlain. Mrs Churchill has been known to attack his sympathizers like a tigress. And who can blame her?'

'You were going to tell me. Why we're here.'

He hesitated.

'It's a little clandestine. But I trust you.' He shot her a sideways glance. 'I *can* trust you, can't I? After all, we are friends.'

*Friends.* The word reminded her, as perhaps was intended, of the time when she had answered his final letter with a card, printed with watercolour flowers, and a deliberately bright valediction, in the tone of a pen pal writing a thank you note after a fortnight's vacation.

'*I will always consider you a friend.*'

'The fact is, the Prof and Churchill are aghast at the way things are going and we're running out of time. They feel the country's unprepared and the French and British governments must face up to Hitler's true intentions. But if Churchill's going to make his arguments convincingly, he needs information, he needs documents and figures, particularly on the strength of our air force and their rearmament. Our essential military capabilities. There's an absolute terror that the Air Ministry is simply failing to grasp the gravity of the situation. They tie everything up in red tape and bureaucracy while our enemies steam ahead building planes and tanks. In particular, the Ministry underestimates the strength of the Luftwaffe. So various . . . channels . . . have undertaken to provide Churchill with the necessary technical knowledge. One of them, a man I used to work under in the Foreign Office, Ralph Wigram, was particularly helpful in providing Churchill with a flow of detail about German rearmament. But that stopped.'

'What happened?'

'He died. Killed himself, probably. Out of depression at what he thought was coming.'

There was a moment's silence between them. Tom's fingers in their kid leather driving gloves gripped the wheel tighter.

'Luckily, there are others who fill the gap. A whole network of people anxious to provide Churchill with whatever information he needs to turn the tide on this appeasement. That's where the Prof comes in.'

'Lindemann.'

'As I said, various armed services personnel have decided the best thing they can do is to bring documents and details to Churchill directly, so he can challenge the government with the proper authority. Like an alternative intelligence network. They bring it here – Chartwell is the nerve centre of the opposition – but it's highly technical most of it, and there are simply tons of papers, so the Prof has taken it upon himself to go through all the information and condense it for Winston. He produces clear charts that show exactly where the weaknesses lie in our defences and what strategy we need to improve. My boss, North, is involved too. And that's where I come in. Someone has to courier documents back and forth, and Lindemann asked me.'

'Why you?'

'Who knows?' He shrugged. 'Perhaps because, like him, I'm a physicist by training.'

'Did you work in the same area? I never actually knew what kind of physics you worked on.'

'Do you really want to know? Not just being polite?'

He gave a deprecatory smile.

'Oh Tom! Really I do!'

'Well, I'll explain as simply as I can. I was working at the Cavendish Laboratory in Cambridge in the field of atomic and nuclear physics. We were examining the behaviour of atomic nuclei under duress. Within all atoms there's a delicate balance between stability and explosive fragility, d'you see?'

'I think I do.'

She recalled Roland Finch's remark. '*It has to do with the most basic building blocks of life. Atoms.*'

'Put briefly, we were studying the very structures of the universe. It probably sounds very dull but you can have no idea how exciting it was.'

It was the first time that his voice had lightened all day.

'If you loved it so much, why on earth did you leave it?'

'Ha!' he laughed gruffly. 'Good question. I often regret it. Physics is a world with no politics. It is a universe free of all the dogmas we lay on it, it has nothing to do with societies and customs and art. It is composed solely of the real, deep stuff that makes us up. You need that kind of perspective, especially at a time like this.'

She stared out at the passing countryside. The dry grass heads at the roadside were lit with a fine, blond light and spun with spider webs. Nature had never seemed more delicate or more beautiful. She tried to imagine what it was like instead to see a world made up of atomic particles charged with explosive fragility. A universe of systems, interlocking and working seamlessly together according to laws that no one properly understood. Equations and symbols fizzing invisibly in the air.

Then she frowned.

'I still can't see how I'll get a chance to meet Lindemann. Surely everyone will be wanting to talk to him.'

'Quite the opposite. As I said, Lindemann doesn't suffer fools. He possesses the ability to unite all quarters against him and he's capable of arousing hostility in the most humble of souls. Most of them are jealous of him because he has Churchill's ear. But it does mean nobody's falling over themselves to engage him in polite conversation.'

'Even so, I don't imagine he'll want to talk to me.'

'From what you've told me, you have little choice but to try.'

The road wound into a valley, ran through woodland dense with rhododendrons, and a large red house came in view, perched on the side of a hill like a galleon.

'There it is! Chartwell. Not classically beautiful, but Winston loves it here. Spends all his time building walls and making lakes. He says a day away from Chartwell is a day wasted.'

It was a rosy manor house, its architecture a melange of Tudor brickwork and later additions of stepped gables and oriel windows, as though each generation had contributed its own signature, like names in a family Bible.

'Do you know, Lindemann brought Albert Einstein here to meet Churchill.'

'Einstein!'

'Yes. That's something you may not have heard about him. When Hitler came to power in 1933, Lindemann got the idea to tour Germany in his Rolls-Royce collecting Jewish scientists.'

'What do you mean, collecting them?'

'Literally that. It was like a shopping expedition for brilliant minds. In 1933, Hitler decreed that Jewish academics were "undesirable" and should be dismissed from their university posts instantly. He calls physics "Jew science". He actually said, "If the dismissal of Jewish scientists means the annihilation of contemporary German science, we shall do without science for a few years." So Lindemann took the initiative and went off on a tour of German universities. He managed to persuade a number of people that it would be highly dangerous for them to stay and he came back with some of the biggest brains in Europe. He installed them in Oxford – world famous physicists. Not only Albert Einstein. He got Erwin Schrödinger into Magdalen.'

The name Ernst Grunfeld came to her.

'*One of his scientists.*' That was how Harvey, the valet, had described him.

'Whatever else people say about Lindemann, you have to admit his fascination with science has been nothing but pure, unalloyed good for Britain.'

The Morgan pulled up on the forecourt alongside several other cars, including the same Rolls-Royce Stella had seen outside the Lamonts' home, with a peak-capped chauffeur in the front seat, one hand extended out of the window. A tinny rendition of 'Me and My Girl' issued from a wireless and the chauffeur's fingers tapped along against the car's burnished flank. He didn't look up.

Tom escorted her through a pair of vast oak doors into a hallway. It might have been a government department for the amount of bustle and activity it contained. The place was busy with men, some in uniform, and young women who looked like secretaries, coming in and out. Loud male voices, fruity and upper class, emerged from an upper room and for a trepidatious second Stella wondered if they were about to come face to face with Churchill himself. She caught a glimpse of a drawing room, painted duck-egg blue and hung with oil paintings. Two telephones rang in the distance and there was the sound of a door slamming, followed by an irascible growl.

'God's sake, woman!'

Tom led her through the house and onto the back terrace, where the land rolled away into a wide vista of the Weald of Kent. Swallows darted from the eaves of the building. The air was filled with the scent of stocks and punctuated by the distant whack of tennis balls.

'Ah. Here she comes,' murmured Tom.

A young woman wearing a white Aertex shirt and short skirt was approaching the house. She must have been around nineteen, with a wide, good-natured face, and dark hair rolled back from a complexion flushed with exercise. A black poodle danced around her feet.

'Oh, the invisible men are back!'

'Morning, Miss Churchill,' said Tom.

The young woman stretched out a hand to Stella.

'Hello! I'm Mary. Are you a friend of Tom's?'

Quickly Tom said, 'May I introduce Stella Fry.'

'Pleased to meet you. Are you staying the weekend?'

'I'm afraid we're not,' Tom interjected. 'I won't be here long. I'm on an errand for Professor Lindemann.'

'That man! We've just been playing doubles with him. He's paired up with my mother. He's a wizard. He drops the ball just over the net with a spin on it, so it doesn't bounce and it makes him impossible to beat. I advise you not to even try. Now, you'll both have to excuse me, I'm afraid, because I've a lunch to attend today, and I'm in a frightful hurry to change. Come on, Sukie, keep up!'

As she and the poodle disappeared into the house, Stella said, 'What did she mean, invisible men?'

'That's her word for us. Lots of people coming and going at the moment. It's not always possible to introduce them all.'

He looked around, savouring the view.

'Amazing here, isn't it? I can see why Winston comes here as much as he does. Now, it seems the Prof is still on the tennis court, so if you wait here, you can catch him as he returns. It's your only chance, so make sure you take it.'

Just then, from further along the path, the sound of voices rose.

'Hang back a moment. I'll speak to them.'

Round the corner came two figures, a woman and a sandy-haired young man, touting a racquet and a bag of balls.

'Ah! Tom! It is Tom, isn't it?'

'Good morning, Mrs Churchill.'

Her face was an older version of her daughter's, with tight iron-grey curls and eyes glinting with enthusiasm.

'How nice to see you. The Prof was just telling me what a saint you are. Are you staying for lunch?'

'I can't, I'm afraid, Mrs Churchill. I'm just on an errand for the Prof.'

'Will you have a drink, then? A gin and tonic? Or maybe you've time for a game yourself? We've plenty of kit to spare and Neville here can find you a racquet.'

The sandy-haired man intervened.

'I warn you not to try your hand at tennis with either the Prof or Mrs Churchill. They beat us fair and square. Six–three, six–two. Mary and I were run ragged.'

'Now you're flattering me,' she laughed.

'Another time, perhaps,' said Tom.

'Well, I hope you can spare a few moments to see Winston's latest project. He finished it this morning. It's a drystone wall, the other side of the kitchen garden.'

'Don't know where he finds the time,' said Neville.

'Oh, he says he likes to do two hundred bricks and two thousand words a day.'

Mrs Churchill peered at Stella, but quickly Tom said, 'I'll come in with you, if I may. I just need to deliver these documents. It will take me no longer than five minutes.'

He cast a backward glance at Stella as they headed into the house.

★

She sat on a bench in the sunshine looking out at the beech-wood valley, interwoven with lakes and streams. A green arabesque of jasmine, cascading over a nearby wall, exuded a heady scent that mingled with the gentler fragrance of wisteria and roses. Hollyhocks pressed against a warm brick wall and a peacock butterfly zigzagged across the path. A ginger cat trotted along and jumped up beside her, butting her gently to have his head rubbed.

It was the most peaceful prospect she could imagine, yet it was impossible to relax.

The crunch of footsteps heralded the approach of a tall man in tennis whites. Despite the heat, Professor Lindemann was wearing a long-sleeved shirt and a knitted white vest. He carried a bag of tennis balls.

Stella jumped up and stood in his path.

He started, but recognized her – she could see that immediately. He even remembered her name. His face twisted in annoyance.

'Miss Fry? What on earth are you doing here?'

'I'm sorry to surprise you like this, Professor Lindemann. I came with Tom. Tom Lamont.'

'Lamont? He's a good fellow. Trinity man, if I remember.'

He was baffled, scrutinizing her with an intense, dispassionate gaze, as though she was an alien species on a specimen glass. She sensed that he was a scientist to the core of his being, and yet she realized in that instant that perhaps this impersonal, logical mind might be an advantage to her. Maybe it would help him recognize the value of what she had to say.

'I've come because I need to speak to you about Ernst Grunfeld. Who disappeared from his lodgings the other day.'

'What about him? Are you telling me you know where he is?'

'No. But I know that just before he vanished, he was visited by a man. A journalist called Roland Finch.'

'I see.'

'Finch went to Vienna. So, I went to find him.'

'You did *what*?'

'I lived in the city for years so I know my way around. But the point is, I did find him.'

Lindemann stared at her, appalled.

'Who exactly are you? Is there something I should know? What is your purpose in all this? What agency enables you to engage in this Continental gallivanting?'

Stella's throat swelled with nerves and she swallowed hard to prevent the words emerging in a rush.

'There's no agency. I'm not an official, or from any agency, or anything more than a bystander really. I only met Hubert Newman because I answered an advertisement to type up a manuscript for him. I do freelance transcription and copy-editing. It's not my main job but . . . anyhow, the same day that we met, Mr Newman died. In the cloisters of Westminster Abbey. And the next morning I received his manuscript in the post and found he'd dedicated it to me. So, I got caught up in this quite by accident.'

'Then I strongly advise you to remove yourself again. This is not an arena for females.'

The curt tone was designed to silence her, but urgency and desperation propelled her forward.

'Please, let me finish, because there's more to tell you. When I talked to him in Vienna, Finch told me he was a Communist. And that Hubert Newman was an Austrian Jew.'

'My God.'

She saw Lindemann's knuckles whiten as he gripped his racquet. His demeanour darkened.

'I know that when Mr Newman came to you, he made allegations of some kind. I just—'

'Wait. Not here.'

Lindemann looked around, then gestured for her to follow him away from the paved area and further towards a patch of lawn that offered a panoramic view of the Weald, rolling lush and green before them. Some distance away in the rose garden, a gardener was tending the late blooms, but he was too far to be in earshot. Behind them in Chartwell, Churchill and others were congregating in the dining room, debating an encroaching war. There was nobody else in sight.

Lindemann was silent for at least a minute, and when he spoke again, his tone had completely changed.

'I think, Miss Fry, I owe you an apology.'

He cleared his throat.

'I still have no idea what your part is in all this or why you should take it upon yourself to investigate the circumstances around Newman's death. I don't know you from Adam, but you've come here with Lamont, whom I trust, and you've put yourself in some danger by travelling to the Continent at a time of very great turmoil. So, I'm going to give you a little information in return.'

His fingers were worrying away at a thread on the racquet handle as he spoke.

'I'm not sure you know, but a few years ago I took it upon myself to visit Germany to meet Jewish scientists who were threatened by the National Socialist regime.'

'Tom told me. You brought Albert Einstein back here.'

'Yes. Though unfortunately he was not so enamoured of England to stop him going off to America. However, one of the men who did stay was *Doktor* Ernst Grunfeld. Grunfeld has been a great asset to our nation. He is a visionary physical chemist focused on molecular structure. I met him at the Humboldt University in Berlin, where he was already supreme in his field. He is a highly talented man and we were extraordinarily lucky to get him.'

'And Grunfeld was the subject of Newman's allegations?'

'Yes. Hubert Newman told me that Dr Grunfeld was a Soviet sympathizer. A Bolshevik. That in itself is not . . . entirely unknown among Jewish intellectuals. But Newman urged me to have the man interrogated.'

'Yet you dismissed him.'

At this, a flash of anger sparked in Lindemann's face.

'Damn right, I did. Who was this chap? He meant nothing to me. A cheap thriller writer. If I listened to every crank and conspiracy theorist who crossed my path, I would never have time for real work. How could a fellow like that possibly have any insight into the kind of work we're engaged on? How would he even be acquainted with Grunfeld? I put it down to the flights of fancy that these trashy novelists entertain. For all I knew, it was actually some kind of jape – a kind of extended practical joke for a play or a story. Maybe the fellow was researching some element of plot. The fact that he refused to explain how he came by his information only confirmed it for me.'

'Then he died.'

'Yes. Then he died.'

He hesitated.

'I confess when you informed me of that fact, it gave me pause.'

His expression was difficult to read.

'As I say, I trust Tom Lamont. He's a sound man, and he's been enormously helpful to us. So, if you're a friend of his, and he brought you here, I am prepared to take you at your word. I assume Lamont has given you some indication of the extent of the crisis we face. The situation is so serious that I am going to trust you with information of the highest secrecy. This requires you to be more than discreet. I'm aware that women like to gossip and tittle-tattle, but this is not a matter for ladies' lunches. This is information of grave importance. You understand I'm speaking to you in strict confidence?'

Softly, Stella said, 'I understand.'

'As I say, I found Ernst Grunfeld at the University of Berlin, where he had moved from the University of Vienna.

He was what I would call a genius of the first rank. This is a very exciting time in science, Miss Fry, for reasons that need not concern you, and when I first brought Grunfeld over to Oxford, he became immediately immersed in work at the Clarendon Laboratory. But in 1935, he moved temporarily to a government facility called Porton Down in Wiltshire. Its official name is the Chemical Defence Experimentation Centre. People there carry out applied research in all kinds of chemistry, physics and engineering. The team that Grunfeld joined was engaged in developing a new kind of weapon.'

'A weapon?

'I can't be more specific than that, nor should you expect me to be. Suffice to say, it is one that could have momentous implications. It's not an exaggeration to say that if it was misused it could affect many thousands of people.'

She could barely speak. Her voice emerged in a whisper.

'And you think that Grunfeld was planning to divulge this knowledge?'

'I can't say. I would hope not. But the fact remains that Grunfeld has disappeared and there's nothing you, Miss Fry, can do. He's gone, and who knows what knowledge he has taken with him. We stand at the cliff edge of great peril, and enormous dangers surround us. Your information about Hubert Newman has been useful, and it is certainly intrepid of you to have searched it out. But Newman is dead, and it's up to others, not you, to work out how we proceed with these facts, if indeed we proceed with them at all. The best thing you can do, Miss Fry, is go back to your . . . transcription work . . . and forget you ever heard anything about this.'

On the journey back both Stella and Tom were lost in their own thoughts. Stella's mind was full of complicated suppositions that she could scarcely fathom. Physics and chemistry and weapons that would affect millions of people.

She longed to tell Tom. He was a scientist, after all, and would understand far more than she did. He must be aching to know what Lindemann had said. Yet he did not ask, and she knew there was no way that she could tell him. Lindemann had talked in confidence, and the last thing she wanted was to compromise Tom in any way. Besides, he seemed preoccupied by another piece of news.

'The German resistance has passed a message confirming that Hitler plans to invade Czechoslovakia imminently. The highest-ranking people in the German Foreign Office are attempting to persuade us that Hitler is insane. They're on their knees asking for our help in attempting to defeat his plans.'

'Isn't that what Chamberlain is trying to do?'

'Chamberlain is being taken for a fool. Hitler has issued a memorandum on the meeting at Bad Godesberg. It demands an immediate military occupation of Czechoslovakia by the German army, and that the Czechs accept an ultimatum to give up the Sudetenland by two o'clock on September 28th.'

'That's four days from now. What happens if they don't?'

'Then we really are in a dark place.'

# CHAPTER 26

Harry opened his eyes blearily and saw a figure looming out of the shadows.

'Who are you?'

'Mickey Mouse. Who the hell do you think I am? We were supposed to meet at Luigi's, remember.'

Harry groaned as a shard of pain lanced through his abdomen, and sank back on the chair.

It was Malone.

Harry did not go in for friends as such. Apart from a series of raffish characters with whom he interacted around Soho, friendship was an abstract notion with no relevance to his life. In his line of work, you could not tell outsiders what you did, or trust the people you did it with, which was hardly conducive to being pals or swapping pleasantries in the pub. If he ever thought about friendship, he would accept that Malone of MI5 was the person who'd come closest to the concept, even if most definitions of friendship would include knowing the friend's marital status, or at the very least his Christian name, and Harry had no idea of either.

To him, Malone was simply Malone.

Malone was tall, with a stoop and, unusually for a Watcher, a distinctive lurch, like someone with a stone in his shoe. It was down to being shot, or shooting himself, in the foot during the last war. His features were haggard, and his demeanour gloomy. He was part of a floating cadre of surveillance operatives whose curriculum vitae was obscure; whether they had gained their skills in the military, the police or somewhere more nefarious was unclear. What mattered was that like Harry himself, Malone was at the top of his game.

They had first encountered each other in 1936 when Harry was tailing Wallis Simpson. Malone had a high-level, jewel-in-the-crown contact within the German embassy, so it was to Malone that Harry turned with the interesting news that Wallis Simpson was making regular visits to the new Nazi ambassador, Joachim von Ribbentrop – both to his home in Eaton Square and to the embassy at Carlton House Terrace. Judging by the pink flush on Mrs Simpson's normally pale complexion after these visits, the meetings were not of a purely diplomatic nature.

Sexually, at least, Mrs Simpson was extending her repertoire.

On receiving this gem of intelligence, Malone's reaction was as close to animated as Harry had ever seen him.

'If you're right, Harry, it's dynamite. The Prince of Wales's lady friend carrying on with the German ambassador. Until now, it was just the old guard against the divorcée, but this changes things. It's more than just some Romeo and Juliet stuff about two households at war. It's a national security crisis. Who knows what she's telling them?'

Malone's suspicions proved right. The German diplomatic bags were opened to reveal information coming straight from Edward's private papers. Mrs Simpson was sending more than love letters to her German admirer.

The whole operation was a triumph. A career high for both of them. But hubris, as Stanley Fox might have told his son, was always followed by nemesis. Two months later Malone killed a man, and it was Harry who took the blame. For a long time, he waited while his future was decided, until, like the abdicated King himself, he was consigned to a murky and ignominious exile.

Yet out of this drama, a friendship was born, and while it was not the kind of friendship that involved mutual trading of confidences, or convivial evenings round the fire, it was enough that Malone knew where Harry lived and was able to effect an entry at the modest Victorian terrace in Battersea where he lay collapsed in an armchair.

'How are you, Harry?'

Malone's cadaverous face was crouched a little too close to his own, causing him to flinch.

'Why are you here?' he managed.

'We had an appointment, you fool. When you didn't turn up, Luigi insisted I look you up here.'

Harry blinked as his surroundings came into focus. Hard sofa, cheap coffee table on which rested two used cups, and everywhere stacks of paperbacks – precarious piles of thrillers and murder mysteries in colourful towers.

'Going to tell me what happened?'

Harry lifted his shirt and touched the side of his ribs where a plum-coloured welt was spreading, and tried not to breathe.

'Somebody hit me.'

'Looks like somebody doesn't want to be your friend.'

'I was thinking, perhaps it was the neighbourhood.'

'Nah. Looks personal. Something to do with the job? What was it?'

'I was doing an adultery. Bread-and-butter job.'

'Maybe the husband dislikes you.'

'He's the one who's paying.'

'Boyfriend, then?'

'I don't even know who he is.'

'Blimey, Harry. I thought you were supposed to be a professional. Anyway, forget that. Why did you want to see me?'

Harry shook his head as if physically to dislodge the fog that had settled in his brain.

'I had a question.'

'What is it?'

'Make me some coffee, and I'll tell you.'

Malone made him a cup of coffee, black as sin, and dumped it on the table.

'There's milk, too. On the counter.'

Malone found the bottle, decanted the milk delicately into a jug with the kind of hands that might break a neck, and rearranged his unfriendly figure on the chair.

'Remember Gino?' said Harry.

'Gino Lombardi? What about him?'

'He's following me. Saw him skulking around in Soho watching me.'

'How long's that been going on?'

'Not sure. But I'm a good Watcher, so I reckon I'd have seen the signs. I'm always on the lookout. Park benches, beggars, dog walkers, nannies with nothing in their prams. It's what we do, isn't it? It's habit. Like cleaning your teeth.'

A glance at Malone's blackened fangs reminded him that this was not the best comparison.

'So you think Gino did this?'

'I don't know. Probably not. But he's on my tail and I'd like to know who put him there.'

'What can I do about that?'

'I'm in Siberia, on a need-to-know basis. You're in Thames House. Ask around. Find out who set him on me and why.'

'I don't know if . . .'

Harry gave his friend a straight look and didn't need to say any more.

'Sure,' said Malone.

★

The dues of friendship paid, Malone left. In time, darkness fell and the neon sign on the fish and chip shop opposite flickered through the window at Harry like an incipient migraine. He pulled the curtains and peered through a crack to see whether Gino's cadaverous figure might be lurking somewhere in the street. His abdominal wound hurt a lot, and not even several fingers of Johnnie Walker could take the edge off it. The concussion, however, was worse. His mind was spinning and spinning like a pub fruit machine, spitting out variations of the same question, but never hitting the jackpot. Why was Diana Sowerby visiting the East End? Was Vera some relation who had left Herne Hill? A foreign branch of the family?

Above all, who had hired Gino? Who wanted to follow him, and why? Could it be Flint, or did it go higher up?

He could not shake the feeling that all these questions were, in some way, connected to the death of Hubert Newman. Or at least his investigation of it. Two weeks ago he had never encountered the names Frederick Lindemann or Stella Fry. He had never heard of theoretical physics or given Vienna a second thought. His life was progressing on its own, underwhelming path and its most exciting novelty was the arrival of a pretty new barmaid called Susie in the Seven Bells. Now his existence had descended into a state of chaos. He had no idea what he was doing, but someone had tried to break his ribs to stop him doing it.

These ruminations brought the ancient voice of his maths teacher into his head.

*'Show your working, Fox! How else will you solve anything!'*

That was all he needed to do. He was a detective, after all, and a patient, methodical assessment of the facts would take him to the answer. He was on to something, of that he had no doubt. It was a hunch solidified by Flint's warning: *'Step away from this one. There's plenty of trouble in the world without you going looking for more.'* He was haunted, too, by the words of Abel Edwards in the mortuary. *'It was unnatural, almost. As though he was frozen. It was like he had become his own statue.'* If Hubert Newman's death was like something from a detective novel, there were plenty of people keen to turn the page.

Painfully, Harry got to his feet, reached for a tin on the shelf emblazoned with the name McVitie's Digestives, and slid out a photograph. It was the picture he had taken from Newman's flat in which the novelist was sandwiched between a man and a woman. Even in a photograph it was possible to sense the other man's commanding presence. He was well-dressed, in his forties perhaps, with intelligent eyes that bored into the camera, thick, fleshy lips pressed together and a sweep of wiry, black hair above a low brow.

Who was he?

Harry shook his head and the movement caused wafts of alcohol to rise from his pores. He reached over for his mackintosh and checked his pockets. His wallet was there, with a pound in it, but, by design, nothing that might identify him. One box of Swan Vesta matches and a small tin of aspirin tablets. The notepad etched with the letterhead of Weatherby and Co. However, the miniature camera he used for his shadowing work was gone.

He trudged across to the kitchenette and poured himself a glass of water but it failed to stop the rising tide of nausea and he had to steady himself against the sink. Then, the room began to lurch and jitter around him, and to calm himself he lit up.

As the nicotine seeped into his bloodstream, he stared down at the photograph again, and nodded. It was time to ask a lady on a date.

# CHAPTER 27

It was seven o'clock by the time Tom parked his Morgan outside Evelyn's flat. London had been washed by a shower . of rain and the street gleamed with puddles.

'Would you like to come in?'

He leaned back and smiled apologetically.

'I'm going straight back to the office, I'm afraid. I'll be burning the midnight oil.'

'I hope you get some sleep eventually. And thank you, Tom.'

As she got out of the car, Stella was secretly relieved. Lindemann's remarks were both frightening and confusing. The idea of Ernst Grunfeld and the weapon sounded fantastical – like something from a novel or a film – yet she could not forget the expression on Lindemann's face as he stared out over the Kent Weald as though he was surveying a far darker horizon.

She walked up the four flights of stone steps and fitted her key in the lock. Yet again it jammed and the key refused to turn. The same thing had been happening for a week, and the key needed to be jiggled before it would yield. As she went in, she listened for a second, and could tell at once that her flatmate was out. The space registered vacancy. Evelyn must be at a rehearsal, or at dinner with Roger. Or, wait. Hadn't she said something else that morning?

'*You remember I mentioned Alexander Korda? That director who has a company called London Films?*'

'*No.*'

'*Well, he's having a reception at Claridge's for Vivien Leigh. She's just appeared in his latest movie and now she's disappearing off to America to make* Gone with the Wind. *And I'm going! Diana Sowerby invited me. She says there's a chance she can introduce me to Korda and he might sign me up. Isn't that awfully kind of her?*'

Stella's guilty rush of pleasure at being alone was short-lived. The sitting room door opened to a scene of disarray.

The flat was in turmoil. Books were scattered across the floorboards and a pair of jackets lay scrunched on the armchair. Records were strewn beside the gramophone. A couple of letters – one an early birthday card and another requesting the return of several overdue library books – had been ripped from their envelopes and tossed aside.

She sighed and peered into Evelyn's bedroom, where the chest of drawers hung open and a sheaf of clothes lay askew on the bed. The Bakelite jewellery box was open, and a string of pearls hung out. A half-full cup of tea stood abandoned on the floor and a tin of Leichner face powder was spilled carelessly across a Persian rug.

Anyone would think they had been burgled.

Stella sighed. It was nothing new. Evelyn was always like this. Tom used to say there was a scientific term to describe his sister.

'*Entropy – it means an endemic state of disorder and randomness. That's what Evelyn generates. Entropy.*'

She put on the kettle and made tea. The kitchen was messier than usual too, with the cupboards open and dirty plates sitting in the sink, so she took the tea through to the sanctuary of her own room, which was, by contrast, its usual orderly self. Her brushes, lipstick and powder were arrayed on the top of the chest of drawers, in front of the tilting mirror. Her spare shoes were lined up on the floor of the wardrobe. Her small collection of books was ranged on the windowsill and her Royal typewriter sat on the desk exactly as she had left it.

She flung herself down on the bed, closed her eyes briefly, then opened them again.

Something was wrong.

She stared around, trying to detect a difference. She could smell nothing but a lingering trace of Lanvin's My Sin, a recent gift to Evelyn from Roger. Evelyn came into her room all the time, borrowing clothes and make-up, so had she, or one of her lovers, entered and rooted through her belongings? There was, however, no sign of disturbance.

So why did Stella sense a turbulence in the air? What was it that she could not see?

On the mantelpiece stood a red geranium that had been flowering away valiantly all summer. The pot was slightly askew, which bothered her, but as she stood to straighten it, she realized that she had straightened it just before she went away. Which meant that someone else had moved it.

She performed another inventory of the room, past wardrobe and desk and chair to bedside table, and it was then that she realized what exactly it was. The manuscript. She had left it on the bedside table but now it had vanished.

Where on earth had it gone?

The room spun before her. The jammed lock. The sense – no, the conviction – she had that someone other than Evelyn had entered the house. The air seemed to quiver and the hairs on her neck stood up as though something liminal, just outside the edge of her vision, was waiting to pounce.

She pulled on a jacket, stepped back into her shoes and grabbed a bag. Then she dashed down the stairs and left the flat.

All she could think was that she had to find Evelyn and warn her.

# CHAPTER 28

To the sound of Tommy Dorsey's orchestra playing 'All That You Are', Stella slipped into the pillared foyer of Claridge's Hotel and looked around her.

Vivien Leigh and Laurence Olivier were in love. Everyone knew. Both were already married with children and for that reason they were supposed to be keeping the relationship out of the public eye, but the lovers were twining hands and brushing shoulders at every opportunity, luminous with a shared electricity that radiated to everyone around them. They were laughing at each other's jokes and finishing each other's sentences. In the mint-green salon, dazzling with art deco mirrors, glinting silver and vases of flowers, they shone with a vivid, lacquered intensity. The actress was as brilliant as a diamond – though a pretty flawed diamond, if reports of her temper were true. Olivier was watching her with the same hungry sexuality that their host, Alexander Korda, had so successfully exploited in a number of films.

'They're supposed to keep the affair secret, but if that's what Laurence Olivier thinks of as secret, God help us if he ever has to work in intelligence,' murmured the man beside Stella.

'You forget, darling, he already has,' said his companion. 'He played a spy in *Fire Over England*. Besides – spies, actors, don't they just do the same thing?'

At any other time, Stella would have been starstruck, but instead, her body ached with fatigue. She had eaten nothing except a sandwich at a roadside café at which she and Tom had stopped on the way back from Chartwell. The turbulent emotion of the day, mingled with her agitated state, only heightened her nerves.

As she looked around for Evelyn, the tenor of the party began to change. Conversations quietened, and people fell quiet, hushed and expectant. Laurence Olivier was declaiming an impromptu performance of *Hamlet*, his most celebrated role thus far.

'If it be now, it is not to come; if it be not to come, it is now; if it be not now, yet it will come. The readiness is all.'

'He means war,' murmured Evelyn, coming to her side with a small man in tow. 'So powerful, isn't he? Oh, Stella, this is Ian. He's a screenwriter. He's written a piece called "The Role of Art at a Time of Crisis". It's going to be published in *The Times*.'

The small man, whose receding chin was covered with a straggly beard in the way that an ugly building is covered in ivy, nodded eagerly and opened his mouth to explain further, but Evelyn deftly interposed. She had already lost interest in the role of art. And in the small man too. She was like a child with a new pet, already half resentful, half bored.

'Isn't Vivien Leigh marvellous? They're so in love. They're need to make the most of being together because she's been cast in a Hollywood movie called *Gone with the Wind*, and they'll be thousands of miles apart and hardly see each other.'

'Evelyn, we need to talk.'

'Yes, where've you been all this time? I have delicious gossip.' Evelyn always offered up gossip like home-baked cake. 'Diana Sowerby's having an affair. The man's an admirer of Churchill. God forbid her husband finds out. Walter Heap would be even more offended that his wife's lover was a friend of Churchill than he would by being cuckolded.'

There was no point telling Evelyn about Tom or Chartwell or anything else about the day.

'Diana's invited me here on the basis that she will slip away at some point, and I'll be her alibi. If anyone asks, I'm to say she was here all evening. Isn't that romantic? She thinks her husband has a private detective on her.'

'Listen. I think the flat's been burgled.'

'Is that a joke? I know I should tidy, but frankly, if we're about to go to war we need to enjoy life. Live in the moment. There'll be plenty of time for tidying.'

'No. I mean it. When I came back, I could tell. Someone's been in the flat.'

'It's my fault. I was panicking about tonight. I didn't have a thing to wear.'

'No. I don't mean untidiness. I mean a real burglar.'

'Are you serious?

'I could sense at once. Someone's been there.'

'How could you tell? Have they touched my jewellery?'

'No, not at all.'

'So that's all right, then.'

'The only thing they've touched is Hubert Newman's manuscript.'

A merry peal of laughter escaped from Evelyn, at a joke Stella did not know she had told.

'That's so funny.'

'What is?'

'That's not a theft! Or at least not in the strictest sense. It was my mother.'

'You're telling me your mother burgled the flat?'

'No. Yes and no. When you were away, she mentioned that she'd like to read the last Hubert Newman book. You'd told her you had it, and she was desperate to be the only one of her friends to see it. She wanted to be the first person in England to read it. Think how she could dine out on that! So, she came round to collect it and promised to whizz through it while you were away. Mummy's a very quick reader. She reads a book in a day.'

'You're saying you gave her the manuscript?'

'Please don't be cross, Stella. It hasn't come to any harm. The fact is, Mummy didn't even read it. She said it isn't a novel at all. She said it was very esoteric and she couldn't make head nor tail of the handwriting. And it seemed to end awfully abruptly. Here, have a drink.'

Relief cascading through her, Stella took a glass from a passing tray. The alarm at the potential burglary, and the intrusion she had sensed in the flat, gradually abated. One glass was followed by another as the drama of the day began to blur into a soft fuzz of exhaustion.

As she relaxed enough to look around her, her glance fell on Alexander Korda, holding forth in his heavily Hungarian-accented English, and theatrically waving an eight-inch cigar. He was saying his goodbyes and preparing to leave. It occurred to her that this, surely, must be the man with whom Diana Sowerby was having an affair. She knew the film producer was a powerful man, not only a friend, but an employer of Churchill, having engaged him to write several screenplays. He had spent time in the Austrian and German film industries before arriving in London, and he was a fierce critic of the Nazis. His recent film, *Fire Over England*, about Elizabeth I and the Spanish Armada, had been a panegyric to patriotism and self-sacrifice. And his sci-fi fantasy, *Things to Come*, had prophesied world war. That must be why Diana Sowerby was there, and consequently Evelyn herself.

She went to find her friend.

'There you are. Diana's just left. It's lucky I noticed. I can't concentrate on a thing. We open in a week and I'm a bag of nerves. But then if you're not a bag of nerves, you aren't doing your job properly.'

'So, who's Diana's lover?'

Evelyn had a high flush and her eyes were dancing with excitement.

'Can't say. It's a big secret. Terribly scandalous.'

Stella knew her friend wanted the secret prised out of her but at that moment, she had more pressing concerns.

'All right, then. Never mind. Anyway, could you ask your mother to return Hubert Newman's manuscript?'

'But she already has.'

'Where did you put it?'

'Back where I found it, of course. Just this evening. Before I came out.'

'Where, exactly?'

'On your bedside table. Precisely where you'd left it.'

'You can't have done.'

Stella knew that the champagne that she had drunk was thickening her brain, yet every sense was straining to understand what Evelyn was telling her.

'Don't look at me like that! I did! I know how you're obsessed with tidiness so I replaced it in exactly the same spot. I guessed you might make a fuss. It's right there where you left it. On your bedside table.'

'But it's not. It's vanished.'

# CHAPTER 29

'*You're good, Harry, but even you aren't capable of tailing a dead man.*'

That was what Flint had said, but God knows, Harry was going to keep on trying.

The morning after the assault, he woke from a fitful sleep, observed that one side of his face had acquired the size and consistency of a worn boxing glove, and consoled himself with the old Russian saying that if you wake up feeling no pain, that's when you know you're dead. He was certainly alive, then; indeed a catalogue of competing pains were registering their presence, from the low throb of his cheekbone to the breathtaking stab of a bruised rib. He felt desperately alone. He longed for a reassuring female presence to lie at his side, emitting the regular sound of breathing and the humid smell of sleep. A soft, warm body, with lingering traces of perfume, shifting into his arms.

He thought again of the character in *Midnight in Vienna*.

Ludmilla Mandlikova. A film actress of stormy, East European heritage, who tangled with Peverell Drake when he accused her of murder. She had thick, dark hair, a husky voice and green eyes that flashed with danger and defiance. A silk dress that caressed a body of perfect proportions, and a proud, pouting mouth that every man – even the buttoned-up Drake himself – imagined kissing.

That was the kind of woman he had in mind.

Instead, he got up, looked at his father's own grizzled jaw glowering at him in the mirror and shaved, tenderly navigating the bruise, running the blade along his cheek and upper lip until he had managed to remove a decade.

Then he brushed his teeth, cauterized the sour taste in his mouth with a savage rinse of coffee and headed off for his date.

B4a, as she was universally known after the section she headed, was a fraction older than him, in her mid-forties. She wasn't really his type but attractive all the same – slight and dark haired, with the trim build of a keen tennis player.

She was the only woman officer in MI5 and Harry was scared of her.

Everyone was scared of her, which was crazy when her special skill was to put men at their ease. Her real name was Jane and she had trained as a barrister, graduating top of her year with first-class honours. Her connections spread across Whitehall and the secret world, as well as several branches of the aristocracy. It was unheard of for a woman to rise to the rank of officer, let alone head of a division. She was high table compared to Harry, who was not so much below the salt as beneath the table altogether; yet, in the warped marketplace of the shadow world, she owed him.

The favour had been earned two years earlier when B4a had summoned Harry to her office in the branch of B division that covered Soviet affairs, to investigate the flat of a writer, Christopher Foxton. Foxton – Eton and Cambridge – was fey and short-sighted and not a successful author, far from it. But when he'd accepted an all-expenses paid trip to a conference in Odessa in 1934, B4a's alarm bells rang. Despite his mail being opened daily, his telephone tapped and his apartment regularly spring cleaned, B4a's agents, including Harry, had turned up very little. Foxton had been to a talk in the upper room of a pub in Islington on the subject of Joseph Stalin's Five Year Plan. He had written an approving review of Eisenstein's *Battleship Potemkin* in a local Suffolk newspaper. He had attended a meeting for the Society for Cultural Relations with the USSR in Wimbledon. His post contained nothing more damning than fan letters from a young man in Paris.

The conclusion was that Foxton was little more than a mild-mannered birdwatcher who loved Continental travel, young men and the Essex Marches. The binoculars and camera found in his flat were the accessories of a lover of the natural world. B4a didn't believe it, but budgets were tight and further investigations were abandoned. Harry, however, agreed with B4a. He had a hunch, and he continued his surveillance in a freelance capacity.

A few months later, patience paid off and he found something. It was a letter concealed in a 'cut-out' – a book whose pages had been carved out to create a cavity for hidden material. The book itself, *Nights out in Norfolk*, was deliberately boring, even more boring than Foxton's own output. But it got more exciting in the middle. There, Harry found a wad of classified documents which were due to be delivered in the course of an Anglo-Soviet cultural cruise to Leningrad that Foxton was shortly to undertake. The documents were traced to a well-known Soviet agent, whose typewriter had a faulty 'e' key. Sometimes, Harry thought, this work was insultingly easy.

The fact that B4a owed Harry didn't make the meeting any easier, but he had no choice.

An uncomfortable mix of anticipation and apprehension churned in his guts as he sat in the saloon bar of the Rose and Crown. He had a mental image of the perfect pub, full of mahogany ale and polished horse brasses. Old friends at the dartboard, and a beaming barmaid at the counter. If that was perfection, then this place was the precise opposite. A low-ceilinged dive purveying undrinkable stout. A fug of smoke and a carpet sticky with spilled ale. A pervasive gloom enhanced by the fact that the landlord had decided to paint over half the windows in preparation for a blackout. A clientele made up entirely of the poor and huddled masses, plucked straight from a painting by Hieronymus Bosch.

The pub was as familiar to him as his own skin.

He almost didn't see her come in. Entering unobserved

was a virility contest among his colleagues and despite her good looks, B4a was able to assume invisibility armed only with a handbag, a headscarf and a mac.

She slipped into the seat opposite, sat down and sipped the gin and tonic he had already bought her.

'Have you been walking into doors again, Harry?'

'Occupational injury,' he said, touching the eye, which was mutating into a rainbow of yellows and greens. What with his scar and bruise on opposite sides of his face, his appearance was not exactly monkish.

'So what's this about? I don't have much time.'

'Hubert Newman.'

She arched one perfectly plucked eyebrow.

'Dead. I thought.'

'Yes.'

'And not one of ours, unless I'm mistaken.'

'Not on the list.'

'Then . . .?'

'The evening before he died, Newman went to an event of some kind. Something happened between that time and when he died. I have evidence that suggests he was killed.'

'Evidence, or proof?'

He paused. B4a could spot a lie at a hundred paces.

'It's still evidence right now. But I'm going to turn it into proof if it kills me.'

She leaned fractionally forward, and he saw the pupils of her eyes widen in empathy. How was it possible for her to do that? To control her body's most automatic reflexes?

'That sounds very dramatic.'

She crossed her legs and shifted fractionally closer to him.

'How are *you*, Harry? In yourself?'

He knew then what it must be like for those poor saps who found themselves across the table from her, looking into those kindly eyes, feeling the sympathy in her voice, longing to unburden their heavy souls. Fighting every urge to confide and cough up every secret into her maternal arms. Battling the desperation not to disappoint her.

'I'm fine. Doing well. Very busy.'

'That young lady, Violet?'

'I might look her up again sometime.'

'Ah. *Cherchez la femme*. You're good at that, I hear.'

He allowed a wry grin.

'It's always been my undoing.'

'I've heard you've had plenty of success too.'

He took a gulp of Scotch and wiped his mouth.

'And your sister. Joan, isn't it?'

'Good,' was the sound that emanated from between his gritted teeth.

'The lad?'

'Doing well. Very advanced at school. Big reader. He's a clever boy.'

'I'm sure he is.'

She leaned the chair back a little, glanced around the pub, then trained those bright appraising eyes on him again.

'It must be in the blood. They say, though obviously I never knew him, that you take after your father.'

'Who says?' he asked, genuinely astonished.

'The people in the Service who worked alongside him.'

'Alongside . . . my father? Stanley Fox?'

'When he was with us. There was a lot of respect for him.'

'My father was a businessman.'

'Yes. Of course, he was.'

'Are you telling me—?'

'Oh, did you . . . did you not surmise?'

*Surmise.* Never know, because the Service was all about hints and nudges. But surmise. Deduce, assume, conjecture. That was the Service lingua franca.

So, all those rendezvous, disappearances, the sudden business trips to the Continent, they had their reason, then? If what B4a was telling him was the truth, then Stanley Fox had been no wayward chancer – no businessman with a bent for import/export, but an agent of the British government. Or, at the very least, an asset. Not merely a hapless man who used his charm and charisma to deflect every reproach, but an active servant of the British state.

The suggestion that his father's life was entirely at odds with the one that his son had believed was too much for Harry to take in just then. He was being asked to rewrite his life's whole story at a moment's notice and he had never been able to write that fast.

'I've been meaning to mention it for some time.'

Years reeled before him, turning themselves upside down. His mother's reluctance to condemn her husband for his vacillations. His own moods and rages at his father's absence.

As a teenager, he had been so scornful of her tolerance. Once he had even called her a doormat. But what had she known? He recalled his father's unexpected pride when his son had come out of the army and straight away found a job at Scotland Yard.

'You're a lot like him you know. You're an enigma, too.'

'That's usually code for an uncooperative bastard.'

'It means people make up stories about you, to fill the gap in what they know.'

He had heard a few of these. That he was running a black market operation with a gang of Italians in Soho. That his scar had in fact been the result of a duel with a Polish prince over a woman.

B4a gave him her most empathetic smile.

'I suspect Stanley would have been proud of you.'

Harry understood absolutely why B4a would disclose the information just then. It was designed to disorientate him and put him off the matter in hand. He therefore needed to ignore it, or at least file it away for later digestion. It took all the composure he possessed to say, 'Anyhow, as I mentioned, I'm busy.'

'All the more reason to forget this nonsense, then.'

'Nonsense? Why would it be that? I'm just asking some questions.'

'Harry, I know things have been hard for you. Leaving your job, so suddenly, must have been a wrench. Sometimes, that kind of thing can leave a mark on the mind. It can make us get things out of proportion. Lose perspective.

The modern thinking – the more enlightened thinking – is that people who have undergone these episodes should be given help. Psychological help. Just to get their heads straight.'

'So they don't hang around in pubs cursing the Security Service, or falling down in the street with a bottle of Scotch in their hands yelling about the government abandoning its own?'

'Listen Harry, I'm on your side. I always have been. And your side is a pretty lonely place to be sometimes. I happen to believe that your actions were in a lot of ways . . . understandable. But that doesn't make them right.'

She had mentioned it. Of course, she had. It was an elementary technique. Confront the subject with the episode he refused to interrogate himself. Drag the dark thing out into the light. She was referring to the manslaughter, Harry's personal mark of Cain, that was emblazoned in letters of fire not just on his file, but on his own cringing soul.

He threw back more of the Scotch and forced himself to remain impassive as B4a surveyed him.

'What I'm wondering is,' he went on, 'might there be anything on file to suggest that there's more to Hubert Newman's death.'

'Why do you want to know? What was Newman to you, or you to Newman, as the playwright might say?'

'Nothing. I met him once. I liked the man.'

He was not going to admit that he had been hoping for a

new sideline as literary advisor. He guessed that B4a would take a cool view of that.

'Well, as I said, I can assure you we have nothing on him whatsoever. We don't have a file on him at all. It's not as though we don't have enough to contend with. We're up to our necks in work. The politicians might be focused on the threat abroad at this moment, but our eyes must remain firmly on the threat closer to home.'

'Yeah. I'd wondered, on that subject – if war with Germany's on the way, whether the Red List . . .?'

'That's a fair question. You're understandably concerned about your livelihood, Harry. Counter-espionage resources are quite rightly being expended on the activities of the German regime, but the Soviets have not gone away. I have at times been a lone voice arguing against complacency. And they assure me that the Red List will continue, at least for the time being.'

She flashed him a smile of her neat white teeth.

'And be assured, despite current circumstances, you're one of our most treasured operatives. I hope that puts your mind at rest.'

'Thank you. But not exactly. There was something else I wanted to ask.'

He pulled out the photograph. As he handed it to her, he noticed that his fingers had left a bloody print across the snap. It was the picture that he had found in Newman's flat. The one in which the novelist was pictured between a man and a woman.

'Ever seen this chap?'

'Your novelist pal?'

'No. The other one.'

It may have been a glint of sun straining its way through the grubby windows, but something seemed to kindle in the depths of her eyes.

'What makes you ask?'

'Idle curiosity.'

She was finishing the gin and collecting her handbag.

'I'm not sure, but as it's for you, Harry, I'll see what I can do. Why not try the usual place tomorrow? In your lunch hour – if you have one.'

# CHAPTER 30

*September 25th*

Stella woke early after a restless night. Evelyn must have decided to discuss The Role of Art more intimately with the screenwriter, because she had not returned to the flat that evening. Nor did she appear in the morning. Stella assumed she had gone straight to rehearsals because *Troilus and Cressida* was due to open in a week's time.

She drank a cup of Nescafé and turned on the wireless. Chamberlain and Hitler had held a second meeting, this time in a place called Bad Godesberg, a spa town on the Rhine. Hitler had taken Chamberlain's hand, apparently, and ushered him up the steps of the Dreesen hotel. The French had mobilized half a million men. Americans were leaving Britain in unprecedented numbers. Blast-proof steel bomb shelters were to be provided for every household in the country, easily installed and to be embedded in gardens under a layer of earth.

She paced the length of the room, unable to settle. She had no doubt that Evelyn's mother had taken the manuscript, but no doubt, either, that Evelyn had been sincere about putting it back. And yet it was most certainly missing now. Which meant only one thing.

Between the time that Evelyn had left, and Stella returned, a stranger had been in the flat.

They may be watching her even now.

She went over to the window and scanned the street below. A line of people stood at the bus stop opposite, variously bored, patient, or absorbed in their newspapers. A pair of housewives with baskets were heading for the shops. A young man leaned against the wall of the block opposite, smoking. A boy was mending a puncture on his bicycle at the side of the road. Might one of them be watching her? Or more than one?

Sitting down at the table, she took out a pen and paper, then jumped up again restlessly, and went yet again to check the vacant spot where the manuscript had lain. Perhaps there was a completely innocent explanation, but if so, it eluded her.

Why would anyone want to steal Hubert Newman's manuscript? There was always the chance that it was for the same reason as Sidonie had wanted to read it. It represented the final work of the celebrated author. Even unpublished, the manuscript of *Masquerade* would no doubt be worth something on the black market.

Yet even as she rationalized it, she chided herself for

worrying about a burglary when so much else was on the horizon. The encounter with Roland Finch in Vienna, and Frederick Lindemann's words: '*We stand at the cliff edge of great peril, and enormous dangers surround us.*' Europe's nation states were engaged in a chess game of immense import. Every move mattered. It was certain, if Chamberlain's negotiations failed, that the whole Continent would be plunged into war.

What would a dead detective novelist or his unpublished manuscript matter then?

She decided to clean the flat. It was just the kind of mindless work to soothe her jittery state, and living with Evelyn meant there was always plenty of cleaning to do. Amid the usual detritus – Tangee lipstick in 'Red Majesty' with the top left off, and an opened tub of Max Factor Satin Smooth foundation – a sweep of Evelyn's room added yet more to the backlog of washing-up that sat in the sink. As Stella worked, she thought again of what Sidonie had said about Newman's book and a phrase snagged in her mind.

'*It seemed to end awfully abruptly.*'

Dishcloth in hand, she froze. There was a reason that the book ended abruptly. Sidonie would have only seen Part One of *Masquerade* because Stella herself had removed Part Two, comprising the final two chapters. She had stowed them in her suitcase to read on her journey and promptly forgotten all about them.

Heart racing, she retrieved her suitcase from its place beneath the bed, and opened it.

There, at the bottom, the brown envelope lay untouched.

Extracting it, she placed the manuscript on the table and separated out the two chapters, 'The Pretenders' and 'The Stratfordian', and forced herself to focus on the scratchy handwriting. The chapter titled 'The Pretenders' began ponderously:

*How little we know about background, and yet how vital is background in understanding the mission, the ability, the ambition of a man. Can it be possible that a simple actor from Stratford, with scant knowledge of philosophy or classics, of medicine, theology or astronomy, could have penned England's greatest literature? Or is it more likely that another candidate, with reasons to hide his own identity, authored this great achievement? Does the true Shakespeare exist under a cloak of secrecy?*

She had a notebook and pencil beside her, and as she went along she made marks and corrections, just as she had in her brief stint of copy-editing after university. It was a reflex action – no more – but all the time, Hubert Newman's dedication rang in her head.

'To Stella, spotter of mistakes.'

What had he meant by that? Mere grammatical inconsistencies, or something deeper? Was she hunting for what the manuscript contained, or what it didn't? She focused harder on the text.

*Of all the questions surrounding the legacy of Shakespeare throughout the centuries, the subject of his identity is the one which has occupied scholars the most. Shakespeare's plays are filled with actors in disguise, with swapped or hidden identities, and with things that are not what they seem. Yet this tendency does not stop at the plays. From almost the moment that he finished writing, alternative candidates have been vouchsafed for the playwright himself.*

*This obsession is not confined to the ignorant. Many reputable scholars have toyed with their own theories as to the playwright's true identity. The lauded novelist Henry James once said, 'I am sort of haunted by the conviction that the divine William is the biggest and most successful fraud ever practised on a patient world.' Such luminaries as Sigmund Freud, Charlie Chaplin and Mark Twain have joined him in that belief.*

*Perhaps we should not rush to judgement. All history asks us to question our assumptions. How do we know what we think we know? After all, it cannot be denied that numerous Renaissance writers habitually adopted pen names or concealed their true identities.*

Stella struggled on. The handwriting was dense and slanted, sloping forward like a mass of black reeds flattened in the wind. After the first introductory paragraphs there followed a series of subheadings devoted to the candidates who had been vouchsafed as the true Shakespeare. In all, eighty-seven potential Shakespeares had been volunteered to date, the most popular being Francis Bacon, the Elizabethan philosopher and statesman for whose potential authorship an entire society had been formed.

Others favoured the Jacobean playwright Christopher Marlowe, who, Newman pointed out, could not have written plays dated 1614 because he was killed in a brawl in 1593. There followed the seventeenth Earl of Oxford, Edward de Vere. De Vere was advanced for his aristocratic heritage, which would have enabled him to travel to all those places – Verona, Padua, Venice – in which the plays were set. But he died in 1604, which meant that he could not have written *Lear*, *Macbeth*, or another eight of the plays.

Further paragraphs were devoted to the Elizabethan diplomat, Henry Neville, and William Stanley, the sixth Earl of Derby. Lancelot Andrews, the cleric, Richard Burbage, the Elizabethan actor, and even a woman known only as the Dark Lady.

The chapter continued on a consensual note.

*The authorship question is a perfectly credible one and there is no shame in advancing alternative candidates as the playwright. In every society there are those who seek to hide their identity because of what may happen if they were publicly unmasked. Some may shield their true persona because they are engaged in a great mission and do not want to be distracted by public acclaim. Others may fear public misunderstanding of the ends that they pursue.*

At this point, Newman's tone sharpened.

*Yet in studying the history of this controversy, we must also be aware of forgeries and deliberate deceptions. Of figures who are advanced for reasons that are far removed from scholarship. There are, among the throng of scholarly contenders, a number of people who have been promoted for reasons of cunning or gain. Like the Dark Lady, they are false, and should be denounced. One might point to Green, Byrd and West as part of this masquerade. The reputation of these pretenders does not deserve to endure.*

The final chapter, 'The Stratfordian', set out Newman's reasons for believing in the authenticity of the Stratford Shakespeare, 'the glove maker's son' and concluded:

*I will not be the first to venture that the Shakespeare authorship question resembles a detective story. Perhaps, my readers will think, that is why it appealed to this author. I could not possibly demur. But I hope that, like any detective, I have provided evidence that points to the truth.*

Deflated, Stella sat back, squared the pages and tidied the edges. She had an obscure sense of failure.

Once again, she recalled the dedication.

'To Stella, spotter of mistakes.'

What mistakes? There weren't too many – apart from the elementary mistake of thinking this book might attract the attention of a nation on the brink of war. Even if the rest of the manuscript reappeared, publishing it was only likely to disappoint Newman's fans, who would surely be keen to read anything he wrote and would no doubt find the book a terrific let-down, just as Sidonie had.

Stella had noticed the odd misspelling and winced at the strangely pompous, leaden writing which was so unlike the shorter, choppier prose of Newman's thrillers. But on his central thesis as to whether Shakespeare was the writer of his plays, she felt no better qualified to judge than before.

A clatter on the street outside made her jump. It was not only Newman's ponderous tone that had made it hard to concentrate; all the time she was reading, her skin was crawling with tension. She got up and looked outside again and noticed that the young man who had been smoking outside the opposite block had disappeared – perhaps he was on his way to apprehend her. She heard a rustle on the stairs, which was probably the upstairs neighbour passing, but what if an intruder returned to the flat now, while she was there? How could she possibly defend herself?

She realized there was one person she needed to find far more urgently than the real William Shakespeare.

That person was Harry Fox.

# CHAPTER 31

Harry ambled across to the bandstand in Clapham Common. The weather was dull and brooding. A suffocating bank of cloud pressed down on the city. Above, planes passed in the sky. Not far away, anti-aircraft searchlights were being set up and the air was cut by the bark of a sergeant major directing a band of troops implementing civil defence measures. These took the form of trenches in which were sunk steel-lined air raid shelters complete with narrow wooden benches and topped with a roof, which was then covered over again with a layer of earth.

He looked across to where the soldiers were digging. Weren't the politicians all doing the same, in effect? Digging away with hope and crossed fingers, as though they might actually shelter from the grim matter approaching? Harry had no time for the news, but he had heard the Prime Minister's sepulchral tones on the wireless that evening.

'How horrible, fantastic, incredible it is that we should be digging trenches and trying on gas masks here because of a quarrel in a faraway country between people of whom we know nothing. It seems still more impossible that a quarrel which has already been settled in principle should be the subject of war.'

If Chamberlain was saying it on the wireless, it had to be coming. Even if he was saying he was reluctant to fight. All military personnel had been ordered to return to their barracks. The navy had been mobilized and the French were manning the Maginot Line.

And if war was coming, perhaps Flint was right when he said that this whole business with the Communists needed to end. Whatever B4a had told him about the Red List continuing, surely the prospect of a Nazi invasion was infinitely more important than an ideological conflict waged in the minds of artists and writers. When had a poet ever posed any serious threat? Let alone the poets Harry followed, with their patched overcoats and down-at-heel shoes and earnest literary evenings. He didn't fancy Auden's chances in a pub brawl, let alone a world war.

If Harry was right, whatever B4a might say, the entire Red List unit would shortly be wound up, the Watchers dispersed, and he would have to focus on other employment opportunities.

He might even join up, if his curriculum vitae did not preclude that.

The prospect of war brought a surge of guilt and the face of Stella Fry, never far from his thoughts, came to mind.

He had neither seen nor heard from her since he urged her to travel to Vienna and provided her with the means to do so. Was she still on the Continent, or had she returned? Was she in danger? The previous evening he had visited her flat in Oakley Street and waited as the doorbell echoed emptily. If she was back, she might have gone to his office, or at least telephoned, but he had not been there since the assault. He had been hunkered down in his basement, licking his wounds and nursing a pounding headache that no amount of Scotch seemed to dissipate.

The truth was, he had been hoping that he and Stella might really make a team. They complemented each other – his experience and her attributes. It was all very well using rough diamonds like Malone, but Stella Fry was a cut above. Her Oxford education and refinement were as good as a skeleton key and a crowbar in gaining access to elite establishments. He had already begun thinking what they could accomplish together.

God knows what would become of that partnership now. The entire venture was his responsibility and if he didn't find her soon, he would go out there himself and look for her. How could he ever have put her at risk for the sake of a dead man?

He passed the bandstand, with its pretty Victorian zinc cupola and cast-iron balustrade. It could only be a matter of time before it was dismantled, like everything else, in favour of Spitfires. A small crowd had gathered to watch the trench digging but Harry averted his eyes. Even now, he could barely look at a trench without a shudder.

The usual place was next to a playground, furnished with a slide and a couple of swings. There was also a climbing frame, like an upturned colander, on which infants could exercise their tiny biceps, and a rusting metal merry-go-round where they could dizzy themselves before falling off and scraping their knees. This playground had first been used for assignations with a particular informer; a clerk at the War Ministry who was a covert member of the British Communist Party. One of the department secretaries would visit the playground with a couple of children and the clerk would call the group across to offer the kids sweets from a tin of Quality Street. The children would pick out their sweets and the secretary would pick out a film canister containing intelligence information.

Next to the playground stood a council noticeboard, pinned with messages, both hectoring and municipal. Instructions about dogs and not walking on the flower beds and asking for civil defence volunteers. Beside the noticeboard was a litter bin.

The location of the dead letter box was critical. It needed to be the kind of place that could be visited for seconds and emptied in a way that was entirely inconspicuous.

Two seven-year-olds were kicking a ball listlessly as their mothers sat on a bench gossiping. It was not until the boys began squabbling about a goal that the mothers reluctantly detached themselves and ushered the children away. Harry squatted down and slid his hand on the underside of the bin. He felt around for a second, then detached and retrieved a half-torn packet of Senior Service cigarettes. His own brand. This personal touch from B4a made him smile, despite himself. She had not let him down.

He pocketed them, then paid threepence and sat in one of the hard little chairs around the bandstand, before taking out the packet and its contents. There were three cigarettes in the packet, but he knew better than to smoke them. He unrolled each one, and it was the third that contained the message.

*Anton Vladimir Sokolov. Born St Petersburg 1890. Ran a tea importing business in Charing Cross. NKVD officer. Recalled to Moscow and executed in the Lubyanka May 1937.*

He looked down at the flimsy cigarette paper and read it again. Harry didn't like it when unexpected facts turned up. No detective novelist would stand for it. There was, of course, no suggestion that Hubert Newman had any knowledge of his friend's true identity. The two men (he found himself hoping desperately) might have come together through a mutual love of fine tea. And besides, the man had died more than a year ago, so he couldn't possibly have had a hand in Newman's killing.

All the same, it was disquieting.

He rolled the cigarette up once more and lit it.

The little crowd that had gathered to watch the digging

were drifting away. A woman with a pram passed, followed by a local newspaper photographer who had been taking pictures of the digging, lugging his case. Harry got up and walked westwards, almost too preoccupied to bother checking for a tail.

He took the bus to Hammersmith and walked down the Fulham Palace Road. Children were trailing home from school, happy and chattering, oblivious to current events, because who cared about the news when there were conkers to collect. Someone was practising the piano – sending the scales up and down again, over and over, in a reassuring rhythm that seemed to suggest that this routine of quotidian homecoming might carry on forever, uninterrupted.

He passed a church advertising a service for peace, an opportunity for parishioners to pray that the Czechs would abandon their obstinacy and accept Hitler's ultimatum, and on a mad impulse he stepped inside. In the soft gloom, flickering stubs of candles were ranked along the walls on iron grilles, and up at the altar a service of some kind was taking place, voices tangling indistinctly like a low, confidential conversation. Presumably they were asking God to arrange a peaceful compromise, and yet surely any deity worth his salt would agree that Hitler had questions to answer. Harry considered lighting a candle, but changed his mind on the basis that it would take more than candles to ward off the darkness ahead.

He sat in a pew, head bowed, as the violet and ruby light coming through the stained glass windows painted his hands blood red. He looked at the long, slender fingers that were capable of such surprising force, as if seeing them for the first time. He wasn't praying – he and religion had parted ways a long time ago. His faith was buried somewhere in Flanders, along with several of his friends, but the words of the liturgy still had the power to thrill him. He supposed people turned to religion the same way they turned to detective fiction, seeking refuge in a narrative where someone had already sorted out the ending and tied up all the loose threads. Where bad people were punished and the innocent vindicated, and detectives, like saints, performed their magic tricks.

He stared down at the tessellations on the tiled floor, as though they were pieces of information that might re-arrange themselves at random into some kind of rational explanation. He was thinking of what B4a had said about his father. Stanley Fox had liked church. He had cherished a deep love of the King James Bible, not to mention the prayer book, and he would declaim his favourite passages as he walked around the house. 'For as much as it hath pleased Almighty God . . . In the midst of Life we are in Death.' He had the manner of an Old Testament prophet, even if his morals sprang from the Bible's darker parts.

A padre of some kind, dressed in a black tunic, had reg-istered his presence and was approaching in an attitude of benevolence.

Horrified, Harry stumbled from the pew and hurried out.

★

To his surprise, Joan met him at her door. She didn't comment on his black eye, perhaps because her own face was a mess of tears.

'The school says the kids are going to be evacuated. He won't have to leave, will he, Harry? You'll do what you can to stop it? He's all I've got.'

Without thinking, he enfolded her in his arms.

'Nothing's certain.'

'They sent us a letter. Because we're near the river, we're at greater risk. But Jack wouldn't want to go and live with strangers. He'd want to be with me, whatever.'

From upstairs, Harry could hear the sound of Jack moving about. Although every word of their conversation would be audible through the flimsy floorboards, it was not like Jack to intervene. While he hated to think of his mother suffering, the boy would endure whatever was necessary. Possibly, because he was a resilient lad, he might even welcome a change of scene. Living in a cramped little house with only his mother and her nerves for company was no picnic.

Joan said, 'He's ten now. He's not little any more. He's got more wit about him than anyone. Can't you do something?'

'Think of it like a boarding school. Rich people, they send their kids off to boarding school and they think it's doing them some good. They pay the earth, don't see them for months at a time but the kids come back, don't they? They might send him to a farm. Cows and sheep. He likes animals, doesn't he?'

Fleshing out this fantasy only prompted a fresh shudder of sobs.

'I won't let him go. He's all I've got. You have contacts, Harry, don't you?'

Then, more ominously, she added, 'You owe me that, at least.'

'It probably won't happen.'

It probably would. They said there might be half a million casualties on the first day of bombing and the country had been divided into zones – Evacuation, Neutral and Reception – and he had heard that children might be evacuated much further afield – to Canada, Australia, New Zealand or America even. There was a plan that kids should not be parted from their siblings, but Jack didn't have a brother or sister so he would be on his own. He wanted to say to Joan, be thankful Jack is only ten. The kid might be sent to the countryside, but that was infinitely better than being sent to war.

'What if he's given a new family? What if he loves them more than us?'

'Now you're being hysterical.'

Harry detached himself and moved into the kitchen. Joan resumed her position at the stove where she was frying something sweet in a pan.

'I'm making apple dumplings. They're his favourite. Want to stay for supper tonight?'

He shook his head.

'I've got a job on later.'

She poured a cup of tea and pushed it towards him, strong and malty.

'Tea and toast, then. To keep you going.'

He considered telling Joan what he had learned about their father and his work with the Security Service. It would give her something else to focus on, and the revelations about Stanley Fox might go some way to recoup a little pride in their family tree. Heaven knows there was little enough to go around.

Instead, he stared down at his teacup – an incongruous piece of blue and white Meissen that his father had brought back from his travels and which outclassed all the rest of their crockery – and peered at the tea leaves. It was as good a way as any other just then to work out the future. But the tea leaves looked a lot like a crooked cross, so he got up and emptied them down the sink.

At that moment his nephew clattered down the stairs, brown eyes bright as chestnuts.

'Tell you what, lad. Why don't we go down to the allotment?'

'It's late,' said Joan, automatically. 'He has his homework.'

'Let me go, Mum. We can pick the last of the raspberries.'

The allotment was down towards the river, via a narrow mud path bordered with bramble bushes. Harry loved it there. The patches of ground, so carefully cultivated, transformed each year from wintery rows of leafless branches into fat quilts of summer abundance: runner beans, potatoes, onions and leeks. Even now, at the end of September, tomatoes and cucumbers were still bursting from their plots, and over-grown marrows were writhing crazily beyond their borders. Some of the neighbouring growers had indulged themselves with dahlias, blazing showers of violet and orange and pink in the Indian summer sun.

His own patch was more neglected than the others, but still he came whenever he could, hacking away at bindweed with a fork, setting the canes for the berries and turning the earth as though it represented something more than mere London clay. This was England to him. It was of this mud that he had been dreaming when he staggered through the trenches at Passchendaele.

A pair of pigeons whirred up with a clatter of wings as they approached.

'Damn things. Looking for berries.'

'Mum's worried they'll evacuate me.'

'What about you? Are you worried?'

'Dunno. It might be an adventure. What do you think, Uncle Harry?'

He looked down at Jack. His coat was too small, and tight across his chest, and his socks sagged to his ankles. A smear of ink was visible on his cheek and his bitten nails were grimy but he exuded an air of irrepressible excitement. Harry experienced a jolt of what could only be explained as paternal feeling. If the boy was billeted with another family, they would be lucky to get him.

'Yeah, I think it will be an adventure. If it happens. And

most boys like adventures. But just make sure you always look after your mum. You know that, don't you?'

He nodded.

A few raspberries remained, clinging like stubborn drops of blood to the withered cane, and Jack began to pick them. Harry smoked and massaged the bruise on his face that his nephew had not asked about. The child's tact was just one of the things that made him seem older than his years.

'I've got another book for you, by the way. A Hubert Newman.'

'Is it a good one?'

'It's his last one. *A Shot Across the Bows*. It's set on a transatlantic liner. A wealthy man who has made his fortune in guano—'

'What's guano?'

'Bird droppings.'

'Eeew.'

'Anyhow, this man is British but he's travelling to America because . . .'

Because the businessman thought war was coming and would decimate his homeland. This motive was implied, rather than stated, but Harry hoped that Jack would not understand the allusion.

'Because he wants to make a new life. But before he can, he's found dead in a deckchair.'

'Don't tell me who did it!'

'I won't. But I promise you'll never guess the murder weapon.'

'That's the bit I like best. The murder weapon. They're always good. I wonder how he chooses them.'

At that moment, an idea flitted through Harry's mind and he froze, the way a bird pecking on the earth freezes, hearing a whisper on the wind.

He would catch that idea, if only it would stand still.

They returned with a jam jar of raspberries, tomatoes wrapped in newspaper and a string bag of windfall apples. To his immense surprise, Joan reached up and gave him a kiss.

'Look after yourself, Harry, won't you? Come over at the weekend. I'll make something nice. Casserole. You like that, don't you?'

He went upstairs and said goodnight to the boy, then headed for the Tube, buying a bar of Cadbury's Dairy Milk from the machine on the platform which gave him the opportunity to check for any shadows, before he headed back to town.

# CHAPTER 32

The charm of Luigi's Café and Bar was, to say the least, understated. London soot blurred the signage above the door and the green paint on the door was cracked. But unlike Stella's previous visit, when Harry Fox had accosted her on the way back from Evelyn's wake, it was comparatively busy, occupied by groups of men smoking acrid cigarettes and conversing in low murmurs. Behind the swing doors to the kitchen, the sound of loud Italian melded with the clash of cooking pans, and the smell of coffee and tomato sauce mingled in the air.

After trying Harry Fox's office again, and getting no answer, Stella went to the only other place she could think of. Behind a glass counter piled with sandwiches and buns, the proprietor, Luigi, in white apron and bow tie, was conducting a dispute with an underling, a wiry, dark-eyed man who was holding a saucepan.

'I no believe you lived in Italy! You have never cook pasta.'

'I do it exactly as you say!'

'It's rubbish. This spaghetti is as soft as a sponge. It falls apart in the water. It should be *al dente. Al dente!* I might have known a Pole would boil it to death.'

As Stella approached, Luigi's entire demeanour changed.

'Forgive me, miss. He is a refugee, I take him in from the kindness of my heart and he can cook nothing but sausages. Pork and cabbage, that's all these people know.'

The refugee smiled. It was clear that the pair were friends.

'I wondered. Have you seen Mr Fox? Mr Harry Fox?'

'But of course. Mr Fox is one of my best customers. He's here all the time. If you sit here, he'll be in, I'm sure.'

She ordered a cup of tea in a thick white china cup, and a bun, placed the manuscript in front of her, and waited.

Fifteen minutes later the bell clanged, and the door opened with a draught, sending a sheaf of foolscap fluttering from the Formica tabletop. Stella bent quickly to collect it up from the grimy floor and when she straightened up a familiar figure in a grey trilby was looming over her.

'Stella!'

'Harry Fox.'

It was hard to say which of them was more shocked, as both were so adept at concealing their emotions. But Harry froze, as though he could not quite believe his eyes, and stood staring at her, until she cleared the manuscript aside and motioned for him to sit down.

'When did you get back?'

'Two days ago.'

She peered at him more closely.

'What happened to your face?'

Harry slid into the seat opposite.

'It doesn't matter. You're here now. And safe, thank God. Tell me everything.'

He sat, with quiet intensity, as she related her journey. She told him of her days in Vienna, and the sense all the time that she was being watched. About her discovery of Roland Finch, their late-night conversation and his revelation that he was a Communist. How he had suddenly disappeared when the soldiers approached, vowing that she would never see him again. And claiming that there were others who she would never find.

'Finch guessed that I had come to find him. He was certain that it had to do with Hubert Newman. I had a copy of Newman's novel in my bag. I was so careless.'

'What did he tell you? About Newman?'

'He knew him. They'd known each other from their student days. They'd knocked around in the same literary circles. And Harry . . . this will surprise you. Finch said that Newman had been born in Vienna. He wasn't English at all. He was Austrian.'

'Austrian? That can't be true!'

Yet his astonishment was pierced by a memory. The jagged Modernist paintings in Newman's flat which had seemed so out of place amid the typical chintzy British decor.

'It's true. His family were Jewish. They were called

Neumann. When he was thirteen his father decided they should move to England, and they changed the family name.'

Harry shook his head, trying to take it in.

'He never talked about it, and by the time he was an adult, nobody knew. Finch said, "*Neumann became Newman. Changing a name can do so much. People rarely look below the surface.*"'

'So what about Newman's allegations? His visit to Oxford? What did Finch say about that?'

'That's the thing.'

She hesitated, eyes down, fiddling with her cup. Then she looked up.

'I'm sorry, Harry. I didn't get a chance to ask him. While we were talking, as I told you, some German soldiers came past and he walked away. I tried to follow but he had completely disappeared.'

She hurried on.

'As soon as I got back, I tried to find you. I went to your office. You weren't there and I realized I had no idea where you lived. Then I had another thought. I went to Evelyn's brother, Tom. He works in the Foreign Office and he knows Frederick Lindemann. And, you'll never believe, yesterday he took me with him to Chartwell.'

Harry's eyes widened.

'Churchill's home?'

'Yes.'

Sitting there in the café, with its fraying net curtains and cracked tiled floor, it was almost impossible to believe that just twenty-four hours previously she had been walking through the grand surroundings of Churchill's stately mansion.

'Lindemann was there. They play tennis together. I got the chance to speak to him, just briefly, and I explained about going to Vienna and meeting Roland Finch. He was shocked, but he told me something in confidence. It was about Ernst Grunfeld and the construction of a weapon.'

She could not convey the expression on Lindemann's face. The mixture of utmost gravity and dawning horror.

They fell silent as Luigi appeared and slipped a cup of coffee onto the table. Then Stella said, 'There's another thing. It sounds crazy, but the manuscript I was supposed to type up has disappeared. It has simply vanished from the flat.'

'The Shakespeare thing?' said Harry, as though he had already forgotten it.

'*Masquerade*, yes.'

'The one he dedicated to you.'

She indicated the pile of paper on the table beside her.

'When I say it's disappeared, the fact is, I had kept these last two chapters in my suitcase. I meant to read them on the train but I forgot about them. I was so certain Hubert Newman wanted to send a message. I kept thinking of the dedication. "To Stella, spotter of mistakes."'

'Did you find a mistake?'

She shrugged, despondently.

'Nothing at all, bar the odd comma. This chapter, "The

Pretenders", is just a succession of names of people who have been advanced as the real Shakespeare. Marlow, de Vere, Neville, Bacon. You know, all well-known people.'

'If you say so.'

'Some people claim the real Shakespeare was a famous person, or an aristocrat who wanted to keep their real identity covered up. And then there's a little bit about other candidates who were suggested for fraudulent reasons and should be denounced.'

Harry frowned at his coffee.

'Fraudulent reasons?'

'For profit. Or to suit some hidden agenda.'

'Read me that part. The part about the frauds.'

She turned back to the front page of Part Two, and rifled again through the chapter.

*Like the Dark Lady, they are false, and should be denounced. One might point to Green, Byrd and West as part of this masquerade. The reputation of these pretenders does not deserve to endure.*

'Most of the alternative candidates are totally plausible, and suggested in good faith. But Newman says some men were advanced as the true Shakespeare because people wanted to flatter their ancestors or lay claim to some renown they didn't deserve—'

Harry interrupted.

'Who are they?'

'Who?'

'These men. Green, Byrd and West. Are they well known too?'

'I've never heard of them. But then I'm not familiar with the minor characters of Elizabethan literature because I studied languages, and although an Oxford language degree does encompass a certain amount of literature . . .'

But he was waving her expertise away, as though she had never spent nine hours in the Examination Schools sweating over papers on Goethe and Dante and the *Chanson de Roland*.

'Newman changed his name, you said. Do you think, maybe, he changed other people's names too?'

'What do you mean?'

'In my line of business that's standard procedure. Codes, pseudonyms. I've had more false identities than I've had hot dinners. Never take a name at face value. Never use a real name if you can help it. This man Green. Who was Green? Was he a genuine historical figure?'

Stella paused for a moment, then sat up with a jolt.

'Grun!'

'What?'

'Grun is German for Green. Could Newman be referring to Grunfeld?'

Suddenly her mind was racing like an encryption machine, full of potential codes waiting to be combined.

'And Byrd. It could be Bird. Finch is a bird. That must be Roland Finch.'

The blood was draining from her face to her rapidly

beating heart. These, surely, were the mistakes she had been asked to spot.

Harry said, 'If Byrd is Roland Finch and Green is Ernst Grunfeld, then who's the third? Who's West?'

Stella tried the word out in her mind.

'I just don't know.'

'What if you translate it to German? Or French?'

'Westen? Ouest? It doesn't mean anything to me.'

'West. West.' He stared out of the windows at the bustle of the Soho street outside.

'W.E.S.T.' She clicked through the letters like the dials of a safe. 'Maybe each letter stands for something.'

Harry glanced up at the wall, where, in an effort to impart a sophisticated, international air to the establishment, Luigi had hung a framed poster of Italy, publicizing the South Italian Railway.

'South,' he murmured. 'South, East, North, West. The points of the compass.'

The breath caught in her throat. Impulsively she reached out a hand to his.

'*Our dear friend Aubrey North. Aubrey is very close to Churchill.*'

'North. Aubrey North!'

She felt a gulp, a twist of nerves. The knowledge that was flowering inside her was terrifying.

'And he is? Remind me.'

Stella glanced around. The people on the tables around them seemed absorbed in their own conversations. Murmured discussions, in a whole Continent of languages. There was no sign that any of them were eavesdropping but all the same, she lowered her voice yet further.

'Aubrey North is a senior official in the Foreign Office. He works closely with Winston Churchill. He's the ultimate insider. He has access to all kinds of confidential documents. He's been channelling secret information to Churchill on Britain's military preparedness for war. Our defences and our air capacity and so on. The information's fed by people in other ministries who are worried that we're not in a fit state to take on Hitler. North processes the documents and takes them to Churchill and then Lindemann boils down all the facts and figures so that Churchill can understand and make use of them.'

'How do you know all this?'

'Tom Lamont works for him.'

'And you think Hubert Newman is suggesting that Aubrey North is not all he seems?'

Stella's head was pounding with the implications. Ernst Grunfeld, Roland Finch, Aubrey North. A trio of pretenders taking part in a masquerade, who needed to be denounced.

'I'd say he's suggesting that Aubrey North is a Communist. A Soviet sympathizer operating at the heart of government. Do you see what this means?'

Harry took off the Himmler spectacles and rubbed his eyes.

'Harry? Tell me. What do you think?'

He paused longer, then eventually, with slow deliberation

he took out a cigarette, found his lighter and lit it. He pulled the ashtray towards him and sighed.

'It sounds far-fetched. But even if it is true, who's going to believe any of it? There's no hard evidence. Codes in a manuscript. It makes sense to me, but I promise you nobody has the slightest interest in any of this. They won't listen to us.'

'But if it's right, what Hubert Newman says—'

'What exactly is he saying? That these men need to be denounced? Roland Finch has already denounced himself. Ernst Grunfeld has vanished. And good luck with suggesting that one of Churchill's closest associates is a crypto Communist. Whose word do we have on it? A detective novelist? Someone whose entire livelihood involved dreaming up conspiracies and plots?'

'That was exactly Frederick Lindemann's response. He called Hubert Newman a cheap thriller writer. But Harry, if you could have seen him yesterday. He apologized for not taking me seriously.'

'And who is making these allegations, apart from a dead man? Me, who was dishonourably dismissed from my job, or you, who is, with respect, an unknown young woman who might be said to possess a vivid imagination? And if Newman really wanted to level an accusation, the question remains, why not go straight to the police instead of scrambling it in code inside a book?'

'He did approach Professor Lindemann.'

'With allegations against Ernst Grunfeld. But why not the others? Why not Finch and North?'

Slowly she said, 'Remind me what his last novel was called?'

'*A Shot Across the Bows.*'

'Maybe that's what he was launching. A shot against the bows. Or maybe he was sending a message. He wrote this before he decided to approach Lindemann. This must have been a precaution, in case something happened to him.'

'Try telling that to Scotland Yard.'

The sleepless night and the coffee were conspiring to make her heart race. Stella's dismay was obliterated by a rising tide of anger.

'I don't understand, Harry. You were the one who was so keen to investigate. And now that we actually have found something, you're talking it down.'

'I'm playing devil's advocate.'

'Is that what you call it?'

'It's essential, in any investigation, to probe the case.'

'Really? Is it? What kind of detective are you? You said you should trust hunches and this is more than a hunch. This is direct evidence in black and white.'

'In code.'

'I'm starting to see why you lost your job.'

'You don't know anything about why I lost my job.'

'Perhaps it had something to do with failing to see what's staring you in the face.'

'All I'm saying is, every allegation needs to be—'

But Stella was jumping up, grabbing the pile of papers and stuffing them into her satchel.

'Where are you going?'

'To find someone who's prepared to take this seriously.'

'Stella. Wait . . .'

But already the door was closing behind her.

# CHAPTER 33

You notice a lot of things when your body is flooded with adrenaline. Tiny details. It had rained again, and Stella was viscerally aware of the specks of water on her skin. The oily rainbows in puddles. The mist rising off the paving. Everything around pressed in on her densely, packed with sensation and information, as she hurried out of the café and through the streets.

Shaftesbury Avenue was swelling with early evening crowds, as though Londoners sensed that this was their last opportunity for relaxation and enjoyment and were determined to take full advantage of it. In her state of hyper alertness, the bright promises of the advertisement hoardings blazed into her brain. 'Bourn-Vita Tonight Makes Tomorrow Just Right'. 'Lifebuoy Soap'. 'Boots Number 7: Loveliness That Defeats the Years'. They summoned a world where women were always beautiful and stockings never laddered and everyone slept soundly.

That world had never felt more fantastical.

The feeling she had had for days of being observed was stronger than ever. It buzzed in her ears like lift music. It sang in her blood.

Stella had always believed there were more than five senses. Who said that the human experience should be confined to just five? Harry Fox had said that she had intuition, and she felt it now – the sixth sense that raised the hairs on the back of your neck and made you alert to something that your animal body knew before your mind could register it. An awareness of a world beyond that human faculties could barely perceive.

She had no earthly evidence, yet still she knew. The person who had killed Hubert Newman was on her trail. She might have expected the greatest peril lay in Vienna, but instead it was right here, on the streets of London.

Despite the oppressive weather, pedestrians clogged Whitehall as they had for weeks. Some were laying flowers at the base of the Cenotaph. Others already had gas masks slung over their shoulders. A workman on a ladder was painting over the windows of an office building with black paint. Outside Horse Guards an anti-aircraft battery had been installed, with the muzzles of the guns pointing menacingly at the sky. The tree trunks in the park were being whitewashed in preparation for a blackout, and a pair of Coventry Climax fire trailers and a couple of portable water pumps had been parked in front of Downing Street.

She wove through the jostling crowds, around a municipal truck unloading sandbags, and turned into King Charles Street, heading for the Foreign Office. She needed to find Tom Lamont.

The interior was as serene as a cathedral after the bustle outside. As she entered the forecourt, she glimpsed a long, cadaverous figure whom she recognized, with a shock, as Lord Halifax, the Foreign Secretary, surrounded by a retinue of young men. His arrival prompted a slight commotion in the lobby which enabled her to slip past and follow the same route as before, up the same stairs and along a corridor until she came to the office on the top floor. Tom had said he was burning the midnight oil every night, and while it was nowhere near midnight, she prayed that she would find him there.

The outer office was empty. The secretaries had already gone home, leaving their typewriters shrouded in their covers. Stella opened the door to find a room with drawn blinds, whose dusky gloom was lit only by a green shaded lamp on the desk. Tom's eyes were down, his chin propped in his hand. A cigarette smouldered in the ashtray.

'I have to speak to you. Urgently.'

He leaped up when he saw her.

'Stella, what on earth is the matter?'

He came across and put an arm round her.

'You're shaking.'

She put the envelope containing the manuscript on his desk.

'It might be nothing, but can we talk?'

'I'm afraid it's not a good time. I'm about to have a meeting with the permanent undersecretary. Tomorrow maybe? I have lunch with an absolute bore at the Travellers but after that?'

'No. It needs to be now. It's important.'

'I can see that . . .'

But even as he was speaking, a figure appeared in the doorway.

# CHAPTER 34

Because he could think of no alternative, Harry went back to work.

Diana Sowerby was attending an early evening party in an art gallery in Chelsea. The gallery's long glass windows spilled light and laughter and the soft chink of glasses into the King's Road. Watching from his habitual berth in the shadows, Harry was overcome with an unfamiliar urge to go inside. Just for once, he wanted to be among people, enfolded in chatter and meaningless conversation – anything to distract himself while he processed Stella Fry's disclosures.

In the window, on a gilt stand, one of the gallery's collection of old masters was displayed, and moving nearer, he made out a Bruegelesque scene of a medieval village, whose inhabitants were celebrating the harvest. The painting teemed with life. Its centre ground was taken up by a party, where heavy-footed peasants danced to the sound of a fiddle and others raised tankards around a bonfire; further away, children fed geese, lads tended pigs and women milked cows. In the foreground, a thief made off with a sheep across his shoulders and women gossiped around a cooking pot. Tucked away in the far-left corner, however, in a barn stuffed with staves of newly threshed corn, a torture was underway. Two guards were supervising the dismemberment of a man – a villain, no doubt – while the rest of the village carried on their cheerful way regardless. At the sight of this horror so close to the partying peasants, and so unheeded, Harry felt a sudden, terrible recognition.

Thus, he almost didn't notice when Diana Sowerby emerged unexpectedly early and slipped into a telephone box some way down the street. After a brief call, she pushed the cubicle door closed and set off briskly on foot, northwards, across the Fulham Road and up Onslow Gardens towards Kensington. Harry followed.

She was lovelier than ever that evening, with the purposeful, flushed air of a woman en route to her lover, as Harry felt sure she was. For form's sake, he had changed his regular jacket and was wearing the new trilby designed to obscure as much as possible his black eye. At times he came so close to her that he could smell a trace of her sweet, musky perfume; he was amazed that she didn't sense him, but the actress seemed lost in her own world. She wore a light, shot-silk coat of peacock blue, with a matching hat and a crocodile clutch bag clamped beneath her arm, and she was distracted, barely conscious of the people on the street around her. She glanced repeatedly at her Cartier watch, as if late for an engagement.

If she was meeting a lover, then who could blame her? What man on earth would not be better than Walter Heap, fat as a slug in his Fleet Street boardroom, plotting a divorce that would ruin her? Beautiful actresses and rich men went together like a horse and carriage, of course, but when they came apart, the men always found themselves a new horse. Men like Heap invariably came out top, and on the way there they trampled everything else underfoot, be it their marriage, their job or their country.

The thought of Heap, and the lingering impression of the painting, merged in Harry's mind, and before he could catch it, his memory was off and running towards his own personal station of the cross.

It was Sunday, October 4th 1936. The 'Mrs Simpson Problem' or the 'Romance of the Century', depending on whether you were British or American, was gathering pace. The King's private secretary, Clive Wigram, had resigned after Edward had left one too many classified documents lying around like copies of *Tatler* in a dentist's waiting room. The Prime Minister, Stanley Baldwin, had been heard calling Mrs Simpson a 'hard-hearted bitch'. MI5 was tapping the phones of all involved. The Watchers were working overtime. The surveillance operation was to be cranked up to provide as much material as possible for those politicians hoping to engineer an abdication.

Harry had been assigned to follow Mrs Simpson's dressmaker, Anna Wolkoff, a White Russian émigré and fervent anti-Semite who had visited Germany several times in the company of Rudolf Hess and a bevy of other Nazi leaders. MI5 already had her under surveillance as a suspected German spy, but Harry was there because she was a close friend of the King's lover.

His instructions were to follow the mark to the East End, where some kind of demonstration was planned.

The briefing barely did it justice. What Harry found was eight thousand members of the British Union of Fascists, led by Oswald Mosley, massing to celebrate the Union's fourth birthday. They were readying to march through Stepney, Whitechapel and Wapping – all areas heavily populated by Jews. The locals had formed a petition, calling for the march to be banned, but the home secretary had given the go-ahead and seven thousand police officers were on standby to clear the route.

When Mosley arrived, in his new uniform of military jacket, cap with insignia and jackboots, the atmosphere was already feverish. Men with brick-red faces and arms bunched with muscle, straight out of *Oliver Twist*, were handing out leaflets proclaiming 'Oswald Mosley, Tomorrow We Live!' Yet the fascists were vastly outnumbered by many thousands more protestors who had massed for a counter-demonstration. Crowds ten deep lined the road, fists raised, shouting 'Mosley Shall Not Pass!' Each side had already set up casualty stations for the likely victims. The police had panic in their eyes.

Harry understood. This was the district the refugees came to when they made it out of Poland and Lithuania and Germany, escaping from a hundred years of bad history with nothing but the clothes they stood up in. This place was a sanctuary from all the thugs in uniforms who wanted to make their lives hell. So they were damned if they were going to let a different set of thugs in different uniforms set about them here.

At three thirty in the afternoon, Mosley arrived in an open-topped sports car, escorted by Blackshirt motorcyclists, and proceeded along Royal Mint Street. A column of men nearly half a mile long began to follow. Amid the sea of people, marbles were thrown beneath the hooves of a police horse and it was badly spooked, rearing up and wheeling around as its rider attempted to keep control. In the ensuing commotion, Harry lost the mark. Frantic, he shoved his way eastwards through the throng towards Cable Street.

Cable Street was a dingy street in Wapping so decayed that Hitler's bombs might as well have already fallen. Across its narrow strait an army of anti-fascists, trade unionists, Communists, anarchists, Jews, Irish and socialists had erected barricades which the police were now attempting to clear. As Harry thrust his way onwards, in the thick of the crowd a violent scuffle broke out and a pair of mounted policemen advanced, dispensing furious and random blows from their truncheons.

To escape, he diverted sideways into a narrow alley, a strip of slimy cobbles strewn with litter and stinking of urine and waste. It was there, to his astonishment, that he ran slap into a man he recognized. His brother-in-law, Ted. Jack's father.

Ted stood at the head of a knot of men in high-collared black shirts, with British Union of Fascists insignia on their armbands, leather belts with a brass clip, and jackboots. Beside him was a tall, striking blonde woman, wearing a necklace with a swastika charm. To Harry, their outfits made a mockery of all the blood that watered the fields of France and all the poetry that had been wasted on its behalf.

Harry said, 'Hello, Ted.'

'Well, look who's here, lads.'

Ted's bravado was skin deep, but it was undercut with a menacing aggression.

'You following me, Harry?'

He didn't bother to reply.

'That's what you do, isn't it? It's what you call a job. You creep around after people. You skulk in the shadows. Too scared to meet a man face to face.'

Once, after Joan told him of a particular beating, Harry had actually squared up to Ted, but then he had stood down, knowing what he was capable of. It would not help matters. Yet when he had backed off, Ted had been triumphant.

'*Can't even hit me, Harry? Frightened of me, are you, hard man? So much for the army, then.*'

'Not seen you in uniform before, Ted.'

Ted had escaped conscription due to flat feet and other unspecified 'medical conditions', no doubt the same medical conditions that made him beat his wife and knock about his own son. On numerous occasions Harry had seen Ted cuff his son on the back of the head or strike him outright for some trifling transgression. He handed over beatings to Joan the way other husbands handed over their pay packets. Many times, Harry's fists had itched to take Ted on, and many times he had restrained himself for the sake of his quivering, white-faced sister.

'Fuck you, Harry.'

Ted turned to his companions. 'He's always hated me. He's a Bolshie. If it comes to war, it'll be the fault of this lot. Reds, Jews.'

There was a dangerous glitter in his eyes. He held his hands out mockingly, as if for cuffs.

'Going to arrest me, then?'

Harry kept his mouth shut, but registered that the alley was a dead end and that he would need to leave the same way he had come in. Apart from the tall blonde, there must have been four other men, maybe five, blocking his exit.

'Show him what you think of Commies, boys.'

Even given his limited intelligence, Harry wondered what his brother-in-law could be thinking. Presumably that a scuffle in this desolate East End alley would be entirely deniable. Yet even as he tried to process that, the first fist came up, followed by a right hook that sent him reeling. And a second, which was an upward jab with a knuckle-duster chaser.

Then he saw the broken bottle, felt the arms wrestling him from behind, and in a pragmatic, split-second calculation to save his sight rather than his looks, he offered up the other cheek to receive a rip in the shape of a scimitar that would curve ever after up his face, first red then silver.

Then he gave back.

Sometimes Harry Fox felt that there were two of him – himself and his own dark shadow – and it was that shadow which moved from muscle memory, seamlessly and power-fully. He shrugged off the men holding his arms like he was shrugging off his overcoat. But he was still one man against five, maybe six, and no matter how many punches he rained, he received a storm of kicks in return until he was reduced to a foetal curl on the ground. The boots continued thudding into him from all sides. His face was a sheet of blood and it occurred to him that he was about to die.

Then, from nowhere, came Malone.

Malone aimed his first punch, causing Ted to double over, grunting. A ragged moan escaped him as he slackened and sagged, turning his back and enabling Malone to land another, heavily, in the kidney. Then he turned to the others, or what was left of them, with more jabs, before returning to Ted, fists pummelling, battering his face into a mess of skin and blood.

Ted jerked like a puppet before collapsing directly back-wards onto the cobbles as though his strings had been cut. The other men vanished. From where he lay on the filthy ground, his neck twisted awkwardly and squinting to one side, Harry vomited, then hauled himself to his knees.

'Ted!'

It wasn't as though he hadn't seen injuries before. He'd seen boys with their legs blown off and friends with half a face. Yet still, it appalled him to look at Ted.

He lay in the gutter, his broken body spread awkwardly, his legs splayed, and one hand to his brow as if trying to recollect a name.

'Ted!'

It was Harry shouting because Malone had vanished as swiftly as he arrived.

'Ted!'

His brother-in-law did not respond. He lay on the ground, utterly motionless, his eyes closed and all the dark thoughts leaking from the back of his head.


Harry had woken in a place with grey walls and white light slicing through heavy blinds. The walls bent and swayed like fairground mirrors, lurching so much he had to close his eyes again. Joan was there – a look of anguish on her face.

'What have you done, Harry? What the hell have you done?'

He never mentioned Malone, and nobody asked. Malone had been at the demonstration, shadowing, just as he was, and could have no idea that Harry and his assailant were related. Therefore, Harry saw no reason to bring him into this. He bore the weight of Ted's death on his own shoulders and even after all was done and dusted, and the question of criminal charges dropped, the guilt still threatened to destroy him.

Just a week later he was back on his feet. His body was recovered, but his career never would. Not to mention his soul.

He quickened his pace behind Diana Sowerby. Drops of rain were gathering on the Himmler spectacles, which together with the trilby, badly obscured his view. At the top of Onslow Gardens, she turned left along the Old Brompton Road and he trudged after her, but what with the weather and the emotion and the encroaching darkness he was barely able to focus on his prey.

# CHAPTER 35

Tom sprang to his feet.

'Have you met Mr North? Aubrey North. Sir, this is a family friend. Stella Fry.'

North took a step into the room and extended a hand.

'Delighted to meet you, Miss Fry.'

Almost immediately, he turned to Tom, lowered his voice and said,

'I've just come from Valentine Lawford, Halifax's office. Apparently, Halifax just said to the cabinet, "Hitler has given us nothing . . . it's as if he had won a war without having to fight." So Chamberlain is not happy, to say the least. Which makes it all the more important that we get on with that information I was discussing . . .'

'Yes. Of course.'

'I thought it might be wisest to scrutinize the papers at my home. If you're not otherwise engaged. My car is outside . . .'

Tom said, 'Stella, I'm sorry, but I have to leave. If I could catch up with you later? Tomorrow, maybe. I could find you a taxi.'

'Heavens, no.' North turned and smiled graciously. 'It will take no longer than a few minutes. Why doesn't Miss Fry come with us and I'll drop you both somewhere later?'

'In that case, thank you, sir.'

Tom was pulling on his jacket and pushing some papers into his briefcase.

'Stella, why don't we do that? I'll take you to dinner afterwards. Then we can talk properly.'

She hesitated. The thought of being with Tom provided a crumb of security, but every instinct told her to refuse. Before she could say anything, however, North had turned on his heel and led the way out of the door.

The car, a black Humber Pullman, was parked in King Charles Street. No chauffeur was to be seen and North climbed into the driving seat himself.

'I let Derek go early. His wife's birthday. The poor woman might as well enjoy it. Who knows where we'll all be this time next year.'

Tom and Stella slid into the back. The interior smelled of expensive polish and the dark red leather of the seat was smooth against her thighs. She edged closer to Tom, as though his physical presence was enough to keep her safe.

She had recognized North immediately. The fair, oiled hair and suave, knife-edged voice. The vulpine smile with the glint of gold in it belonged to the man who had bent down towards her in the Athenaeum. The man Hubert Newman had refused to introduce.

Yet she had no idea if he recognized her. They had met only briefly after all, in the most fleeting of encounters. North could not possibly know that she had read a section of Hubert Newman's manuscript, which seemed to spell out a coded warning against him. Surely he could know nothing, other than that she was a girlfriend of Tom's, a family friend of the Lamonts, on her way to dinner.

The car purred through the streets of Knightsbridge and along the perimeter of Hyde Park to Kensington. Nobody spoke. She stared out at the houses as they passed, looking into the lighted windows as though they were stage sets peopled by figures coming home, moving about in the glow and warmth, preparing their evening meal or clearing it away. Turning on the wireless and settling down with the evening paper. Maybe even picking up a detective novel, because the news was bad, and everyone needed to escape.

Already she was regretting her furious departure from Harry Fox. She wondered if he had tried to come after her, but the streets had been so crowded and her pace so rapid, she guessed there was little chance.

After five minutes, the Humber swung into a square of tranquil Georgian houses surrounding a private garden and North drew up.

'Right. Here we are.'

Suddenly, he craned around to the back seat and handed Tom a key.

'Lamont, I'm going to drop you off here. Give you a moment to go through the documents and sort out what's what. I've left them on the desk in my study. Why don't I deliver Miss Fry home and then come back so we can talk privately?'

'Certainly, sir. Is that OK with you, Stella? It's Oakley Street, sir. I'll come by as soon as I'm finished.'

She opened her mouth to protest, but already Tom had his back to her and was climbing out of the car. No sooner had he closed the door than North accelerated away.

Instead of turning south to Oakley Street, however, he turned in the opposite direction and said,

'You'll forgive me, Miss Fry, if we make a short diversion.'

She had no idea where they were when North drew the car up and motioned her outside. It might have been any London street in the gathering dusk, where oppressive five-storey houses of red brick crowded out the sky. It was a place of bedsits and lodging houses in varying states of repair. Tidy wrought-iron balustrades at the upper windows and doorsteps with flaking paint. Stella stood, every muscle braced with fear. She tried to reassure herself that Tom was aware that she had gone, and with whom. Hadn't North assured him he would be back very soon? Which meant that this encounter could not last long. Whatever Aubrey North planned to say to her, she must give him no inkling of what she had discovered.

Inside the building, he kicked aside the drift of letters

wedged beneath the door and ushered her through a dimly lit marble hall bearing a mahogany side table and an umbrella stand, up a flight of uncarpeted stairs and into a drawing room. At least, she supposed it was a drawing room, but it had a transient, unlived-in air, as though it was not a home at all. The wallpaper was stained and patterned with faded roses. It was sparsely furnished with few domestic flourishes; no photographs dotted the mantelpiece, no flowers stood on the side tables and the landscapes on the wall, featuring dull, craggy Alps and nameless lakes, had an institutional look. The only gesture towards domesticity was a drinks trolley, crowded with crystal decanters of Scotch and brandy, and a couple of unopened bottles of red wine.

Closing the door behind her, he said, 'Can I offer you something?'

'No thank you.'

'A glass of water, then?'

Without waiting for an answer, he dispensed some into a cut-glass tumbler and handed it to her before pouring a brandy for himself. Then he shrugged off his velvet-collared coat, folded it carefully across the arm of a chair and gestured towards one of the two seats flanking the empty fireplace. His suit was superbly cut and obviously expensive, its fine wool moving smoothly with his limbs. The cuffs were snowy white.

'Why have you brought me here, Mr North?'

'Please. Sit. Don't be alarmed. I want to talk, that's all.'

She remained standing and folded her arms. Any hope

that he had not remembered her was dashed. He knew exactly who she was.

'Smoke?' He proffered an engraved gold case, in which one remained. 'Don't worry, I have more somewhere.'

'No thank you.'

He put the case and lighter down on a side table, and said, 'I must say, you made a rapid return from Vienna. I hope the journey was comfortable?'

Stella kept rigidly silent and her refusal to comment prompted a smile.

'You see, I had a cable from a friend there, alerting me that he'd met a young woman who was in surprisingly energetic pursuit of Hubert Newman's associates. He thought I ought to know. He imagined you were sent from the British intelligence services, but we know that's not the case, don't we?'

'I've no idea what you're talking about.'

An elegant sigh escaped him.

'I hope this isn't going to be tiresome.'

'If I'm boring you, I'll leave now.'

'Oh, you could never be boring. You live such an interesting life.'

'It's relative, I suppose.'

'Hardly. Sidonie's daughter, even if she does spend so much of her time with unsuitable men, sounds fun, if a little rackety. I suspect you two young women have a whale of a time, don't you? You'll miss it if you take that job you've been offered.'

How it was possible that he knew these things? Then Stella

remembered that whoever burgled the flat had searched her room and the letter offering her a job at St Theresa's had been on the mantelpiece. What else did Aubrey North know? Could he be aware that only the previous day she had been to the home of Winston Churchill himself?

'It's a convent school, I understand. It might be a trifle dull, compared to what you're used to. Rather more respectable company than knocking around with Evelyn Lamont and a discredited policeman, but no fun with nuns.'

The line amused him enough to repeat it.

'No fun with nuns. Worth considering though. The air on the south coast is very bracing.'

'You've been following me.'

'My dear girl, don't be preposterous.'

He laughed, perched on the arm of the chair and took out a fresh packet of cigarettes, lighting one and inhaling.

'That's a ludicrous idea. Of course, I haven't been following you. I'm the best brain in His Majesty's Foreign and Colonial Office at a time of grave national crisis. You can have simply no idea what a workload we're under right now. I've been extraordinarily busy. I spend every day of the week from eight until late in the F.O., attending meetings, sending memos, advising Lord Halifax. Circulating executive telegrams and reports from embassies abroad. It's true I enjoy spending time with beautiful women, but there are only so many hours in the day.'

He smiled a brilliant, diplomat's smile.

'No, the glory that is the British Security Service has been deployed in your honour. They can be quite thorough, in their straightforward, plodding way, so long as they're not asked to do anything that requires intellect or cunning.'

Moments flashed before her. The bicycle that had nearly knocked her down in the King's Road. The lock at home that jammed. That sense she had of being watched at all times – it had been neither nerves nor neurosis. Her instincts were correct.

'To do him credit, my man there has managed to put you and your policeman friend on a list of suspects and string together a timeline. On Monday, September 12th, you met Hubert for lunch at the Athenaeum. That was where I saw you. He has no idea how or when the pair of you had met before that. Two days later you went to the office of the discredited Mr Fox, and shortly afterwards you left for Vienna. My chap informs me that you arrived in Britain in March, and that you've lodged with Evelyn Lamont since then, but true to form, he has failed to answer the most pressing of my questions. Most importantly, why did Hubert choose you? Who do you, and your Mr Fox, represent? Are you working in a freelance capacity, or do you report to some agency of which I am as yet unaware?'

Summoning a coolness she did not know she possessed, she took a sip of water and said, 'If anyone has questions to answer I'd have thought it was you. Why on earth have you brought me here? I'd like to leave right now.'

A quiver of irritation crossed North's features, and the

patrician face tensed slightly, before the mask of gentility descended again.

'All in good time. Before that, I'd like to know how you came by the name of Roland Finch. As well as everything else that Hubert told you.'

'He told me nothing.'

'So you conjured Finch's name from thin air? You went to Vienna on what, a whim?'

'There's no law against it.'

'And when you lunched with Hubert that day, you discussed the weather?'

'No. We talked about Shakespeare.'

To her surprise, this response drew a delighted cackle of laughter.

'Shakespeare! I don't doubt it for a second.'

He motioned her to the chair opposite and crossed his legs.

'How consoling to think that Hubert spent his last hours on his favourite subject. He always loved Shakespeare. I'll tell you a little about Hubert, if you like. I mean, if you have the time.'

She tried not to react. She was wondering exactly how much of this North had planned. He could not have known that she would be in Tom's office that afternoon, at that precise time, so he must be improvising, and that was better.

North continued, in the same languid, amused drawl.

'I can't remember where he and I met – either in a punt or over a pint – but wherever it was, what I do recall is his extraordinary twin passions – both for the cause and for Shakespeare. Some of us thought he should show the same enthusiasm for Tolstoy, but Shakespeare was safer. Tolstoy could at any time become ideologically unsound, but everyone loves Shakespeare, don't they? And Hubert genuinely did. He could be utterly boring about it. What he especially hated was the idea that the Bard might not be a simple chap from Stratford but an aristocrat, an educated man. Someone who had travelled and was familiar with the philosophy of the day. Always very protective of the common man, that was Hubert. Whereas I, who have dedicated my life to the service of the proletariat . . . well, I tend to bat for the Earl of Oxford. It makes so much sense, and I prefer ideas that make sense.'

'His passion for the cause? Are you saying . . . that it was Newman's cause too?'

'I am. Hubert was not what you call in England a "parlour pink". Until it all went wrong, he was a man of profound dedication. A penetration agent, working in the Soviet interest. In that bankrupt merry-go-round which passes for the literary world in Britain, that despicable circle of critics and poets and little magazines, he sought out writers he thought might be sympathetic and pointed them in our direction.'

Stella thought of Harry Fox, whiling away evenings listening to talks on the future of socialism, tailing Auden and Orwell and C. Day Lewis, when all the time the man he was looking for was right in front of him.

'You said, "until it all went wrong". What went wrong?'

'Who knows? Maybe, the subject matter of his work affected him. Or the society he chose. All those aristocrats with their house parties and shooting weekends. One can't deny that the English country house is a very seductive place to be. Perhaps the poison of the class system rotted his soul. At any rate, he became disaffected. He started making disparaging comments about Stalin, whereas most of us accept that Stalin's current activities are justified by the ends of the system we serve.'

She wondered how long it would be before Tom realized that something had gone wrong. Would he telephone Oakley Street and raise the alarm? Then she thought of Harry Fox, and where he might be now. How she regretted storming out of Luigi's café. Despite his eccentricities, she sensed in Harry a quality of strength and resourcefulness that would be good in a crisis.

But Harry would never know she was here, and Tom would assume that North had done exactly what he had said: dropped her at the flat in Oakley Street before heading back to convene over the papers they had been aiming confidentially to discuss.

'You see,' said North. 'The interesting thing about Shakespeare . . .'

But what the interesting thing about Shakespeare was, she would never know because at that moment, there was a ring at the door.

North tensed.

The bell rang repeatedly, first in long rings, then with the staccato insistence of one who was annoyed, and determined to have an answer. On and on it went, for a minute or more.

The two of them remained motionless as the echo of the bell floated up from the hall. North's eyes were fixed on her own, as if to mesmerize. All he said was, 'I advise you to stay completely silent.'

# CHAPTER 36

Diana Sowerby turned left into Rosary Gardens and when she reached number 3, she patted her hair, clutched her coat more tightly about her, and trotted up the steps. She glanced around, as if wary of being seen.

Then she rang the bell.

Ten yards away, Harry took cover and lingered, allowing the soft symphony of sounds that made up the autumn evening to wash over him; the bass rumble of traffic and the arpeggio of a motorbike approaching and passing in the street. High soprano laughter from a variety show on the BBC National Programme and the staccato cough of a car starting handle as a motorist tried to fire their engine. He took out a Senior Service. He imagined she would be some time.

Diana Sowerby rang again. And again, but there was no answer. The delay intrigued Harry. It wasn't often you saw a woman like Diana Sowerby kept waiting. But greater than this vague curiosity was his own mounting disenchantment. For one thing, he had not managed to replace his stolen camera, so if an adulterous liaison was on the cards, he would not be able to capture it for posterity. And for another thing, it didn't matter any more.

Because the recollection of Cable Street had made up his mind.

He would not betray Diana Sowerby to Walter Heap.

He didn't care what golden fictions she had spun to her ogre of a husband, or who she was seeing or why. Harry may be guilty of cheap and clichéd emotions, as Violet had said, but he was prepared, in this case, to forgo the fee. He would say he lost her. That there was nothing to see. Because he knew, when the balloon went up, as it would, and if the country was occupied by a foreign power, that Walter Heap would be in the vanguard of those running the show. And men like Heap were everything he despised. A letter to *The Times* that morning from a man called Ian Fleming said it was 'time to organize this country on a wartime basis'. Well, let this be the first shot in Harry's war.

After a few minutes waiting on the doorstep, the actress turned disconsolately and continued back the way she had come. Harry shook some life into his limbs and prepared to follow.

Suddenly, another resolution occurred to him. He would not only abandon the task of shadowing Diana Sowerby, he would inform her exactly what her husband was up to.

She was halfway down the street when she heard his feet pounding after her and turned. A look of hope on her face died when she saw it was not the man she was expecting.

'Miss Sowerby.'

She hid her uneasiness beneath a smile of composure and he realized that she assumed he was a fan. Her voice was a sweet, breathless coo.

'Hello. Can I help you?'

'No. But I can help you.'

A frown creased her lovely brow.

'I'm sorry. You must have made a mistake. I don't need any help. I'm just out for a stroll. My husband will be meeting me any minute. He's just around the corner.'

'In that case, we should talk before he arrives. It's your husband I want to talk about.'

Harry shifted out of the street light to the shade beneath a tree, and she followed him.

'Who are you exactly?'

'I'm your shadow.'

For a beat, she was transfixed, sapphire eyes wide, as though Nemesis in person had risen from the underworld and made a visit to the backstreets of Kensington.

'What are you talking about? Are you trying to frighten me?'

Then, as a car passed, and its headlights sent a blade of light across his face, she said, 'I think I recognize you! I do, don't I? It was you. Driving the taxi?'

He nodded.

'So, it's true. Damn him. I might have guessed he would pay some cheap lowlife to have me followed.'

Harry decided to let that go.

'Miss Sowerby. I admit your husband's been paying me. He wants to see if he has grounds for divorce. He believes you've been having a love affair, but he doesn't know who with.'

'An affair? How dare you!'

'With respect, Miss Sowerby, if I wanted to see you act, I'd buy a ticket and watch you on stage.'

'You've got some cheek.'

'But as I say, your husband doesn't know who the gentleman is and nor, as it happens, do I. Who is it?'

'Call yourself a detective? You think I'm going to tell you if you can't find out yourself?'

'That's what I hoped.'

'I've had enough of this. This conversation is over.'

She began to walk away, but he came after her.

'Wait!'

'Leave me alone or I'll scream. I'll call the police.'

'I am the police. Sort of.'

This had the desired effect and she stopped and quietened, though her chest was still rising and falling rapidly and her breath coming in gulps. She was looking left and right up and down the road, as if for rescue.

'Please. Forgive me for alarming you. You see, you have to understand, I'm not planning on telling your husband anything. I'm not working for him any more. I've decided he's not a model employer.'

She pulled her silk coat more tightly around her and looked at him quizzically.

'Then why are you still asking questions?'

'Professional curiosity, I suppose. Just . . . don't be frightened.'

'How am I expected to feel when a man with a face like Boris Karloff comes up to me in a dark street?'

'Sorry if I alarmed you.'

'For all I know you've taken photographs of me. If you're not selling them to Walter you're probably selling them to the *News of the World*. You haven't, have you? Taken a picture of me with him? Are you trying to blackmail me?'

'I told you. I don't even know who he is. Who is he?'

'What kind of idiot do you take me for?'

She folded her arms defiantly.

'I'm not standing here being questioned. I'm a busy woman. Did you come in your taxi?'

'No.'

'Well, I'm going to the underground, then.'

'Thought you were meeting your husband round the corner?'

Her eyes narrowed. The barmaid in her was coming to the fore.

'This is ridiculous. I don't believe you're the police. Where's your warrant card? If you've dumped the job, and you're not trying to sting me for money, why are you bothering me?'

'As I said, professional curiosity. I've been following you for weeks. I've watched you leaving home and going to the theatre. I've followed you to your hairdresser and your dressmaker—'

'What do you want? A medal?'

'. . . and what interests me, Miss Sowerby, is this. In my line of work, you get interested in anomalies. The anomaly that interested me, the other day when I gave you a ride, is you went to Bermondsey. Why would a lady like yourself be carrying on with a man who lives in a dump like that?'

She rolled her eyes.

'He doesn't *live* there.'

'So he lives back there? Where you rang the bell?'

'No. His home's somewhere else.'

'Then why don't you meet at his home?'

'Work it out, brainbox! He's an important man. And in case you hadn't noticed, I'm not an entirely unknown actress. We don't want anyone to see us.'

'But Bermondsey?'

'It's not just there. We meet in different places. Not hotels, but . . .'

'Love nests?'

She gave him a disgusted look.

'People's houses and other places. He said we'd be safe in Bermondsey. Nobody would see us. He has a friend who let us use her house.'

'What friend?'

'I don't know.'

'Did you not ask?'

A long-suffering sigh.

'That's not the kind of thing you talk about when time's limited.'

'What do you talk about?'

'Oh, international affairs, the future of Europe, my husband's political opinions. Are you being serious? What do you talk about when you meet up with a lady friend? No, on second thoughts, don't tell me.'

'So, despite using her house for your liaisons, you know absolutely nothing about this friend?'

Diana Sowerby looked again up the street, as though her errant lover might, against all hope, emerge.

'Not that it concerns you, but she's a bookseller, actually. She's away a lot, quite often at book fairs and so on, meeting international dealers, and the rest of the time she's at the bookshop.'

'What bookshop?'

'She runs a bookshop in the Charing Cross Road.'

'This lady and your friend. Are they close?'

It was a shot in the dark, but even the most random shots occasionally hit the target.

'What are you suggesting? You think he's with her tonight?'

'There must be something holding him up. If he's not where you planned to meet.'

A thunderstorm of emotions crossed her face, then, more softly, she said, 'I used to think he'd had a thing with her, but he denied it. He could have, he said, quite easily. But she was far too important to him in other ways to mess around like that. If he wanted a woman, he wouldn't have chosen her. That was just like him, really. He thinks he's better than other people. He thinks he rules the world.'

She shrugged her fine shoulders, as if she could shrug off all the callousness of men, and Harry watched her, entranced. He admired her, not only for the beauty of her face, which glowed so luminously beneath the lamp post, but for her composure. He meant it when he said he might buy a ticket to see her on stage. She reminded him of the actress in *Midnight in Vienna*, Ludmilla Mandlikova. The same flashing eyes and proud defiance. As it turned out, it was Ludmilla who had killed the wealthy tycoon, Randolph Cavendish, not the impoverished American playwright, Abe Larson, who had been cheated of an investment in his new play. Except that Ludmilla Mandlikova had been of Russian extraction, with raven hair and scarlet lips, whereas Diana Sowerby was a delicate honey blonde with the body of Aphrodite and the eyes of Medusa.

'And does he? Your man? Rule the world?'

'I suppose he does, in a way. He works in Whitehall, after all.'

'What's his name?'

She hesitated.

'When you said you wouldn't tell my husband . . . did you mean it?'

'Absolutely.'

'Well, I'm sick of it already, to tell the truth.'

'Understandably.'

'And the fact is, he told me once . . . He said he didn't really mind if our secret got out because everyone knows powerful men attract hordes of beautiful women.'

'So he's romantic too.'

She smiled at that, then surprisingly, almost offhandedly, she said, 'His name is Aubrey North.'

CHAPTER 37

When the doorbell sounded, Stella had wanted to shout, but the breath stuck in her throat. After a few minutes, the persistent ringing ceased and there was only the sharp tattoo of heels ringing emptily down the street.

North retained his posture of languid relaxation but she could tell by the rigidity of the shoulders and the slight tightening of his jaw that the interruption had bothered him. He was a man of layers, and beneath the civilized, unruffled demeanour of the English gentleman, she perceived a disdain for her and for anyone else who stood in his way. He got to his feet and went over to the mantelpiece.

'Our dear friend Hubert, with his inherent sense of melodrama, would probably describe this meeting like a showdown in the library, where the wretched Peverell Drake explains everything to a cast of characters and his fatuous assistant. How the victim was stabbed or drowned or thrown into the sea, and who exactly wielded the candlestick or the pearl-handled pistol. Fortunately, this is real life, not fiction, and I have no intention of explaining any more than necessary. Though I will, if you like, and for my own gratification, explain why I brought you here.'

Stella said nothing. She was expending all her energy on concealing signs of fear. Fortunately, she was good at hiding her emotions; she had her mother to thank for that. Nancy Fry had a strong distaste for demonstrative attachments, believed displays of affection were vulgar and had never told her daughter that she loved her.

Now, Stella was grateful for that hard-learned emotional restraint. Besides, the more North talked, the better.

'When you met Newman, I had no idea what the two of you were discussing. You seemed as thick as thieves. But I did know that Hubert was disenchanted. More than that – I don't mind saying we'd had a stand-up row a few months earlier. He said he was abandoning our valuable work because of Stalin's purges. Someone had come back from Moscow, bleating about show trials. Stalin had ordered the execution of Osip Mandelstam, a poet whom Hubert admired, and last year a man we knew – a man who had been important in all our lives – had been recalled to Moscow. He was found to be a traitor and was executed.'

'Was he a traitor?'

North shrugged his impeccable shoulders.

'I assume so, if the court found him to be. That's not my concern. But Hubert was incensed. He thought we should all renounce our allegiances. It was useless pointing out to him that we follow a system – an idea – not Stalin himself. At least, Hubert said that was his objection, but if you ask me, I suspect the true cause of his about-turn was vanity.'

He went over to the drinks tray and poured himself another slug of brandy. The fine features were flushed and a beading of sweat dappled his hairline. She noted that his eyes were red-rimmed from fatigue.

'It's funny, really. I made a little joke. A *jeu d'esprit*. But the trouble with foreigners, especially Austrians, is that they have absolutely no sense of humour or irony. Hubert could never take a joke. Not like us English. I'm sure you'd have found it amusing.'

'Try me.'

'It goes like this. When we send . . . communications, documents, information . . . to the Continent, we use special cameras – a German invention as it happens – that can shrink photographs quite dramatically to something called a microdot. This microdot is so tiny you can store a whole document in the full stop at the end of a sentence. Isn't science wonderful? You can fit fifty complete Bibles on a spot the size of a postage stamp.'

'I don't imagine you were sending copies of the Bible.'

'Nothing so dreary. But the point was, these microdots would be embedded in copies of books, and then shipments of books were taken to a designated bookshop in Vienna to be rerouted to Moscow. Exactly which books one uses doesn't matter in the slightest. And that's where my joke came in. You see, Hubert's books are very popular on the

Continent. Mostly in translation, of course, but there are some who prefer the original English versions. Rumour has it that von Ribbentrop is a fan – he buys them for his English library - and while I'm not sure about *Gruppenführer* Heydrich, he is known to adore the British detective novel. He's gung-ho for Agatha Christie, they tell me. So it amused me, I suppose, to use Hubert's own novels for the purpose.'

'And he didn't find it hilarious?'

'Sadly, it seemed to irk him. He regarded his books as works of art. Incredible, really. That kind of tosh. I mean, have you ever read them?'

'I've skimmed.'

'Precisely. I think they come under the category of "light reading", which seems ironic, considering that they're so heavy going. Anyhow – that's beside the point. Whatever the cause of his disaffection, the fact remains that Hubert had threatened to endanger our endeavour, and that could not be allowed to stand. So, it was resolved that we must act in everyone's interests.'

'You mean, murder him.'

North blew a cool jet of smoke.

'It was going to be difficult. Senior civil servants don't go around strangling their friends. Or stabbing them. The police might be utterly useless but even they are capable of noticing if someone has been shot. I can't take credit for the solution – that was someone else more familiar with Hubert's work.'

'Who?'

'It doesn't matter. But in one of those novels – sorry if I'm spoiling it for you – the victim dies by poisoning. As part of his research, Hubert had been in touch with an old friend.'

'You're talking about Ernst Grunfeld.'

This startled him, she could tell. His eyes widened, recalculating. His voice hardened.

'You *have* been busy.'

'How did Hubert know Ernst Grunfeld?'

'As it happened, their families grew up alongside each other in Vienna. They were neighbours, childhood friends.'

She recalled what Lindemann had told her.

'*I found Ernst Grunfeld at the University of Berlin, where he had moved from the University of Vienna.*'

'When Grunfeld came over to England five years ago, a mutual friend brought him and Hubert together again. It was a kind gesture – it's lonely being a genius in exile. Most people don't want to know you and those that do, don't understand you. Added to which, Grunfeld is not the most sociable of chaps. Not the kind of fellow you want to share a drink with, or take on a house party weekend. Scientists can be like that. Too much time with their test tubes.'

This thought ignited a smile.

'Anyhow, their reunion was useful in all kinds of ways. Hubert was writing a novel, and he wanted a murder weapon. He needed to find a poison that would kill slowly and undetectably, and as it happened, Grunfeld was able to help. He'd been working on a government project to develop a nerve agent for a weapon. A biological toxin.'

'A toxin? You mean a poison? What kind of weapon is that?'

'A chemical weapon.'

'But I thought—?'

'You thought chemical weapons were outlawed. Their use is outlawed but not their development. Be assured – everyone else is working just as hard. The Germans, after all, made chlorine gas, and they have a new agent being developed as we speak. The Russians have long been involved in creating toxins. Lenin possessed a "special office", which was an entire laboratory for developing poisons, and Stalin's people are actively engaged on intensive research to make new ones. Until now, the British have been adamantly opposed to the idea of chemical weapons. Who could forget the mustard gas in the war? But recently, international relations are such that in the national interest, the British government has decided that it cannot afford to ignore them.'

'What is this toxin?'

'It's called substance X. Its scientific name is botulinum toxin. Botox, for short. It works as a nerve poison. It paralyses the nerves so that muscles can't contract. It is the deadliest substance in the world. If you manage to administer it, a couple of drops can kill hundreds of thousands of people.'

His gaze was fixed, unseeing. He spoke as if mesmerized.

'Astonishing stuff. It's absorbed through the eyes, mucous membranes, respiratory tract, or any place on the body where the skin is not intact. The effects take hours to show themselves, but when they do the neurological results are drastic. The eyelids droop, swallowing is impeded, muscles grow weak. If left untreated what follows is paralysis and respiratory failure. Death, in other words.'

Paralysis. Stella had a sudden vision of the figures she had seen once at Pompeii during a visit with the Gatz family. The bodies paralysed, arms clutching the air, frozen in time, their lives ossified in ash.

'Apparently, just the tiniest drop is enough to cause total neuro-paralysis. I see you looking alarmed, Miss Fry. Do you need a light?'

He nodded towards the cigarette beside her, but she didn't trust her trembling fingers to take it. She remembered something Evelyn had told her about stage fright, that when you froze on stage, time became elastic and every moment seemed to last an hour. For her, fear was its own paralysis now, coagulating within her, slowing every movement and clouding her thought. She sank down onto the armchair while North towered above her, brandy in hand.

'Grunfeld told him that it was an entirely peaceful death. Nothing agonizing, like cyanide or strychnine. So, years later, when we discovered Hubert was about to betray us, it was the least we could do for an old comrade to give him an easy exit. Poetic, really.'

'More like Greek tragedy.'

'Yes, yes, very good. Sophocles. It certainly appealed to the classical scholar in me.'

'Why did he need to die?'

'Because if he'd lived, many more lives would have been lost. And it matters very much – for the future of the world, and for peace, that we are not betrayed. The only issue was how to execute it.'

She felt her way along the memory. Newman in the Athenaeum. Fiddling with his glasses. The bitten finger-nails. Rubbing his eyes. *This is my spare pair.*

'The spectacles. You used it on his spectacles. They were in a case, so you didn't need to touch them.'

'That's right. Properly applied, a single drop can kill ten thousand apparently. Incredible, isn't it? After Grunfeld had dealt with the spectacles, I returned them to Hubert at our club. And that, of course, was when I saw you. Huddled across the table conspiring, discussing who knows what. I had no idea what Hubert was telling you. For all I knew, you might be some kind of journalist. As soon as you left, I procured your name from the porter and he mentioned that Hubert had asked him to post an envelope. It didn't take a genius to work out that he had sent you some com-munication, and that I needed to see it. Though the fact was, when I did finally see it yesterday evening, I could barely hide my disappointment. That new manuscript is a terrible bore. If that's Hubert's gift to posterity, posterity may well return it.'

He poured more brandy, but she noticed his hand was trembling and the tremble gave her a sliver of hope. He had his own nerves, and that was a weakness. She scanned the room for any kind of weapon with which to defend herself, but saw nothing. No lamp stand. No poker in the fireplace. It meant that she needed to keep him talking.

'Why did you ever get involved in this?'

'You mean the Honourable Aubrey North? Member of the Amici Society at Marlborough and classical scholar at Balliol College, Oxford?'

It had been a good guess. North was longing for a switch in focus. She sensed that he was enjoying himself, indeed that he welcomed the chance for a little self-exploration. She had met so many men like him – at parties and dinners – who required very little prompting to spend a whole evening talking about themselves. Perhaps North wanted to prolong the encounter. That was good. Any extra time was good.

He leaned back, one elbow on the mantelpiece, like a philosophy don untangling a knotty dilemma. His eyes were glossy with reminiscence.

'That's an astute question. At the beginning, when I was young and bright, I wanted to go straight to Moscow and serve in some way – even be a tractor driver if necessary – but they insisted I would be more useful in another role. That's how they think. They plan a career for you. In government service, in academia. Something long established, dull even. Where you might be of use decades later. I resisted at first.'

'Because you didn't want to be dull?'

He laughed and swilled the alcohol in his glass.

'Who does? Dull's not my style. I'm the kind of man who

requires constant distractions. In happier circumstances I would prefer to invite a lovely woman like you to dinner at Quaglino's.'

'Instead of . . .?'

'As you say, instead of.'

Lightly, as though they were indeed exchanging cocktail gossip across a restaurant table, she said, 'How can you bear to do this? To betray your country's secrets at a moment like this? To kill a man?'

He slammed down the brandy balloon sharply on the mantelpiece.

'Oh, please. Here we are, a tiny island that was once an empire, glorying in our past. Our literature, our heritage. I hate all that. Empires fall, that's what any student of the classics will tell you. But working towards it is slow and painstaking. It requires real dedication. It's not a pleasant business. Newman knew that. Why do you think he took refuge in Shakespeare and all the scholarly stuff? The same reason one might find solace in late Beethoven, or, I don't know, Poussin. One seeks sanctuary in the civilized because the requirements of the job are not always edifying.'

'And where will you go now?'

'Go?'

He cocked his head, questioningly.

'What are you talking about? What do you mean, go? I'm not going anywhere. I'm staying here. The corridors of Whitehall may be endless, but they lead to power. I have the utmost dedication.'

The word seemed to prompt a further bout of rumination.

'Dedication. Yes, that's what we all shared. We were dedicated servants of the greater good. We were – and most of us still are – dedicated to the work of peace.'

'With Germany, you mean?'

'So much more than that. There's only one system in the world which can guarantee peace to mankind, and we do her service. You see, Stella, our side works deeply. The Russian national game is chess. Never underestimate a nation whose habit is to think three steps ahead. Our plans are laid years in advance. We have agents in place who might not be active for ten, even fifteen years. We're prepared to wait.'

Quietly, guessing the answer before she had even asked, she said, 'Are you not worried? Telling me all this? I don't understand. Why would you implicate yourself in murder?'

For an involuntary second his eye flickered towards the side table and she knew. The water glass. She had taken a single sip. Who could say what was in that glass? Especially now that she knew Hubert Newman had been killed with poison. Clearly, Aubrey North had no intention of allowing her to leave this place alive.

She jumped from her seat, but North was too quick for her. He sprang up, barring her way, and grabbed his coat.

'You'll have to excuse me, I'm afraid. I'd love to stay chatting, but I have government business to attend to. I'll be back within the hour.'

Then he dashed from the room, locking the door behind him.

Stella sank back in her seat, frozen, as if poison was already working in her veins. If it had happened, how long would it be, before it took effect? In those fractured seconds, she pictured Hubert Newman staggering to his death, like a soldier stumbling in the line of fire. She thought of Evelyn's flat, and the dear, tiny jumble of her possessions – the shells, the photographs, the mementoes. She thought of Alan and her mother, and then of Harry Fox, who had set her upon this terrible venture.

This would be her end. She was ending when she had barely begun.

# CHAPTER 38

Once the actress had disappeared up the street, Harry flung away his cigarette and turned back towards the house. Even if North wasn't there, it would do no harm to take a look.

To begin with, it seemed impossible. Although number 3 had plainly been converted to bedsits, these Edwardian houses might as well be medieval castles, so solidly were they built to repel invaders. Five-storey towered terraces of thick walls and triple-locked doors six inches thick. A red-brick cliff face impossible to scale, and open on all sides to net-curtained windows and prying eyes. He had none of his usual equipment, not even the skeleton keys, but Harry enjoyed a challenge, and he had never yet come across a building that did not yield to his most determined advances.

After sizing it up and taking a hasty glance around, he slipped over the railings at the front, dipping down into a basement well that was dark and unkempt, strewn with leaves and rubbish. A beer bottle rolled beneath his foot.

Close up, he was relieved to see that his first instinct was correct; as was often the way with bedsits, the exterior was unloved and badly maintained. Cracks yawned in the mortar and the edges of the sash windows were rotting.

Peering through a soot-flecked pane and seeing nothing, he exerted an experimental force on the centre of the frame. It was not even locked, only fastened with a rusty latch that would give way, he knew, if subjected to determined force. He was about to try again when the smart tap of footsteps at pavement level caused him to freeze and press into the shadow of the wall. He waited until the trousered legs, complete with polished brogues, had passed, then with a single heave forced the window up and clambered into the unlit basement.

Inside all was darkness, but in the gloom he discerned a pair of chairs, a desk and a filing cabinet. Crossing the room, he mounted the uncarpeted stairs skilfully, avoiding the battery of creaks that such ancient floorboards always threatened, and creeping catlike through a short corridor until he came to a door at the level of the ground floor. He hesitated for a second, then slowly and noiselessly turned the handle.

The hall was empty. Street lamps threw bars of light across a deserted vista of black and white chequered marble tiles, illuminating an umbrella stand and a side table. But no dog erupted in a frenzy of barking, and nor did any house-holder put an inquisitive head around the door.

Harry stalled for a moment in doubt. His nerves were as

tense as piano wire as he wished, not for the first time, that English detectives, like Americans, came equipped with guns. There was nothing so warming as a shaft of cold steel in the hand. Instead of which he had no weapon at all, bar his own quicksilver brain and a body full of adrenaline. Bent double, he crept across the hall and towards the stairs,

A misplaced brass stair rail caused him to stumble, and he could not suppress a curse. It was just a single, soft syllable of Anglo-Saxon, but it was enough. From somewhere above came a sudden rustle of movement, then a shout. Too swiftly to consider who or what awaited him, he accelerated, taking the steps two at a time to the first floor. The shouting continued, from behind a panelled door. It looked locked. Very locked. He tried the knob and, when it didn't yield, he took a deep breath and flung his shoulder against it with full force. The first blow sent him reeling backwards, pain ricocheting from his collarbone to his elbow. He tried again, and the door scarcely quivered, but when he redoubled his strength for a third assault, part of the panelling splintered and gave way. At the fourth attempt the lock yielded with a crunch and the door swung open. The shouting had stopped. He stared into the room and swore again.

Stella Fry was standing in front of him in the fading light.

# CHAPTER 39

'How would I know?'

For some time, they had not spoken. Harry had brought her back to his office, sat her on the chesterfield and covered her tenderly, in a blanket, like a child. He had seen people with shell shock in the war, and understood that they needed careful handling. That wasn't anything he had done personally, but he knew how to make a mug of tea and stir in three lumps of sugar, and how to provide a packet of digestives and a bottle of Teacher's Highland Cream.

She had taken a couple of gulps and gradually her throat, constricted with fear, began to relax.

'How would I know? If I'd been poisoned?'

'You're fine,' he said, with a certainty he did not feel. 'I saw people who'd breathed mustard gas in the war. It takes effect immediately. I'd know. Look at you – you've got the colour back in your cheeks. You're right as rain. Besides, North said he was coming back, didn't he?'

'What happens when he does? When he finds out?'

'I've put in a call to Flint.'

'Flint?'

'Just a man I've worked for. You'll have to tell him every-thing you know. Meanwhile, you're safe here.'

She clasped her arms round her knees, still wondering if the poison was seeping into her blood.

'He gave me water. I only had one sip . . .'

'Anything else?'

'Nothing. Except . . .'

Her brain was starting to gather pace.

'A cigarette. He offered me a cigarette from a gold case. It was the last one, and he said not to worry, he had others. But when he smoked, he took them from a fresh packet. And he left the case beside me. He must have assumed I would take it.'

'Clever. Nobody would expect poison in a cigarette.'

Hope revived her. Although she was still dazed, and her eyes bruised with tiredness, the tea, and Harry's cheer, was restorative. She had stopped shaking, and the whisky was wonderfully bracing, and adrenaline was racing through her veins.

'You really think I'm OK?'

'Trust me. You look a picture.'

Moving on quickly from this false confidence, he said, 'What puzzles me is how North thinks he could have got away with it. You say Tom Lamont knew you had gone with him.'

'I suppose, if I had smoked that cigarette, I would be poisoned. Unconscious probably, but paralysed anyway. Then North would have been able to take me back to Oakley Street and nobody would be the wiser.'

'Tell me again about this stuff. The poison.'

'It's called botulinum toxin. Botox, for short. It kills slowly. It freezes the muscles. But it's undetectable.'

Musingly, he said, 'That's what he meant.'

'Who?'

'Abel Edwards, the mortuary attendant. I went to see if Newman's body was still there and Edwards said he looked frozen. He looked like his own statue.'

'Poor Hubert. I remember something he said to me when I met him. He said, '*It behoves us all to pin our colours to the mast.*' He must have decided to start the process with Ernst Grunfeld. Approaching Lindemann was an inspired idea because he was anti-Bolshevik and close to Churchill. And it was Lindemann himself who rescued Grunfeld from Austria in 1933.'

'What do you mean, rescued?'

'After Hitler outlawed Jews in German universities, Lindemann brought several brilliant Jewish scientists to England. Theoretical physicists. Men like Albert Einstein. He got Erwin Schrödinger into Magdalen.'

'Who?'

'Schrödinger. The Austrian physicist. He's famous for that theory about a cat.'

'What cat?'

'The theory's hard to explain. It's about being alive and dead at the same time.'

Harry was familiar with that concept. In the no man's land of his career he knew how the dead lived and he walked among them.

'Ernst Grunfeld was a genius in his field, apparently.'

'And where is he now?'

'Long gone. Abroad, no doubt. Maybe in Moscow already. But he must have been active for the last five years.'

She shivered, and drew the blanket more closely around her.

'You know, Roland Finch was so confident they would never be uncovered. He said, *'You may have tracked me down, but there's others you'll never uncover.'* At least he was wrong about that.'

Harry was prowling the short length of the room, pacing over to the window and back again, while Stella ruminated, putting all the pieces together in her mind.

'No wonder Newman was terrified. After he had changed his mind about Stalin and rowed with the others he would have known it was a race against time because he'd seen what happens to dissidents in the purges. That must be why he put their names in his book. It was a precaution. There was every chance he would be killed before he had a chance to alert the right people. These are ruthless men, Harry, and they act without delay. North said another man was executed last year, the moment he returned to Moscow.'

At this, Harry stopped his prowling and looked round.

'What did you say?'

'A man who had been important in their lives, that's what North said. The Russians decided he was a traitor and sentenced him to death.'

He was regarding her intensely. Then he said, 'Sokolov. The man's name was Anton Sokolov. I found a photograph of him in Newman's flat.'

He strode over to a drawer and pulled out a picture which he thrust before her.

'This is him. He set up a tea-importing business, but was recalled to Russia and executed in the Lubyanka.'

'Who's the woman?'

'That's his wife.'

'She's very beautiful.'

Harry realized what had been playing at the back of his mind. It was his conversation with Dorothy Sayers.

'*There's a description of a woman in one of his novels which I think could only have been written by a man who had once been in love.*'

It had puzzled him at the time, and it still did. He had never taken Hubert Newman for a romantic. Even his publisher said, '*The only ladies I ever saw Hubert with were his mother and his secretary.*' But his encounter with Diana Sowerby had reminded him of the depiction of Ludmilla Mandlikova. Harry had spent enough of his life with pining lovers and infatuated men to recognize love when he saw it.

He had been about to eat a biscuit, but now he stopped, with the digestive still in his hand.

'Where's the manuscript? The Shakespeare book?'

'I left it on Tom Lamont's desk. At the Foreign Office.'

'Can you remember what it said? The part where he names the pretenders or whatever he calls them?'

Stella had been blessed with a highly retentive memory, which had been a great help in the year she studied medieval French verse. Now, she said,

*Like the Dark Lady, they are false, and should be denounced. One might point to Green, Byrd and West as part of this masquerade. The reputation of these pretenders does not deserve to endure.*

'Green, Byrd and West. In other words, Ernst Grunfeld, Roland Finch and Aubrey North.'

'No,' he said. 'That's not it.'

His thoughts were tumbling like litter in the wind. What had Stella said about losing his job? '*Perhaps it had something to do with failing to see what's staring you in the face.*' He put down the biscuit and shook his head. He, Harry Fox, who spent his life thinking about women, had failed to think about them when it mattered most.

'That's not it at all. We've missed the entire point.'

# CHAPTER 40

Along a row of nondescript south London houses, their windows so mottled with soot that there would scarcely be any need for the prospective blackout precautions, a woman was walking. She was in her forties, with high cheekbones and glossy dark hair that was drawn back and covered with a bright red and yellow headscarf. Her frame was slender and her shoulders high. Despite the uneven paving, there was a sense of dignity in the way she carried herself. Even in her cracked, low heels and shapeless coat, she comported herself with the demeanour of a catwalk model. At her throat, the street lamp caught the unlikely gleam of a pearl necklace.

She was remembering Vienna, and happiness.

In her mind it was 1931 and she was in a room on the top of a house in Vienna's tenth district, the rough, working class suburb of Favoriten, eating *Käsespätzle* and laughing. It was late – almost midnight – and she was surrounded by a group of others in their twenties, sharing a steaming dish of cheese noodles, drinking cheap beer and chatting. The discussion was about politics, because they were all enthusiastic and committed idealists, burning with passion for the Comintern, the international branch of Communist revolution throughout the world. To be a young political activist in Vienna just then was to be alive, and on that particular evening they were celebrating their success in smuggling eight Communist fighters out of the city, right under the noses of the *Heimwehr*, the home guard. At some point in the evening a new member arrived and took the seat next to her. The newcomer was older than her, with finely wrought, angular features, and behind his wire-rimmed glasses, eyes that seemed to penetrate her soul. He was a Russian by birth who had studied psychology at the University of Vienna; almost immediately, he took command of the conversation, with a charismatic stream of wit and anecdote. Every face turned towards him, and every woman was held in the palm of his hand. Anton Sokolov was Jewish, intelligent, domineering and charming, and she fell instantly in love.

It was Anton who brought her here, a few years later, to this grimy south London district, full of warehouses and dock workers' houses. Everything about England felt alien: the fug of breath on the packed underground trains and the odour of unwashed clothes on the buses that was so different to the distinctive sausage and sweat smell of Vienna's trams. London's dirt-stained, medieval buildings were nothing to the gracious dazzle of Vienna. And she could never forget that England was an empire built on blood and bones.

Anton had set up a bookshop as cover, so she spent most of her time there, manning the counter and auditing the accounts, while he recruited and ran his agents. His training in psychology had been useful in identifying which well-born university graduates in the civil and diplomatic services, and in academia and journalism, would be receptive to his approach. As a psychologist, Anton knew the varieties of childhood neglect that predisposed people to betray their country. He could unfailingly pinpoint the natural outsiders, and those who abhorred bourgeois morality. The outwardly conventional young men whose emotional repression had bred an eternal contempt for the West.

Vera owned a typewriter, so to bring in a little extra cash, Anton decided that she should become a secretary. She called herself Mrs Harris, and she would type up manuscripts for authors whom they met at functions and through literary societies. This also proved perfect cover for regular liaisons with Party members, whose communications would be passed to Moscow via exported copies of books. The information would be condensed with the use of special cameras, and printed in the pages of popular novels. Sometimes the agents met here, and sometimes at the bookshop or the Kensington house. This was how she'd first met Hubert.

Poor, rotund, pedantic Hubert Neumann, reciting Shakespeare and declaring love whenever she picked up yet another indecipherable manuscript and began the toil of typing it up. Calling her the Dark Lady and boasting of his undying passion. So much for wanting to be the ultimate buttoned-up Englishman; Hubert loved with all the florid eloquence of the Viennese.

Life was cruel really, because who could possibly love Hubert Neumann when men like Anton Sokolov walked the earth? And yet it was Hubert's other passion that had piqued the attention of Moscow Centre and led them to dub this band of agents the 'Shakespeare Spies'. And it was Hubert's ingenuity that had proved his downfall, when Vera chose the manner of his death from the pages of his own book.

The voice that broke into her reverie came out of nowhere.

'Mrs Sokolov?'

She started at the dim figures in front of her, and did not answer.

'Vera Sokolov?'

Nothing betrayed her alarm, except the trembling fingers as she fumbled in her bag for her door key. Then, because she had been so deep in her daydreaming that she had forgotten her usual checks and routines, she said, 'You have the wrong person, I'm afraid. My name is not Sokolov. My name is Harris. Mrs Harris.'

They followed her into the house and the three of them stood in the kitchen. To keep from shaking, she folded her arms, set her jaw taut and leaned against the stove. The man and woman were called Harry Fox and Stella Fry. They levelled their questions at her as if they were expecting her eyes to flicker, or her gaze to falter, or a confession to come tumbling out. How little must they think of her. She was not some discombobulated little widow, or fragile middle-aged woman who could be intimidated. She was Vera Sokolov, born Vienna, 1894, educated at Vienna University and a member of the most secret arm of the Comintern, the International Liaison department, or OMS. A Red Queen whose ring of spies had brought information of the highest value to the motherland. Did they honestly expect her to burst into tears? Could they possibly imagine that she, who had withstood the interrogation rooms of the Austrian fascists, would stoop to talk to them? That she would say yes, Hubert Newman was in love with me, and yes, we had him killed.

All the same she was panicking inside, and calculating wildly. Several days ago, Byrd had sent a telegram, warning her that a woman had come to Vienna asking questions. West had also been alerted. If this was the same woman standing in front of her, how much did she know? What evidence might these people have, and would Byrd's warning have reached the Centre, activating exfiltration for the others, as had already happened with Green?

The man, who had shown her a Special Branch card, went out to telephone, leaving her alone with the girl, Stella Fry. Vera watched her eyes move, darting around the place, taking everything in, observing. She was not a girl but a woman really, barely in her thirties, the same age Vera had been when she arrived here. She was pretty, too, and even resembled Vera a little, with her slender figure, pale, sober demeanour and chestnut hair.

Vera's cat, a sleek three-year-old tortoiseshell called Pushkin, came in and wound herself around her legs but she didn't respond. She loved the cat, and worried what would happen to her, and hoped that, like her owner, Pushkin would prove a resourceful creature in a crisis. When Anton had been recalled to Moscow the previous year, Vera had wanted to go too, but he refused. The Comintern needed her here – she would take his place and run the agents as normal. A month later, reports of what had happened to him filtered back to her. She dreaded imagining what Anton had suffered in the dank basement of the Lubyanka building, enduring the interrogation from his own side with all the skills he had been taught to face the enemy. The same questions, fired at him with varying force and brutality, which he must have countered patiently, calmly, with the same truthful answers.

It was perverse, but in the bleak aftermath of Anton's cruel death, knowing that she was carrying out his wishes was all that kept her going. Despite the injustice of it, she burned all her photographs of him, as she knew he would have wanted, and went through the motions of their usual work. Yet still she fretted that she had handled the Hubert Newman problem disastrously. Anton would have been more skilful, and then they would not be in this predicament. She, Vera, was guilty of compromising the Shakespeare Spies, the most successful Soviet spy ring for a decade. She and these two people, whoever they were.

Fox returned and said someone called Flint would be arriving shortly.

'Has she said anything?'

Stella Fry shook her head.

It was not until later, when the man called Flint arrived with two policemen and she was being shuffled out of the house, that Vera spoke. The girl was still regarding her steadily, curiously, and Vera couldn't help herself. She said, 'You will never understand.'

Without taking her eyes off her, the girl replied, 'Then you will have to explain.'

# CHAPTER 41

*September 30th*

The weather was preposterously beautiful. The sky shone
like shot silk and the light was pure and glossy. A bunting of
'Special Edition' front pages flapped lightly on the railings.
In Trafalgar Square, sunlight shimmered on the iridescent
feathers of the pigeons and made rainbows in the fountains'
spray. A holiday air prevailed, as if for a coronation, or a
jubilee. It was relief: that life might go on as normal, and
the wind had changed, pushing the black cloud that hovered
on the horizon quite out of sight.

Harry emerged from the Tivoli Cinema on the Strand
where he had been watching the newsreel. Even Pathé's
jaunty tone could not make the scene any less funereal:
four men – Hitler, Chamberlain, Mussolini and Daladier –
sitting in dictator-sized armchairs at the Führerbau in
Munich, surrounded by silk lamps, agreeing a peace pact.

A quartet in the Führer's chamber, pretending to be in tune.

This was followed by footage of Chamberlain stepping out of his Super Lockheed 14 brandishing a piece of paper. 'We regard the agreement signed last night and the Anglo-German naval agreement as symbolic of the desire of our two peoples never to go to war with one another again.' On the paper was Hitler's signature, which had already sent thousands to their deaths.

Then came the Prime Minister and Halifax driving straight from Heston aerodrome to Buckingham Palace where the sashes of the windows were thrown up to receive the adulation of crowds.

It was bewildering to Harry to see so many people cheering their own defeat. What did they imagine? That caving in to brutes would not encourage them? He knew brutes. He had been brutish himself. Did they think the best way to prevent Germans taking things was to give them everything? This felt like sitting in a dentist's waiting room, reading magazines dating from 1914. He could almost smell the dust settling on the rubble of his own city. One would think they had won a major victory instead of betraying a minor country.

Still, this foreboding was not quite enough to dent the glow of good humour rising through him as he crossed the square and headed down the Mall. For the first time in years, entirely without the aid of alcohol, he sensed an emotion that might be happiness. He could not quite explain it, except that things were going well, the excitement of the last couple of weeks had led to more commissions, and he had the entertaining memory of Flint attempting to make sense of Hubert Newman's longhand version of *Masquerade*.

Also, Stella Fry had come into his life. It was hard to describe the mix of emotions he had felt when he had brought her back to his office the other night and covered her trembling form with his blanket. It was not the kind of feeling you came across much in detective thrillers, and besides, Harry had never been good with words. But she was different from the women he had known before, let alone those he had courted. She was not a *femme fatale*, or an extraordinary beauty. She had the kind of face you wanted to wake up to, and eyes that seemed to understand you, and a mind you wanted to entertain. His urge to please her, not out of guilt or duty, or any of the usual prompts, surprised him.

If he ever lit a candle in a church, it would be for her.

'Break a leg, Evelyn.'

Backstage in dressing room number two of the Westminster Theatre in Palace Street, Stella was watching Evelyn apply her make-up. She leaned forward into the mirror, dabbing panstick in *pointilliste* fashion on her face, sponging circles of rouge on her cheeks, then taking a small brush and outlining her lips in heavy crimson lipstick. The mirror had light bulbs all around it, just like in the movies, and the dressing table was a fragrant jumble of lipsticks, mascaras and kohls.

'Thanks, darling.'

'Helen of Troy! And on the first night, when all the important people come. This is your big break. What did Diana Sowerby say?'

'She said she couldn't face working tonight, not when all the press would be here, gossiping about her,' said Evelyn, pausing, lipstick in hand. 'She's totally distraught, poor thing. What she minds most is the implication that Aubrey North was only seeing her to get an insight into her husband's circle. She must have really loved him. Either that or it offended her vanity. But she'll be back tomorrow, so this is my one shot.'

'There are important producers coming. Film people. It's a great opportunity.'

'I know. And I'm humbled,' said Evelyn, who was hiding it well.

As the dresser entered and began fussing with Evelyn's hair, she said, 'How's your man? Harry Fox?'

'He's not my man.'

'I know. But rescuing you from an abduction! That's pretty gallant.'

'He's a professional detective. It's routine for people like him. Just another job of work.'

Stella wondered why she was so reluctant to credit Harry Fox with courage or gallantry. The memory of him standing in the doorway, swearing, would be forever imprinted on her mind, as would the scene later, when he had taken her back to his office and listened to her story without interruption, tenderly dispensing whisky like aspirin. Instead of exploring her feelings she had tidied them all into a compartment, with characteristic neatness, for reflection at a later date.

She made her way back to the front of the theatre. The porticoed entrance was bathed in flashlights as the first-night celebrities began to arrive. She looked across the throng for Sidonie Lamont and Tom, who would be joining her, and as she searched, across the street she caught sight of a figure she recognized. It looked a lot like Harry, in an Aquascutum trench coat, but he had his back towards her and was walking north, towards Victoria. She thought of calling out, yet he was too far away, and as he went a jubilant woman ran into his path and accosted him.

'Haven't you heard? It's peace. We're going to have peace!'

But Harry Fox, if it was him, took no notice and just kept walking away.

# EPILOGUE

In a country churchyard, amid the deep silence of the trees, lichen-covered cherubs sank, half noticed, into the long grass. Long spears of meadowsweet thrust between the graves, and at the uncut edges, purple loosestrife waved in the autumn wind. A distant rumble of thunder threatened to break the unseasonal humidity of the past week. The air felt like a bated breath, waiting to see what the next few days might bring.

Harry and Stella were standing beside a mound of freshly dug earth.

'Flint loves me now. I'm his golden boy. Turns out Rosary Gardens was a Soviet safe house and they found all sorts of documents there implicating North. Finch and Grunfeld, too, though they're long gone. Flint couldn't believe it when he heard about North. That man had the most intimate access, not only being so senior in the Foreign Office, but being close to Churchill. Apparently he had access to huge amounts of documents. Papers on Britain's military pre-paredness. Scientific espionage. Submarine designs. Who knows what else? All of it being sent to Russia in the pages of Newman's books.'

'Flint must feel pretty guilty. After all, it was North who instructed him to have you followed. Probably to have you assaulted too.'

'Guilt's not in his repertoire.'

'What about Aubrey North?'

'He's under arrest. To his credit he wanted it made clear that your friend Tom Lamont had no idea what his boss was up to.'

'Has Flint said anything about Mrs Harris?'

'Only that she's not talking. Not even to MI5's best inter-rogator, B4a. There's no doubt that her husband, Anton, was the agent runner who recruited the three of them. When he was executed last year, she took over the operation.'

Stella frowned.

'Obviously, Newman could never have let her see the manuscript. She would have understood that he was about to denounce her. But what puzzles me is that he told me, *"Mrs Harris is getting on a bit and her eyes are going"* when she's not an old lady at all. She can't be much more than forty. And she's a beautiful woman.'

'That's why he was in love with her. And love makes people do crazy things.'

'Does it?'

'So they say.'

Harry looked down at Newman's grave, where a couple of bunches of roses lay, already wilting.

He was thinking of his father, Stanley Fox, lover of horse racing and the King James Bible, and how his entire life might need to be rewritten. Stanley, like Hubert Newman, had tried to control his own story when he was alive by hiding the truth. But truth had a stubborn habit of emerging, like a splinter beneath the skin.

'You know what I said about us making a good team?'

'I assumed you were joking.'

'About the way the Security Service like to put together a classy woman and an older man. Want to know why?'

'Why, then?'

'Because the girl will fancy the bit of rough but won't break up his marriage.'

'First, don't flatter yourself. Second, you're not that rough. Third, as far as I know, you're not married.'

'We complement each other though. We're like oil and water.'

'More like petrol and matches.'

Even as he spoke, he thought, she's too bright to be the sidekick, and I'm not doing that.

Stella was thinking of the night in Vienna and the terrible dream she had when it was only the face of Harry Fox who came into her mind.

He looked around him at the deserted churchyard and said, 'I like women. I think they're underrated.'

'Well, thanks.'

'And the people I work for, they'd like you too, you know. If you were interested. They want people who can speak other languages.'

'It wouldn't work. And as for you and me, I don't even know anything about you, Harry. Not really. You haven't told me anything about your family.'

'I have a nephew. He's a great lad. He's ten.'

That was the only snippet of information he was going to give out, it seemed. Yet its sheer brevity was telling. Did the nephew not have parents? Why were they not mentioned?

Was Harry Fox yet another man who hid the important parts of his life?

'You're going to miss him if they evacuate the kids, aren't you?'

'It won't come to that.'

'It might.'

The heat had broken. The first drops of rain were falling. Slowly, with intent. A storm was coming – eventually, a storm that might engulf the whole Continent. But for that moment the low trees offered shelter, and the tea shop in the village called, and the rain ran down the name on the wooden cross and refreshed the flowers they had placed before it.

# AUTHOR'S NOTE

The Red List was the informal name of a list collated by a joint unit of MI5 and Special Branch in the 1930s to monitor Communist subversion among the British cultural elite. The many notable intellectuals and writers who were shadowed by the domestic Security Service included George Orwell, Christopher Isherwood, W.H. Auden, Stephen Spender and C. Day Lewis (subsequently Poet Laureate).

Frederick Lindemann, 1st Viscount Cherwell, was Churchill's chief scientific advisor during the Second World War, director of Oxford's Clarendon Laboratory, and also a competitor in the Wimbledon tennis championships of 1920. After Hitler banned 'non-Aryans' from teaching in German universities in 1933, Lindemann set about facilitating the relocation of a number of physicists to England, raising funds for them and finding support. As a result, some of the most brilliant scientists of the time, including Albert Einstein, Erwin Schrödinger, Kurt Mendelssohn, Nicholas

419

Kurti, Franz Simon and Heinrich Kuhn came to England and led the rapidly developing field of nuclear physics.

Before the war, when concern was expressed in different government departments about Britain's lack of preparedness for conflict with Germany, Lindemann undertook to help Churchill by analysing confidential documents and boiling information down to data points so that Churchill could express himself more powerfully in the House of Commons.

In 1938, as international relations deteriorated, the UK government authorized the development of offensive chemical warfare research. Until then, the 1925 Geneva Protocol had permitted the use of chemical warfare agents only in retaliation. Research on the potential weapons, conducted at Porton Down in Wiltshire, included work on a new neurotoxic agent called botulinum toxin which ultimately proved difficult to weaponize. It was the same substance which is today used as a cosmetic aid, in the form of Botox.

Michael MacOwan's modern-dress version of *Troilus and Cressida* opened at the Westminster Theatre in September, 1938. It was a great success. The dramatic lighting and dark background caused some critics to recall Picasso's *Guernica*, which had just gone on display at the Whitechapel Gallery. Dorothy L. Sayers wrote, 'if ever there was a play for the times, it is this.'

Number 3, Rosary Gardens in Kensington was one of a number of safe houses established in London by agents of the USSR.

JT, January 2024

# ACKNOWLEDGEMENTS

As ever I am hugely grateful for the support and encouragement of my agent Caradoc King, as well as Millie Hoskins, Becky Percival, and all at United Agents. At Quercus, it has been a joy to work with Jane Wood, a much-admired editor, as well Florence Hare, Emily Patience and the rest of the team. I am indebted to the following authors and books; David Caute's *Red List: MI5 and British Intellectuals in the Twentieth Century, British Writers and MI5 Surveillance, 1930-1960* by James Smith and *Prof, The Life of Frederick Lindemann* by Adrian Fort. And lastly, thanks to my children, William, Charlie and Naomi, for their interest, advice, and long-suffering willingness to discuss the turbulent 1930s.